LESSONS IN ENCHANTMENT

SCHOOL OF MAGIC, BOOK 1

PATRICIA RICE

Lessons In Enchantment

Patricia Rice

Published by Rice Enterprises, Dana Point, CA, an affiliate of Book View Café Publishing Cooperative
Cover design by Kim Killion
Book View Café Publishing Cooperative
P.O. Box 1624, Cedar Crest, NM 87008-1624
http://bookviewcafe.com
ISBN 978-1-61138-868-8 eBook
ISBN 978-1-61138-869-5 POD

INTRODUCTION

Can a straitlaced engineer, three psychic children, and a lonely witch find love?

"You mistake me," a plummy feminine voice declared in icy hauteur from the foyer.

On his way up the stairs to wash before attending yet another business meeting, Drew hesitated.

The rounded vowels continued, "I am Lady Phoebe Malcolm Duncan. I will *not* use the servants' entrance." The lady's cool tones conveyed imperiousness without once raising her voice. "If this is how I am greeted, then you may tell your master that he may find someone else to educate his children."

Oh no, he wasn't losing another nanny before she was even hired! He'd had to throw out the last one when he'd found her drunk in the kitchen after the episode with Clare and the ghost.

He hastened down the stairs despite the fact that he was missing jacket and cravat and his shirt was coated in oil and his worst nightmare was at the door.

The apparition in his foyer almost brought him to a halt. He had expected aristocracy at its worst—billowing skirts and soaring tresses and condemnation permanently engraved in her expression.

Instead, the visitor had no resemblance to any female he'd ever encountered. He couldn't precisely gauge her height since she appeared to be wearing high-top shoes with heels beneath her too-short skirt, and her porkpie hat—adorned with roses—teetered above a stack of chestnut curls. A black duster hid most of her gown, but he was positively certain it didn't conceal layers of petticoats. In fact, he was quite convinced the skirt was somehow. . . divided.

She was holding a high-wheeled bicycle. And her pocket was. . . squirming.

Now he was mesmerized.

AUTHOR'S NOTE

Writing fictional history is an interesting amalgam of fact and fiction. Thanks to the University of Edinburgh, I have a veritable treasure trove of old maps and photos to work with. But fiction requires action in areas that fit the story—without forcing my characters to spend hours traipsing all over Edinburgh. So for the sake of condensing time and pages, I have not attempted precise historical accuracy in street structure. Margaret's Wynd did not exist, for instance, but others like it did. The veterinary schools were located near what is now Multree's Walk. They not only existed, but they were located a short distance from each other, just as in the story. New Town was established as a system of Georgian terraces, so while Drew's house might be imaginary, it represents the beautiful areas of town that can still be seen today.

The Association is pure fiction. Yes, through centuries of history there have always been groups of powerful men who would do whatever it took to have their way. We still have groups like that today. It's human nature to believe one's own beliefs are right and others are wrong. The Victorians were very fond of "associations" of all sorts, good, bad, and indifferent. So I simply combined all the factors I required into a single group and labeled them generically, just as my heroine calls her pets by their generic names.

ACKNOWLEDGMENTS

My extreme gratitude to Laura Vivanco for all the lovely on-line Edinburgh maps, and Monica Burns for the huge assortment of Gaelic and Scots dialect, both insults and endearments. They saved me immense amounts of time and inspired all sorts of ideas I'd never have had without them. And to Mindy Klasky, beta reader extraordinaire, without whom conflict would never happen.

Creating a book is like raising children—it requires a village. I have been blessed with an assortment of friends, family, and fellow writers who understand when I stop and stare blankly at a particularly interesting building or ask what it feels like to fear heights. They're my heroes.

ONE

LYING FLAT ON HIS BACK UNDER THE WORKTABLE HE'D BUILT FOR THIS project, Andrew Blair applied his screwdriver to the undercarriage of the frustratingly useless pterotype. "My cousin should have accepted the bank's offer, then blown up the mine," he said absently, focusing on his newest mechanical contraption and not his partner's business discussion.

The wrench he reached for drifted into his hand. Frowning at the anomaly but still concentrating on his work, he continued removing the recalcitrant key.

"Blowing up the mine would have put Simon's miners out of work, an effect I thought our consortium is attempting to prevent." Hugh Morgan nudged Drew's shoulder with his boot. "You need to come out from there and sign this contract for the demolition of the tenements in Auld Town before they fall down."

"Simon would rather the dastards blow *him* up? He's been hunting for evidence for almost a year now! If he'd give up on the mine, I could invest his money in the restoration project, and he wouldn't have to be living in fear of cowards—"

A floating screwdriver slammed into the table leg and toppled to the floor. Finally drawn from his work, Drew shoved out from under the table to glare at his cousin's six-year-old son. What in thunderation was the brat doing in here?

"A wife, my kingdom for a wife!" Drew muttered, shutting his talk of the lad's father.

A wife would keep the blasted *weans* where they belonged, right?

"You won't have a kingdom if you don't sign these contracts," Hugh informed him in the perfunctory tone that warned he was losing patience. "And if we don't start work soon, we'll go broke, and you'll never find a wife."

Hugh had a mathematical mind in the muscular body of a black-smith. He didn't socialize well, but he spoke fluent business. Any form of social commentary indicated rebellion on the horizon.

The tool-shifting brat slipped into a corner of the workroom and closed his eyes, as if that made him invisible. Generally, the children didn't exist to Drew, but they were easier than contracts. "Enoch, get back to the nursery where you belong! Where's your damned nanny?"

"Nanny says *damned* is a very bad word, and you will go to perdition," the boy said, eyes closed and forehead furrowed in concentration. As if drawn by imperceptible strings, a screwdriver rose unsteadily from Drew's neatly organized toolbox.

Not making any progress on the pterotype, Drew caught the inexplicably floating screwdriver, stood, and brushed at the dust on his trousers. "Be damned to nanny. You're too young to be in here. Where are your sisters?"

Holding a stack of papers, Hugh blocked his access to the brat. Where Drew was long and lean, Hugh Morgan was barrel-chested and shorter. They'd fought with fists as boys, neither of them coming out the winner. Now, they tangled over stacks of legal documents. Being an adult didn't have a lot to recommend it.

"Nanny has a megrim. The twins are in the attic," Enoch announced, scampering out of the workroom before Drew could haul him out.

"What's a megrim?" Drew asked idly as he scrubbed his oily hands on a rag.

"Something nannies get, apparently. I'll never understand why your family thought you should take care of the three-headed monsters." With more assurance now that they were back to business, Hugh showed him where to sign.

"My family believed I was getting married," Drew said with a shrug.

Hugh snorted. "And they wanted to scare her off? Brilliant."

His partner knew Drew's cousin, knew his circumstances, and that Simon had gone mad crazed with drink and vengeance after his wife's death. There were times when Drew had wondered if the children had driven his cousin to madness first.

Drew couldn't really blame his ex-fiancée for not wanting to set up housekeeping with an instant family. Now that he considered it, Rose probably would have had megrims and retired to her room too.

He didn't need a wife. He needed an army sergeant—at least until such time as Simon regained his senses and took the weans back, which might be never.

"You'll not find a wife willing to put up with them," Hugh said darkly. "We need to start this project so you can someday afford a dozen nannies. Right now, the tenants don't pay enough to cover the enormous maintenance. We're losing buckets of money. And you have a meeting with the consortium in an hour."

"That entire medieval cesspool of derelicts and rats should be razed to the ground," Drew complained, shrugging into his cutaway tweed jacket. "I fail to perceive how sinking all my funds rebuilding will earn me enough to buy food." Although he had ideas of mechanical improvements. . . That had been one of the reasons he'd agreed to investing in the project—a mechanical lift.

Hugh was his investment manager. Without him, Drew would be living in a garret. Tinkering with ideas was not a sound financial policy, he'd learned. Some of his inventions paid off well, some not at all. He had to eat in between. He had to listen when Hugh spoke. He didn't always understand. He simply went to business meetings and hoped to learn.

"Because you'll be involved in restoring a historical city. They're demolishing the old wynds and money is pouring into High Street. We'll start in Canongate, where the investment is lower. Imagine rows of new terrace houses winding up the hill. You'll earn more than on that tatty machine you're working on." Disgruntled, Hugh shoved the contract back into its folder.

Aye, right, that's what he'd been thinking—refilling his coffers for his ever-needy family.

"My pterotype has universal applications more important than money. Just imagine how much faster your fancy contracts could be prepared if they could be written by my machine." Drew looked around for his cravat, and not finding it, stalked toward the parlor door.

A man with his plebian background couldn't step outside his house without a cravat and polished boots, looking like the gentleman he wasn't. He'd have to go upstairs and straighten his attire before he went anywhere. He should probably check on the nanny and the children while he was there. By the time he attended the meeting, he'd have to forget lunch, again. He didn't want to have to hire another cook, but this one had a schedule that never suited his.

He reached the foyer just as the maid let in his neighbor— *Blood and thunder!* Aware of his non-existent cravat, Drew felt like a half-naked barbarian. A pale young thing peered out from behind his broad-beamed neighbor, and his stomach cramped.

"Mr. Blair, I'm so glad I caught you." Mrs. Dalrymple rustled across the parquet. "I'd like you to meet my niece—"

A scream reverberated down the stairwell, rattling the excellent foundation. Almost relieved at the excuse to ignore the little mouse and her aunt, Drew dashed for the stairs, leaving his visitors gaping in the foyer.

"THERE YOU ARE, MRS. MAC, A LETTER THAT WILL MELT THE HEART OF THE most heartless son." Phoebe Malcolm Duncan capped her fountain pen and shook the linen notepaper to be certain it dried without smearing. The old lady liked to pretend she lived in a fancy house by using Phoebe's stationery.

The hunched pencil seller in faded mourning and black lace gloves curled her fingers into her palms and shook her scraggly gray curls. "You send it, my lady. I daren't touch it."

Spoken through toothless gums and in a broad accent, her request was barely comprehensible, but Phoebe had heard the language of the slums since childhood and understood enough to nod and fold the letter for later mailing. Mrs. Mac's son never responded, but a mother never gave up hope.

Picking up her penny farthing, she climbed on the towering seat and arranged her split skirt to fall over her high-top shoes. Before she could continue on to her next stop, Phoebe heard Raven screech a warning overhead. She froze and opened her senses.

The rats were rushing out of Margaret's Wynd as if their tails were on fire. Even the simple-minded pigeons were aflutter. Holding on to her porkpie hat, Phoebe tilted her head to search the sky. There—right over the wynd where she'd grown up—flocks of pigeons surged upward, circling in panic. Her stomach clenched in alarm, knowing the pigeons only performed that aerial act if seriously disturbed from their roosts.

The only home she'd ever known was in the center of that medieval winding lane. Pumping the bicycle pedals, balancing the high wheel, Phoebe raced into crowded Canongate in the direction of the palace. On this main road, she dodged carts and pedestrians and curses, then shot across in front of a carter's horse, into Margaret's Wynd.

All looked normal in the grim dark lane of towering ancient edifices. A business-suited patron smoked outside the cigar store. The professor in his aging black coat lifted his top hat to her, heading for the university. An urchin played in the gutter. Clothes fluttered from the lines strung across the narrow alley.

Only she noticed the silent pigeons circling frantically in the almost invisible sky and the rats racing from their tunnels in the courtyard middens.

She heard the ominous rumble before she could see around the narrow curve to her tenement. *What in all the holy saints—* she pedaled faster.

A horrendous crash followed by a thick cloud of dust nearly pitched the bicycle over. Raven screamed imprecations. Even Piney whimpered a sleepy protest in her pocket.

Phoebe halted, planting her boots firmly on the shaking ground. In horror, she watched as the front of her home crumbled into a mound of brick and stone. The professor raced back down the street to join her.

People spilled out of the shops and taverns. The noise nearly drowned the screams and cries of the tenement inhabitants in their now wall-less building.

Gaping, not quite believing her eyes, Phoebe gazed upward at the eight-story edifice she called home. Her flat—and all the others—were completely exposed to the September wind. The medieval façade had simply fallen off the structure.

How the holy. . . By all the saints, what did she do now? Panic sank into her bones. How many people were hurt? Acting instinctively, she set aside her bicycle and headed for the rubble.

In the back of her head, a voice wailed, *Where will I go? Everything I own, everything I love, gone, crushed. My books! Daddy's portrait!*

A woman's screams halted any further hysteria.

Neighbors crowded around Mrs. Tarkington, holding her back as she tried to reach the mound of rubble still emanating centuries of thick, rock dust.

"My baby!" the mother cried. "My baby!"

Oh no, not Evie! Phoebe had watched little Evie grow from infancy. The child wasn't entirely right in the head—her mother was an alcoholic prostitute who may have passed on some disease—but that didn't mean the bonds of love weren't strong. She might not be able to save her home, but *Evie. . .*

Biting her finger, Phoebe fought past her rattled nerves. Her flat was laid bare three floors above—all her family's cherished heirlooms, her mother's treasures—but what mattered was the people here in the street.

She slipped the pine marten from her pocket, whispering soothingly, and mentally focused on an image of Evie's golden curls. "Please, Piney, find her." She knew the animal didn't understand the words so much as the pleading tone and the image she planted in his head. A member of the weasel family, Piney could squeeze into the most impossible crevasses. Maybe, if they could find Evie quickly enough. . .

She set the marten free in the shadows. She'd raised him since she'd found him as a baby in a deserted nest in one of the few remaining trees down by the ancient cemetery—a dying pine. She'd hoped to someday find him a mate, but his natural habitat had been nearly eradicated by the growing city. She didn't stand much chance of finding another pine much less a marten.

The slender mammal wiggled from her hand and scampered over the stones to squirm under the mound of debris. Mrs. Tarkington's screams reverberated over the echoes of the crash. The neighbors not in shock tried to steer the distraught mother away. Phoebe could say nothing that might console her. All she could do was pray and concentrate on tracking her pet.

And not think about the appalling loss of her only home.

She had to focus on Piney so she didn't lose him. Overhead, Raven squawked and complained. The old bird had a right to protest. He'd made his home on the tenement roof. With the front wall gone, he'd be subject to every cold wind that battered the crumbling mortar. He'd lost his mate last winter, despite all Phoebe's efforts to keep them warm.

The wind seemed chillier than usual. Phoebe wrapped her arms around herself, grateful for the old coat she wore over her fraying gown. She had a little money, but living here, there was no point in flaunting the fact or wasting her meager savings. She had resisted applying at the veterinary college—called Dick's Vet School by the locals—for fear her mother might need more funds if her consumption worsened.

After Phoebe's father had died, her mother had created their nest egg by selling the entire tenement building to a consortium that could manage the tenants better than she could. Malcolms had lived in the once grandiose edifice for centuries—behind the ornate facade that was currently collapsed in the street. Part of the sales agreement had given them a life estate in that flat. It was the only home she'd ever known. Phoebe started to shake.

Concentrate. Follow Piney through the dust and debris—*hear a child's whimper.* Evie was alive!

Not daring to raise anyone's hopes, Phoebe slipped over to old Michael and gestured at his shovel. The cemetery worker frowned but signaled his younger assistant. As the crowd gathered in the street, wailing, arguing, or just gawking, Phoebe led the diggers to the farthest end of the rubble, where she sensed Piney nosing what could be the child's skirts. She started pulling at the crumbling stones with her gloved hands, showing the men where to dig.

These people had known her from birth. They knew her family. She didn't have to explain herself here. Men instantly followed her actions, gently pushing her aside so they could paw at the gravel and debris with their bigger, rougher hands, helping the grave diggers.

She hadn't realized she was crying until a wet spot dripped onto her dusty sleeve. She rubbed her eyes and cried more.

Piney slithered out of the debris, and she gathered him up, hugging the tiny animal as the men shouted and a mat of filthy hair appeared. Hearing Evie's whimpers, Phoebe shuddered in relief. She was no physician. She could do no more but pray.

If she'd learned nothing else in her hard world, it was that she had to act swiftly and think later. Her life, all that she owned, was in ruins at her feet. She had to keep moving.

While the hysterical mother swept in to gather up her child, Phoebe slipped Piney back into her pocket. Everything she loved and treasured —except her mother—was in that building. And her mother might die of heartbreak if she should learn they'd lost even the family portraits.

Shivering so hard that she could barely move her feet, Phoebe crawled over the crumbled mortar and stone blocking the lane. She didn't dare attempt to enter the tenement through the gaping front, but the rear staircase in the outside tower should still be solid, if she could reach the alley further down.

Around her, people wept and cursed and bewailed their wretched fates. She wanted to weep with them, but she had no one to rely on but herself. Crying would not protect her books and the artwork. She'd save hysteria for later, when the impact of homelessness fully hit her. She'd sit down and have a good howl then, when there was nothing left to be done.

She had no idea how she would cart a few centuries of belongings down three flights of crumbling stone stairs.

She did, however, know what she had to do after she'd accomplished the impossible. She simply hated sacrificing her independence to do it.

That produced a fresh spate of useless tears.

TWO

Wiping the sweaty grime from her forehead, Phoebe closed the lid on a trunk holding her meager wardrobe. She'd squeezed in the cloth rabbit her father had given her as a child and the ink sketch of her mother and as many small items as she could manage, but she couldn't afford to be too sentimental.

She was relieved that her mother had the cottage in the south of France so she needn't see this. Phoebe wanted her mother to get well and come home—but not just yet, please.

She looked around through a blur of tears. The mahogany inlaid vanity was covered in dust and debris. The Chippendale chairs she'd always hoped to have re-upholstered were buried in rubble. Portraits of noble ancestors. . . she'd saved the best. Grief gnawed at her middle more than hunger.

And the worst was yet to come. She mentally berated herself for thinking like that. At least she had a place to turn. Most of her neighbors did not.

As the laborers gathered to haul the last of her boxes down, she gestured at several lifetimes of family belongings and told the men to help themselves in payment for their work. The place would be scavenged by daybreak in any case. Her boxes of books, artwork, the family silver, and her mother's wedding china were in the cart already.

Back in the street, she paid the carter and his ancient mule with a beautiful pewter oil lamp.

Using an almost-clean handkerchief to smudge the dust from her face, Phoebe took one last glance at her home. Raven circled overhead, hunting for new territory. She stroked Piney in her pocket, blinked back a threatened waterfall of tears, and walking beside the mule, gulped and nodded at the carter to proceed.

She led the way from Margaret's Wynd, down Canongate, and through a maze of backstreets to the small close near the palace where her aunts lived. Like Phoebe's mother, her aunts had each inherited an entire building inside the medieval walls of the old town. The family had built in Edinburgh centuries ago, when the town had first started growing. Unlike her mother, who had married a handsome, courageous, and penniless earl, her aunts had married well enough to retain their neighboring townhouses.

Over the years after their husbands passed on and Cousin Max disappeared, Lady Agnes and Lady Gertrude had remained in their gothic horrors. They'd knocked out walls and combined their two homes to form a School for Malcolms. They might as well have called it a School for Witches. Everyone who knew their family understood Malcolms weren't normal.

The school's street level floor had been turned into a giant repository of books and artifacts few thieves would wish to steal. Praying there was room for her belongings, Phoebe entered the stairwell in between what had once been shops. She climbed to a brightly-painted blue door and rapped the ornate brass knocker.

A young girl answered, bobbed a curtsy, and gestured her inside. "You're expected, Lady Phoebe. The ladies are in the parlor."

She could hear the laughter of young girls in a schoolroom overhead. Still in her filth—she couldn't exactly have changed in a building without a wall—Phoebe curtseyed to her aunts. Sitting around a parlor table with their flowered tea set and plates of crumpets, her mother's older sisters beamed welcomingly but wisely didn't stand to hug her.

"Phoebe, there you are! Come sit down, child. Let the staff carry your belongings inside. We've cleaned a space in the library for your books while we were waiting. There'll be room below for your boxes, but I'm afraid if you want many of your things in your room, you may not be able to turn around. We'll leave that to you. We're so glad you finally came to us! That building has always been a disaster waiting to happen. The mortar should have been maintained. You should have rented out that flat. You were never meant to *live* there!"

This recitation bounced back and forth between her prescient aunts. They had a habit of speaking as one. Phoebe had often wondered if they read each other's minds as well as everyone else's. She waited patiently until they wound down before she answered.

"You are all that is kind, my dear aunts. I shall try not to impose upon you for long. I've decided I must find a solicitor to demand reparations. A lifetime lease cannot be absolved simply because the owner did not maintain the structure. I need to wash before I can sit down with you. I apologize."

She'd learned at an early age to push past her aunts' chatter to what she wanted or she'd go quietly mad. She was quite convinced that was why her beloved Cousin Max had taken off for darkest Africa and never returned. She loved her mother's sisters, but they were. . . overwhelming. She curtsied again and followed a student—she was pretty sure the school didn't have maids—to her assigned room, leaving her aunts still protesting and explaining and weaving a world of their own.

The tall, narrow townhouses were a warren of tiny rooms cut up even more as the family grew and the school expanded. The address had once been prestigious. Like much of old Edinburgh, the neighborhood had been deteriorating since the English came into power and the palace fell into disuse. At best, these days most of the area inside the city walls could be called a slum, but everyone knew her family. Phoebe had never felt threatened.

Her aunts might not be wealthy, but they maintained their house well. The threadbare tapestries on the walls kept out the damp and cold. The thick old glass in her bedroom window was covered by heavy velvet draperies. The poster bed was laden with downy covers so only a minimum of coal would be needed in the grate on a chilly night. All in pretty shades of blue and adorned with forget-me-not prints, the bedchamber had obviously been chosen for Phoebe.

She couldn't stay here. She'd suffocate. She'd spent the last five years on her own, with an entire flat at her command and all of the old city as her dooryard. Under her aunts' roof, she'd have to obey their expectations and pretend she was a proper lady, wearing corsets, crinolines, and bonnets and never going out unattended. She would fail, of course. One could not tend ailing animals in crinolines. And she'd have no place where she could tend to them. She might as well be locked inside a cage with her creatures.

She needed a windfall to set her free, preferably one that would allow her to attend Dick's—the Highland Society's Veterinary School. Maybe if she sued the consortium she could obtain a lump sum to pay the tuition. Then she need only find a closet somewhere to sleep.

An elderly housekeeper and her young son carried up her clothes trunk. One of the students brought hot water. Wearily, Phoebe realized the entire day had gone by without time to eat. She hugged Piney and settled him into a dresser drawer with his box of pine branches and a dinner of berries she'd saved for him. Night was his most active time, but she didn't know if the students would appreciate him stealing into their rooms in search of bugs and rodents.

Changing into a gown and petticoat from her adolescence that fit a little too tightly across the bosom, she traipsed back to the parlor, where her aunts had arranged dinner.

"I will help tutor, of course," Phoebe announced as she spread her skirts on the faded stripes of a Regency chair. "I will gladly help with correspondence or in any other way to return your kindness in taking me in on such sudden notice."

Short, rotund, with her graying hair piled in loops and ribbons to better show off her enormous earrings, Aunt Agnes waved away Phoebe's prepared speech. "I'm sure you will be an asset to our little school. But we have been talking while you dressed."

Aunt Gertrude nodded, her dyed black tresses bobbing precariously. Taller than her sister, she was more stout than round, and the pince-nez she wore on a chain gave her an air of authority. "We have received a request for a nanny. It's most unusual, admittedly. In the past, we haven't actively recruited students, but it seems our gifted family has achieved some claim to fame."

"Terrible, of course," Aunt Agnes said. "Ladies should never be noticed or talked about."

"But we're Malcolms," Gertrude continued. "And people are becoming more interested in the spiritual."

To prevent her head from bouncing like a ball, Phoebe interrupted. "Spiritual, as in the fake clairvoyants and mediums who rob people of their money and their faith, you mean? That's preposterous. We're not carnival shows. We do not *sell* our gifts."

"Of course, we do, dear." Aunt Agnes patted Phoebe's hand. "We simply do it in a more genteel manner. Our family is our foundation, so we needn't actually sell our gifts for *money*. But we do use them in various ways that enhance our fortune. You deliberately give away your gift rather than expose it to the world, but the knowledge you obtain from animals earns you the respect of your neighbors."

"And perhaps a little fear," Aunt Gertrude acknowledged. "The lesser sorts do not harm you because they believe you're a witch. Word is already spreading that you saved that little girl's life, even though they have no inkling of how you did it. Anyone attempting to harm you would be thrashed within an inch of their lives. People are not stupid."

Phoebe squirmed and concentrated on her food. She was starved, after all.

She had never wasted much time wondering how people thought of her. Her life was simply too busy taking care of her animals and her neighbors and her mother and. . .

"But this letter offers us an opportunity to branch out," Agatha continued.

"It offers *Phoebe* an opportunity to branch out," Gertrude corrected. "She is young. She needs to see more of the world than these crumbling walls and a past that will never be resurrected."

"Queen Victoria is extensively renovating Holyrood," Phoebe argued, not wishing to be talked around. "The kirk is being rebuilt on High Street, and they're razing entire blocks to modernize the streets. We are more than crumbling walls."

"We are not blind to what has become of our home. The old town is an overpopulated slum," Gertrude said bluntly. "Poverty and disease are rampant. There are scientific reports declaring the death rates are beyond control. You have no idea what life is like outside these walls, and you need to learn."

Yes, she did. The new part of town had veterinary schools. Phoebe had bicycled there, studying the neat buildings with longing. She'd never seen a woman near them, and she'd lost her courage to go up and make inquiries among so many men, knowing she hadn't the funds to pay tuition.

But the direction of this conversation had taken an alarming turn that she must cut off at once. "My friends and family live inside these crumbling walls," she protested. "Why would I have any interest in fancy terrace houses and parks where I don't belong or in shops I can't afford?"

Or a college she couldn't get into. . .

Aunt Agatha produced a letter from her pocket. "Because we wish to broaden our horizons, dear. Our little school has no room to house more students. This offers us an opportunity to teach the gifted *outside* our limited space."

Phoebe scanned the small, neat lettering. The writer did not include a single flourish. Each letter was as precise as a printed book. Tedious. She frowned as she read it a second time. "He wants a nanny for his cousin's children? And he writes to you, why?"

"Because he recognizes our family, of course," Gertrude said with satisfaction, raising her pince-nez and taking the document to re-read. "We have verified his credentials, naturally. Until you came along, we've been uncertain how to proceed."

"Mr. Blair is an engineer, a very wealthy one," Agnes said. "His family is from Glasgow, but he attended the university here and has made quite a name for himself. It is a credit to his character that he took in his cousin's children after they lost their mother."

"But why us?" Phoebe asked in genuine bewilderment. "There are other perfectly respectable agencies who hire out servants."

"His wards are *gifted*, dear." Aunt Gertrude folded up the letter and regarded her with severity. "Their mother was a Malcolm descendant, although the relation to us is far in the past. Her family has recommended that the children be sent here, but they are much too young for classes."

Terror yawned wide as Phoebe recognized the direction of this conversation. "I am not a nanny!"

"Of course, you're not, dear." Gertrude patted her hand again.

"You're a gifted teacher," Agatha said complacently. "But instead of tutoring the poor in the streets, you will be teaching gifted children. Present yourself as a governess. You may tell Mr. Blair that once his wards are prepared for school, we will welcome them. Until then, they are no more than young heathens and simply not acceptable."

Appalled, Phoebe realized her aunts were serious. They meant to send her into the new city to mix with the elegantly garbed ladies and gentlemen of *business* who lived there. She wouldn't know a single soul. Her freedom would vanish, and she'd be trapped like an animal in a zoo.

That thought almost caused her to brighten. She *was* an animal to those staid citizens. They'd recognize that the moment she darkened their doorsteps.

And they'd shoo her away as if she were no more than a mutt of little consequence.

She actually smiled as she envisioned how she'd assure that outcome.

And then she would knock on the door of Dick's Vet School and ask if they took scholarship students.

THREE

"You mistake me," a plummy feminine voice declared in icy hauteur from Drew's foyer.

On his way up the stairs to wash before attending yet another business meeting, he hesitated. The tone was more refined than his meddling neighbor's. Mrs. Dalrymple and her niece hadn't returned since the hysterical screaming incident he'd blamed on a nanny afraid of mice.

The rounded vowels continued, "I am Lady Phoebe Malcolm Duncan. I will *not* use the servants' entrance."

Lady? Aristocrats did not darken his doorway, especially ones with the condescending speech of royalty. He had the urge to duck and run.

The lady's cool tones conveyed imperiousness without once raising her voice. "If this is how I am greeted, then you may tell your master that he may find someone else to educate his children."

Oh no, he wasn't losing another nanny before she was even hired! He'd had to throw out the last one when he'd found her drunk in the kitchen after the episode with Clare and the ghost. He hadn't found another since. He didn't even know where the damned children were at the moment.

He hastened down the stairs despite the fact that he was missing jacket and cravat and his shirt was coated in oil and his worst nightmare was at the door.

The apparition in his foyer almost brought him to a halt. He had expected aristocracy at its worst—billowing skirts and soaring tresses and condemnation permanently engraved in her expression.

Instead, the visitor had no resemblance to any female he'd ever encountered. He couldn't precisely gauge her height since she appeared to be wearing high-top shoes with heels beneath her too-short skirt, and her porkpie hat—adorned with roses—teetered above a stack of chestnut curls. A black duster hid most of her gown, but he was positively certain it didn't conceal layers of petticoats. In fact, he was quite convinced the skirt was somehow. . . divided.

She was holding a high-wheeled bicycle. And her pocket was. . . squirming.

Now he was mesmerized.

She glanced over the maid's shoulder and spotted him. "Sir, are you aware that the children are playing on the roof?"

How the devil did she know that? Did she fly in on a broom? No, on a *bicycle*.

When he didn't instantly respond to her warning, she brushed past the maid and headed directly for the stairs—and him. She might look as if she'd just emerged from the gutter, but there was no disguising the aristocratic arrogance with which she looked down her—rather enchanting—nose at him.

Good Gad, like the veriest bampot, he was falling into a pair of huge cornflower-blue eyes enhanced by lush dark lashes. What the devil was the matter with him?

Drew hastily stepped aside to let her pass. She smelled of roses, and he glanced at her hat to be certain those were silk. No, they weren't. She had *real* roses on her hat. And she was marching past him as if he were wallpaper.

He wasn't a vain man, but he knew he wasn't exactly invisible. Intrigued more than panicked, he followed her swinging duster up the stairs. How the devil did she know where to go? She lifted her ankle-length skirt to reveal trim ankles in striped stockings. Striped. Red and white. To match the red roses?

This was *Lady* Phoebe?

He didn't mix with the aristocracy. He had a working man's distrust of inherited power and wealth. But he was fairly certain, no matter how she styled herself, that nobility did not ride penny farthings and wear striped stockings.

Not that he'd ever divested any aristocratic ladies of their stockings. He spent his few spare hours with working girls.

Tilting her head as if listening for the children, his uninvited guest unerringly located the doors to the servants' floor, the attics, and the roof. Even *he* hadn't known there was a door to the roof. Of course, he didn't spend much time in the attic—but the children did.

Lady Phoebe scampered up the rickety stairs to the roof as if she were one of the brats. More reluctantly, Drew followed.

He'd spent a bad few hours clinging to the crow's nest of a towering mast in a storm as a stupid young man. He'd learned the sea wasn't for him and had turned his ambition to his studies. But hours of watching the wind and waves roil madly had left him unable to shake his fear of heights. He was a man who kept his feet solidly on the ground these days.

He could hear a crow squalling on the roof. Lady Phoebe's skirts temporarily blocked the scene outside, but he heard her gasp. She nearly threw herself into the channel between the slate peaks of the roof in her rush to reach whatever the scamps were perpetrating now. Accustomed to his young wards' depredations, Drew forced himself upward at a more pragmatic pace.

Apparently Simon's son and heir had taken to levitating one of his little sisters. Drew supposed the next step would be flying, which might be interesting, except the lady was behaving as if Enoch were committing murder.

"You dropped her!" she scolded the shame-faced boy. The tranquil pond of the lady's blue eyes now blazed with unholy fire. "What if you had lost concentration while she was over the parapet, and she dropped down four stories? Did you think of that?"

She was hugging one of the twins. Drew thought it might be Catherine. Cat was the more bold of the two and looked a little perplexed at the commotion. Clare, the quieter one, sat feeding pigeons and watching the scene with interest.

"No, ma'am," Enoch muttered. "I didn't mean for her to drift."

Drift? *Blood and thunderation.* . . Floating wrenches was one thing, floating his sister off the roof. . .

Drew narrowed his eyes at his young cousin. "Would you like to know what it's like to levitate?"

Enoch glanced up, surprised. "Yes, sir, I would."

Drew grabbed him by the seat of his pants and hauled him into the air so fast the child didn't have time to gasp. While the females gaped, he swung the boy back and forth until he looked as if he might puke. "Now imagine floating off the roof like that." He dropped the boy's feet to the ground.

Enoch sat abruptly. The lady glared at *him*, instead of the boy. "Mr. Blair, that is completely inappropriate."

"Not if he thinks twice before doing it again. Will you think before you act next time?" Drew demanded of the boy. "You could have killed your sister."

Still looking green around the gills, Enoch nodded.

"Mama said the angels won't take Cat until she's very old," Clare offered.

"Mama didn't tell us the angels were taking *her*," Cat argued after the lady returned her to her feet. "I want to see Mama."

That plaintive statement nearly brought Drew to his knees. The four-year-old twins seldom spoke. He had not once considered how these orphaned children felt. He'd simply inserted them into a nursery, hired servants, and went about his business. They were *infants*. Infants were of no interest until they reached an age of comprehension.

Simon's children were there already.

"Your mama watches over you, even if you can't see her," Lady Phoebe admonished. "Do you want to make her sick with worry? You are not to practice any of your talents unless an adult is there to guide you."

The girls looked blank. Enoch spoke for them, as usual. "Nannies scold us if we try. Clare talks to mama sometimes, and they spank her for saying so."

"Spanking is *not* acceptable," Lady Phoebe said, taking the hands of the twins and glaring at Drew. "You did the right thing by writing my aunts. You did the absolute wrong thing by disregarding what ignorant servants were teaching them. Now, let us go down and have a spot of tea."

As the lady swept his wards downstairs and dragged him along in their wake, Drew had the distinct notion that his household had been hit by a tempest worse than any he'd met at sea.

STILL QUIVERING WITH INDIGNATION AND A TOUCH OF HORROR AT ALMOST watching a child fly off a roof, in the presence of a gentleman who could upend a reasonably stout little boy with one hand, Phoebe chose the time-honored defense of steadying her nerves by hiding behind a teacup. What would have happened had Raven not seen the children? And if her host's walls had not been filled with mice to tell her in which direction to go? Nannies weren't an answer.

She took another steadying sip of excellent tea.

The children were much too young for the parlor, of course. She'd settled them into the nursery with their nursemaid and ordered tea and biscuits.

Now she was attempting to figure out, by all that was holy, how she would deal with the children's guardian and her own situation. Mr. Blair had taken time to don a stodgy tweed jacket and proper cravat and looked every inch the stiff, staid gentleman she despised, but she'd seen him in dishabille—and in action. *Mr. Blair was no gentleman.*

Mr. Blair was the most gorgeous male animal she'd ever set eyes on. The taut, sinewy muscles of a true thoroughbred, the black eyes and coat of a temperamental stud, the square whiskered jaw of. . . a pure Scottish warrior. All he needed was a plaid. She gulped and sipped the scalding tea.

She needed to flee like the wind.

She couldn't desert those children to ignorance and superstition, not any more than she could have abandoned Piney in his dead tree or left

Raven crying on the ground after being thrown from his nest. The young needed nurturing.

Her wretched, manipulative aunts had known that.

"I believe we have not been properly introduced," Mr. Blair said, in his stiff Glaswegian accent. He'd pulled his chair out from the tea table to give his long legs room and sat with his back straight, giving an impression of an authoritarian prat.

Phoebe didn't deal well with authority. She nodded, and a rose petal dropped from her hat. "As I said earlier, and I believe you heard me, I am Lady Phoebe Malcolm Duncan. You wrote to my aunts at the School of Malcolms requesting aid with your wards. They sent me. They do not have the facilities to work with young children. They have asked me to speak with you in their stead."

Mr. Blair tilted his head in acknowledgment of her introduction. "I am Andrew Blair, guardian for my cousin's children. As you have ascertained, they are gifted in ways most nannies cannot comprehend, but your family seems attuned to. I am a man of business and do not claim to understand their talents, but I acknowledge that the children have been raised. . . to be unusual. Talking to ghosts and levitating objects are the activities of foolish spiritualists in my book."

She supposed she must give him credit for not calling them *weird*. When he let down his defenses, he spoke with a delightful lilt and rolled his r's.

Idly, she plucked a raisin from her biscuit and fed it to Piney in her pocket while she sought the right words. "I have never tutored young children and certainly not gifted ones."

There, she could hope he would send her on her way. Surely her aunts could find someone more adept at schooling. She'd only taught street urchins their letters and numbers and occasionally attempted to instruct their elders. Teaching was not easy. Teaching gifted children with talents beyond hers. . . would be an enormous task.

Her host considered her words, irritatingly unoffended by her eccentric attire or her refusal to cater to his whims. Of course, the man was no doubt desperate.

"You have already taught them a lesson and settled them in where they belong, a task no one has successfully accomplished to my knowledge," he countered. "They have inquiring minds. Curiosity is a family trait, I fear. I'm prepared to offer room and board and a salary commensurate with the task, that is, if *ladies* accept salaries."

She heard a hint of spite in that last part. She needed to ask her aunts more about Mr. Blair's antecedents. They had only told her of his accomplishments, which were considerable. He'd come from no family worth mentioning, managed a university education, and had invented contraptions for the railroad that had launched him into the highest circles.

"I am in need of funds to pay tuition," she said, not revealing her desperation but her goal. "I am prepared to take a position until I've earned what I need. I owe my aunts a great deal, and if this is where they send me, then I'm obliged to consider the offer."

"Taking a paying position with a single gentleman cannot be considered respectable. Will you require a maid or companion?"

Despite looking like a hot-blooded warrior, the citified engineer still sounded like an officious mug. Phoebe bit back a laugh at his concern. He might as well know what to expect. "If my attire doesn't give you a hint of my opinion of proper protocol, perhaps Piney will." She produced the marten from her pocket and smoothed his ruffled fur.

Mr. Blair didn't quite drop his biscuit—he made a quick catch.

"I talk to animals," she merrily continued. "Although *talk* is a human word and doesn't actually define what I do. *Communicate* is probably a better description. I can tell you that Piney is interested in testing everything on the table. I have taught him to eat berries and nuts, but he will happily rid your house of rodents and insects."

"Anyone with knowledge of animals could say that," he objected.

"Yes, of course. If you will put some raisins in your pocket, I'll show him where to find them. He won't jump in your pocket without incentive, I fear." Phoebe was perfectly aware that no one understood her gift. She'd always been happy to leave them in ignorance. She didn't know why she was attempting to impress—or frighten—this man.

"I'll take your word for it," he said dryly, eyeing the animal on his tea table. "I assume pockets are not where he normally lives."

Not certain how to take his acceptance, Phoebe explained, "He belongs in a pine forest, but there are few trees left in the area."

"There is a small pine in the park," he said, looking more interested than he had since they'd sat down. "He would have to dodge dogs and horses and stay out of the road though."

"Small pines are unlikely to have hollows for nests, and he will be very lonely, but if I can keep him with me, I can introduce him to the concept," she agreed. In some ways, the newer part of town had advantages her medieval stone village did not, unless she wished to trespass on Queen Victoria's grounds. So far, she'd resisted the temptation.

"I will have my business partner draw up a contract. How soon can you start, my lady?"

A contract. She gulped. That didn't sound like something she could escape from easily. Hastily, she looked for wiggle room. "As I said, I wish to take classes. A restrictive contract might interfere. Can we not simply agree to go along as we must?"

"I don't do anything without a contract. Discuss your requirements with Mr. Morgan. My housekeeper will show you available rooms if the nursery doesn't suit. You will need to park your bicycle in the mews. I have appearances to keep up if I'm to retain my investors. It would be preferable if the children are taught not to display their. . . talents. . . in public."

Phoebe didn't often get angry, but her temper flared. "You want them to hide who they are? Are you ashamed of them?"

He looked taken aback. "No, of course not. They're children. But the world is full of dangerous characters, and I don't want some sick mind to think a child who speaks to spirits or levitates objects might be marketable."

She deflated again. She had never considered the world a particularly wicked place, but she could see the potential in the elevated atmosphere of New Town. In her part of the city, the wealthy mixed with the poor and everyone knew everyone, so there was no clear class distinction.

On this side of the gardens, the poor saw expensive clothes, enormous townhouses, and purses of gold, and coveted a bit for themselves. She nodded thoughtfully. "That's very sad. I had not thought in those terms. Our family is well known in the old part of the city, but here. . . It's a different world. I shall try to adapt."

"My cousin's wife was gifted. The village where she grew up appreciated her abilities. But talking to the dead and the Sight are acceptable traditions. I'm not certain even Simon realizes what his son does. I don't suppose you know of any male tutors who might have better insight into what a boy like Enoch needs?" He almost sounded human with that question.

"I'm sorry, no, I don't. Our world tends to be peculiarly female. It may be up to you to show him how a man's world works. But he's young yet. Let's bring him up to snuff on the basics and then you may decide what is best." She regretted using flash vocabulary when her new employer winced, but she grew up in the gutters. She didn't see the need to change. He'd have to adapt as well.

"Very well. How soon can you start? And will you need a clothing allowance?" He glanced at her unfashionable attire.

A clothing allowance! Money solved everything? So much for frightening the wretch. Maybe she'd have the twins summon ghosts and scare him into sending her away.

From what she could see, ghosts would merely annoy the dratted man.

FOUR

JACKET SHOVED BACK, HANDS IN HIS TROUSER POCKETS, DREW STUDIED THE pile of rubble that had once been the façade of the tenement he apparently owned. "Convenient," was all he said.

"The stone can probably be reused?" the property manager suggested.

A portly old fellow with the reddened nose of a heavy drinker, the manager had done little about maintenance, until the buildings had become little more than worthless—*dangerous*—piles of rock.

"Brick is more modern and easier to use," Drew said off-handedly, still studying the situation. Aging furnishings remained in the naked flats above. "Are the other buildings in similar shape?"

The neighboring tenements appeared to be tilting toward the damaged one already. Medieval construction had involved labor and materials and very little engineering. Like the city walls surrounding the old town, the ancient edifices were crumbling. It was only a matter of time until someone was killed. More likely, dozens, if the building fell at the wrong time.

Hugh was right. The buildings had to come down.

"I'll have the tenants moved out within the month," Bennett said eagerly. "Dangerous to live in. They'll all be suing us if I don't."

Drew doubted the downtrodden inhabitants of this slum even knew the term *sue*, or had the wherewithal to hire lawyers. His father hadn't. His father had spent the last decade of his life in bed with a broken back. The mine hadn't even sent his last week's wages after the accident. If Drew hadn't already graduated and found work. . . His parents would have ended up in the street.

His mother still could, if the consortium didn't make a profit soon. Every day they delayed tearing down this slum cost them interest.

Drew watched a duster-cloaked figure enter one of the endangered buildings. Perhaps top hats and striped stockings were the fashion for women in this part of town.

Lady Phoebe had refused to take the position until she'd seen his contract.

"That's her," Bennett growled. "That's the one threatening to sue. I'll have to drag her out of there afore they all get riled." He stomped off after the eccentric female.

Drew studied the squalid alley and hummed tunelessly as he calculated the equipment required to demolish an entire block and the woman in the duster who threatened to sue. A woman who might have a family solicitor?

Surely not.

His partner hurried down the street, folders of papers flapping in the breeze his pace created. "See?" Hugh cried. "It's perfect. We're not far from Holyrood. A row of terrace houses will be snapped up by statesmen, at the very least."

"How many of those flats are empty?" Now that he had time to consider, Drew was pretty damned certain the poor devils living in that squalor wouldn't know where to find a solicitor, even if they could afford one, which they couldn't.

Hugh blinked, pulled out his reports, and shook his head when he couldn't find the answer in his numbers. "I don't know."

"If people are still living in flats with no wall, then they're desperate, and I'm going to assume every room in every building is taken." Counting the floors in the three buildings, Drew made a hasty calculation. "Not counting the shops on street level, I estimate seven floors of ten rooms each, times three buildings, minimum one person per room—at least two hundred people. Quite likely two or three times that."

Hugh glanced nervously up and down the alley. The street was so narrow that women had hung clotheslines across it. Skirts and long underwear flapped briskly in the breeze. A gaggle of children kicked a rock down the street. Drew waited for his assistant to grasp that people *lived* in these piles of crumbling stone.

Surely Lady Phoebe didn't. If that was her he'd seen, she must be one of the bored philanthropists determined to improve what couldn't be improved. She had no case.

Hugh was no doubt right. Tearing down these cesspools would be doing everyone a favor.

Loud voices emerged from the tenement Bennett had entered in pursuit of the eccentric female who might or not be Lady Phoebe. A shoe flew out an open window, followed by a flower pot. The shoe was a man's.

"Will he throw the tenants out the window next?" Drew asked, watching with the morbid fascination of a spectator unable to prevent two vehicles from colliding.

An enormous raven swooped low, screeching in its raspy voice, landing on the rotten frame of the open window. The argument escalated. Drew wondered if he should intervene, but he wasn't entirely certain if he'd know which side to take—the story of his life these days.

A moment later, the raven screeched and entered the building. The shrieks that followed were decidedly masculine.

"Looks like it's Bennett who will be flung out," Drew decided.

"Do we rescue him?" Hugh asked, staring at the building with incredulity.

Drew considered it. "No, I think we insist that Bennett relocate the tenants. We can't afford to be sued."

He walked away, leaving the manager to whatever fate the odd female chose for him.

STILL FUMING OVER THE EARLY MORNING ENCOUNTER WITH BENNETT, PHOEBE pedaled furiously across the bridge, toward the almost rural environs of the veterinary schools. Before she even considered committing herself to servitude, she needed to speak with someone in charge of the schools. Perhaps she could *owe* the tuition.

And if nothing could be worked out now, she needed to remind herself of why she must accept Mr. Blair's damnable contract in hopes of her future education.

There were actually two schools for animal doctors in the same area. She had heard that the university was now accepting women, even if they wouldn't give them degrees. The vet schools were private, but they associated with the university. Times were changing. Maybe it wouldn't matter if she was female.

Heart pounding so hard she feared she might pass out, Phoebe entered a door marked OFFICE. A woman sat there, and her hopes rose.

She walked out five minutes later, shattered. They did not take women. They did not have scholarships, even if she were a man. They taught courses on horse anatomy and breeding, which were not at all proper for women. They gave their degrees to farriers with the ability to deal with large bovines, not to frail females who would undoubtedly faint if they smelled dung.

Trying not to weep in frustration and despair, Phoebe walked her bicycle toward the newer veterinary school, when she heard a mewling cry. Students brushed past her, too caught up in their own affairs to notice or even care. It was quite obvious these *men* didn't consider small animals worth studying.

Never having had a need to stick to any schedule, Phoebe lingered, listening.

Would she be able to wander and linger once she had a *contract*? She was supposed to be on her way to speak to Mr. Blair's partner now.

Heedless of the time, she leaned her penny farthing against a wall, lifted her skirt, and clambered down a grassy hillside. A tiny wet kitten clung to the bank of a stream. It appeared to be a lovely ginger. Glancing up at the bridge she'd crossed earlier, Phoebe uttered as many curse words as she could summon while gathering the poor creature into her skirt to dry it off. She didn't need to read the creature's mind to know that it had been flung into the water—possibly with its siblings.

There were no signs of other kitty survivors. She hoped they'd escaped on their own. Distracted from her own woes, she wrapped the trembling creature in her handkerchief. The castle's one o'clock gun went off as she did so. She was late.

Striding up the bank, she tucked the kitten in her other coat pocket and reclaimed her bicycle. "Where will I keep you if I sign this contract?" she asked Piney and the new kitten. They didn't answer, of course.

Above, Raven screamed, and she frowned in memory of the morning's confrontation with Mr. Bennett. Her pets needed a home.

"Mr. Blair has a lovely rooftop," she told the bird. "I'll bring you treats. You were brilliant today."

The raven was smarter than the marten. Phoebe didn't know exactly how much the bird understood, but he'd known to attack Bennett when she called him.

"He thought he could *threaten* me," Phoebe said, still amazed at the landlord's audacity. "I think we showed him. Maybe I should ask the lawyer about the other tenants. Surely they have rights too." Only her pets would listen to her radical notions.

Maybe she couldn't be an animal doctor anytime soon, but she could see about suing her landlord and the consortium. She would visit the family solicitor right after she met with Mr. Morgan, which gave her another idea.

Remembering Mr. Blair's admonition about hiding her bicycle, Phoebe chained it to a decorative fence in the park rather than wheel around to the carriage alley and traipse back to the front again.

Mr. Blair lived in a row of attached terrace houses constructed of ashlar stone, each one with identical windows and pilasters and steps up to the first floor. Pretty, but boring, Phoebe decided as she climbed the well-scrubbed marble.

She'd had Raven check the roof as she rode up to be certain the children weren't attempting flight again. The only thing interesting about this position was the children. For them, for her aunts, for her future, she would go through with this. Somehow.

The same petite maid answered the knocker. This time, she didn't argue with Phoebe but bobbed a respectful curtsy and led her down the hall to a small dark office.

Phoebe tried to reach out to the children with her mind, but she'd never been successful with anything other than the simple thought-images of animals.

A large, auburn-haired man with mutton chops and spectacles stood to greet her, looking vaguely uncomfortable. "Lady Phoebe? Hugh Morgan. I was expecting you earlier. I have another meeting and don't have time to go over the finer points of your contract now."

Feeling rebellious and not ready to be pinned down, Phoebe nodded knowingly. "Of course. I'm only here to pick up the papers and deliver them to my solicitor. I never sign anything without his advice."

Her family solicitor would fall on his face in shock if he heard that bouncer.

Mr. Morgan blinked in surprise, removed his spectacles, and polished them. "Naturally, yes," he spoke slowly, as if finding his way around the words. "I suppose that is wise. He can explain the details, although he may not understand their necessity. Mr. Blair is most concerned about the welfare of his wards."

She needed to remind herself of why she was even touching these papers—the children.

"Commendable. In that case, perhaps you could show me to the nursery floor and whatever accommodation you have in mind? We shouldn't delay the children's education over minor details like pieces of paper." Without giving the poor man a chance to protest, Phoebe turned on her heel and headed for the stairs.

Having no memory of the earl who had fathered her and died adventuring, Phoebe was a stranger to discipline. Her mother had been an invalid in Phoebe's adolescent years. Their servants, such as they'd been, had no hold over her. She knew exactly how to get her way.

Poor Mr. Morgan didn't have a chance of holding her back.

She swept into the nursery where Enoch idly bounced a ball without touching it, and Clare and Cat whispered to a wall, while a bewildered nursemaid looked on.

"Are you ready for a walk in the park?" Phoebe cried, appalled that their active minds had been reduced to such tedium.

As the children shouted in excitement and raced for their coats, poor Mr. Morgan coughed and sputtered. "Mr. Blair doesn't want them introduced to the public just yet."

With a militant gleam in her eye, Phoebe tightened the ribbon on her hat. "And *that* is why a contract will not suit at all."

FIVE

WITH MISS HIGGINBOTHAM'S GLOVED HAND ON HIS COAT SLEEVE, DREW matched her small steps and strolled—minced might be a better word—toward his neighbor's house. Miss Higginbotham was everything a wife needed to be—quiet, thoughtful, well-versed in society, fashion, and etiquette, the kind of well-bred female who would support his projects and impress his investors. She would mind his household while he devoted his attention to inventions.

Maybe she'd even persuade Cook to feed him when he was ready to eat.

Behind them, her aunt, Mrs. Dalrymple, drilled holes in their backs. It was damned difficult to court with the scheming besom watching their every move.

Miss Higginbotham was a pale blonde with a generous dowry from her deceased merchant father. Her uncle, his neighbor Dalrymple, had helped Drew when he'd arrived in the city. He also belonged to the investment consortium. The lady was a respectable match.

As Rose had been, but she'd vanished the instant Simon's brats had descended upon him. He needed to introduce Miss Higginbotham to his household under controlled circumstances that wouldn't send her screaming into the street.

How likely was that?

Hearing childish squeals, Drew frowned. The nannies had been *told* to keep the children hidden, for excellent reason. He'd have to see that this never happened again.

He hurriedly steered the lady up the stairs to her aunt's home. The lady resisted, peering over her shoulder to the park. "I never hear children playing. This neighborhood is so very staid and elderly."

Her formidable aunt glared in the direction of the fenced patch of greenery shielding the respectable terrace houses from the noise of the street. "Children should be seen and not heard," Mrs. Dalrymple announced ominously.

"I'm sure they'll be in a classroom soon," Drew said, eager to park the ladies so he could redirect the children. "I had a lovely time this afternoon, Miss Higginbotham. I hope you will allow me to call on you again."

"What is that woman doing, *climbing a tree?*" Mrs. Dalrymple continued to glare at the park. "Since when are riff-raff allowed in the park? Isn't there a key to the gate?"

Drew desperately tried not to look in that direction. "I have a meeting shortly and must leave you at your door. I will send a note around tomorrow, shall I?"

It was no use. Mrs. Dalrymple sailed off to clear the park of riff-raff, which Drew was pretty certain meant his wards and their new governess.

Lady Phoebe was a teacher, so he couldn't call her a nanny, right? Never having grown up with them, the complexities of servants eluded him.

"My aunt is quite opinionated on the matter of proper behavior for children," Miss Higginbotham murmured apologetically.

Since those were more words than he'd heard from her all afternoon, Drew was forced to heed them. "I've never given the behavior of children any thought," he admitted. "But I should think they ought to be allowed to play."

"Oh no, that encourages rebellion," she whispered. "They must be taught to mind at an early age."

For the second time that day, he heard heated voices raised in argument.

"This park does not belong to you, madam." Lady Phoebe's ringing vowels were apparently meant to carry over the din of screaming children. Polite remonstrations didn't stand a chance against her foghorn voice when she chose to use it. "If you continue to frighten the children in such a manner, madam," the governess continued with ire, "I shall be forced to call a constable. Come along, children, we shall sing a merry tune and disperse all angry vibrations."

Vibrations? Drew winced as the governess launched into a nursery song that his wards knew well enough to scream at the top of their lungs, however untunefully.

Since the dainty woman on his arm wasn't in any hurry to miss the circus, Drew surrendered in defeat and turned to watch Lady Phoebe and the weans marching from the park, singing at the top of their lungs. The tawny-haired twins were adorable in matching pinafores. How could anyone scold them? Enoch. . . well, the sturdy lad looked just like his dark father, who had the devil in him.

The governess had removed her faded duster and flat hat. Considering what she was wearing, he almost wished them back.

Today, she wore a completely unfashionable short walking dress in cherry-red with no ruffles, crinoline, or panniers to conceal her boots. Admittedly, the pretty striped bodice accentuated her girlish figure. She did not sport the puffed-up foolery other ladies wore, so he could see her slender bosom and waist were as nature made them. He discreetly glanced down at the pouty pigeon bosom of his companion and wondered how much was lace and wire and how much was real.

As the children marched toward him, he faced his doom.

"Ah, Mr. Blair," his new governess called happily. "You are home in time for tea. The children wish to show you what they have learned today."

"Mr. Blair!" Mrs. Dalrymple cried in horror, waddling after them. "Surely these creatures do not belong to your household."

Damnation. He'd hidden the *creatures* for nine months. One rebellious governess. . . and the secret was out. He could strangle her.

Lady Phoebe didn't look the least concerned as she approached his fashionably dressed companion. Like any other privileged aristocrat he'd ever known, she stuck out her gloved hand as if everyone would be pleased to meet her. "Hello, I am Lady Phoebe Duncan. You must be Mr. Blair's neighbor. I hope we will become better acquainted."

Dashitall, the woman had more nerve than a carnival barker.

Miss Higginbotham automatically bobbed a curtsy. "Dahlia Higginbotham," she whispered, in obvious awe of being addressed by a noble.

"Dahlia, go inside at once. This is no lady." Mrs. Dalrymple swung on Drew. "And you, sir, are no gentleman to keep such. . . *creatures*. . . as this in your household."

Ow.

With a big, bright smile, the governess addressed her nearly apoplectic accuser. "You may write my uncle, the Earl of Drumsmoore, to verify my identity, but I warn you he will find it extremely obnoxious behavior. Our family is well known, although due to their courageous and often reckless behavior, my father's side is small."

Lady Phoebe turned her smile away from Mrs. Dalrymple to Drew. "We shall meet you over the tea table."

Turning to the children, she gestured for them to hustle up the steps next door. Eyes wide in curiosity, they hastened to obey.

Drew wondered where the ferret was. Or weasel. Or whatever.

He glanced at the lady's skirt but couldn't see if she had pockets. He could tell, however, that she had well-rounded hips that swayed delectably. How the hell did he reprimand an earl's daughter?

"Is she really related to an earl?" Miss Higginbotham whispered as her aunt grabbed her elbow and dragged her toward the door.

"And probably half the aristocracy, including the queen," Drew said with a sigh. Hugh had looked up her genealogy. Lady Phoebe very definitely existed.

Both women managed to look horrified, for different reasons, as they retreated inside.

Muttering about aristocratic arrogance, Drew stomped down his neighbor's steps and up his own.

∾

PHOEBE HELD BACK A SIGH. SHE REALLY NEEDED TO LEARN TO RESIST temptation. But the children had looked so bored, she'd impetuously set aside her intention to visit her solicitor. And then she'd seen the imposing Mr. Blair walking with that insipid piece of fluff and the dragon lady—and all sense had flown out the window.

She'd mentioned her *uncle*. She never did that. She despised the old miser.

But she'd taken an instant dislike to the harridan calling her students insulting names, and one thing had led to another. . . and here she was, with Mr. Blair glaring down at her as if she'd developed two heads and horns.

She tugged at her gloves and smiled mindlessly up at him. Even though she'd worn her best heels, he was taller. "Are you too busy for tea? I can teach them proper etiquette in the nursery, but they are very eager to make you proud of them."

"Doesn't a governess belong in a nursery?" he asked with what almost sounded like genuine puzzlement.

She suspected from Mr. Blair's less-than-polished accent that he'd never had a governess or a nursery. She really shouldn't take advantage of him, but she simply did not approve of pretending children didn't exist.

"Perhaps an ordinary governess and ordinary children might be hidden from sight," she said brightly. "But I am a *tutor*, and your wards are not only gifted, they are exceptionally intelligent. They require extra attention. As I said, we can have tea in the nursery, if you prefer. But you might wish to know what they are learning."

She saw his struggle and clenched her fingers into her palms. Due to straitened circumstances, she'd often been neglected as a child. She loved learning, but there was only so much she could teach herself after her governess had left. When her father traveled, and after his death, her mother had had more time to attend to Phoebe's instruction, but then she had been struck ill. Her neighbor, the professor, had brought her books and taught her when he could, but there had been no one to appreciate her achievements.

Phoebe wouldn't let Mr. Blair's wards be ignored or their achievements looked down upon. Children needed adult encouragement to thrive.

Her employer pulled out his pocket watch, checked the time, and scowled. "Give me a few minutes to send a message. I suppose I can miss a meeting for this occasion. Does this mean you and Mr. Morgan have come to an agreement on the contract?"

"Oh no, this means I'm missing a meeting with my solicitor so he may read the contract for me," she said with as much self-importance as she could summon. She'd meet the man on his own terms, by gum.

His dark eyebrows soared but he had the grace to nod. "In the parlor in fifteen minutes?"

AFTER DISPATCHING A SERVANT TO CANCEL HIS MEETING AND JOINING LADY Phoebe and his wards at the tea table, Drew wished he'd spared a minute to spruce up.

Despite having spent the afternoon romping in the park, Lady Phoebe smelled of sunshine and roses. Her shirtwaist was no longer crisp—he dutifully attempted not to notice her round bosom. Her abundant chestnut hair had become somewhat disheveled, but the tousled look seemed more inviting than neatly styled curls.

But mostly, she exuded high spirits and energy that made him feel old and staid.

"We have shown the pine trees to Piney," she announced, pouring the tea with expertise.

"He does not approve," Clare said with more vigor than he'd heard her use since her arrival.

"There is no hollow for his nest," Enoch explained, not to be outdone. He practically swallowed his quarter sandwich whole and reached for another.

"Piney needs a box," Cat declared. "So does Kitty."

Kitty? Drew glanced at his new—yet uncontracted—governess. . . tutor. Blue eyes danced with mischief.

Unused to servants, refusing to fall for blue eyes, he practiced being stern. "Who is Kitty?"

"We couldn't call her Cat. That's my name," his ward said complacently.

The twins were frail four-year-olds with tawny hair like their mother's. Drew had scarcely heard them speak two words before Lady Phoebe's arrival. They didn't smile or bounce now. They just regarded him with those big, shadowed, blue eyes and waited.

"The children say you have a workshop," Lady Phoebe added expectantly.

Enlightenment ensued. Drew almost sputtered into his tea. Use his highly technical workshop and his valuable time to build a foolish crate? He congratulated himself on a swift recovery. "You wish me to build boxes for a weasel and an invisible kitten?"

"She's not invisible," Enoch said, politely holding up his plate for a refill. "Clare tried to make herself invisible like a ghost, but it didn't work."

"I don't think we can make ourselves invisible," Lady Phoebe said sympathetically. "We'll need to consult the Librarian. I shall write to her this evening."

The *Librarian*? Hearing the capital L quite distinctly, Drew chewed his sandwich and listened. For young children, his wards seemed remarkably well behaved, although Cat was getting a little squirmy. He kept a wary eye on her.

"Do you know if their mother's journals were sent to the Malcolm library?" the lady asked.

"I didn't know they existed," he admitted. A frisson of fear followed. Could Letitia have left a journal?

"Will you stay with us tonight, my lady?" Clare asked. "Mama can't always visit."

Since her mother was quite dead, Drew swallowed his biscuit wrong and coughed.

The question didn't faze Lady Phoebe. "I'm sorry, not tonight. I played with you today instead of visiting my solicitor. I shall move my boxes in once your guardian and I have settled our business. You must sing if you are afraid or lonely. Do you know any brave songs?"

The conversation continued in this inane but edifying fashion until all the food was consumed and the children began to look weary.

Rather than let the flibbertigibbet governess escape, Drew called for the nursemaid to lead them off for baths and bed.

Lady Phoebe rose as if prepared to depart. Drew pointed at her chair. "Sit, my lady. Explain, please."

She sat, folded her hands in her lap, and demurely cast her lashes down so he couldn't read her expression. "Yes, sir?"

He wasn't entirely certain if she was questioning his command or his title.

"One of the clauses of our contract expressly states the children *will not be removed from the house* without my permission," he said sternly.

"I have not yet read your contract, and I will most certainly strike that clause before signing it." She spoke matter-of-factly, without a hint of ire. "Children cannot be confined to four walls like animals in a cage, especially ones with minds as active as theirs."

Hard to argue when he felt the same, but there were more important considerations. "They cannot be associated with this house." The whole point of bringing them to Edinburgh was to hide them. He'd been successful until this intrepid female came along. "Take them in the carriage to the gardens, if you must, but either Mr. Morgan or I must accompany you."

Her chin shot up. There was the blue blaze of defiance he expected.

"Are you sure you're not ashamed of them? Or perhaps you don't wish your suit hampered by children?"

Well, there was that, too, which was why he'd mentioned the public gardens. But his main reason was their safety. "My affairs are none of yours," he asserted. He was as angry at himself as with her. He *ought* to be able to handle this conversation with more authority.

"Then perhaps this arrangement will not suit. If I cannot be in charge of their education, you may as well hire someone more suited to servitude."

And there it was—she wasn't a servant. She would never obey his orders.

Drew ran his hand through his hair while he sought words. "I have no good way to put this." That was an understatement. "But we have some reason to believe their mother's death was not an accident. I'm not yet ready to let down my guard against the potential of assassins following them here."

Her eyes widened into huge saucers. "Oh my. You should have told me from the outset."

Dung beetles. Here it came. His one chance of obtaining an understanding governess, and he'd ruined it. He waited for her to throw her napkin at him and stalk off.

"I'll have to enlist Raven." Looking as if she was running mental lists, she stood and rang for the maid. "I cannot possibly move in this evening, but I'll leave my pets. Piney and Raven are trained at least, and the children are acquainted with them. They can learn to heed their warnings. We'll start to work on the kitten and any other creatures I find in the morning."

She asked the maid for her coat as Drew rose in confusion. "Train? Other creatures?"

"Do nae fash yersel'," she said absent-mindedly. "You'll not notice until it matters."

He doubted that, but if she was reduced to dialect, her mind was obviously not on him—as his was on her. He'd best remove temptation from his presence.

"The nights come early. Let me take you home in my carriage." Drew tried to keep the question out of his voice and off his tongue. Sometimes, restraint was the better part of valor.

She raised her expressive eyebrows. "I'm not certain a fancy carriage is safe in the close, but I suppose you may let me off in High Street, if my penny farthing will fit on back."

"It will fit. And I'll return in the morning to help with your boxes."

Yes, he mentally shouted. Yes, she was coming! He could have his life back!

Not until he had delivered her to her aunts' old but very respectable townhouse did he realize there had been no further mention of a contract.

SIX

"OH, MY, WITH ALL THAT DARK HAIR, IT'S A GOOD THING HE DOESN'T WEAR a mustache!" Olivia, one of Phoebe's distant cousins, said with a laugh. Still wearing mourning, she peered from the upper story window at the gentleman on the doorstep below.

"He is very handsome." Merry—still another of Phoebe's extended family—sounded envious.

"And twice your age," Phoebe scolded, pulling on her gloves. "Mr. Blair already has three children on his hands and doesn't need a fourth."

Merry stuck her tongue out at her. "I shall be seventeen next month. And I'm already teaching three children."

"Well, I shall be certain to recommend you should I not suit the position. Mr. Blair and I do not see eye-to-eye on many levels."

"Including height," Olivia said with a laugh. "If you did not wear those ridiculous boots, you'd barely reach his shoulder."

"My boots are useful. One of the advantages men have over us is size. I merely seek to equalize my position." Phoebe picked up her carpet bag and glanced around to see if she'd forgotten anything.

Servants were already carrying her trunk downstairs. Her cousins' nonsense was a welcome distraction from the knowledge that she was making a giant, possibly irrevocable, step into a frightening new world. She tried very hard not to shake in her maligned boots.

She had to remember she was a woman of the world who had a meeting with a solicitor over contracts and lawsuits.

"Phoebe kicks and stomps," Merry explained to her more-sheltered cousin. "You've never seen her in action."

"The streets are sometimes rough and not everyone knows me." Phoebe adjusted her hat. "Sometimes, a polite introduction isn't sufficient."

Olivia covered her mouth. Phoebe didn't worry if she concealed laughter or horror. Her cousin had lived gently in the country until circumstances had changed, and she'd sought refuge at the school. Life happened, as they all knew too well. Life *kept* happening. They had to adjust or starve.

Finding a worthy goal helped push past fear. She would *earn* her own education.

Leaving her cousins to watch from windows, Phoebe sailed down the stairs, hugged her aunts, and followed Mr. Blair to his waiting carriage. He'd managed to turn it around at the bottom of the close instead of forcing her to walk to High Street, as she'd feared.

She tried not to imagine what he thought of the neighborhood. At least her aunts' home looked reasonably respectable. No clothing hung on a line in this lane.

"I built boxes," he said stiffly as he helped her to a seat.

It took her a moment to follow the path of his thoughts. He'd built boxes for the pets! "That is most excellent, thank you." Phoebe waved at a carter passing by, then admired a trinket a child ran up to show her. She'd known these people all her life. The back lanes of the medieval town were her home.

Somehow, for the sake of Mr. Blair's orphaned wards, she must make a new home. She tried to console herself by knowing she wouldn't be far from the veterinary schools, but she was feeling discouraged about them teaching her how to help the small animals she found.

"And kind of you to fulfill the requests of children," she acknowledged. "I know you cannot understand my relationship with animals, so it is generous of you to listen to your wards and their concerns for pets."

"Letitia, the children's mother, had the Sight. She saw danger. We didn't listen," he said gruffly. "I try to listen now." His tone was remorseful.

"The Sight is difficult to interpret. Knowing there is danger doesn't provide sufficient guidance," she said when he climbed up and took the reins. "What happened?"

He sat silent for a moment, as if unwilling to explain. He shook the leathers and put the horse in motion before speaking. "Letitia and Simon were in a carriage. They'd meant to visit an ailing tenant and do a little shopping in the village. The children went with them everywhere, but they were feverish that morning and were left behind. The axle gave out going downhill. Simon swore it was cut. Letitia was thrown from the carriage while he struggled to halt the horses."

"Praise all that is holy," Phoebe whispered. "Either the saints watched over the children, or Letitia heeded her instinct."

"That's what Simon said, once he was coherent. He blames himself, which is patently ridiculous." Mr. Blair sounded more angry than sorrowful.

"Why would he believe it was no accident?" Phoebe hadn't been in a carriage in ages. Distracted by the man beside her, the view, and the tragic story, she didn't know which way to turn. New Town sprawled below as the horse sedately clopped down the hill. What would it be like if the axle broke as they turned toward the bridge?

She gripped the side, just in case.

"The carriage was new," Mr. Blair said. "Simon had checked it over carefully and driven it himself before allowing his family in it. He claims they hit no rut to cause the rod to snap. You'd have to know Simon to understand his caution."

"But his whole family could have been killed," she cried, understanding the gravity. "Why would anyone wish to harm children?"

Phoebe watched as her employer's handsome visage darkened into a frown. He'd be ferocious in defense of what he considered his. The notion caused an inexplicable thrill. She knew too few people with that core of strength.

"I tell you all this only so you will understand the danger. Simon is having difficulties with his neighbors," he answered grudgingly. "He's a fair employer, unlike some I could name. He is part of my investment consortium. We planned to build an iron manufactory on his land that would use his coal with a better return than the current market. There are people who despise factories. And other mine owners who lost workers because they resist Simon's willingness to pay for good labor. I do not claim to understand such ignorance, but neighboring landowners resent him. The bank recently offered to buy him out to prevent us from continuing with the project."

He expertly steered the horses over the bridge and into the wider— safer—streets of the new town. "Industry must come if we are to feed families. If nothing else, the Clearances proved that agriculture only feeds landowners."

Phoebe nodded a grim understanding, even as she admired the shiny new shops and mansions they passed. "People resist change. It's human nature. But I doubt that is reason for killing, unless one is quite mad."

He frowned but acknowledged that. "It almost has to go back to money, doesn't it? But why not just kill Simon without risking innocents?"

"Well, they have effectively killed him if he's drinking himself to death." She shot him a hasty glance. "I'm sorry. Servants gossip."

He shrugged. "It's common knowledge that's the reason the children are with me."

Something in the way he said that caused Phoebe to pause. If their father was anything like Mr. Blair— then there was more going on than met the eye. "Did the children bring anyone from home with them?"

"The nursemaid. She's an old family retainer, and they needed some semblance of familiarity."

"Then it is not likely they are in danger here—unless the *children* know something they shouldn't." She had to say it. Her own family had been harmed in too many ways because of what they knew or could do.

"You and your kind are downright spooky. I do not claim to under- stand," Mr. Blair said with a sigh. "Clare took an instant dislike to one of the stableboys. He'd been with the family for years. She yelled at him. You've met Clare. She does not yell. He left shortly after Clare refused to go anywhere near him."

Phoebe picked at her gloves, fearing what a gifted child might see to cause this reaction. "It's hard to say what she sees or how much she understands. He may have just kicked a horse when he thought no one was looking." She knew what it was like not to be understood or not to be believed. Understanding a gifted child took patience.

That a killer might believe Clare *knew* something seemed hard to accept, but if her mother had sensed danger. . . It was possible someone might be superstitious enough to fear the children as well. "Or, I suppose, very bad men might think harming the children will drive their father completely mad or drive him from his land."

Mr. Blair considered her notions as he guided the rig down the carriage alley. "Either is possible. We're searching for the stableboy. He certainly had the opportunity to tamper with the axle and his disappearance is suspect."

"Have you looked for their mother's journals? Most Malcolms keep them."

His dark eyebrows drew down in perplexity or a frown. "I have no notion. I can't imagine Letitia could write anything that predicted her death or a possible killer."

"We often write our fears and the reason for them. There might be clues." Phoebe turned over other possibilities in her mind. The children needed a different sort of defense than the ones she'd erected around her mother's home. "I will begin training the animals at once. I may make some odd requests. I would appreciate it if you would inform your servants that they are for a special project."

As he stopped the vehicle in the carriage lane behind his house, he shot her a peculiar look, the kind with which she was most familiar when she said things like that. But he didn't mock.

The carriage swayed as he climbed down. An aging stable man staggered up to take the reins, and Mr. Blair offered his gloved hand to assist Phoebe. "You will not take the children out again?"

She accepted his assistance and took a moment to admire her new employer's broad chest and masculine scent before replying regretfully, "No, I make no promises. They must learn to navigate their surroundings and be aware of dangers. Surrounding them in cotton batting only turns them into mice."

She walked off, leaving him to deal with her bags.

DREW WAS STILL STEWING OVER THE LADY'S HIGH-HANDED COMMENT WHEN he strode out later that morning, already late for the transportation board meeting.

He almost collided on the doorstep with a bespectacled fellow with graying mustache wearing a low-crowned, curled-brim hat from a prior decade.

"My pardon," the older man said, stepping aside. "Is this the residence of Mr. Andrew Blair?"

"It is. I'm he. You'll have to make an appointment," Drew said, impatiently stepping toward the street, expecting the gentleman to follow.

"I have an appointment with Lady Phoebe. Good meeting you, sir. I'm Thomas Lithgow, Esquire, the family solicitor." He hung his umbrella over his left arm and offered his right hand.

Hell and tarnation. She was still going to argue over the contract? "Pleased to meet you, Mr. Lithgow. I'll be off then." Drew lifted his top hat in farewell.

He hadn't expected his life to become this complicated when he'd agreed to take the children. A governess who had a lawyer! The end of the world must be nigh.

He'd always avoided the aristocracy with their inherent belief that blood made them better than people who worked for a living. The privileged few had had their own way for so long that they'd become unreasonable in their expectations. A governess who had her own lawyer! There was a gulf a mile wide between his upbringing and hers.

Drew believed in hard work and education. The upper class apparently believed in the magical power of connections. Maybe they were right. Since he didn't know any powerful people in aristocratic circles, he wasn't likely to find out. He'd settle for the middling class businessmen who understood profits.

Where in damnation did *Lady* Phoebe fit into this equation?

He had just reached the main thoroughfare when Dalrymple's carriage pulled up beside him.

"Climb in. We'll go to the meeting together," the older man suggested.

Drew had wanted to clear his head with a brisk walk, but he climbed in anyway. Sometimes his neighbor had valuable insights. Drew had quite a bit invested in the consortium with Dalrymple, so he liked to keep on top of what was happening.

"The meeting is just routine business today, isn't it?" he asked, settling onto the cushioned seat.

"As far as I know." Dalrymple made a dismissive gesture with his chubby hand. "The women tell me you have children. I hadn't realized that. Your own?"

Simon shrugged, uncomfortable with explaining his family to outsiders. "My wards."

His neighbor nodded knowingly. "Family can be an imposition. You have to put them to use, although I understand yours are a little young yet. I wanted to bend your ear about the new education bill the women are championing."

Relieved that he needn't explain, Drew studied his new boots with the elastic siding instead of buttons. They saved time, he supposed, but they needed to be broken in. "Can't say I've paid attention. Education is always a good thing, isn't it?"

"They want to take education out of the hands of the kirks and made free for *all*," Dalrymple objected. "They'll need buildings and teachers and those don't come free. You know what that means."

"The kirk schools aren't regulated in any way," Drew said, not sure what this topic had to do with anything. "I understand the legislation simply establishes a school board to see that all students receive a proper education, and not just lashings at the whim of some misguided reformer."

He'd been on the receiving side of some of those poor kirk schools. He'd been large enough to intimidate teachers, and smart enough to work his way up to better schools. That didn't mean everyone had his advantages.

"Let the kirks reform, then. We don't need to be paying our hard-earned money for the thieves and scalawags in the slums. Just think of those lazy Irish in Cowgate! I'll pay my tithe to the kirk. The government has no place wasting it on some chumpy goody two-shoes notions."

Drew had the uneasy feeling that he'd been one of the scalawags in the slums in Dalrymple's world, so he just grunted noncommittally, letting the older man rant.

"Then you'll support me when I run for the council?" Dalrymple finished as he pulled up at their destination.

Startled by the demand, Drew didn't have an appropriate response prepared. Dalrymple was a useful man to know, but he was receiving the impression that his neighbor wasn't precisely open-minded.

"I'll certainly think on it," he said enthusiastically, shaking the older man's hand. "I appreciate the ride. There's Northolt. I need to speak with him. I'll see you inside."

"I'd rather build boxes and pound nails," Drew muttered later as the meeting drew on over some infinitesimal argument.

He liked making money, he reminded himself. His family relied on his money. His mother couldn't work. His sisters had growing families. Simon's ambitions required cash. His wards would need schooling.

He'd turned a few boring valves and screws into patents and manufactories which had produced his first success. He couldn't count on everything he did achieving the same level of profit. So he had to invest with men who understood money better than he did, which meant working with the consortium. Not being able to putter and play was part of growing up.

A fact Lady Phoebe didn't acknowledge, he concluded as he returned home that afternoon to find the children and the new governess running about the house, apparently in a game of hide and seek. How the devil could he work in these conditions?

Drew growled at Enoch crouching under his worktable. Before he could order the brat out, the boy held a finger to his lips and pointed.

A whiskered nose quivered and sniffed from beneath a stack of rags Drew had left on the floor. The weasel?

Torn between wanting to work and discovering what the hell was happening, he waited impatiently.

Satisfied the room was safe, the creature—a mouse!—scampered from hiding and under the table, where it chattered enthusiastically, then fled under a far cabinet. His house had mice or was the lady bringing them in like the cat?

"It found me," Enoch cried, grinning from ear to ear. "I gave him seeds as a reward."

"I see," Drew said, although he didn't. "And the purpose of this exercise?"

"First, to teach him not to fear me," Enoch said, crawling out and dusting himself off. "Lady Phoebe says her mice chatter to let her know when there is trouble. But she can hear them in her head. She wants them to come find us so we can hear too."

She heard mice in her head? Maybe he should rethink the suitability of the new governess.

But he wanted to work and this seemed a harmless game. "You'll need to find better hiding places than here. I have sharp tools you can hurt yourself on. Did you learn anything else today?"

"We are writing a letter to the Librarian. The twins don't write their letters well, but I finished mine," he said in evident satisfaction. "Is it time for tea?"

"Maybe you should ask the mouse," Drew said dryly. "Run up to the nursery and see."

He was deeply immersed in aligning the pterotype's keys when Hugh arrived, waving papers as usual.

"Your governess and her solicitor have made mincemeat of our contract," his partner complained. "We might as well have no contract at all."

"Which I suspect is the lady's intention." The mention of food made him realize he was feeling peckish, and he pushed away from the table. "Can we discuss this over tea?"

Hugh wrinkled his broad nose. "If we can find anything to eat, we will have to take it to your office or the dining room," he said stiffly, with disapproval. "The lady and the children are playing a game with the kitten in the parlor, and cats make me sneeze."

"Then tell them to play elsewhere." Drew strode down the hall past the windowless office to the sunny parlor. He and Hugh never used the formal dining room. They had organized their boxes of supplies and files there.

The children sat on the floor, watching as a brown and gray tabby slept in a cozy nest they'd made in a basket.

With her unruly tresses uncovered and pinned in loops that were already falling into temptingly touchable curls, Lady Phoebe beamed at their arrival. "Kittens need a lot of sleep," she informed them.

Drew dragged his mind back to the situation at hand. "I see that. Could he sleep elsewhere? Felines are an irritation to Hugh's nostrils, and we need the parlor for discussing the changes in your damn—" He cut off the curse and amended, "In your contract."

"Our apologies, Mr. Morgan." She stood and handed the basket handle to Enoch. "I think Kitty has done an astounding job of locating all the intruders. She needs her rest."

Intruders? Drew refused to ask. It was obvious the only intruders here were animals.

"Children, why don't you run up and fetch your favorite book and practice finding your letters and words you know in it? I'll be up after I speak with your guardian."

Feeling a little more confident that the lady had heeded his request, Drew watched in approval as the children obediently curtseyed, bowed, and trudged upstairs with the kitten, only bickering slightly over who got to hold the basket.

Lady Phoebe brushed off her crinoline-free skirt—in bright blue wool today—and beamed at them. Drew knew better than to fall for her wide-eyed, deceptive smile. He waited for the ax to fall.

"Piney and Raven have been exploring the neighborhood. You have a vagrant living behind the stable, and the Dalrymple cook has been feeding him. You might wish to learn more. And there is an infestation of squirrels in your attic. I dislike letting Piney use his predator instincts, but squirrels are destructive and do not belong inside. I'd rather they fled outside where I might put them to better use."

"You're asking my permission?" Drew asked in confusion, fretting over the vagrant.

"I'm trying to show you that your contract does not exactly apply to all the ways I might be truly dangerous. Use your imagination, gentlemen." She bobbed a brief curtsy and departed.

"How destructive can a squirrel be?" Hugh asked.

"Have you ever seen one gnaw through a gas valve?" Drew asked ominously. "Let's go find the vagrant and not worry about rodent infestations."

Or what Lady Phoebe might do with them.

SEVEN

Feeling uncertain and out of place, Phoebe tried to keep to as much of her usual routine as she could in this strange new world. She knelt beside her fluffy new bed to say her prayers in a pretty blue room on the nursery floor. Admittedly, the space was lighter than her old rooms, the furniture much fresher and more comfortable. But it wasn't home. She hoped prayer would stifle her urge to weep. It had been a long, trying few days.

The nursemaid, Daisy, slept in the room next to the children. She could answer their calls for drinks and their cries at night, if needed. The children were familiar with Daisy. It would take time before they completely trusted Phoebe, so her separation from the nursery presented no difficulty and offered an illusion of freedom.

Vagrants in the alley didn't bother her too much. Madmen who cut axles and might kill children. . . gave her cold shivers. If she told her aunts. . . but she couldn't desert the children. She had to stay.

Mr. Lithgow had not been very confident about Phoebe's desire to sue the tenement owners over the loss of her home. The knowledge that she might be permanently homeless had made him anxious to appease her on her employment contract.

The contract was very generous. Her expenses here would be almost nonexistent. She could turn her earnings into a little nest egg. Maybe in a year or two, when she had enough money, she could try the other veterinary school. Admissions policies could change.

Although she feared she might have to disguise herself in trousers. And she would, too, if she thought they would teach her how to look after small animals, not just cattle.

Planning seldom worked well in her world, but it didn't hurt to dream. Having a goal prevented the dismals.

The kitten rustled in its basket, hungry. The marten had been active all day, learning his new abode, but his habits were normally nocturnal. He was prowling the house, keeping the mice in the walls. The mice told her the men were still below, doing whatever men did at this hour.

She should be feeling secure and exhausted. She wasn't.

Oh well. She bolted the door and turned on a lamp to read one of her books. That should make her sleepy.

The bed was extremely comfortable. So were the pillows. But she was so used to a hard mattress, and the racket of horses and wheels, shouts and brawls carrying up from the street, that she couldn't adjust to the quiet.

She got up and fed the kitten from the scraps she'd brought upstairs for the purpose. "Mr. Blair is very handsome, is he not?" *Andrew*, she'd heard his friend call him. "It was brilliant of him to build your litter box, wasn't it? And give you this nice home? Even if Mr. Morgan doesn't like you."

Intent on eating, the kitten didn't reply.

"I did not realize men can be so attractive when they're clean. Perhaps I should spend more time studying the students at the university so I can learn not to notice my employer."

The kitten condescended to lick her hand, but it was evident that exploring was on his mind.

"I think he notices *me*," she whispered.

That was the part that thrilled and frightened her. Even when he regarded her with annoyance, Mr. Blair was *seeing* her, despite her lack of elegance.

How could she intimidate a man like that into ignoring her?

Raven shrieked a warning. Still not sleepy, Phoebe donned her wool slippers and the sheepskin-lined robe her mother had given her one Christmas, and headed for the attic.

ANNOYED WITH HIMSELF AND THE WORLD, ANDREW DUSTED THE STRAW OFF his coat and shucked his hat at a hook at the back door. "Could we ask Queen Vicki if she'd install the brats in Holyrood?" he grumbled. "She's never there anyway."

"Wouldn't help if the miscreants believe the bairns can tell you anything incriminating. I still think your family is dicked in the nob for worrying over them. Who'd believe a babe?" Hugh shrugged off his coat. "If you start imagining spooks around every corner, we may as well all move to the palace."

His partner was a practical man who didn't believe in Letitia's Sight or the children's gifts, even when wrenches floated past his face. Hugh lacked imagination and saw everything in terms of physics and numbers.

"What other reason is there for that stranger in the alley, studying our door?" Disgruntled, Drew called for coffee to ward off the chill from their stint in the stable. The stranger had run off before he could be confronted. "Is Lady Phoebe still awake?" he asked the maid. "Ask her to come down if she is."

"You're a savage," Hugh remarked, heading for the stairs. "It's late. You don't entertain governesses at this hour. I'll take my coffee in my room, where all sensible people are at this hour."

Drew wasn't ready to sleep. The search for the vagrant and the result had left him unsettled and restless. He supposed he could take another look at the pterotype. Maybe he'd suffer a sudden stroke of brilliance.

The maid returned and bobbed an apologetic curtsy. "Lady Phoebe is not in her chamber, sir."

Not in her chamber, at this hour of the night. What the devil did that mean? Was there something wrong with the children?

Alarmed, he headed for the stairs before he realized that's why he was paying for a damned governess—so she could watch over the children. Undeterred, he continued upward.

The children were sleeping snuggly in their beds. The kitten peered up at him from beneath Clare's cot. Wasn't it supposed to be in a basket somewhere?

Where could a governess go in the middle of the night? Had he unwittingly hired a spy for Simon's enemies? He couldn't think of another good reason strangers were watching his house.

He stalked down the hall, noting the nursemaid's closed door and the governess's open one—which probably explained the kitten's escape.

And then he saw the open door to the attic.

Now that he knew the way, he went directly to the roof. Lady Phoebe sat huddled in an ungainly robe against the parapet. Was she crying?

Panicking at female tears, Drew wanted to back away, but he simply wasn't that kind of coward. The aristocratic governess looked much too vulnerable in slippers and tumbling curls.

Figuratively girding his loins, he crossed the roof and slid down beside her, dragging his own coat around him. She hastily wiped at her eyes.

"Your vagrant finally showed up. He's nephew of the cook next door. He lost his position, has no references, and can't find another, so he's been sleeping in the stable."

She nodded, and Drew noticed she'd wrapped her hair in rags, making her look like a street urchin. He'd have to remember that image when she pulled the haughty act on him.

"I gave him a job guarding the stable," he offered when she said nothing.

She finally turned liquid blue eyes in his direction. "You're *paying* him for a roof over his head?"

"And peace of mind," he reminded her. "A villain is less likely to cut axles if there's someone to notice. The carriage driver goes home before dark."

"Of course, very wise of you." Her voice cracked as if she might still be holding back sobs.

"And both Henry, our new stableboy, and the carriage driver report strangers skulking about the alley today, watching the house." His teeth grated at the news. He was developing his cousin's fears for the children, on no grounds whatsoever.

She nodded. "You need a dog." She finally glanced up at him. "Why are you up here?"

"Where else would I find you?" he asked. "Has anyone said anything to upset you?"

She pulled her robe tighter. "Raven must have seen you in the alley. He sent a warning. And when I came up to see what he did, I. . . I don't know. It's all very strange over here. I think I miss the noise."

"I take it you've never lived in the country if you think this is quiet." He stretched his legs and inspected his new boots, but it was too dark to see if they needed polish.

"No, I cannot recall ever leaving the city, although I suppose I may have as a child, when my father was alive. Mama was never strong enough for long journeys. She had to take a nurse with her when she traveled to the south of France for her health."

That explained why Lady Phoebe lived with her aunts. They had ill parents in common, he supposed, but that didn't bridge the gulf between their upbringings.

"When he broke his back, my father refused to leave his house. He'd have shot me for suggesting France." Drew couldn't explain their differences any better. France might as well be the moon to his parents.

"My mother went to school in Switzerland. She wasn't always poor. And I don't know why I'm telling you this. I'm quite sure this is improper." She adjusted her robe so she could stand without tripping.

Drew was reluctant to give up the moment of. . . just existing, without any expectation or thought. He stood, glancing up to see if there were stars, but of course the clouds hid them. He offered his hand to help her up, and she accepted it as if it was the most natural act in the world. Her fingers were warmer than the chilly air, small boned and narrow.

When she stood, she just reached his shoulder. That answered one question.

He reluctantly released her hand and led the way back to the attic stairs. "I thank you for your vigilance, but I really do not expect you to sit guard on the roof."

"It's what I do," she said simply, if puzzlingly.

"Send a servant to fetch me next time," he suggested, taking her hand to assist her into the attic from the high step.

He was in an unlit room with a beautiful woman and discussing household duties. What the hell was the matter with him? When was the last time he'd been alone with a woman? All right, if a courtesan counted. . . But alone with a *lady*?

Never. He'd never been alone with a respectable female. They shouldn't be alone now. And still, he wanted the moment to linger. At least the governess had more conversation than Miss Higginbotham, but if he were to marry, it had to be to someone who understood that his business was more important than *pet boxes* and who could handle tea parties without him.

"Thank you for looking for me," she said softly. "It really wasn't necessary, but it was. . . nice. I was feeling a little lonely, I suppose. I'll do better." She gathered her long robe and hurried down the stairs, leaving him in the attic, with only a lingering trace of her heather-scented soap.

Drew took the stairs at a slower pace, telling himself he'd wasted enough time on the governess. He had a business to run, inventions to finish, and no interest in social niceties. He needed to apply his nonexistent spare time to finding a wife who could handle society for him, and that was most definitely not a capricious madcap who sat on roofs listening to birds.

WASHING IN THE AMAZING LUXURY OF WARM WATER DELIVERED BY A MAID the next morning, Phoebe attempted to block the scene on the roof from her mind. She'd been alone and missing her home and succumbed to a moment of weakness. She would have been fine in a few minutes. It was highly embarrassing that Mr. Blair had discovered her.

He'd been remarkably kind about it, sharing his father's injury and obstinacy with her—and letting her know about the poor boy sleeping in the stable! Wealth might be rather useful if one shared it. Although even wealth couldn't always buy safety. She'd need to help with that. Strangers skulking in the alley meant she'd have to keep the children inside. She hated that.

She had breakfast in the nursery. Teaching the little ones etiquette would have to wait until after she'd taught them to actually sit at a table.

"No, Cat, you cannot feed Kitty your bacon on the floor. It will make him ill and you dirty before the day even starts. Enoch, put the chair down before it topples. If you wish to use your talent to make it easier to lift the chair and pull it out for Clare, that's fine, but are you certain you wish to exhaust your energy on trivial things? Wouldn't you rather wait for your lessons?"

"You will give me lessons on levitation?" Enoch asked, eagerly taking his seat without helping his little sister into hers.

"If you do your other lessons well and quickly. Cat, please come sit down before your eggs are cold. I'm sure your mother is trying to tell you the same."

The twins looked so sad and pale, they broke Phoebe's heart. What did one say to motherless children who'd been ripped from the only home they knew? If she'd wept on the rooftop, she could only imagine how they felt.

"Do you really think Mama is watching us?" Clare asked forlornly.

"I cannot see into the spirit world, so I cannot speak to that," Phoebe said, straightening the child's collar and pushing her braid out of her food. "But I know mothers love us, and they're always with us in some way. Mine is many miles away, but I feel her right here." She touched her heart. "And I hear her in my head, scolding me to eat before my food gets cold."

"Mama used to say that," Enoch said knowingly, shoving food into his mouth. "And she'd say not to eat too fast."

"And she said not to talk with your mouth full," Cat added.

They perked up a little as they reminded each other of the things their mother said. The nursemaid looked up from making the beds and winked at Phoebe over their heads. She hoped that meant approval.

She had the children writing their letters on their chalkboards when Mr. Morgan warily peered in, a wad of documents in his hand. He looked as if he'd entered a dragon den as he fiddled worriedly with his spectacles and waited to be noticed.

She took pity on the poor man and stepped into the hall. Mr. Morgan was the kind of solid man who would have fit in nicely back in her part of town. He was only half a head taller than she, although her heels gave her that height. She wanted to tap the curved hump of his nose and assure him she wouldn't bite.

She hadn't felt remotely sisterly with Mr. Blair last night. She wasn't at all certain how to deal with that flutter of expectation he'd engendered.

"I've amended the contract," Mr. Morgan said almost apologetically. "If you'd like to discuss the changes, I'd be happy to go over them with you."

Her solicitor had explained all the chains the contract placed on her. She wanted the salary, but she couldn't sell her soul and promise all the things Mr. Blair seemed to think essential to the welfare of his wards. She needed time to show him how ridiculous he was being.

"If you will send the contract to my solicitor, please, he'll let me know if it's ready for my signature. A lady must be careful of the terms to which she agrees, you understand," she said, adding a flap of her lashes and a pretty smile.

Mr. Morgan stumbled all over himself and backed away. "Of course, my lady."

He was much too easy. She shouldn't play games with him like that. But she'd been feeling vulnerable after last night and needed to regain her equilibrium.

She returned to the children and had them finish up their letters to the Malcolm librarian, asking for information on their gifts.

"Books go in libraries, don't they?" Clare whispered, holding her pencil as if it were a hammer she must use to put words on paper.

"When we're not reading them," Phoebe agreed, helping Clare to adjust her fingers.

"Clare has Mama's book," Cat said, drawing a picture of a book on her paper.

Mama's book? Phoebe took a second to register the implication. Their mother had been a Malcolm. Malcolms kept journals. If Letitia had the Sight—what might she have kept in that journal? The children couldn't read. . .

"Did your Mama give the book to you?" Phoebe asked, trying for insouciance as she continued to help with their writing.

Clare nodded. Cat ran to the cot and produced a leather-bound book. "Can you read it to us?"

With trepidation, Phoebe took the heavy tome and peeked inside the front cover. *The Journal of Letitia Malcolm Montgomery Blair* read the frontispiece. The following pages were written in a hand so tiny that it took a moment to realize it was Latin.

Phoebe flipped through to the end. "It's all in Latin, I fear, and mine is very rusty. I will have to find a dictionary to translate."

"Latin?" Enoch looked up. "Cousin Drew knows Latin."

Clare violently shook her braids. "Mama says no, no, no! Lady Phoebe must read it to us."

A woman didn't want her words read by men. Phoebe understood that. She set the book on the table. "I'll start on it this evening. It may be very boring recipes. Now let's finish our letters to the Librarian. We'll tell her about your mama's journal, shall we?"

They weren't old enough to appreciate the books of Malcolm knowledge, but if there was anything of importance to be found in the library, the librarian would let her know, and she could decide if a trip to the castle library would be worthwhile. But she hoped Letitia's journal held the answers she needed.

Would it hold the answers to why Letitia had been murdered?

EIGHT

ENGROSSED IN THE OILY INSIDES OF HIS CURRENT PROJECT, CONFIDENT THAT the new governess had his wards in hand, Drew ignored the whispers and patter of little feet outside his workshop.

He couldn't ignore Hugh, who once more hovered with a packet of papers in hand.

"I've found additional investors for those buildings. I want to be in on the ground floor of rebuilding that slum." Hugh stood immovable over him.

Applying his screwdriver, Drew tried to ignore his friend's desperation, but unlike the children, Hugh was too big to disregard. Hugh was determined to find a way to wealth, but his funds were limited—the main reason he stayed with Drew. "The tenants?"

"The landlord swears they're moving on. The place is a rat-infested slum! No one should live there. I've talked to some of them. One's a university professor. He's agreed he could find rooms closer to the school. He was simply reluctant to move his library. There are elderly widows in there with pensions. They could do better."

Drew knew Hugh wasn't ruthless, just unenlightened. And it might even be possible they'd be doing some of the tenants a favor by forcing them to look for better quarters. But he was pretty damned certain Hugh hadn't talked to *all* the hundreds of tenants. They'd take one look at a large man in a business suit, see trouble, and hide.

He ignored a rap on the open door. He knew his bank account was bleeding money into Hugh's project, but his past warred with his present. He couldn't put people out in the cold. "Do we have to tear down all three buildings at once? Could we repair one and only tear down the other two?" Drew knew that would create hopeless over-crowding, but it was better than no housing at all.

A child wept in the hall and the rap became more demanding.

"No," Hugh said firmly. "Removal of the destroyed one will cause the other two to collapse. We'll have to brace the other attached proper-ties as it is or the whole block will tumble like dominoes. The tenants need to leave *now*."

The governess—who stood one whole head shorter than himself—entered and glared at Drew as if she were a Valkyrie. "While you fling poor people into the street, your ward seems to have misplaced her sister."

He'd stayed awake half the night dreaming of this termagant and what he should have done when he had her alone. He needed her out of his sight. "The children are your business and tenants are mine. The brat isn't in here."

Drew brushed by her, aiming for his office to look for his copy of Sholes' patent application for the useless American version of the pterotype. Maybe he had missed some detail. He lit a lamp in the windowless room—and noticed a mountain of books on the floor behind the door. Glancing up the bookshelves, he discovered one of the twins apparently sleeping on a top shelf. A chair propped precariously on some of his largest volumes indicated how she'd climbed there.

She probably thought herself quite hidden that far above her siblings. Drew shook his head at the precarious position. All she needed to do was toss in her sleep. . .

He disliked scaring her. He disliked watching her fall even more. His life had become a series of uncomfortable choices.

Hearing the other twin following him down the hall, crying, accom-panied by Lady Phoebe's whispered assurances, Drew sighed and picked up the sleeping child.

She was so tiny he feared he'd crush her. Had he not held them once since they'd arrived? Probably not. He'd left them to the servants. He knew nothing about children.

This one yawned and squirmed, cuddled up against his shoulder as if she belonged there, and promptly returned to sleep, nearly twisting his heart out of its socket. He didn't have time for this.

He carried her out to the hall, where the usually unflustered Lady Phoebe looked just the least little bit perturbed as she led the other twin toward the stairs.

"Your stray, I presume?" he asked.

She swung around and relief briefly lit her expression, before she assumed her haughty air. "Ah, she fell asleep. I see a flaw in the process."

"That's so unfair," the twin holding her hand said, pouting and sounding much older than she should. "She scared me."

Drew now recognized the voluble one as Cat, so the one in his arms had to be mousy Clare. "She scared me too. She could have hurt herself. I don't think they're ready for scampering around alone, my lady."

Instead of taking the child from him, the governess swept past to investigate his office. She chortled as she discovered the cubbyhole his ward had created. "She has a bit to learn about hiding, I fear, but she's smart and a hard worker. That was quite a task."

"I'm a hard worker," Cat declared obdurately.

"Then you may attempt to put those books back where they belong," Lady Phoebe said with a low laugh that shivered Drew's timbers. "I'll watch."

Cat determinedly climbed the staircase of books to the propped up chair and tried to put one heavy volume back on the empty shelf. She tipped precariously. Lady Phoebe stepped in to push the book onto the shelf for her.

"We should wake Clare so she learns it's harder to put things back than to take them down, but she apparently wore herself out." Lady Phoebe finally held out her arms for the sleeping child. "Thank you for finding her. We are testing the extent of their abilities, but four-year-olds are not reliable subjects."

"They should be learning their letters. That would be safer." He shifted Clare into her arms.

Today, the lady was wearing a most ungoverness-like bright green gown that emphasized her natural—uncorseted—waist and bosom. He should be grateful that she appeared to be wearing a small petticoat and not a split skirt that caused indecent thoughts.

The front door knocker rapped. Drew passed Clare over, prepared to hide himself in his workshop again. The little maid raced to answer the door.

"I'm not home to visitors," Drew told her. Abby bobbed a curtsy, knowing this was his usual preference.

Apparently still unhappy with him, Lady Phoebe scolded, "Don't be foolish. People are more important than things. Abby, take the twins to the nursery, will you, please? I'll answer the door." She passed the sleeping child to the maid and shook wrinkles out of her skirt.

Looking a little befuddled, the maid followed the governess's orders instead of Drew's, hurrying up the stairs with the children while Lady Phoebe sailed down the hall to the door.

He'd wanted a governess to maintain order in the nursery, not a ring-master for the circus his life had become. Drew watched in trepidation as the lady opened the door and merrily welcomed. . . Dalrymple from next door, and his niece, Miss Higginbotham. Drat, now he'd not have time to return to the machine before he had to leave for the manufactory board meeting.

He supposed if he were to court Miss Higginbotham, he should. . .

"Blair, there you are." Accustomed to the familiarity of a middle-class household with few servants, Dalrymple set his hat down on the hall table. "I wanted to speak with you a moment, if you don't mind. We need to talk about the real estate investment in Old Town, and my niece wished to become better acquainted with Lady Phoebe, if she is not too busy."

Lady Phoebe and Miss Higginbotham? Before Drew could panic, the lady sent Drew a sharp look, and declared, "I was about to order lunch and naps for the children. And I'd love a coze with Miss Higginbotham, if she is willing to accompany me into town while I run a few errands."

Drew had the icy notion that despite her mild tone, she was about to undermine everything he was attempting to establish.

"I LOVE YOUR HAT, MISS HIGGINBOTHAM," PHOEBE DECLARED AS SHE SWEPT the younger woman down the street toward town. She was still stewing about the overheard conversation and worried about the journal she'd hidden in her room. She hoped walking out might clear her head.

Besides, if Mr. Blair was courting this bit of fluff, she should learn whether Miss Higginbotham was a suitable mother for his wards. Men didn't think like that, if they thought at all.

Her companion shyly touched the bouquet of blue flowers dangling over her hat brim. "Don't tell anyone, but I trimmed it myself," she murmured. "It seems such a waste to buy new when I so dearly loved last year's style."

Phoebe wouldn't know last year's style if it spit in her eyes, but she nodded knowingly. "I would love to learn how to do that, but I am not creative in the least." She'd placed a bird feather in the band of her hat, next to the bedraggled and faded rosette with which it had been originally adorned.

"I'll show you where I buy my flowers. Mama says I am not very clever, but I do know how to make a pretty hat." Miss Dahlia Higginbotham walked with more purpose.

"There are many kinds of cleverness. I'm sure you're quite good with children as well."

To Phoebe's surprise, Miss Higginbotham slowed down and knitted her hands together in uncertainty. "I have no siblings. I have no notion if I even like children."

Phoebe hid her frown. "Well, I'm certain once you have them, you'll be fine. You simply need a little experience."

Miss Higginbotham went completely silent.

Phoebe wasn't fond of silence. If this was the woman Mr. Blair considered wife material, he was in for a rude awakening. She probed deeper. "I, myself, would prefer to attend the university than to marry and have children. Have you considered that?"

"I am not clever," she repeated sadly.

"Nonsense. You can make hats, and that is exceedingly clever. Having children takes fortitude and patience but even witless mice manage to look after their young. I'm not sure children require cleverness, just a willingness to learn." Phoebe stopped to admire a shop window of pretty hats.

"I don't think I'm willing to learn," Miss Higginbotham whispered. "Men are hairy, crude creatures. I simply want a little shop of my own and to be left alone."

Phoebe fought her eyebrows to prevent them from shooting upward. After rearranging her thoughts about the girl's desire to marry, she said, "Well, then, you must apprentice in a hat shop, mustn't you? Do you have any income of your own?"

"A small stipend from my grandfather's estate. I use it for ribbons and such. It is not enough to live on," she said sadly, barely acknowledging the colorful display in the window.

"If it is enough to feed you, then you might look for a position that offers a room while you learn the trade. Once you start attracting customers, you could ask for a commission. That's what I would do, if I were clever with hats." Phoebe had meant to pick her neighbor's brain, not send her down the road to perdition. But if Miss Higginbotham did not like men. . . She desperately needed a friend.

"My aunt would hate for me to be a shop clerk," Miss Higginbotham murmured. "She thinks I should marry well and help advance my uncle's business. Mama just wants me out from under foot while the grocer courts her. I don't think she'd mind if I set up a shop. But I wouldn't know how to go about it."

She glanced up at Phoebe, and her rosebud lips tightened. "I've never had anyone to talk to about this before. You will not tell my aunt?"

"Of course I won't. Are you quite certain you'd prefer a shop to a husband?" Phoebe waited, giving the girl time to think about it.

Miss Higginbotham nodded vigorously. "I am very certain. I've thought about this for years. I do not like boys or men. Just the thought of marriage and children appalls me. Is that very wrong?" she looked to Phoebe anxiously, as if she might be a woman of the world who had all the answers.

Phoebe wasn't precisely a woman of the world. She was probably no more than five years older than Dahlia Higginbotham. She did, however, have considerably more experience than the sheltered miss. She knew, for instance, that there were many reasons a woman might not like men. She didn't need to know Miss Higginbotham's reason, just the disastrous outcome if she were forced into marriage. As angry as Mr. Blair made her —putting tenants in the street!—she could not in good conscience allow him to marry an unwilling woman.

"If you are quite certain, then let's do something about it. Shall we go in here?" Phoebe gestured at the hat store. She'd not be able to afford one of those hats even if she saved her earnings back in the streets for a year. And she didn't intend to spend her new salary on fripperies. But she saw no purpose in dreams unless one took action to make them happen.

Miss Higginbotham looked up, almost startled to notice the window they stood in front of. "Those are very fashionable," she said tentatively.

"And won't look well on anyone," Phoebe declared. "I'd look like an ostrich in that feathered thing."

Miss Higginbotham giggled. "And I'd disappear under that straw. Hats should be made for the individual, shouldn't they be?"

"Exactly. Now keep your chin up and be brave and let's see what we can do." Phoebe pushed open the shop door and sailed in, Miss Higginbotham in her wake.

"Good afternoon, ladies." She nodded at the clerks at the counter and the lone customer. "I should like a new hat, but none of those in the window will suit. I've asked my friend here to tell me what I need, if you do not mind? She is an excellent milliner, just back from France, and she's always advised me well."

Miss Higginbotham shrank behind Phoebe's narrow skirt.

The clerks looked askance at Phoebe's battered porkpie hat, rightfully so. She took it off and twirled it around her finger. "Dahlia trimmed this for me back when we were children, before she had any experience. I wish to remind her of how far she's come. Now, Dahlia, choose the right style for me, and let's see what you can do with it."

"The lace with the slight veil in the window," Miss Higginbotham said quietly. "You have lovely hair and shouldn't hide it. And the angle of the veil is slightly rakish and suits you."

Oh yes, rakish did sound fine. Phoebe waited expectantly. One of the clerks edged over to the window. She pointed at a lovely green confection that almost matched Phoebe's dress. But it didn't have a rakish veil.

"No," Miss Higginbotham said. "The pretty blue one that will set off her chestnut hair. Just to your right."

By now, everyone in the store was watching them. The clerk picked up the correct hat, and Dahlia nodded approval. "The rosette is too large and disproportional to the brim. This is an autumn hat. A sprig of berries like those there. . ." She pointed at a chip hat on the counter. "And just the smallest red bow, perhaps, to set off the green of the leaves."

"I vow, I'll need a whole new wardrobe to go with anything that magnificent," Phoebe crowed as the clerk rearranged the trim. "May I try it on?"

The clerk offered up the newly-adorned lace hat, gazing at Phoebe's unruly stack of hair with trepidation. Phoebe wasn't much inclined to be careful when pinning it up.

Dahlia took the hat. "Duck down so I may reach, my lady. You should wear it dipped slightly toward one eye for the full effect." She pulled and pinned and fastened the scrap of hat in place. "There, a mirror, please."

"My lady?" the clerk whispered as Phoebe leaned over the counter to peer in a mirror.

"Lady Phoebe Duncan," Dahlia whispered back. "Of the Malcolm Duncans."

Phoebe heard the customer whisper to another clerk. "The *eccentric* Malcolm Duncans, very old family, well respected."

Phoebe pretended not to notice the remark as she admired the confection on her head. It really was a very nice hat.

"It is ideal for. . . for the shape of your face," the clerk who had helped them said.

"Yes, I do like it. Dahlia, perhaps you should help the lady choose what looks best for her." Phoebe nodded at the matronly customer dithering between two old-fashioned bonnets.

Miss Higginbotham persuaded the lady into a more fashionable chapeau, then suggested changes to more of the stock so that it suited current colors and better proportions. Even Phoebe, knowing nothing of hats, recognized that the results were far superior to the original.

More customers entered and joined in the entertainment. While Dahlia was center stage, Phoebe regretfully removed her pretty chapeau, set it aside, and sidled over to the older woman who appeared to be the shop owner. She was frowning but didn't appear averse to the spectacle.

"Dahlia is looking for a new place," Phoebe murmured. "Do not tell her I said so. But the milliner in France. . . well, he was not good for young girls, if you know what I mean. I had to bring her home. I don't know what I would have done without her when I was a child. But we are all grown now, and she must make her way in the world. If you would be so kind as to recommend a position somewhere nearby, I'd be forever grateful."

The proprietress nodded grimly. "I understand. She is very young, but creative. I will have a word with her, if it's all right with you."

"Certainly." Phoebe tilted her head in acknowledgment, hiding a smug smile, her mood considerably improved. She really did enjoy meddling.

NINE

DREW FLUNG HIS HAT AT THE BACK-DOOR HOOK, LOOSENED HIS CRAVAT, AND shrugged off his coat, fully prepared to return to the challenge of creating a machine that printed without snarling keys. If only he could make his pterotype work better than the American typewriter, he could earn a fortune. Unfortunately, investing in tenements had a faster, more certain return.

More for his own conscience than Lady Phoebe's altruistic outrage, he'd sent Hugh back to Margaret's Wynd to talk to tenants. If he married Miss Higginbotham, he'd have her uncle's support when it came time to contract out jobs. He had time to consider that.

Remarkably, the house was actually still. Abby rushed to take his coat. The children were presumably in the nursery, eating dinner and preparing for bed. At moments like this, he appreciated the well-oiled machinery of a proper household. Money might not buy happiness, but it could buy organization and contentment.

Even knowing Cook wouldn't obey, he ordered dinner to wait until Hugh returned, then started for his office. The boy he'd assigned to the stable popped out of the kitchen stairwell carrying what appeared to be a hatbox. At seeing Drew, he tugged his forelock apologetically, handed the box to Abby, and vanished back down the stairs.

Drew looked questioningly at the maid, who curtseyed, flustered. "Cook says as her knees are too old to be carrying packages up and down the stairs. She told Henry he could earn his keep by helping out."

Drew shrugged. "Fair enough. I hadn't realized Cook was having problems with the stairs." He knew better than to mention a woman's *knees*. Back home, he'd have thought nothing of it, but here in the city, gentlemen did not mention body parts. "Is that a package for Lady Phoebe?"

As if summoned from on high, the lady herself appeared on the staircase from the upper stories. She'd apparently taken time to brush and pin her heavy tresses into some semblance of decorum for a change. She still wore the bright green wool of earlier. It didn't appear any more or less the worse after a day with the children. . . Which was when Drew realized that a lady trailing crinolines, petticoats, and yards of flounces would be thoroughly frazzled after a day spent romping with weans.

Nursery maids and proper governesses were expected to wear simple black and few furbelows. Lady Phoebe was a damned *lady*. So she'd combined both expectations of governess and lady with her ridiculous costume—the very model of a modern female.

And he was staring as if he had nothing better to do.

Before he could remove himself, Abby presented the lady with the hatbox. Lady Phoebe froze. She glanced nervously to him, then back at the box. This ought to be good. He didn't see her flustered often enough. He propped his shoulder against the door frame and waited.

He had to give her credit. She recovered swiftly. Opening the box for all the world like a princess being offered a crown, she removed a blue confection of lace and berries. Dropping the princess mode and exclaiming in delight, she set the box down on the stairs. Applying the adornment to her hair, she rushed to the hall mirror to adjust the angle, then swung around to confront him.

"What do you think?" She swirled, giving him a view of front and back.

The rakish veil dissolved the waif-like image of the porkpie hat she'd arrived in. In fact, it made him very aware that she was a grown woman with seductress beauty.

Berating himself for his wandering mind, Drew straightened. "It is very. . . blue."

It was an enticing bit of frippery, drawing the eye to the lady's delectable lips and rosy cheeks, teasing with glimpses of mysteriously shaded eyes.

"Indigo. Dahlia calls it indigo." She rummaged in the hatbox on the stairs and found a note, handing the box to Abby to carry away. The maid disappeared back to the kitchen.

As Lady Phoebe read the note, Drew watched her mobile expression go from surprise to delight to. . . concern? She checked the mirror again, steadied the hat, and took a deep breath before turning to him.

"You may be hearing from Mr. Dalrymple shortly. I shall not apologize to him, but I shall to you. You do not deserve whatever comes of my rash behavior."

"That whets my interest even more than that improbable fluff on your head. Dalrymple is a bit of a stick-in-the-mud, but he's helped me find my feet here. I'd rather not be at odds with my closest neighbor. What have you done?" He waited with more curiosity than concern.

She bit her bottom lip, apparently parsing her words before speaking. "Miss Higginbotham wishes to become a milliner, not a wife." She took off the new hat and approached to show it to him. "She is very talented. She put this together in minutes."

Drew didn't see much talent in sewing pieces of fluff to a bit of lace, but women liked that sort of thing, he supposed. "I see. And this has what to do with me?"

"Mr. Dalrymple wishes Dahlia to marry you. I. . ." She shrugged, looking embarrassed. "I encouraged her to follow her heart, and she has. She sent this as a thank you gift to let me know she's found a position in a hat shop and has taken rooms above the store."

A hat shop. His hopes for easy support for the tenement project exploded. He'd be fortunate if Dalrymple didn't have him tossed off every board and committee in the city.

Hugh chose that moment to slam in the back entry. "Progress!" he shouted as his big feet pounded down the hall.

"Later," Drew warned the governess. "We will talk later."

After he learned how much trouble he was in if his biggest investor chose to sell out.

Upstairs in her room, regretfully admiring the first brand new hat she'd had since childhood, Phoebe wondered if she should start packing.

It had been a hasty impulse to drag Dahlia into that shop. It had been providence that the owner needed new talent. Phoebe didn't think Mr. Blair would look at matters quite that way. He'd appeared ready to rain down thunderbolts.

But she'd been right to help Dahlia, she was convinced. The girl had simply needed an understanding ear to give her the confidence to do what she'd wanted to do anyway.

So Phoebe would have to pack her bags and return to her aunts' house in disgrace. She hated to fail at an assigned task. Knowing she'd done the right thing was cold comfort, especially if the children came to any harm because she was not there to help—which reminded her of Letitia's journal.

Should she tell Mr. Blair of it before she left? If the twins really did speak to the ghost of their mother and Letitia didn't wish it read. . . Awkward. Very awkward. She peeked inside the book, at the tiny lettering and foreign words. Perhaps she should start at the back.

Some time later, she'd translated enough to know she couldn't abandon the children. Letitia had received warnings from the ladies in the village—nothing specific enough for Phoebe to act on but enough to be concerned. She'd have to keep translating to see if she found anything more concrete, but she hadn't seen any names. What if Letitia's ghost could pass on names? Was that possible?

With a sigh, she donned her coat and set out for the attic. Piney had taken a liking to Mr. Blair's wooden box. Phoebe had carried up a few pine boughs from the park and the marten was happily gnawing on them and carrying them into his new abode on the roof.

It was the wrong season for Raven to nest, but he needed somewhere warm for his old bones. She'd piled up some sticks and old bits of wool near the chimney in hopes he might call it home.

She'd have to move her pets again if Mr. Blair ordered her to leave. She needed to tell him about the journal. If she simply told him without giving him the journal, would he believe a ghost might pass on names of killers? He'd need proof. The children had trusted her—a dilemma.

She leaned against the sloped slate roof near the front parapet and admired the gaslights sprawling into the valley toward the gardens. The castle promontory was far in the distance, along with her home in its shadows. Her home was gone, she reminded herself.

"The stars are out," Mr. Blair said from the attic door. "Winter will be here before we know it."

"Just tell me if I must leave without a reference. My aunts will be very disappointed, but I am not ashamed of helping someone who needed it."

He leaned against the slate with her, blocking some of the wind with his bulk. "Was Miss Higginbotham in any danger from her uncle?"

That startled her. She turned to stare, but he was too uncomfortably close. She returned to gazing at the lights and stars. "She was in an awkward position, that's all. Some women really do not wish to marry. I know that's difficult for a man to understand."

"It's difficult to understand why a woman with no means of supporting herself would give up the opportunity for a sound roof over her head and a man to look after her, granted. I will try not to take it personally," he said with what almost sounded like amusement.

"Good, because her decision was not meant to be about you." Phoebe shoved her hands in her coat pockets.

"I can understand why a sheltered child like Miss Higginbotham wouldn't be interested in a family that already includes three eccentric children. They would be enough to scare off the most intrepid of women. They *have* scared off an assortment of better-prepared women."

She turned and glared at him. "There is no reason to be afraid of *children*. Now tell me what happens when Mr. Dalrymple learns his niece has run off because of me."

"If Miss Higginbotham has any brains at all in her pretty head, she won't tell him about you. What she chooses to do is a family affair, and none of our concern."

"Your concern must be for the children. I will leave for university as soon as I am able. Finding a wife who loves children and will accept a ready-made family will not be easy."

"I think I am capable of handling my own affairs," he said dryly. "Do not concern yourself with me. What do you mean to study at the university?"

She was a failure at directing conversations. "I wish to be an animal doctor. I thought if I entered the university, the veterinary college might allow me to take courses. It is not easy for women to overcome the prejudices of the past, but Edinburgh is very enlightened in some matters."

"An animal doctor, of course. That makes good sense. It will not be easy for you," he warned. "Men are distracted by beautiful women. It isn't prejudice but common sense to keep order in the classroom by keeping women out of it."

Even calling her *beautiful* did not mitigate the inanity of that statement. She sighed. "I know you do not mean to be discouraging, but I want to smack the snot out of you when you say things like that. Women are not responsible if men are too weak-minded to control their urges."

He laughed, a belly-deep laugh that roared over the rooftops.

She relaxed a fraction. Perhaps he understood, even if he was laughing at her. Few took the time to know her well enough to laugh at her admittedly eccentric world-view.

"You might actually talk your way into school with that attitude," he said when he stopped laughing. "I expect you'll simply wear them down until they accept you so they don't have to listen to you anymore."

"But something must be done about the children so I won't feel guilty in leaving them. If you cannot find a wife, then you must discover who might cause them harm. I can try to persuade Clare to speak, but she needs to learn to trust us first."

"I have people working on it," he said with a shrug. "There is little I can do from here, and I must stay in the city to earn the money that provides for the children and my family."

"Have you made a list of suspects?" she asked, eager to solve his problem without revealing the journal. "Surely it cannot be long."

"And what, pray tell, would I do with such a list? Knock on doors and ask if they may have murdered an innocent woman?"

"If you had a list, I could ask my family to help!" she said in excitement. "We may not be closely related except in our differences, but my family communicates with each other."

"That does not sound like a good idea," he said in a low rumble that warned she was exceeding her boundaries.

"Oh, but you do not know us! I have one cousin who *finds* things. He helped the queen find a lost earring and a duke to find his long-lost half-brother. He is quite good. There are many more of us like that. Let's go inside where it's warm—"

Mr. Blair caught her in his arms before she could hurry for the stairs. Startled, Phoebe froze where she was, aware of the encompassing heat of his big body and how very. . . strong. . . he was. She looked up questioningly.

And without permission, he bent to kiss her.

TEN

DREW KNEW BETTER THAN TO GIVE IN TO IMPULSE, BUT HE HATED HEIGHTS and had distracted himself with noticing the enticing woman beside him. He had this terribly perverse desire to see if Lady Phoebe tasted like a real woman—as opposed to chocolate or vinegar, perhaps. He'd never met a female like her, and he needed a better sense of where he stood in her universe. His notorious need to experiment made him do it.

She froze, as she often did when caught by surprise, he'd noticed. But then her lips warmed and grew soft, and she was very definitely a real woman, one who tasted of mint and honey and melted like hot wax in his arms. He could feel her perfect breasts pressed into his shirtfront, and if he pulled her any closer, she'd learn more of male anatomy than was decent.

Fortunately, she was a woman of more fortitude than he. She pressed her hands against his shirt and shoved away. He was quite certain he heard her gasp.

"I haven't decided if I should apologize," he said before she could slap the snot out of him. He grinned again at the vulgarism her rounded vowels had produced earlier. He felt remarkably good, almost carefree, for the first time in centuries. "We are both inviting temptation by meeting like this. It just seemed a good idea to remind ourselves why we should not be alone together. Unless, of course, you find me as appalling as our neighbor apparently does."

She stepped back and briskly adjusted her coat. Maybe next time, he could divest her of that damned ugly thing.

"You are not appalling," she finally said, back to proper. "But you *are* my employer. I must insist that we do not do this again. It is most awkward." She headed for the door.

"Oh, I grant it's awkward. I will have difficulty listening while remembering your mouth against mine. And once we start down this road, it becomes harder to stop. So perhaps we should simply send each other written notes." He knew that would never happen. She was too alive and volatile.

He watched her sway down the narrow stairs into darkness and wanted to tug her back into his arms again, even if it meant staying on the dratted roof. If he didn't look down. . . The lady provided an ideal distraction.

"Perhaps I should seek another position," she said stiffly as he followed her down to the attic. "But I cannot recommend sending any of my younger cousins here under the circumstances."

That knocked his confidence straight out of him. "Don't do that. The children need you. I almost feel comfortable leaving them with you. We'll work out something."

"Almost." She snorted and proceeded through the attic to the stairs to civilization. "That's reassuring. You consider me *almost* safe with your wards."

"Be fair. You haven't exhibited exemplary comportment so far. You are obviously not a trained governess, but you're apparently a good animal trainer, and that's almost as good with my wards—for now. But there's a world of difference between animals and children, hence my hesitation." Drew wasn't entirely certain what he was doing here—putting her off him so she'd keep out of his company?

"Hmpf." She entered the light of the narrow nursery hall.

She looked utterly delectable in that ancient coat, with her hair wind-blown and curling around her long, elegant face with its perfectly rounded chin. He didn't dare lower his gaze to the firm bosom that had been pressed into him just a few minutes earlier. He waited for her condemnation.

Instead, she glowered. "Are you aware that Malcolms keep journals?"

He tried to work out how they'd gone from kissing to journals and couldn't. "You mentioned it before."

"Your cousin's wife was a Malcolm. She kept journals. There may be some chance that she wrote something in hers that could incriminate her killer. Talk to your cousin, ask. And you, sir, need a wife, one I can speak to about the children without being in the same room as you. Find someone a little older than Dahlia." She spun on her heel and marched off.

He'd hired *her* rather than marry, he wanted to shout. But he'd wake the children and the nursemaid, and it was all too complicated. He'd just have to arrange to have a maid in the same room with them when they discussed the children.

If only the damned woman would stay upstairs and out of sight.

He'd be dreaming of that kiss for months. Maybe he should go out and seek relief elsewhere.

He didn't want paid kisses and pretend caresses. But harassing employees was never a good idea.

What the devil had she meant about a journal? That sounded damned dangerous.

Cursing, Drew traipsed downstairs to write to Simon.

Hugh waited for him—with a stack of papers in hand. "As I was trying to tell you before you went haring off. . . The tenants are filing a lawsuit. They don't have a leg to stand on, but—"

"You found an empty building to house them in?" Drew asked cynically, marching through the dining room to his workshop, previously known as the withdrawing room.

"I'm still looking. I can't build Rome in a day." Hugh sounded offended.

"Sorry. It's been a long day. All right, I understand another builder might come along with less interest in doing what's right. We'll move forward." He took the packet of papers and returned to his office.

"Our neighbor and his wife are having a screaming argument," Hugh said conversationally.

Hugh never made small talk. Drew shot him a shrewd look. "Eaves-dropping, were we?"

Hugh shrugged his big shoulders. "Didn't have to try. They're loud. And the new stableboy said he was in their kitchen with his aunt and heard them. Sounds like their niece ran off rather than marry you. You'll have to hunt further afield for a wife."

Drew signed his name with a flourish and flung the packet at his assistant. "No, we need to hunt for a killer so Simon will be satisfied the children are safe, and we can send them back where they belong."

STILL STUNNED AND NERVOUS ABOUT LAST NIGHT'S KISS—AND HER REACTION to it—Phoebe stayed in the nursery the next morning. What on earth had she been thinking?

She hadn't. She'd behaved like every silly woman on the planet in the presence of an attractive man. She knew better. She certainly wasn't opposed to men as Dahlia was, but they just weren't on her agenda. Not in that way. She wanted to go to school and learn to do what she did best. She didn't have time for dalliance.

But Mr. Blair had been so solid and alive and. . .

She cut off that thought. Marriage was a trap even worse than servi-tude. She'd translate more of Letitia's journal and see if she found names. Maybe she wrote in code.

She returned to teaching the children their letters. "Levitating the chalk removes the weight needed to produce a mark," she warned Enoch. "It might be possible to levitate an ink pen and write without hands, but you'll need to prove yourself with a pencil first."

Enoch scowled and returned to determinedly completing his alphabet.

"We do not need to write," Cat said fretfully. "We talk."

"What about your father? Would you not like to read a letter from him?" Phoebe asked.

The twins studied her with suspicion. Cat, of course, was the one to reply. "He would not write us. We're *little*."

"But you will not always be little. If you sent him a letter showing how big you're growing, he would send one back." If she had to write it for him, Phoebe mentally vowed.

The twins frowned, then apparently coming to some silent agreement, returned to their chalkboards.

Kitty prowled the room, pouncing on dust balls and imaginary monsters. Time ticked slowly. Phoebe was used to being on the streets, greeting people, helping where she could, trading and offering services where they were needed. She didn't like confinement.

Neither did the children. They wiggled restlessly, their attention spans easily diverted by kitten antics. Enoch proudly finished his alphabet and handed it over for inspection. Phoebe fussed over it appropriately and decided he needed to be rewarded with more than a pencil.

She would not believe evil men would seek children over a *journal* they most likely did not know existed.

"You may have a small recess to play with the kitten while I arrange an appropriate celebration of Enoch's graduation to the next level of education. Do not become too rowdy while I am gone."

Refusing to go downstairs where the men were, Phoebe jotted a note and handed it to Daisy, who carried it down to Abby. It was a ridiculous system and took twice as long as it would for her to run down and make the request herself, but she was determined to be proper. She had apparently given Mr. Blair the wrong idea. For the sake of the children, that must be rectified.

Daisy returned to report, "Mr. Blair says the carriage will be ready soon."

The children cheered and ran for their wraps.

The nursemaid was a plump, sensible, older woman who carried on her work quietly in the background. She would never presume to be asked on an outing, but Phoebe saw no reason she shouldn't join them.

"Would you care to come with us, Daisy? I've asked if we might have a picnic lunch prepared. While the days are still fine, we should take advantage of the outdoors." Phoebe helped Clare tie her bonnet.

"If you think I might help, mum." Daisy looked uncertain. She hadn't quite adapted to calling Phoebe *my lady*, but she hovered over the children as if they were her own.

"Can we take Kitty?" Cat called, stalking the kitten around the perimeter of the room.

Phoebe pushed her old porkpie hat over her hair to keep it from flying about, jabbed a pin in it, and mentally consulted the kitten. "No, I think Kitty would like a bit of lunch and a nap. She's not quite as old as you and needs more rest."

"Are we going to the garden?" Enoch asked. "May I take my ball?"

"Yes, you may bring a ball." Dealing with a barrage of questions, coats, hats, and toys, Phoebe managed to herd everyone down the stairs and out the back past the kitchen garden to the mews.

The carriage waited. Instead of a servant in the driver's seat, Mr. Blair held up his whip and greeted them by touching it to his curly-brimmed silk hat. The children cheered. Enoch immediately climbed up beside him and asked if he could hold the reins. Phoebe lifted the girls into the small seat in back and joined them, leaving the nursemaid to the front with Enoch.

She had not anticipated sharing a picnic with her employer.

Mr. Blair lifted one dark eyebrow at her position but merely urged the horse into motion once Daisy had hauled herself in.

He was just so. . . so *manly*. From this angle, she could see the jut of his square jaw, the cut of his cheekbones, and the dark curls of his sideburns beneath his hat brim. She'd felt those chiseled lips on hers last night, and she shivered a little.

Phoebe wasn't much at describing how she felt, even to herself. She liked keeping busy, not pondering impossibilities. She'd never had time for whispered exchanges with other girls about the attributes of suitors. She'd never had a suitor. It wasn't as if she socialized among her own set, whatever set that might be. She'd had to put food on the table or go hungry.

She simply didn't have the necessary experience to deal with self-assured men of business. What the devil was Mr. Blair doing taking time out from his busy day to go picnicking?

"Was I remiss in asking for the carriage for the children?" she asked tentatively as they clopped slowly down the street. "Did you need it?"

He kept his attention on the road. "Not at all. I generally walk to my meetings and the horse needs exercise, as do the children."

He gave no further explanation for his presence. Surely he had not heard from his cousin already.

Refusing to fret, Phoebe turned her attention to the twins, who were practically bouncing in their seats in excitement. She had to grasp the back of their coats to keep them from tumbling out as they tried to watch dogs running alongside the wheels and horses passing by. Being unfamiliar with this side of town, it took a few minutes before Phoebe realized they were moving faster than other carriages and taking side streets that did not lead directly to the green space dividing the two parts of the city.

Pulse accelerating, Phoebe studied her surroundings. The narrow alley they currently traversed wasn't wide enough for anyone but pedestrians to pass the carriage. There were few of those and the horses easily left them behind.

When they entered a wider avenue, Mr. Blair expertly maneuvered around slow carts, staying well ahead of any other vehicle. But horses could easily follow. While keeping half her attention on the children, Phoebe sorted through the various animal minds nearby. Even if she couldn't see animals, she could identify their. . . *presence*. It was rather like being aware of people while walking down the street.

Several horses outpaced them and turned corners in different directions. One stayed a steady distance behind. Phoebe caught at her hat and pretended to glance around and wave at someone so she might look over her shoulder.

There, the old roan wearing blinders, plodding along beneath a shabby-looking country gentleman wearing spats and a worn hat even more disgraceful than hers.

It could just mean the man was lost and looking for an address, but she kept watch for him as the carriage turned a corner.

The roan turned the corner with them.

Before she did anything drastic. . . Phoebe leaned over the front seat, close enough to Mr. Blair that she could smell his pine-scented shaving soap. "Is the gentleman riding the roan horse and wearing a battered bowler a friend of yours?"

"No," he murmured tersely. "He's been following since we left the house."

Phoebe thought a few curse words but concentrated on locating susceptible animal minds. The roan was tired and hungry. So was the stray dog sniffing the gutter. A farm cart filled with hay waited on a corner ahead. Past the cart was a portly man eating a meat pie from a vendor.

Mentally apologizing to everyone concerned, Phoebe placed the picture of the meat pie in the dog's head. Part hound, he lifted his snout and sniffed the air. Finding the scent, he dashed in front of the roan, causing it to rear. Phoebe offered the image of the delicious hay to the blinders-wearing horse, which was prancing nervously as its rider shouted at the dog.

Rearing again, the roan managed to throw his inept passenger and head straight for the cart.

Mr. Blair drove the carriage down another street, leaving chaos behind. Phoebe sat back, not satisfied but fretting. She needed to interrogate the roan's owner.

"Stop, please," she whispered to Mr. Blair. "I will meet you by the Scott monument shortly."

He shot her a scowl, but she was already leaning over Daisy's shoulder. "If you would see to the twins, please, I saw some old friends back there. I really must speak with them."

The carriage pulled to one side, Phoebe scampered down, leaving Daisy to manage on her own. She gathered her walking skirt and petticoat and hurried toward the shouts. From his contentment, she could tell the horse was still eating. As she turned the corner, she could hear the carter shouting in outrage. She didn't know how the man with the pie had fared. The dog was long gone.

If only she could read the minds of people! But she couldn't. So she looked for the countryman in the crowd, tugging at his horse's reins. She didn't recognize him. She didn't want him to recognize her. She shrugged out of her old redingote, removed her hat, and concealed it under the coat draped over her arm. It was a pity she couldn't carry her pretty new veiled hat with her so she could don it now. Instead, she settled for wearing her most sympathetic expression.

"What a good horse," she cooed, mentally telling the horse to back up while patting its nose. The roan tossed and shook its head. Spooked, it backed away from the hay.

The men arguing in the street turned to stare. She gave them a vapid smile. "Are you a stranger to the city, sir?" she asked, still calming the horse and taking advantage of the sudden cessation of argument.

"Mayhap," the middle-aged rider said cautiously, gathering up his horse's reins. The broad country accent gave him away.

"It's best not to take a hungry horse through the streets. The apple cart might have been next," she said merrily. "Are you taking him back to his stable?" She patted the old thing affectionately and scratched behind an itchy ear. The roan twitched it in approval.

The carter growled something irascible and returned to his seat to move his load out of reach.

"Not so it's your business," the rider said in suspicion.

"Oh, but you see, it is," Phoebe said sweetly. "My aunt owns a stable behind the old walls. I thought if you were looking for a place, you might be interested. This old boy is looking mighty tired. Where are you from? Do I detect a Glaswegian accent? That's a very long trip by horseback."

"I come by train," the rider said, indignantly. "Rented this hack. Now if you'll let 'im go, I'll be on my way."

"My aunt's place is in Canongate. Ask for Auntie Mable. Everyone knows her. If you'll give me your name, I'll tell her to give you a discount." Everyone knew Mable's Stable. Phoebe simply didn't intend to let Mable know she'd sent a scalawag her way. Mable wouldn't care.

"Ebenezer. Just tell her it's Ebenezer. Now I gotta be on my way." He swung up awkwardly on the restive horse and yanked it away from Phoebe's caress.

He was from Glasgow and wasn't an experienced rider, which meant he wasn't a countryman. Interesting.

Phoebe took the straighter path to the garden, down lanes a carriage couldn't go.

Surely a simple man like that had no reason to hurt small children? What if it was Mr. Blair he wanted?

ELEVEN

DREW THOUGHT HE MIGHT HAVE AN APOPLEXY WHILE HE PARKED THE carriage, found an urchin to look after the horse, and tried to keep the children reined in while he waited for the thrice-cursed governess to return. What in all that was holy could she do on her own?

He didn't dare let Daisy take off with the children. They'd soon be out of sight. He couldn't know that the rider meant harm, but he was taking no chances with the weans. He had them play a jack-in-the-box game in the carriage while they waited.

He breathed a sigh of relief when he saw the lady's long strides down the street. She was pulling on her redingote as she walked, struggling with her hat, and dodging passersby in her haste. People turned to stare. Lady Phoebe was not exactly ladylike in her demeanor, and he smiled. The lady was nearly as direct as a man.

And then he quit smiling, wondering what kind of upbringing she must have had that she'd been allowed to behave in such a manner.

She pinned her rumpled hat on as she greeted them. "Sorry for the little delay, my sweets. Shall we inspect the monument first? The view is said to be spectacular." She helped the twins down.

Drew considered wringing the lady's neck as he followed with Enoch in tow. The boy was eager to toss—or levitate—his ball, not look at a horrendously ugly monument. "Daisy, will you watch the children while I speak with Lady Phoebe?" His irritation made the question more of a command, but he lacked patience for niceties.

The twins happily skipped past Daisy, and Enoch sat down to launch his ball. Lady Phoebe almost stopped to correct him, but she apparently caught the look in Drew's eyes. He could see her hesitation. That was his fault after last night. But he planted his boots between her and the children and refused to budge until she acknowledged his presence.

"His name is Ebenezer," she whispered, almost angrily. "He's from Glasgow. He does not know horses well. That was a rented hack. He arrived by train. I cannot offer more than that. Did you do anything that would cause him to follow us?"

Glasgow! That was Simon's base of operation. "Stay here. I'll look for the bastard."

"His horse is trying to drag him onto the park grass," she called after him. "Raven is circling him."

He glanced up to spot the bird and wanted to kick himself all over again for listening to such babble. But there was the damned old crow circling, just past the monument. He picked up speed. Behind him, he could hear Lady Phoebe calling cheerfully to the children, rounding them up for a race—in case there was danger?

The scoundrel in the shabby green waistcoat was just dismounting from his horse. Phoebe was right—he wasn't a horseman by any means. He slid off like a dafty arse, then looked around as if uncertain what to do with the hack.

Prince's Street did not generally cater to riff-raff. Gentlemen frowned at the shabby interloper. Ladies crossed to the other side of the street. Drew would not normally be caught speaking with him, but he bore down on the bastard with determined step. Ebenezer didn't look his way in time to be alarmed.

Drew grabbed the ruffian's tattered collar and dragged him into the shadow of a hackney coach. "Who sent you?" he demanded.

Ebenezer wriggled, but Drew caught his arm and yanked it behind his back. An elderly gentleman passing by frowned through his thick white mustache and hurried past.

"Noo jist haud on, I ain't nobody," Ebenezer whined. "I widnae do nuthin' but mind me own bizz."

"A Weegie like you widnae come a'this way for nae reason," Drew taunted, falling into familiar dialect. "And widnae follow me from my house unless he means harm. I'll have ye behind bars if you don't tell me who sent ye!" He shook the older man for emphasis.

"It'd be my life to tell ye," Ebenezer whined. "I'll go away."

The brass buttons and rounded cap of a city policeman crossed the street, coming toward them.

Drew tightened his grip and spoke properly. "You'll tell me who sent you, or I'll tell the policeman you tried to rob me. Who do you think he'll believe?"

"The Association sent me," Ebenezer whispered. "I dinnae know more."

The Association? The world consisted of associations. He belonged to a few. And the only one he knew of from Glasgow—had been deadly dangerous and long defunct. "What Association? What did they want to know?"

"If the bairns be with ye, that's all."

Black temper boiled up inside him, and Drew bodily lifted the man from his feet and whispered harshly. "Ye clatty mongrel, tell the bastarts that I'll rip off their baws before I rip off their heads if they come within a mile of my wards, do ye ken?"

The policeman halted in front of them. Drew had no choice but to release the bastard while lying in proper accents—"He insulted my wife, officer. I apologize for causing a scene, but I could not let the insult go uncorrected."

Ebenezer scurried back to his horse. The constable frowned, nodded, and continued on his route.

As Ebenezer attempted to cluck his tired hack away, Drew wished he had a way of ordering the raven to follow. Then he rolled his eyes at the thought. Still furious, he stalked back to the monument. From there, he could see Lady Phoebe on the lawn watching his wards try to hide from. . . a pigeon?

She noticed him instantly. Out of frustration, Drew circled his hand in the air, indicating the crow. She nodded and miraculously, the creature glided off in the same direction as Ebenezer. He'd start believing the stars directed the moon shortly.

By the time Drew reached her, Lady Phoebe had the children throwing the ball to one another, encouraging Enoch to use his abilities to guide the rubber into the small hands of the twins. They were so thrilled with the game that they barely acknowledged Drew's return.

"Is that bird really following him?" Drew asked in disbelief that she'd not only interpreted his message but been able to pass it on to a *bird*.

"Raven amuses himself. If he tires of following, he'll return. At the moment though, if I'm interpreting what he's seeing, Ebenezer is headed for the train station in a frightful hurry. What did you say to him?" Holding on to the flat top of her hat, she cocked her head to study him.

"I threatened him with the police." Drew didn't want to tell her more until he'd had time to investigate what the spy had said. He didn't wish to explain the danger of a powerful group of men who should no longer even be alive. "I'm reassured that he listened and is heading back where he belongs."

She waited, but when he didn't say more, she shrugged her narrow shoulders. "Fine. If you can spare the time, it would be good if you rewarded Enoch with a little attention. He has mastered all his letters and is ready to read. I'd like to work a little more with the twins to understand how they communicate."

"Do I just throw a ball?" he asked, watching the children play.

She looked at him with incredulity, then nodded as if he were a simpleton. "I take it you invented things rather than play in the street at his age. He'll let you know what he enjoys."

Drew didn't intend to explain that the streets he grew up in weren't safe for playing ball. The past was behind him. If he had his way, it would stay there.

Unfortunately, Simon's prodigies might be dragging him back in. *How? Why?*

PHOEBE TOLD HERSELF THAT MR. BLAIR'S BUSINESS WAS NONE OF HER concern. She marched down the lawn to draw the girls aside to play flower dolls. She showed them how to make heads and arms and ball-gowns out of weeds and blossoms. "Should the dolls have a tea party and invite their friends?" she asked as stubby fingers carefully manipulated recalcitrant stems.

"Mary wants to know if she can play too," Clare said, setting her flower doll down beside a toadstool table.

Since the twins had been distracted these last minutes, Phoebe had conjectured there was more on their mind than Enoch's ball. "Of course, although you may have to make a doll for her," she suggested, to see if she'd guessed correctly about their preoccupation.

Clare nodded and began twining another set of stems. Cat was the one who spoke. "Mary is all wet. She needs a towel to dry off before she catches cold."

Anyone else in the universe would believe the children were creating imaginary friends and testing her. Phoebe had cousins who saw ghosts, so her experience was a little different.

She glanced at the worn lawn covered in yellowing leaves, down to where the old canal had been—well before her time. Trains had taken the place of canals. There was no place—now—for a child to fall into water. It wasn't raining today. The twins had no reason to imagine a *wet* child. "If Mary is a spirit, she cannot catch cold, but it's thoughtful of you to think of her. What does she have to say?"

The twins silently communicated. Did one twin see spirits and the other hear them? Or was their silent communication simply a defensive collaboration against adults who didn't believe them?

"Mary says she's not cold, and she's never seen flower dolls. Can we take her home with us?" Cat reached for another weed and held it up to the air, as if for approval.

"I think she would miss her home," Phoebe said, trying to remember what little she knew about spirits from her occasional conversations with distant family. "Don't you miss your familiar beds?"

Both girls nodded vigorously. The poor wee lasses were holding up bravely, but they'd been torn from all that was known to be cast into a cold house containing no loving arms or familiar objects beyond their old nurse. That was enough to cause them to invent invisible playmates, but the detail about the wet hair gave Phoebe shivers.

"We can leave Mary the dolls to play with," she suggested, wondering if there was a way to exorcise a lonely spirit and send her on to whatever awaited in the next world. "Maybe her mama will come and find her here."

"I wish our mama could find us," Clare said in a pragmatic manner as she set a new doll around her toadstool table.

"She *can't*," Cat wailed, abruptly crumpling her doll in a pudgy hand. She got up and ran to join Enoch and Mr. Blair.

"Why can't she?" Phoebe asked, hoping for a clue, any clue, to what went on in the twins' heads.

Clare sighed and continued working on her dolls.

"Clare, could you *try* to explain why your mama can't find you?"

"Cat sent her to the light." Clare shrugged and a tear trickled down her cheek.

That explained so much and so very little. Talking to a four-year-old about spiritual beings was a little beyond Phoebe's curriculum. "Can Cat send Mary to the light?"

"Mary doesn't want to go." Clare looked around for more flowers.

"Did your mama want to go?" Phoebe wished she had her own mama here to help her out.

"No, but she was crying. And she wanted to go back to Daddy. So Cat showed her the light, and she went away."

Impressed that the taciturn Clare had offered that many words, Phoebe didn't dare ask more. She had the uneasy notion that their mother might have wanted to warn their father and couldn't, because only the girls could see her—and they didn't understand.

"Shall we leave Mary with her tea party and join the others? I think Daisy has set out lunch." Phoebe offered her hand to the girl.

Clare solemnly took it and stood up, shaking the grass off her little coat. "Mama showed us the bad men and said to stay away from them. What does *clarty clipe* mean?"

Phoebe's head was still trying to grasp the first statement. The question caught her unprepared. She sorted through the street cant she'd learned from childhood, translated it through Clare's proper accents, and winced. "Dirty snitch. I'd not use that phrase, if I were you. Where did you hear it?"

"The bad men called me that."

Phoebe decided she was taking the children to China. That's all there was to it. Maybe India would be far enough. She was pretty sure France wasn't.

"Can you describe the bad men?"

"Big. Scary." Clare ran off to join the others.

Mr. Blair sent her a worried look when Phoebe wouldn't sit down but checked the sky for Raven. Then she checked the tiny minds all around them, but to wild creatures, all men were big and scary unless they were handing out food.

She needed to *do* something. But her gift was singularly useless.

"Lady Phoebe, might I interest you in the bird in that bush over there?" Mr. Blair asked politely, standing up from the picnic blanket and gesturing at a shrub Phoebe couldn't identify.

She was a city girl. She'd never been in this garden before, even though it was easy walking distance from her home. The only bush she could identify was a pine tree.

She obediently followed him at an angle, so she didn't have to let the children out of her sight.

"You are looking as pale as one of Clare's ghosts. What did she say?" he demanded the instant they were separated from the children.

"That our surmises about the children knowing something are correct but not very useful unless you can translate *bad men* into names and faces."

He cursed and looked despairing before shuttering his expression. "Her exact words, please."

"She's four. There are no exact words. She said Cat sent their mother to the light because her mother was crying and wanted to go to Daddy." Phoebe wrung her fingers and waited to see how much of this he would accept.

He rubbed the hair falling into eyes that seemed to see the depths of hell. "Can we hope that means their mother is in a better place or that she's watching over Simon?"

"Your choice. I'm not sure they even know." Since he accepted that, she took a deep breath and continued, "Clare asked me what *clarty clipe* means and said the bad men called her that."

Dirty snitch. Bad men thought Clare knew something to snitch about.

Mr. Blair's reply was not fit for a lady's ears. Phoebe picked up her skirt and returned to the children, leaving him to deal with his demons while she dealt with hers.

TWELVE

Stripped of his coat and cravat, Drew sorted among the metal pieces he'd ordered, found the ones he wanted, and slid through the straw beneath the carriage. He screwed the tin alloy into place along the axles and checked the undercarriage for any other areas of vulnerability. Then sliding back out, covered in straw dust, he examined the leather reins and tackle.

He'd waited until the aging carriage driver he shared with Dalrymple took his afternoon off before completing this task. The new stableboy presented a different problem. He'd have to trust the adolescent.

Nibbling his bottom lip, Henry watched him. "They're spankin' new, sir. Naught wrong with 'em leathers. I shined the brass meself just this morning."

"And I wish to keep them that way, Henry. When they're not in use, I want them locked up." He nodded at a cabinet he'd just completed.

Henry nodded, puzzled but agreeable.

"Are you comfortable with any weapons?" Drew asked, studying the stable for any other weaknesses.

Henry looked alarmed. "I have me sgian-dubh, sir. I ain't learned to use a whip."

Drew studied the boy. No more than fifteen, he was still a stripling, and not a very tall one at that. He took down a riding crop and threw it to him. "Just think of this as a stick to whack anyone who tries to make you do something you don't want to do. You're less likely to hurt your knuckles that way. How good are you with the knife?"

Henry pulled a short knife from his boot. "I never used it on people."

"That's good. You have to be close to use it. It's a last resort unless you've perfected the art of throwing. I want you to feel safe if anyone comes nosing around the stable who shouldn't be here. Don't believe any tale anyone tells you. It's just me and Mr. Morgan and no one else, got that?"

Henry looked worried. "Yes, sir. What about the lady?"

"Lady Phoebe?" Drew frowned. "I suppose, but I wouldn't like her to go out without accompaniment."

"If I go with her, then there's only old Tavish to guard the stable, sir. He tipples a bit and sleeps a lot. What about a dog?"

The boy caught on quickly. Drew frowned. The governess had mentioned that once. "I'll consult the lady. Let me know if you have any other concerns, and tell me immediately if you notice any more strangers."

He entered the house by the back door and checked the door hinges and bolts, then the windows. He could provide a few spring-activated surprises that would give the household fair warning should anyone attempt prying at the locks. The problem became maintaining locked doors with too many people keeping odd hours.

Hugh emerged from the office with a stack of correspondence. "I'd feel better were I to go back to Glasgow myself to investigate any return of the Association rather than asking others to do my work."

"I know." Drew tried to dust off the straw and gave up. Entering his workshop, he set aside the pterotype to prepare an alarm for the door. "So would I. But if we gallop off to interrogate half Glasgow, who would stay here to guard the children?"

"You're certain the geezer said the Association? I thought they'd died out decades ago, a relic of the old days when landowners controlled the laws. Money is in trains and shipping and factories these days. Estate owners court bankruptcy and don't have the wherewithal for skullduggery anymore." Hugh bounced the letters against his palm and frowned in thought.

Remembering Dalrymple's plan to use his investment partners to run for council, Drew frowned. "So now we have wealthy businessmen wanting to control the laws, maybe a new angle on an old tactic. Laborers are attempting to unionize. This new Association may want to prevent unions. Simon was talking about allowing his men to appoint leaders to bring complaints directly to him, not a union but close enough. I hadn't even considered that a problem until now." Drew tested his spring and lever, then hunted through a selection of screws. "We need to know who hides behind the Association mask these days."

"Sending these letters will start rumors flying," Hugh cautioned, waving the ones in his hand.

"Good. Give them something to do. I telegraphed Simon yesterday to warn him." Drew carried his tools down the corridor.

"The telegraph office will tell everyone within miles," Hugh shouted in alarm.

"Don't be naïve. We have a code. He'll be watching for your letter for explanations. What do you think about bringing in a dog?" Drew studied the door frame, hating to mar the pristine paint.

"I'm thinking you should ask the cat lady," Hugh replied dryly.

Yeah, that's what Drew was thinking too. Except he was also thinking about moist lips and a slender waist and why the damned woman had chosen to walk back from the park instead of taking the carriage with him. And where the hell had she been all morning?

"IF THOSE PROPERTIES ARE TO BE SOLD," PHOEBE TOLD HER SOLICITOR, "THEN whoever buys them must be forced to uphold my life lease on the flat. There is absolutely no question of allowing money to exchange hands without my share being included."

Mr. Lithgow pushed his spectacles up his nose, scanned the original lease she'd retrieved from her trunk at her aunts' house yesterday, and nodded. "Quite right, my lady. If he is selling the property, then this contract specifies a definite obligation. I'll check the deeds office and be certain they are aware of the lien. Will you be signing the employment contract in the meantime?"

To keep a roof over her head, she should. But it felt like servitude, and Phoebe didn't wish to be hemmed in. "I'll take the papers and study them at my leisure." As if she had any leisure. She had a perimeter to establish around Mr. Blair's house, one that strangers couldn't breach without her knowledge.

"Of course, my lady. Shall I charge my bill to your account?" he asked solicitously.

Which meant from the investments they had tucked away against the inevitable rainy day. She supposed it didn't get any rainier than being homeless. "Yes, thank you, Mr. Lithgow. My mother and I appreciate your honest service."

She pulled on her gloves after she left so he did not see the gaping hole in one seam. She supposed she could sew it, if she'd thought to pack her meager sewing things after the wall collapsed. She didn't wish to spend more on fripperies with the solicitor's bill dipping into their small earnings.

She walked slowly up the hill toward the impressive line of attached housing that was now her abode. She wasn't certain she could ever really call it home, but Raven circled overhead, and she was learning the creatures in the neighborhood.

Houses here didn't have dovecotes, but pigeons roosted on the roofs. Their habit of traveling in flocks was useful. She knew where the squirrels nested, although the ones in the attic were a bit resentful of being removed from their cozy nest on the verge of winter. Perhaps she could find them some warm rags.

There were several stray dogs scavenging in the mews and alleys not far from the house. They'd be flea-ridden creatures, but it didn't hurt to enlist them in her defensive barrier. Instead of entering through the front door, she walked down to the kitchen and asked for scraps.

"You shouldn't be feeding them strays, miss, my lady," Cook argued. "Nasty things, they are."

"They wouldn't be nasty with a good bath, but they need to be trained first." She didn't intend to explain that she could reach them with her mind and teach them much faster than it would take the normal way.

Animals weren't dumb by any means. They responded to food and shelter as well as any human.

She mentally reached the nearest hound with an image of the big bone she carried. She didn't think Cook would appreciate it if she left it in the stairwell, so she took the bone around to the mews where she'd stored her bicycle. While she was there, she filled a basin with water.

She slipped into the stable, waved at a worried-looking Henry, and waited. Not too long after, a large hound loped down the alley. She was no dog expert, but Irish wolfhound traits were obvious, perhaps with a bit of foxhound. In any case, he was *large*. That ought to deter anyone sneaking around the door.

"Keep him fed and watered, Henry," she whispered. "He'll be good company."

Henry appeared somewhat taken aback at the dog's arrival but rallied quickly. "Master said as he thought a dog would be good. I'll let him in here with me."

"Not unless you want fleas," she warned.

"I'll give him a bath, I will. I'm good with dogs."

Not wanting to be around when the skinny boy attempted to wrestle a wolfhound into a horse trough, Phoebe hastened through the garden gate, stripping off her gloves and coat as she entered the rear door.

She nearly ran into the broad form of Mr. Blair.

He caught her arms and steadied her. Phoebe didn't want to look at him, but she hadn't been raised to look down. Once he released her, she clenched her molars and looked past his disgraceful dishabille, straight at the prickles of late afternoon beard. The visceral thrill his whiskers caused warned she daren't look further. "Sorry. I was in a hurry to return to the children. I hadn't meant to be gone so long."

She was glad she'd left the solicitor's envelope in the kitchen for Abby to carry to her room.

"I've made a few changes," Mr. Blair warned. "Let me show you what I've done to the door so you do not trip an alarm."

"You've been fortifying the house," she exclaimed as he showed her the hidden latches and springs he'd installed around doors and windows. "Brilliant! Although I do hope no one ever tries them."

"And that's something I need to talk with you about. I'm not certain how much you want to know about the Association. Would you prefer to trust the locks and not know more? I don't want you staying awake all night listening for boogeymen." He led her toward his workshop with its overlook of the tiny kitchen garden.

He'd disappeared yesterday after their visit to the park without telling her what Ebenezer had said. She'd already fretted away one night. Assuming this Association was what he'd learned about, she was relieved he was finally willing to share information.

"I have never listened for boogeymen. I have Raven and my other animals to let me know of strangers. They protect their own, and in so doing, they look after me. Unless you tell me this Association consists of Frankenstein monsters, I'd like to know what to expect. I assure you, they should be more afraid of me than I am of them." She hoped that sounded brave. She'd never had to look out for others before—although Mr. Blair seemed as if he might be a competent partner.

Hands behind her back, she studied the contraption he'd been working on.

"You are an unarmed woman," Mr. Blair corrected. "You cannot possibly stand up to thugs, hence the locks."

She shot him a glance, raised her eyebrows, and declining to engage in pointless argument, waited for explanation. He was most attractive running his hand through his dusty hair and looking harassed.

"This is a modern industrial age. The Association and its kind should be long dead," he said with angry emphasis. "It was a group of powerful landowners who banded together to prevent the common man from gaining the vote by use of intimidation, harassment, and occasionally worse."

"I'm aware of the history, nothing more," she admitted.

"You have no particular reason to know more of that period, although your noble grandfather most likely would have known of them, if he was not one of them himself. The origins of the group were in aristocratic landowners who were convinced common men would lead the country to perdition if they were allowed to vote. But then common men became wealthy running shipyards and trains and factories, gained the vote anyway, and an association of landowners lost its influence and purpose."

"But the Ebenezer-creature said an association sent him?" She processed what he was telling her while examining his fascinating machine. She liked being spoken to as an equal, although she wasn't certain he was aware he was doing it.

"Yes, which makes no sense. These days it is business and industry owners who feel under attack by laborers making demands, not landowners. So far, government has prevented unions, but tensions are rife."

"And by government, you mean the aristocrats, landowners, and wealthy *men* who own shipyards and factories, since women are not allowed to vote." Phoebe understood the results of male manipulation. Laborers might have good reason to complain about working conditions, but at least they had employment. Women either had to marry or starve. And that was how a few men ruled the world—by preventing others from doing so.

"There was a time when I believed women were better suited for the compromise required to run a country. Then I met you." Mr. Blair turned to tinker at his dratted machine.

Phoebe didn't know if she appreciated essentially being called uncompromising, but she liked that he saw her gender as equal to men. "Sewing circles are unlikely to send thugs to follow children. What might an *association* want with the twins? Did you ask your cousin about his wife's journals?" She fretted that the book was what they really wanted, but the *dirty snitch* comment didn't seem to be related.

"I've written Simon about the journals, but they do not explain why Ebenezer was sent to see if the children were here."

Would anyone know the children had a book? Should she tell Mr. Blair? He'd want to read it. She'd promised a ghost she wouldn't let him. She'd found nothing so far that he could use.

"If the old Association has returned," he continued, "then I must assume it is again powerful men who wish to maintain the status quo. Simon may have roiled them with his new-fangled ideas. Our family does not come from wealth, so established gentlemen and nobility would consider him little more than an encroaching mushroom, as my grandfather used to say. There may be powerful men who covet his mine, or simply neighboring mine owners whose best workers have been lured

LESSONS IN ENCHANTMENT 101

away by Simon's newfangled practices." He rolled paper into his machine and began pushing the keys, producing inky letters on the paper.

Phoebe watched but her mind was on how all this applied to the children. "So you're thinking the Association decided to remove your cousin and sent someone to cut his axle—because wealthy men do not crawl under carriages themselves. And in some manner, the children's mother must have known who did it? Told the twins—*after she died*? That's far-fetched by any standards."

"Granted, unless one believes in ghosts, which apparently everyone here does, but the Association? Not reasonable." He hit a lever and part of the machine jumped back to the beginning.

Startled, Phoebe watched in fascination as he hit the letter keys a little faster. He was printing right before her eyes! She wanted to ask a dozen questions, but she had to think about the children first and foremost. "I will ask our Librarian about ghosts. But the twins might know something far more prosaic, like remembering a neighbor in the carriage house who shouldn't have been there.

"If the *bad men* were in the least superstitious, guilt may have played on their minds, and the children running screaming from them would raise all the tales about Letitia's Sight," Phoebe suggested. "I still can't believe grown men would fear children. No one listens to four-year-olds!"

"Simon would, if he thought Letitia told them." Drew cursed as the keys jammed. "Letitia was half the reason he's as wealthy as he is. I can't imagine anyone understanding that, though. I have Hugh learning more about the Association. Once we know who belongs, we may have a better idea of which one might be cowardly enough to fear innocents." Unjamming the keys, he returned to typing with two fingers again.

"If anyone knew that your cousin's wife was half the brains behind his success, they may have intentionally chosen to remove her along with your cousin," Phoebe said softly.

Mr. Blair abandoned his machine to pace the room in agitation. Experimentally, Phoebe touched a finger to one of the keys. It did nothing. She hit it harder, then stepped back, startled, as it produced a smeary letter on the paper. When he did not object to her experiment, she tried another letter.

"That almost makes sense," he murmured, as if thinking aloud. "Letitia's family came up from nothing, but they're ambitious and talented and have fingers in a lot of pies. They are little more than merchants, but they've scraped together enough to buy a bankrupt estate, so now they're landowners. I doubt they're considered socially acceptable by the older generation."

"Or their heirs," Phoebe said absently. "Jealousy is human nature." With one finger, she typed the alphabet and frowned at the awkwardness. "You'd better not let the children see this or they'll tell me they don't have to learn to write."

"It's supposed to write faster than the human hand," he grumbled. "And it would, if the keys didn't have to be unjammed every fourth letter. As it is, it's worthless. I thought I could solve the problem, but I haven't."

Phoebe picked out a sentence but the keys stuck when she tried to type *dear*. "The letters are too close to each other. If the *d* was on one side and the *e* on the other, it might work better."

"Agreed, but besides working out all the possible combination of letters that shouldn't be near each other, it would be impossible to type fast while hunting each letter. The alphabet is more straightforward." He came over to stand beside her and study the machine.

She was entirely too aware of his masculine presence and eased away, but she couldn't contain her excitement when she realized the unleashed power of his machine. "More women might be able to make a living if they could be taught to type documents like inventories and wills! This machine could be the new spinning wheel. We would learn to *memorize* the key placement."

"Like on a piano?" Frowning at the machine, he seemed lost in thought. He was much too attractive when he was playing at mechanic instead of staid businessmen. She couldn't think clearly enough to continue this discussion. She should return to translating the journal.

Hoping it didn't appear as if she were fleeing, Phoebe eased toward the door. "Thank you for explaining. I'll return to the children now." And she fled.

THIRTEEN

"There's a bleidy great hound out there," Hugh complained as he entered the workshop late that night. "And you've taken the machine apart!" He sounded genuinely dismayed at the last.

"Aye right, a hound." Weary, Drew pushed out from under the work table. One of these days, his bones would crumble into dust under there, but work gave his mind better use than imagining what Lady Phoebe was or was not wearing right now.

Having her with him, helping him think through his dilemmas—while wanting nothing more than to kiss her senseless—had inspired him in more ways than one.

"Great monster of a hairy beast, gnawing on bones and growling when I come near. Where's Henry?" Hugh dumped his coat over a chair.

"Maybe our stableboy turns into a beast at night. How in hell would I know? Tell me something I want to hear." Drew tried to remember if he'd eaten. His stomach said he hadn't.

"The contractor has accepted our terms. We're both about to be a lot poorer," Hugh said in his usual pokerfaced manner.

"We're tearing down the tenements? Shouldn't we be celebrating? Where's the whisky?" He could use a long draw of liquid courage as he mentally registered the declining balance in his bank account.

"Save the celebrating until the deeds are filed in the consortium's name. The solicitor is working on them now. Is there a chance of finding a bite to eat in the kitchen? I'm fair starved." Hugh studied the remains of the machine.

"The grocer's bill is enough to believe half the cattle in Scotland are down there, unless it's all been fed to your hound. Let's explore." Drew wiped his oily hands on a cloth.

It was late. The children were long abed, as were the servants. He assumed Lady Phoebe must be also, unless she was haunting the roof again. He was better off aiming for the kitchen and not temptation.

Without coat or cravat, he stalked toward the kitchen stairs, Hugh right behind him. "I should latch that back door now that you're inside. Let me show you the mechanism so you won't be clobbered if you try to enter without properly unfastening it."

Before they reached the end of the dark hall, the door in question opened, and Lady Phoebe entered, her long hair disheveled and her skirt dirty, looking as if she'd been in a fight—or worse. Drew almost had an apoplexy.

"What happened?" he demanded, rushing to her aid—except she proceeded to brush at her dirty skirt and didn't seem to need his assistance.

Which idiotically angered him.

"Hound is still quite skittish, I fear," she announced. "I have him leashed now, and Henry is showing him around the block."

"Hound?" Drew stood there blankly, torn between shaking her for being outside at night and simply drinking in the sight of the lady in dishabille. The top buttons of her bodice had come undone, and she was most certainly not wearing crinolines or corset.

"I told you," Hugh said ominously. "Bleidy great hound."

"You may name him, if you prefer. I try not to become too attached." Lady Phoebe tugged at her hair, pulling it into invisible pins—lifting her breasts higher against thin wool. "I was about to fetch a tray up from the kitchen. The mice tell me you haven't eaten, and I asked Cook to leave you a cold collation. I can't keep the mice out of it much longer."

"I'll fetch the tray," Drew said crossly. "You shouldn't be out at this hour."

"I had to wait for the children to go to bed. I had promised them a story. I'll be out of your way now. You may fetch your own tray." She stalked past him haughtily.

Not a servant, he reminded himself. The lady was not a servant. He could not scold. He damned well couldn't even throw her out. She'd found a bloody damned guard dog and arranged his supper at the same time. Cook never left food out after dinner.

"Thank you, my lady," he called after her, grudgingly. "And don't go out there alone again."

Hugh chuckled. The lady made a gesture that Drew was fairly certain was rude except he assumed she didn't know that.

"Guard dog?" Hugh asked, still chuckling. "She trained that beast overnight?"

"Not even overnight," Drew muttered. "It wasn't out there before we left for the park. She found a damned dog and leashed it this afternoon and evening." He trotted down the stairs to see what food they could rummage.

"Maybe the mice helped her," Hugh said with laughter.

"I can almost understand why men might have wanted Letitia dead, if she was even half so interfering as Lady Phoebe," Drew complained. But the lavish feast laid out on a tray for him—guarded by a sleepy kitten—shut him up.

"Impressive," Hugh agreed, admiring the stacks of beef and ham.

The kitten leaped down, regarded them with indignation, and stalked off, tail high—rather like the lady. Drew muttered under his breath but the lady wasn't at fault for his wandering mind. Mostly.

Cook had left a full loaf of bread and one of her pea salads as well. And candied pears. Drew shook his head in disbelief. The governess had turned his whole damned household upside-down, then organized the kitchen. "It takes a lady to be fed around here?"

"Well, no, it probably takes sitting down to dinner at mealtime," Hugh suggested. "But if you're not prepared to do that. . ."

Drew turned the spigot on the ale keg and filled mugs. "I wonder if she ate?"

"I think the lady is capable of looking after herself. We seem to be the ones lacking. Are we taking this to the workshop or the parlor?" Hugh hefted the heavy tray while Drew carried the mugs.

"Maybe we should clear a place in the dining room. Do lady governesses come down to dinner?" Drew's mind wasn't on the food so much as the sight of the lady wearing next to nothing, with her hair down in fetching curls he wanted to wrap around his hand. He was a tactile man. He liked touching.

"Not with us," Hugh said pragmatically, setting the tray down on a crate on the dining room table and hunting for a match to light a gas lamp. "So let's not work up a sweat moving all these boxes aboot and messing with the order. Tell me what happened to your machine?"

"The lady happened to it," Drew said grumpily, pulling out a dusty chair, shoving a few crates aside, and filling his plate. "She says women would *memorize* a keyboard if I scramble the letters. I had not even thought of *women* using it. I wanted to be able to type reports faster than I can write them."

"You have an execrable hand, which is why you have me," Hugh said pragmatically. "And I'm not memorizing a keyboard."

"You won't always be around to type my reports," Drew argued. "You'll be rich and be gone by next year. I don't have the time to look for someone new."

"I'll hire my replacement before I go," Hugh said, complacently accepting that future, before filling his mouth with a huge bite of bread and ham.

"There's even mustard." Drew smeared his bread. "Cook wouldn't have thought of that."

"Teach the lady to type, and there you are, the perfect assistant," Hugh suggested.

"Just what I need, one more person to worry over. I think I'll tie her to the nursery. I wasn't cut out to be a family man. Look at Simon. He's shattered and chasing hobgoblins. Wouldn't have happened if he'd stayed single."

Hugh gave him an incredulous look and ripped off another bite of sandwich rather than reply.

Right. A governess was not a wife. He wouldn't fall to pieces if anything happened to Lady Phoebe. He'd simply hire another. The notion gave him indigestion.

THE NEXT MORNING, MR. BLAIR ROARED, "PHOEBE!" FROM BELOW, SHOWING his level of disturbance by not bothering with the title she used to maintain propriety.

She donned a smile and set the children back to work on their numbers. Closing the nursery door, she roared down the stairs in a voice she'd learned from fishmongers, "*Andrew*, familiarity breeds contempt."

She needed to read her employment contract to see if insolence was reason for termination.

"Then stop the familiarity of this contemptible hound!" he roared back.

She giggled, sought Hound's mind, and hurriedly descended. "Whatever happened to polite notes delivered by servants?" she called. She really was trying to avoid her employer when possible. He was just too irresistible when he glowered.

"The creature is holding Abby hostage in the kitchen! What the devil is he doing in here?"

"He smells bacon and *someone* left the door unlatched. He is a very smart animal."

"His tail is destroying the house. Remove him, at once!" Mr. Blair emerged from his workshop just as she reached the main floor. His black hair was disheveled, mud streaked his stiffly pressed trousers, and his newly shaved jaw was set as if he were about to go to war. All he needed was a plaid and a dirk. . . Oh, my.

"Hound has shown you the flaw in your defense," she asserted, brushing past to find the dog sniffing the worktable, his tail sending metal pieces flying.

"He's more wolf than hound. He growls every time I try to lead him out. He's not suitable to be around children." Furiously, Mr. Blair began slamming his tools into proper order.

"On the contrary, he's perfect. He's very protective of his pack. The problem is that he regards you as competition for leadership. He's testing you, looking for your weaknesses." She scratched behind Hound's ears, and his wagging tail sent the newly ordered tools flying.

Mr. Blair pinched the bridge of his handsome nose and covered his eyes. "Just remove him, please."

"Since you ask so nicely," she teased. "Squat down, look him in the eyes, and give him the command to leave." She wrapped her fingers in Hound's collar.

Drew kneeled down and scowled. "Wolf, *leave. Guard.*"

The dog growled and bared his teeth.

"Now I have to teach him a new name," Phoebe grumbled, planting mental images of bones in the animal's head. "Heel, Wolf, good boy."

The dog obediently trotted in her wake.

"Hugh, house keys for everybody," Mr. Blair yelled as Phoebe led the dog away. "No more leaving that door unlocked."

Phoebe could have told him that mechanical contraptions wouldn't stop the lockpickers she knew, but she figured he knew that. Mr. Blair simply didn't want Hound—Wolf—in his workshop.

"Abby, Wolf is hungry," she called down the kitchen stairs. "Could you fetch him some scraps so he'll learn to eat outside?"

"Tie him up, my lady, and I will," Abby yelled back fearfully.

"I'm fairly certain proper households do not shriek at each other like fishwives," Mr. Blair shouted from his shop.

"Then invent talking tubes or hire footmen," Phoebe yelled back. She'd been shouting to be heard since birth. It saved many unnecessary steps. And if she was loud enough, she made her point much faster. Besides, he'd started it.

Moisture from the fog collected on her gown as she led Wolf back to the stable and an abashed Henry. "That was fun," she told the embarrassed boy. "But we probably shouldn't repeat the adventure any time soon. Mr. Blair dislikes interruption."

"I'm so sorry, miss. I was putting the leash on him and he smelled the bacon and—"

"Out he went, understood. He's not tame yet, so we have to be careful. How are you faring out here? Is the brazier warm enough?"

"Oh yes, miss. And Wolfie is a good blanket. Is it all right to call him Wolfie? That's what Mr. Blair said."

Phoebe hid a smile. "Did he? Did he come to visit you or the dog?"

"Both, miss. He checked on our coal and taught me how a quirt works. He says I might learn to drive the carriage some day!"

"That would be wonderful. Do you know your letters and numbers? They can be useful for writing down directions."

"I learnt that at school before me ma died. I can write real well."

"Excellent. Perhaps Mr. Blair can hire you for running errands as well and pay you more. I shall suggest it. But guarding the stable is your most important task. Training Wolf to help you is part of that task. You'll need to use the scraps Abby brings up to tame him."

Despite the chilly damp, she lingered outside to teach Henry how to use food as a reward. Using her connection with the dog's mind, she could hasten the process. Wolf was smart, and he caught on to her mental images quickly.

Mr. Blair's roar reverberated through the windows and the mews. It was too muffled to discern, but Phoebe heard her name being taken in vain again. Since Wolf was currently following Harry's command to heel, Phoebe assumed the children were the cause this time.

Living in the streets might be easier. Hoping it was nothing serious, she left Wolf to the stable and hurried for the back door, forgetting to flip the alarm latch. A spring tossed an empty bucket at the door as it opened. Phoebe ducked.

"Use a blanket as the alarm," she shouted in frustration, "before someone is decapitated."

The children raced from the workshop toward her. "There is a bad man by the park," they shouted in various stages of coherency.

Her heart froze in her chest, and she glanced over their heads for assurance.

Mr. Blair was already at the front door, his expression one of controlled fury. "Watch them," he ordered.

"How do you know he is a bad man?" she asked, telling herself that *bad men* could mean almost anything.

"Mama says so," Cat declared.

A ghost said so, of course. She had yet to find names in Letitia's journal. The lady was as vague as her children.

While Mr. Blair stalked out the front door, Phoebe gathered the children and ushered them into the storage/dining area while she assessed the situation. Despite her preference for high places, she decided downstairs offered various street exits and seemed safer than running to the roof. Leaving the children among the boxes, she returned to secure the backdoor latch and return the bucket to its place.

Through Raven's eyes, she watched her employer approaching a businessman in tailored tweed and bowler, younger than the man yesterday, if she could judge through a bird's mind. She mentally woke Piney and sent him scampering along the roof, looking for intruders. These attached houses allowed access from neighboring roofs. She must remind Mr. Blair to lock the attic door.

She needed to hear what was being said. But most animals could not recognize human words, so she couldn't rely on them. She had to be out there to know which of her forces to call on. She hated being confined like this.

She regarded the room she must turn into a fortress. "All right, children, let's practice our hiding. Shall we see what's inside these boxes?"

She opened wooden crates, and the children helped her to lift out tools and machinery and books. After storing the contents beneath the dining table, Phoebe lowered the boxes to the floor so the children could climb in without endangering life and limb.

"Inside. Make certain you can lift the lid when I call," Phoebe instructed.

She was impatient to be outdoors, but the children's security came first. She'd not had time to teach them all the ways they could use their gifts to defend themselves.

Once they proved they could climb out at will, she told them to be very silent and asked them to each make up a story to tell her when she came back. Enoch objected, but she whispered that he needed to watch after his little sisters. That silenced him.

Then, heart pounding in anxiety, she snatched up a coat by the back door and hurried to the stables. She ordered Henry and Wolf to secure the doors and patrol the house's main corridor. Once she'd done all she could, she dragged out her bicycle and set out down the alley, a confiscated whip in her hand.

FOURTEEN

DREW STUDIED THE GENTLEMAN SWINGING A CANE AND PACING IN FRONT OF the locked park fence, apparently unfazed by the heavy mist. The stranger didn't appear to be a hired thug, but he didn't belong here either. Drew knew all the inhabitants of the terrace entitled to use the park.

The grating cackle of a raven passed overhead. Not bothering to glance up, Drew ground his molars and continued his study of the expensively-tailored but not fashionable stranger. As Drew passed his neighbor's house, Dalrymple hurried down the steps.

"Well met, Blair! I want you to meet someone. He's offered to help me with my campaign for council, says he knows a little something about politicking." His neighbor slapped Drew on the back and strode briskly toward the park.

"Why are you meeting him out here instead of the house?" Drew asked in a low voice.

"Wife don't like politicking," Dalrymple murmured back. "I'd hoped to impose on your hospitality if the weather became inclement. Look, Wilkes is joining him. He's a baron and a good man to know."

Drew knew Wilkes from meetings of the consortium. A tall and muscular man in his forties, Wilkes used his wealth and intimidation to command men without needing to say much. He wasn't one of Drew's favorite people, but it wasn't surprising he was involved in politics.

Wilkes and the stranger approached. Drew noted a few pigeons flying down to perch on a nearby fence. His jaw twitched, but he noted nothing else untoward—like a governess with a feather in her hat.

"Wilkes," Dalrymple greeted the baron with respect, then turned to the stranger. "Gareth Glengarry, meet Andrew Blair. He's on the board with me. Good man to know. Blair, Glengarry comes highly recommended as someone who can solicit votes."

Drew shook the man's hand but remained suspicious—*because of a pair of four-year-olds*. He ought to have his head examined. He'd met dozens of men like Glengarry over the years, bored and unambitious, using the vast connections of their aristocratic relations for their own purposes.

"Why don't we take this to your place, Blair? Have a spot to drink and talk in comfort." Dalrymple was already heading back up the street —toward the twins.

"Sorry, I was on my way. . ." Where? Town was the opposite direction. ". . .to meet a lady."

A questionable lady wearing his own damned coat chose that moment to bicycle sedately around the corner—whip in hand? What the devil was the damned woman about? She should be with the children!

"Mr. Morgan can let us in, can't he?" Dalrymple called out, continuing down the street, his back toward the bicyclist.

Glengarry and Wilkes followed in Dalrymple's wake, as if they expected Drew to fall in line. As he might have, just last week.

A flock of pigeons flew up to circle in the odd way of mindless birds. In the mews, Wolf howled, and Drew's hackles rose.

"Dalrymple," Drew shouted after them. "Hugh's not in."

And neither was the damned governess, who continued pedaling fiercely past him as if he didn't exist. From her expression, he thought she might be concentrating on the pigeons. Or the dog.

In exasperation, he hurried after the parade. Dalrymple turned to glare at him. The other two merely waited stoically, although they sent the circling birds puzzled glances.

"I don't want to be seen meeting in town," Dalrymple said in a low voice. "We need privacy. We'll not bother the young 'uns. They've come all this way, and it's the least we can do."

There was no *we* about it. Drew might owe his neighbor some loyalty, but not enough to allow strangers inside his house. "Sorry, sir, but the women won't like it."

"If you mean that interfering governess of yours, I'd watch out for that one, if I were you," Dalrymple warned. "She gave our Dahlia notions, I vow. She'll be teaching the children to be ill-mannered heathens."

Besides irking his temper, this idiotic warning was the least of Drew's worries. He needed to know why the twins identified Glengarry as a *bad* man. And he needed to make him go far, far away—without causing his neighbor to think him mad.

Glengarry looked bored. "We can return to the park, as planned. It's only a little drippy. We won't melt."

Neither man was Drew's guest. He didn't feel the least guilty in denying them shelter. Before he could speak, the hound howled with blood-curdling warning. The pigeons descended *en masse*, blanketing the fence guarding his front door.

And a male shout of fear, pain, and fury echoed from the mews.

Drew looked in the direction of the bicyclist—she was gone.

At Wolf's howl, Phoebe pedaled faster. She'd hoped to hide in the park and listen to the men, but planning wasn't her strong suit. She hadn't anticipated the men heading for the house or someone attacking from the rear.

Releasing the pigeons from her mind, she concentrated on Wolf.

He had an intruder cornered inside the kitchen garden! Oh gadzooks and blasphemy, the intruder might smash through the door just to escape the hound. But she didn't dare tell Wolf to let him go—

Turning into the mews, the high front tire hit a loose brick, and she nearly flew headfirst over the bars. Twisting quickly, she managed to land on her leg and hip instead. Shaken, she tried to connect with Wolf, but he was in full guard mode, oblivious to anything but the stranger endangering his pack. Or his food, whichever.

Unsteadily, she pulled herself up. Going after a bad man with a whip while on a penny-farthing had seemed like a good idea earlier. But the high wheel was now twisted and useless.

Pounding steps approached the mews from behind her. Had the *bad man* hurt Mr. Blair and followed her? She didn't have time to look. Children first. Gathering her courage, she limped down the alley as fast as she could, heading toward the howling hound.

A well-made man in familiar tailored wool raced past, then halted and swung around. "Phoebe?"

"Mr. Blair," she acknowledged, not stopping. "Wolf has a stranger trapped in the kitchen garden. Don't wait for me. Go!"

He studied her limp but to her relief, he heeded her admonition and took off running again.

By the time she reached sight of the house, the two men in the kitchen garden were hugging and slapping each other on the back instead of beating each other to pulp. Wolf lay in the alley, looking puzzled.

"Did ye think I'd leave the bairns unguarded, ye dunderheid?" Mr. Blair shouted, pounding the stranger harder.

"It's better they're eaten by a devil hound?" the stranger cried, punching Andrews' shoulder. His trouser leg had a serious tear in it.

So, *not* hugging. Rolling her eyes, Phoebe snapped her fingers and brought Wolf to her side. Henry was tucking his sgian-dubh into his belt and caught her eye with a question.

Limping down the lane, Phoebe shrugged and tossed him the whip. "Would you run down and bring my bicycle back, please? It met with a slight mishap."

That reminded the manly dolts of her existence. Mr. Blair instantly halted his back pounding and brushed aside his companion's punch to address her. "I don't know whether to dismiss you for abandoning the children or ask if you're hurt." With a frown of concern marring his square jaw, he shoved open the gate.

Phoebe stubbornly refused to acknowledge a thrill at his notice. "Toss me out, by all means. My life would be much simpler. Go inside and see if you can find the children, but you'd best unlatch your trap so you're not decapitated."

Her knee ached abominably, but she maintained a composed demeanor as she'd been taught. A lady did not whine or scream or complain. *Phoebe* did, but her current position required ladylike behavior. Her aunts would expect no less, and failure was not an option she could afford.

"Is *unlatching your trap* a euphemism I've missed?" the stranger asked, weighing her disheveled appearance and probably finding her lacking. Granted, he had reason if Wolf had taken a chunk of his leg.

Shrugging off his visitor, Mr. Blair wrapped his arm around Phoebe's waist. "Put your weight on me. Let's bring you inside. You took a nasty spill."

"Nice of you to notice," she muttered, but that was only to distract herself from how appallingly wonderful it felt having a strong arm supporting her. And how very nice he smelled. And a host of other sensations she was quite certain a lady shouldn't notice.

Mr. Blair turned to the tall man watching them. Both men had similar long-lashed brown eyes, but the stranger was shorter, broader, and less elegant. "Don't be a bampot, Simon, slip the latch. Here's the key." He tossed a key to *Simon,* his. . . *cousin?*

"Ah, the infamous latch. What's on this one? Will a bucket of water immerse me?" The stranger nodded at Phoebe. "My apologies, miss, but I'm eager to see my bairns." He easily found the lever, undid it, then unlocked the door, vanishing inside.

"Did you hide them well?" Mr. Blair asked, helping her limp over the threshold.

She almost smiled at his perceptivity, but her leg—and pride, admittedly—hurt too much to be chipper. "Not from their father. He need only call their names, and they'll be all over him. Wolf may have bit him, and I apologize, but I really need some warning. Did you find the bad man?"

"Just one of Dalrymple's questionable acquaintances," he said, helping her down the hall. "I left them to the park."

Questionable acquaintances didn't seem to be an immediate danger, but she watched in astonishment as the tall visitor crept from doorway to doorway, peering in without speaking.

"You're not the only one to play games," Mr. Blair explained, assisting her into a dining chair. "Letitia did the same. I'll fetch Abby to help you upstairs."

Phoebe could hear the children rustling restlessly. While her employer retreated toward the doorway, she leaned over to open the nearest crate and held a warning finger to her lips. "A surprise for behaving so very well," she whispered to Enoch. "Let your sisters out, then catch the intruder."

Mr. Blair glanced over his shoulder to see what she was doing. Apparently just noticing the misplacement of his boxes, he lifted a questioning eyebrow. Phoebe would like to believe that he hadn't noticed earlier because of her, but her employer had peculiar priorities. He didn't react as Enoch helped the twins from their hiding places. His jaw muscle twitched a little as the children crept into the corridor like a trio of pirates.

Leaning against the door frame, Mr. Blair kept an eye on the *game* his insane family played. Phoebe seized the opportunity to prop her leg on a crate and pull up her skirt to examine her injured limb. She muttered a curse at her badly torn stocking, but blood wasn't dripping, so she calculated she'd survive.

When she set her leg down again, Mr. Blair was watching her instead of the children. Alarmed by her visceral reaction to his attention, she flung one of the unpacked books at him. He caught it and averted his eyes while wearing a grin that spun her off balance.

The front of the house erupted in a chorus of delighted screams and a man's rumbling laughter.

"Your cousin, I presume?" she asked dryly, dropping her muddied skirt.

"I telegraphed him a warning yesterday. I should have known better. Simon hasn't a devious bone in his body. He didn't have to pretend very hard to be a drunken madman after the accident, but he's not normally a weeping-in-his-ale sort. Keeping him away from the children has been a struggle."

"Well, if his enemies know the children are here, there isn't much point in continuing the pretense," Phoebe said pragmatically, wondering if this meant the end of her position.

Maybe she'd be lucky and her aunts would find her a new situation in Outer Mongolia, far away from handsome dark Scots businessmen and inventors who made her heart flutter madly.

"I'll admit I'd rather he be here than risking himself alone." Mr. Blair studied the disruption of his storage room. "The crates were pretty ingenious. I'm the only one who would know they were disarranged."

"Fooling the eye is easy. Keeping children quiet is not. Your cousin and his wife trained them well. Explain Mr. Dalrymple's acquaintance. Why might the children call him a *bad man*?"

Mr. Blair frowned. "I could name a dozen men like him—the sort who likes to manipulate events while never standing up and taking responsibility for his actions. He was joined by one of my investors, a man of some substance, so he's well known in higher circles."

Phoebe paused in her departure, considering all the things he didn't say. "You didn't like the stranger, and you think he's the sort the Association might use."

"Not the sort who cuts axles, but the sort who knows who will. But I could be very wrong and have just taken a dislike because Glengarry supports Dalrymple's narrow view of the world and I don't," he concluded honestly.

"I lost track of Raven for a while, so I don't know how long they stayed out there. They're not there now. If you don't mind, I'd like to go upstairs."

Mr. Blair was tall and wide and filled the doorway with restless energy that resonated with hers. Rather than attempt to push past, Phoebe waited for him to move.

He shifted to the hall with a look of concern. "Shall I send Abby up? Do you need a physician?"

"I've been banging my knees since childhood," she said dismissively, too tired and sore to play lady and pretend she didn't have limbs. "I simply need to rest for a while. Daisy is in the nursery if the children grow tired, which they will shortly."

Feeling out of sorts didn't describe how she felt as she dragged up the stairs. She'd been a complete and massive failure today.

And she might not have a second chance tomorrow.

"I CAN PUT YOU UP HERE," DREW TOLD HIS COUSIN THAT EVENING, AFTER dinner. "While you're in town, I can introduce you to a few other mine owners, and to some manufactory managers who might give you advice on your new enterprise. But at some point, you have to go home, you know that."

Simon rubbed his tired eyes. "I know that. And I'll want to go shortly, once I'm not so shoogly, and I'm assured the bairns are safe. It was good seein' them, to know there's something worth fighting for. I appreciate you taking them in. Do they like their teacher?"

Drew sipped his whisky and screwed up his forehead in thought. "I think so. I don't know much about children, but they seem to take to her." He glanced at his cousin with concern. "She's like Letitia. You don't need to fret about her."

"If you mean that scarecrow who set the dog on me, she's naught like Letitia!" Simon protested.

Letitia had been small, plump, and pleasant-faced, but Drew wasn't talking about the lady's looks. Personally, he preferred Phoebe's more athletic physique and striking features, but he could see where her brusque attitude might put off most men.

"Lady Phoebe comes from the School of Malcolms that Letitia's family recommended," he explained. "She talks to animals. You probably wouldn't have a leg if she hadn't mentally muzzled the mutt she trained to guard the house."

Simon threw back the rest of his whisky. "As long as she isn't mentally muzzling the children. So she takes to their differences awright?"

"More than all right," Drew admitted. "She's teaching them to use their talents, although the twins are still a bit young. They're the ones who had us guarding the house this morning."

"Is that what you were doing?" Simon asked, pouring another glass. "Could have fooled me. She looked pretty comfortable with yer arm aboot her."

"Don't be daft. She fell off a bicycle trying to reach the little ones before you did. The point is that there was a stranger in the street that the twins identified as *bad*, and she was out there trying to find out why. She believed them."

"But neither of you know why they called him *bad*. Maybe I should start there and not with this trumpery about Letty's books. I can't claim to know everyone who might be in the Association, but I wager I can recognize most from Glasgow. Did you get his name?" Simon sat up, looking more alert.

"Gareth Glengarry is what he calls himself. Smooth talker, well-tailored but rural, a wee bit shorter than myself, about a decade older than you, I'd say. Been living comfortable, so he's soft." Drew watched for recognition in his cousin's eyes, but Simon shook his head.

"Sounds like half the people I know. We've come a way from the slums where a man had to work hard to get ahead. I should go down in the mine more often, work up a sweat, remember where I came from." Simon stood.

Before the accident that had taken Letitia's life, Simon had been down in his mine regularly. That he hadn't been back said his cousin still wasn't anywhere near normal. Drew knew better than to comment.

"I'll take ye up on the offer of a bed," Simon said, looking weary. "Maybe in the morning we'll drum up some better answers."

"And you don't think Letitia's journals might tell us anything?"

Simon shook his head. "I looked in 'em. They're recipes for anything from soap to chicken. There's a lot of foreign words, probably Latin. I don't have your fancy education and can't read it. There's naught recent or about people."

So much for that theory. Drew showed his cousin up to the nursery so Simon could check that the children were safely sleeping in their beds. He noted the attic door open—which meant their governess was wandering in the night again. That gave him notions he shouldn't have.

He showed his guest to a spare room and left him there with the rest of the bottle of whisky. Sometimes a man needed more than cold sheets to welcome him.

It wasn't that thought that drove Drew to the attic though. He was fairly sure it was concern for the intrepid Lady Phoebe. She'd stayed out of sight since the earlier incident, and he'd feared she'd truly harmed herself in her attempt to protect the household. He wanted to be furious with her, but she'd looked so forlorn traipsing up those stairs. . .

The rain had let up, but the night wind blew chilly as he climbed out to the roof. The slate was slippery, but the lady wasn't foolish. She'd found a sheltered spot near the chimney to pet her weasel. The raven squawked a warning from the top of the chimney. Drew felt like an interloper in his own house.

"This is how you rest?" he asked dryly, leaning against the slope near her.

"Have you come to tell me you don't need my services any longer?" she asked, not bothering with pleasantries.

"Good heavens, no!" he said in genuine alarm. "Simon is half off his head. He can't look after them. He needs to be able to hunt a killer. He can't do that with three weans clinging to his boots. Whatever gave you that notion?"

"I failed," she said with a shrug. "I'm in unfamiliar territory, and I'm badly prepared. Your cousin could have been the killer and broken down the door while I was out looking for a boogeyman, apparently."

"You did a brilliant job with what little you've been given. I'll grant, I would have preferred you stayed with the children instead of putting yourself at risk, but I do not fault your need to chase boogeymen. I did the same," he admitted. "Why would you think I'd dismiss you?"

She turned and looked at him with a puzzled frown. "I thought, perhaps, your cousin had come with good news and meant to take the children home."

"Even if he had performed miracles, I'd have sent you home with him. Children need attention, and it's difficult for a man to give it while providing the roof over their heads. Simon's children need more tending than most." Drew was uncomfortable with the path of this conversation. He didn't know what he'd intended when he came up here, but it wasn't soul-searching.

"Letitia must have family who could look after them. They're probably better off in the country, where they can be surrounded with people who accept them, without strangers who stare if they behave oddly." She released the weasel, then crossed her arms and studied the night sky.

He didn't know a single woman who could stand on a cold wet roof and look as if she had come to conquer the skies. Drew was starting to wonder if she was part of the elements and might someday blow away with the wind.

"Letitia's family is as much a target as Simon, as far as we know," he argued. "That is not an acceptable alternative. The children are safer here, where neighbors notice strangers and watch out for each other."

"Neighbors who don't understand children and who resent them for making a little noise? But I grew up in a different sort of place, so maybe I have it wrong."

"You think they'd be better off in the slums of the *auld* town?" he asked with a snort. Why on earth were they on this topic? He'd simply wanted to see if she was all right.

"The streets there are alive, day and night. People don't have time to notice children. There are disadvantages to that, I suppose. I just never cared, growing up."

Was she homesick? That might explain her melancholy. He shoved his hands in his pockets and watched as she stood and limped restlessly toward the parapet to look out. He should go back to his rooms, where he belonged.

"I need more than pigeons to work with," she said in frustration.

"I thought that was you behind the pigeons," he said, finally realizing why he was here—because she fascinated him. "You kept Dalrymple off my doorstep. Perhaps you need a forest. I can't give you one. Why don't you come back downstairs where it's warm. I'll give you a draft of whisky to help you sleep."

She sent him a look that almost seemed to be of approval. "A forest of animals would be lovely, thank you. And you would actually offer me a whisky, as if I were a man? That rates a hug, but I fear I don't dare offer that in return."

Staring at her kissable lips and vulnerable expression, Drew spoke before he thought. "I could use that hug aboot now."

FIFTEEN

AND THERE IT WAS, PHOEBE UNDERSTOOD—TEMPTATION PLACED SQUARELY
on her doorstep, and her choice to accept or reject. Mr. Blair requested a
hug. How long had it been since anyone else had held or kissed her or
shown any token of affection? None since childhood. Could she
deny him?

Tears sprang to her eyes. She hated weakness. But she was so alone
and had spent the afternoon terrified not only of being reduced to a
homeless, dependent relation, but of leaving the children in danger. And
here was a man who offered hugs, whisky, and a sympathetic ear.

It simply seemed the most natural thing in the world to wrap her
arms around Mr. Blair's—Andrew's—waist and lean into him. He
embraced her, and they stood there like that for a blissful eternity, just
absorbing the closeness of another human being.

But the attraction was too strong to stay that way. Even innocent as
she was, Phoebe felt the driving need for more. When he leaned over and
brushed a kiss against her cheek, he offered her still another choice. She
could back away.

She wasn't a servant obliged to endure his caress. She was a lady. She
had alternatives, of a sort. Just because she found those alternatives stul-
tifying didn't mean that she wouldn't be better off accepting them.

But she'd grown up in the streets, doing as she pleased, and she didn't have the willpower to deny herself—or him—right now. She longed to know his kiss again, to see if it felt the same as last time.

So instead of backing away, she tilted her head and brushed her lips to his, and there it was, the inferno of desire that they'd kindled the last time they'd done this. It was as if they'd only banked the hot coals so they could flame to full strength now.

His tongue invaded her mouth, and she felt the sensation in her lower belly. She pressed against him, needing to be touched while their lips meshed and clung. He obliged, pushing aside her redingote to caress her breast. They both groaned in unison.

The raven squawked overhead. Abruptly coming to their senses, they pushed away in the same accord as they'd come together.

"I should probably tender my resignation," Phoebe said sadly. "I love the children, but my aunts would die of shame should I disgrace myself while in their care. I'm sorry. I'm not sure what came over me."

She wrapped her coat closer and headed for the door, needing to cut this off before she slid backward and into his arms again. If she looked into his eyes, she'd be lost. Andrew Blair had the most honest face she'd ever seen on a man, and despite their differences, she liked it much too much.

He'd touched her *bosom*! And she craved more of that tantalizing caress—and the tingling sensations it aroused. She was shameless, but she supposed she'd known that all along. She'd never been *normal*.

"Phoebe." He caught her arm and pressed her into the warmth of the chimney. "I don't want you to leave. I know it's selfish of me. I know I've made it impossible for you. I don't know a solution. But please, don't leave yet."

The brusque businessman and stormy Scot pleaded in a way that made him entirely too human. She dared a glance at his expression, but in the cloudy light, she could see little. She simply knew his big body warmed her, and his plea spoke to her heart, and she couldn't move.

"Let me court you," he said abruptly. "Could we do that? I know I don't come from aristocratic circles. My family is humble, I won't lie to you. But we seem to have. . ." He stumbled over the words.

"Animal attraction?" she asked wryly. "I've never wanted marriage. I wish to attend the university. I don't wish to be a man's accessory."

He pulled back, running his hand over his hair and sighing deeply. "And I need an accessory," he agreed. "If I had a title, I could be as eccentric as I like, but I don't. To overcome my background, I must be more proper than a king. I can't afford a misstep or my investors will all desert me. Without investors, I can't turn my patents into machines."

"That's ridiculous," she said in disbelief, reacting to this lack of confidence more than his so-called humble origins. "You are a creative inventor and an intelligent man. You don't need a *wife* to prove that. What is the point of all your hard work if you can't enjoy the fruit of your labor? You seem to take care of everyone but yourself."

She blinked in surprise even as the words came out of her mouth—that's what he did. He made a partner of a childhood friend who needed help. He took in his cousin's children, even though they disrupted his life. He helped a neighbor he didn't like because the neighbor had helped him. But what did he ever do for himself?

He shrugged uncomfortably. "It's what a man does. I've been blessed with a brain that I can use to help others as well as please myself. I don't expect more."

"Then maybe you *should* expect more," Phoebe said more tartly than she'd meant to. She needed to put a distance between herself and this man for whom propriety was more important than having a life , apparently. "In the meantime, hire an upstairs maid so we needn't communicate by shouting."

Or hugging or meeting on the roof. She stomped off, irritated with herself as well as him. Or frustrated would be a better word. She wanted more hugs and kisses. She wanted to know where they led. And he was making her see why her desire to learn was a foolish dream in a world like theirs.

EXPECT MORE? DREW UNSTEADILY COMBED HIS HAIR FROM HIS FACE AND waited until his body had cooled off before following the exasperating female into the house. He had everything he'd ever dreamed of and more—and she thought he ought to expect more from life? *What*? What else was there besides work, a solid roof over his head, food in his stomach?

He didn't want fancy carriages and china or artwork on the walls. He'd never really required a wife as long as he could buy women for his needs. Children were an expensive nuisance, as Simon's brats had proved. A bachelor could come and go and do as he wished without explaining to anyone.

A bachelor went to bed alone while the woman he wanted slept in a room above. *Hell and damnation.*

Hearing a whimper from the nursery, he passed Lady Phoebe's firmly closed door and strolled down the corridor to look in on the weans. One of the twins was awake, sitting up in her bed and cuddling the kitten, her hair down in her face as she smothered sobs. His heart nearly broke at the sight.

Without giving it a second thought, he scooped her up and carried her into the low-lit hall. "Did you have a bad dream?" he whispered.

The kitten leaped from her arms, and the child flung them around his neck to sob into his shoulders. "Mommy's not coming back."

Drew wanted to weep with her. He hugged her and paced the floor while she wept, awkwardly patting her back. He could take her to Simon —except his cousin was probably blootered by now. The man needed his rest. "She's looking out fer ye, noo, isn't she?"

"Kitty walked right through her," she said, sniffing. "She's not *really* here."

How in hell did he respond to that? What would Phoebe say? And why shouldn't Phoebe say it? He turned his feet in the direction of the closed door. "And your mama is in your heart, too, isn't she?" he asked, recalling one of the governess's reassurances.

He didn't even know which twin he was holding. He was helpless here. The child seemed to nod but didn't answer. He ought to just plop her back in bed and tell her to go back to sleep, but he had the urge to rap on the lady's door, so he did. She wanted him to know what he wanted out of life? He wanted someone to solve the human problems he couldn't learn to handle from books.

Money couldn't buy magic genies.

Phoebe immediately appeared at the door, looking a little panicked and wrapping a robe around her. When she saw him, her eyes widened. . . until she saw the babe. Instantly, she reached for his burden.

"Where's Daisy?" she murmured, adjusting the twin over her shoulder and covering her cheek with kisses.

He hadn't thought to kiss the child's cheek.

"Asleep, probably. She wasn't making much noise." He shrugged awkwardly, not knowing what to do now that his burden was lifted.

Phoebe brushed hair off the girl's face and rubbed the tears from her cheek. "Clare, honey, can you tell me what's wrong?"

Clare. This was the quiet one, of course. Persuading her to talk was like pulling teeth.

"She said her mama wasn't coming back and kitty walked through her. Should I fetch warm milk?" He dragged that memory out of the bowels of his long-ago childhood.

She looked at him with such approval that his head bloody-well swelled two hat sizes.

"Did your mama used to fix you warm milk, my bonnie lass?" she whispered in the child's ear.

Clare nodded her head. "Cocoa."

"Will you tell us what you dreamed while we fix your cocoa?" Phoebe handed Clare back to Drew.

The girl went willingly. Her sobs lessened, and she watched with interest as Phoebe donned slippers and tied her old robe in place. Drew watched with equal interest. The lady had long slender feet and pretty toes.

"Was it scary when Kitty walked through your mama?" Phoebe asked as they traipsed down the stairs—as if this were the normal conversation one had after a nightmare.

Clare nodded vigorously against his shoulder.

"Did your mama know your daddy is here?" Phoebe reached over his shoulder to brush a strand of hair from Clare's wet cheek.

Her hand brushed his scratchy jaw—Drew couldn't tell if it was accidental or not, but the touch burned all the way to his core.

Clare nodded again. How the devil did one persuade the child to talk?

"Can you remember what your mama said?" Phoebe asked, in the same brisk tone she might ask what they would like for dinner.

Drew led the way down to the kitchen, so Clare could see Phoebe following behind them.

"She loves us," Clare said with a sob. "I want my mama!"

"It's hard to see and hear and not touch, isn't it?" Phoebe asked, studying the dark kitchen.

Knowing where things were kept, Drew transferred the child back to her so he could light a lamp and hunt a pot. Hunting, he could do.

"Mama is sad," Clare said, accepting the transfer. "She said to tell daddy about the bad men."

Drew listened as he found the chocolate pot and milk and sugar. He'd prepared his own hot chocolate as a child, while his mother worked her fingers to the bones sewing for others. That was before his father's injury, when they occasionally had chocolate.

"What does she want to say about the bad men?" Phoebe asked, taking a chair at the trestle table and nestling Clare in her lap.

The weasel peered out from under a cabinet, then scampered over to the lady. Phoebe scooped him up and placed him in Clare's arms.

"She says ask your *earl*. What's an earl?"

Drew swung to watch Phoebe's face pale.

"The only earl I know is my uncle, unless one counts my dead father. Can she mean Drumsmoore?" Phoebe whispered, glancing to him with what appeared to be panic.

Drew shrugged. "He's the only one I know."

Composing herself, Phoebe returned to reassuring the child. "An earl is an important man. What are we supposed to ask him?"

"About bad men," Clare said impatiently, squirming to watch him at the stove. "I don't want it *too* hot."

Nightmare apparently forgotten, Clare settled into Phoebe's lap to sip her cocoa. The weasel did what weasels do, nosing around the floor, scaring the bugs and mice. Drew poured more cocoa for Phoebe and himself and wondered how in hell his life had come down to this level. He was a wealthy, important man of business, he reminded himself. He should be reading contracts or tinkering with his typewriter or drawing up a schematic for the new—

"My uncle is a grasping miser with no family," Phoebe murmured, setting down her own mug to hold onto Clare's so it didn't slip. "I haven't spoken with him since he refused to help my mother travel to a warmer climate."

"Drumsmoore owns a mine," Drew said. "We tried to persuade him to join us in the manufactory. He refused."

He did more than refuse. Drumsmoore was an aristocratic bigot and one of the reasons Drew didn't look kindly on the class.

Uninterested in what she didn't understand, Clare clambered down to follow the weasel around the kitchen.

"I don't know him well," Phoebe said, keeping her voice low. "My mother seldom spoke of him, but I have the impression that he didn't approve of my father's marriage. When my father died and my uncle inherited the title, he refused to allow us to use the estate, even though he lives there all alone. To be fair, I believe my father left the estate management to Uncle Albert. My father preferred living in town and traveling."

"There's not much estate to manage," Drew told her. "It's little more than a stone watchtower on a hill overlooking a stream and a village, but there's coal underneath the hill, and the land isn't far from the main road between Scotland and Glasgow. It's an ideal location for a manufactory, but the earl has few expenses and the old ways cover them."

"If there's an Association. . ." She whispered his fear aloud.

"Your *grandfather* would no doubt have belonged. Your uncle has no reason that I can see, other than sheer backwardness. He leases his mine, so the workers are of no concern to him. But maybe he *knows* who's in the Association," Drew added thoughtfully.

The governess looked as sad and sleepy as Clare. Drew set their cups in the dishpan. "Come along. I think we all need a good night's sleep."

He picked up Clare and led the way upstairs, wishing he could follow Phoebe back to her room and forget the world for a while.

The Earl of Drumsmoore was a crotchety bastert who opposed every-thing not his own idea on principle. Drew didn't want to believe an old man's opposition to change would take him so far as to attempt to kill an entire family. Clare could just be providing another boogeyman. Or she might be speaking of a different earl.

How the hell did one investigate an earl—based on a child's report from a ghost?

PHOEBE READ THE TRANSLATED PASSAGE IN LETITIA'S JOURNAL AGAIN. *THE church ladies warned me again. I have tried to tell Simon. Men believe they are invulnerable.*

Just not useful. Did she break a ghost's trust and give this to Mr. Blair? What could he find that she hadn't? And what could *bad men* want with a lady's private thoughts? How might the book relate to an *earl*? There was no Latin word for earl. *Noble*, maybe.

When she got up the next morning, Phoebe deliberately avoided going downstairs. Mr. Blair confused her, and she needed to clear her thinking before she saw him again.

Hugh Morgan hunted her down in the nursery, the familiar packet of papers in his hand. "Have you had time to go over your copy of the contract yet?"

She hadn't even looked at it. "I don't think I'll be signing it, thank you. You may ask Mr. Blair why I'm declining."

"You're leaving?" Hugh asked in incredulity, watching her surrounded by three children eagerly working on various puzzles.

"Not unless Mr. Blair insists." She wasn't a failure if she was tossed out for refusing indentures, she'd decided. The result might be the same as being cast out for not doing her job, but ladies did not sign contracts of servitude, she was fairly certain.

Besides, she had to be able to leave at a moment's notice if she and Mr. Blair became too close. She was not marrying him for the sake of someone else's children. His cousin could take the children away anytime, and then where would they be? The whole situation bordered on the ludicrous.

Muttering, Mr. Morgan stomped back out.

As if the world conspired against her, a little while later Abby ran up, looking excited. "Miss, you have guests, very distinguished. They told me I would marry a soldier!"

Recognizing the tactic, Phoebe refrained from rolling her eyes. "Have you been walking out with a soldier?" She leaned over to praise Enoch's math and correct Cat's letter M, while her heart thumped with anxiety. What now? What other brick could fall on her head?

"There's one as lives next door to me ma," Abby whispered. "Very handsome, but he's never home."

"Did he give you that pretty pin you're wearing?" Phoebe stood and shook out her skirt and debated donning something a little more respectable, but she refused to be dominated by her fears—or anyone else.

Abby touched a small insignia pinned to her stiff collar and nodded uncertainly.

"My aunts don't read the future, just the present. Tell them I'll be down shortly."

Abby's eyes widened before she dropped a curtsy and ran off. Life would be much simpler if her aunts could actually read the future instead of teasing people with their observational skills.

In trepidation—her aunts seldom left their home—she straightened her hair into some semblance of respectability. As Phoebe descended the stairs, she heard voices in the parlor—male as well as female. Drat.

She was almost petrified at any reason that might drag her aunts out of their lair. Having them meet Andrew. . .

They might not read futures, but they were perceptive.

Phoebe picked up her pace. She needed to separate them at once or they'd yank her away from the children so fast hair would fly.

SIXTEEN

CONSIDERING WHAT HE'D BEEN DOING WITH THEIR NIECE JUST LAST NIGHT, Drew was extremely nervous about the arrival of Lady Phoebe's possibly prescient aunts. One of the disadvantages of believing in the odd powers of women like Letitia and Phoebe was that it made him mistrustful to the point of superstitious. He hated wasting time looking for ulterior motives in every interaction.

"We're so glad to have a chance to meet you in person, Mr. Blair," the taller, more authoritative of the pair announced. "We hope our niece is filling the position to expectation."

"We apologize for the intrusion," the rounder, more placid one said, settling a flutter of silk shawls and ribbons before reaching for her teacup. "It is kind of you to see us."

The back and forth between the two kept Drew's head swiveling but didn't allow him to say much, for which he was greatly relieved. The two ladies wore the airs and fashion of the *grandes dames* of his childhood, the ones who left charity baskets at Christmas and nodded coldly as they swept through meager schoolrooms. As a child, he'd been taught never to speak to those above his station, which meant he had no notion of how to address Phoebe's aunts.

"Here she comes now," the pleasant one introduced as Lady Agnes said. "You need not entertain us longer if you must return to your work, sir."

"I think Mr. Blair should remain to hear this," Lady Gertrude said in a tone of finality, lifting her *pince nez* to observe as her niece entered.

Drew hid a grin as Phoebe swept in wearing one of her usual crinoline-free gowns, chalk dust on her bodice, and her spirited hair springing in wisps around her face and nape. She determinedly did not look at him but bobbed a brief curtsey to her aunts.

"My ladies, to what do we owe this visit?" she asked in a crisp voice that didn't welcome a repetition of the unexpected call, leaving Drew to wonder about the relationship between aunts and niece.

Lady Gertrude snapped out the folds of what appeared to be a telegram. "Your mother, to be precise."

Phoebe paled, and Drew instinctively took a step toward her, knowing her mother had been ill. A telegram was seldom good news.

Lady Agatha, apparently the more sensitive of the pair, hurriedly added, "She is coming home."

Phoebe held a hand to her bosom and sank into a chair. Since neither aunt offered, Drew poured a cup of tea and handed it to her.

Was this fascinating female about to be swept from his life before he knew what to do about her?

"She's well then?" Phoebe asked in a voice of hope after taking a sip of tea.

"Of course. Did I say otherwise? She's taken one of her notions," Lady Gertrude said disapprovingly, handing over the telegram.

After reading it, Phoebe frowned and looked relieved. "It simply says she's coming home."

"Telegrams are expensive," Lady Agatha said. "She would never have sent one if it weren't urgent. That's why we're here. It means she's concerned about you."

"What have you been doing that would bring your mother home?" Lady Gertrude demanded.

Drew felt his collar tighten, but he wasn't a coward. He wouldn't retreat.

Phoebe, apparently reassured that her mother wasn't dead, coolly lay the paper down, sat back in her chair, and sipped at her tea before responding. Drew had to give her credit for resisting the doughty old dowagers and their blatant curiosity.

"It may be a matter of what *Uncle Albert* is doing. The twins believe he may know the identity of a killer. We have been debating whether I should call on him."

"We are debating no such thing," Drew said decisively, stepping in on this nonsense. "You will go nowhere near the man."

"You do understand that our niece is no servant?" Lady Gertrude responded icily. "She is a woman of exceptional talent who has already identified what is troubling her charges. You and your friends may deal with Drumsmoore as you please, but you will not order Phoebe about. That is for us to do."

Phoebe rubbed at the place between her eyes—as a means of controlling her temper, Drew thought, reading her tension. If he'd learned anything at all about his governess, it was that she couldn't be brought to reins. He waited with interest to see how Phoebe responded.

Apparently controlling her tongue, she replied in uncompromisingly aristocratic tones. "I am a grown woman and will not be dictated to. The question here becomes—what will we do with Mama when she arrives? I cannot desert the children if they are in any danger, but I cannot leave Mama alone."

Drew noted the old biddies nervously gathered their bags and shawls, sending him hooded glances, and behaving as if they'd rather *he* disappeared. He had no intention of doing so. Did they expect *Phoebe* to provide a home for her mother when they had a perfectly adequate one?

Apparently reading her aunts' minds, or understanding what he did not, Phoebe stood, as if in dismissal. "Fine. I shall speak with our solicitor and see what he suggests. I thank you for coming all this way to inform me."

Drew sensed he was missing some underlying message here, but the ladies were not his to question. He assisted Lady Agatha with her shawl, handed her gloves she'd left on the table, and asked if he should bring his carriage around.

They assured him they had a vehicle waiting. Phoebe handed her Aunt Gertrude her umbrella.

"My bicycle is broken, so I cannot visit easily, I'm sorry. I'll have Mr.

Lithgow send a message when he's found a place to settle Mama. I don't know how well I'll be able to divide my time, but I'll wait until she's here before deciding what needs to be done. If you can think of any way of approaching Uncle Albert before she arrives, I'd appreciate it. Once the children are out of danger, I'll feel better about taking time for Mama."

Drew could hear the distance in her voice, and a cold chill iced his blood. She was thinking of leaving—which no doubt meant she had taken some hare-brained female idea of tracking down her uncle and killers first. If her formidable aunts couldn't control her, how would he?

He had the terrible notion that he couldn't, not as an employer, and that was not a state of affairs he could accept.

PHOEBE FOUGHT A SINKING FEELING IN HER MIDDLE AS SHE WAVED OFF HER aunts.

It was good that her mother was feeling well enough to travel was the thought she held uppermost in her mind. She should be jubilant.

But that thought inevitably led to the gaping maw that was now her mother's uninhabitable home. Such loss might cause a terrible setback in the countess's recovery.

She brushed aside her fear for the moment to deal with her puzzled employer. She might not be able to read human minds, but Mr. Blair was an open book most of the time. His puzzlement was understandable. Men liked to comprehend events in their universe, and her family did their best to send up smoke screens to prevent that.

"Couldn't your aunts have simply sent a message?" he asked, reasonably enough.

"Not if they wished to send a warning," she answered absently, trying to think through a dozen problems at once. "I dislike interrupting the children's lessons, but I fear I really must see my solicitor. I'm sorry for my aunts' intrusion."

She started for the door but Mr. Blair blocked her path. She had to think of him as *Mr. Blair, her employer.* To do anything else would completely confuse an issue that was already too muddled.

"What warning did they wish to send?" he demanded.

She sighed and studied his dark expression. She'd really like to believe his concern was for her, but she didn't have the luxury of such self-confidence. And she truly couldn't tell him that her aunts—and possibly her mother—probably suspected what was happening between them. Her family's abilities were. . . exceptional.

"It is impossible to explain the dynamics of my family," she settled on saying. "My mother is the youngest sister, but in some ways, she's the most powerful and upsetting. She would not be leaving a home she's come to love for a Scotland winter if she did not sense a very real danger."

That her mother had not come when the building had fallen spoke more to this than she could explain to Mr. Blair. She didn't wish him to realize they were homeless. Her mother was a countess, the wife and daughter of earls, and once a very wealthy woman. Unlike Phoebe, she did nothing lightly.

"If she senses danger, then I should remove you and the children to a safer place. Perhaps your mother should go with you?"

"The children should spend the rest of their lives in hiding? I don't think so, although I shall try to keep an open mind. First, I must see my solicitor and find a place for my mother to stay." And there went their nest egg and her very distant dream. A solid roof over her mother's head was more important than a university education.

Tears welled. She had so hoped she'd have time to earn money for tuition. . . Paying rent for a home for her mother destroyed any possibility of that. She'd have to spend the rest of her life in service.

She could not deal with that realization now. Defeat hurt too much.

Before he could respond, Mr. Morgan and *Simon*—she didn't even know his cousin's full name—arrived. Mr. Morgan waved what appeared to be correspondence. Andrew's cousin was filing a. . . dirk?

They waited expectantly for her to leave. She dipped a brief curtsey, eager to do so, except Andrew—*Mr. Blair*—grabbed her arm and held her back.

"The Countess of Drumsmoore will be staying here," the dratted man proclaimed. "That will alleviate the proprieties and give us time to regroup and plan."

He enjoyed exploding that little bomb in their faces, Phoebe decided, watching the trio. The other two looked fairly dumbfounded.

"You might at least properly introduce me to your cousin so I may use the correct address when I assure him at least one of us hasn't lost her mind," Phoebe said waspishly.

"Simon Blair, at your service, milady." Older than Andrew, with darker brown hair than hers, the children's father bowed. "We're Sy and Drew to our friends so as not to confuse which one is about to be murdered."

That riposte almost softened her, until Andrew—Mr. Blair—spoke over her head.

"The countess apparently has the Sight, like Letitia, and she knows the earl. She may be our ticket to learning his associates. We'll need to clean up the dining room and pretend we're not a lot of heathens."

"Do not pretend to be what you are not." Phoebe pried his fingers off her arm. "Despite all expectations, my mother is a delicate invalid accustomed to a solitary life. She does not involve herself in quarrels." Quarrels that became *dangerous* if her mother entered them, she could have added, but then she would have to explain the countess's manipulative propensities, and she truly would sound like one of the spiritualist charlatans who haunted low places.

She skirted around *Mr. Blair* and his companions and stalked out, leaving them to their plots and plans. She practically ran up the stairs to her room to fetch her wrap.

After checking in on the children and promising them a romp when she returned—she feared to take them outdoors again—Phoebe gathered coat and gloves. She pinned on her new veiled hat so she looked moderately respectable and took the back stairs. She could hear the men arguing in the parlor as she slipped out the back.

The large wheel of her bicycle leaned against the stairs, looking as if someone had started hammering the rim and spokes back into shape. But the rubber tire was sadly damaged.

Summoning Raven to be certain no strangers lurked, she marched—limping—out to the main street. Despite her bruised knee, she knew how to walk distances, and it was a crisp autumn day, fine for an outing. By taking the mews, she avoided the parlor window and notice by the men inside.

Mr. Lithgow was all that was solicitous when he learned the countess was returning.

"Oh, my, yes, this does complicate things," he admitted. "I've placed the lien on the tenement, and notified the buyer."

"Will our savings tide us over until the matter is settled?" Phoebe asked anxiously, squeezing the gloves she'd removed. She hated looking shabby at times like this.

"Oh yes, yes, but it will reduce your income," he explained anxiously. "Your mother may have to lower her expenses."

Or Phoebe would have to use her income instead of saving it—and not jeopardize her position with inappropriate behavior. "We'll manage. Could we impose on you to locate a small place where she might live comfortably for now?"

He frowned and tapped his pen on his desk. "I shall make inquiries, but it may be that she should take a room in the household of a friend or relation who already has servants. Setting up a new household is expensive."

Phoebe's heart sank. "She won't like that," she murmured. "She has a maid and a nurse who look after her. Perhaps something could be found in the country?"

He brightened. "That might be better. I'll look into it for you."

Phoebe left the office not feeling much better than she had when she entered. If only. . . But that list was a mile long and a mile wide.

She should not have been so hasty in rejecting Mr. Blair's offer to put up her mother, but as she'd told the lawyer, her mother was unaccustomed to sharing with strangers. Besides, Phoebe didn't wish her mother to see how she lived. She knew that was foolish, but she was supposed to be a veterinarian by now, performing miracles.

She resisted the urge to cross the bridge to see how her old home fared. It would never be her home again. She must keep looking forward. Wiping away a tear, she strode back up the hill to the terraced housing she currently called home.

She knew Mr. Blair's house was only a temporary refuge. Perhaps she could move in with her mother once she was settled. *In the country.* She'd never lived in the country. She supposed she'd have more creatures to work with there, but less reason to do so.

Thinking to check on Wolf, Phoebe returned via the mews. As she approached the back gate, a large bicycle rim rose on invisible wings and wobbled in the air above the fence. Enoch! Why weren't the wretched men watching a lonely little boy?

Her bruised knee ached after the morning's excursion, and she wanted nothing more than to sit down with a cup of tea before tackling any more challenges. But she straightened her back and marched through the kitchen gate as the rim crashed into the garden.

Enoch sat forlornly on the back step, one small arm around Wolf's neck as he bravely attempted to right the rim with his mind.

"You know, using your hands in this case would be much more productive," she said crisply, removing her gloves to scratch behind Wolf's ear.

"What am I *supposed* to lift?" he asked plaintively.

"A most excellent question." She sat beside him. "You must learn to be unobtrusive, so people don't know you're helping."

"Or they'll think I'm a freak," he said morosely.

"Well, you must understand that you're the only person people will know capable of lifting things with his mind. I know thousands and thousands of people, and I know of no other like you, so you're very special."

Phoebe crossed her fingers as she said that. She didn't know *that* many people, and she knew of one possibly *capable* of duplicating Enoch's feats, even if she never used the ability. But hyperbole tended to impress children.

Enoch looked interested, if not impressed. "Mama said I should never brag about what I have in front of others who don't have as much."

"That is *exactly* it. It is very rude, and you'll make no friends that way. But if things. . . are made a little easier in your company, then people will enjoy being with you. But that requires that you think real hard about what you can and should do."

"How will I ever have friends if I must hide in the nursery all day?" he asked gloomily.

"You will be going off to school in no time at all. So now is when you must practice. Remember how happy your sisters were when you guided the ball into their hands?"

He nodded. "But they're little. They don't know anything."

"Well, neither does anyone else when it comes to your ability, so you're in charge. Come along, we'll look for tests." She stood and offered her hand.

He took it but dragged his feet as he followed her inside.

Men shouted and cursed overhead. A large object hit the floor, rattling the lamps. Holding Enoch's hand, Phoebe hurried down the back corridor, wondering if the men were engaged in battle.

When she came in view of the front staircase, her eyes widened, and she froze in place. Hugh and Simon struggled to move a large wardrobe down the stairs. She had the distinct impression that was the wardrobe *she'd* been using.

Before they broke their foolish necks, she whispered to Enoch. "There you go. Can you add just a little lift to the wardrobe so they might maneuver it easier?"

The wardrobe slipped and the men shouted as it tilted dangerously.

Enoch scrunched up his little face and concentrated.

SEVENTEEN

"It could have been much worse," Lady Phoebe insisted. "Enoch saved your silly necks."

Drew shoved the wardrobe into the corner of the room he'd meant to impress her with, while the damned woman coddled Hugh's smashed hand and called Drew *silly*.

Enoch's effort to help had unbalanced the furniture and sent everyone crashing into the banister. It was a miracle they hadn't broken their necks.

Instead of banishing Enoch, she had reassured the distressed child and allowed him to hang about underfoot to practice helping with the smaller furniture. She hadn't so much as acknowledged Drew's effort to provide her and her mother with creature comforts.

He damned well ought to send her home with Simon and the children. Then he could return to real work instead of playing at padding his own damned nest.

In disgust, Drew sat down on the fancy carpet to tighten the leg on a vanity. As he wrenched the screw into its socket, the kitten crawled onto his leg and proceeded to purr.

Hugh sneezed.

With exasperation, Drew glanced up at the governess. In an instant, the kitten dashed out of the room in pursuit of the invisible. Phoebe smiled covertly in his direction, then ducked her head as she patted Hugh's hand and told him he would be fine in short time.

Smote by a smile, Drew collapsed on his back and studied the underside of the table. What the *hell* was he doing? Just that brief glance from a woman who mentally talked to *cats* had his gut clenching in anticipation, had him believing she was noticing *him* but was too polite to acknowledge what they both knew they shouldn't.

He shouldn't be wanting to heave the cat at Hugh's overlarge head.

"Mr. Simon, I cannot think small swords are suitable for the nursery," she said as his cousin's shadow blotted Drew's ability to find the screws.

"A man needs a good dirk at his side," Simon argued. "I can halt a rabid dog or cut a lamb loose from the thorns with this blade."

"And should we be in any danger from lambs, that might be useful, but wearing a weapon in town is an invitation for trouble."

Drew watched Phoebe's skirt rise as she stood. From his position on the floor, he admired her pretty black and white boots, then realized the sole was coming off one, and the heels were worn to a nub. Shoving out from under the table, he took a closer look at the lady.

She spoke with the authority of the upper class to which she belonged. She possessed a haughty long nose accompanied by the firm tightness to her malleable lips of one accustomed to giving orders. Her hair might be lively, but it was always clean and smelled of rich fragrances. And then there were those crisp, rounded tones that he'd never attain in a million years. She exuded aristocratic privilege—in his humble mind.

But her gown was nearly threadbare. He hadn't really noticed since she flaunted bright colors and styles no other woman wore. But now he had to wonder if she had stockings to replace the ones she'd torn yesterday.

The fool woman bloody well needed every farthing he paid her, and she still wouldn't sign his contract! He'd never understand the female mind.

Once he was standing, she turned that formidable frown on him. "That is my trunk in the corner. Do I merit an explanation?"

"Simon, use your dirk to herd your brats back to the nursery. Take the cat with you since the twins are on the stairs hunting for it. Hugh, don't you need to check into that problem with the deed the solicitor warned us about?" Drew knew how to give orders too. The room cleared of everyone but him and the disapproving governess.

She didn't exhibit an ounce of annoyance or fear at his highhandedness. She offered no covert glance from under long lashes to let him know he interested her in *that* way. The damned direct woman merely waited, her eyebrows raised in question.

"You need a chaperone," he said curtly. Explaining his thought processes didn't come easily. Explaining his need to ravish her every moment they were alone wasn't happening at all. "This suite will provide you with room for a maid and your mother, if needed. I do not want your aunts thinking I cannot offer you the accommodations due a lady."

"Balderdash." She glanced around at the hodgepodge of furniture they'd moved around to fill the once-Spartan suite. "I was perfectly fine upstairs, near the children. Where will Mr. Simon and Mr. Morgan stay?"

It amused him that she'd reduced his older cousin to Mr. First-name, giving Drew sole claim to the family appellation. Apparently titles of one sort or another were necessary in her circles. "Simon will only be here briefly. He's been relegated upstairs so he may look after his children, as he must learn to do. Hugh has his own room down the hall. Think of him as *my* chaperone."

She frowned and nodded thoughtfully, then crossed the suite to examine the front bay window overlooking the road. A small room between the two larger rooms served as washroom, and they'd installed a cot in an alcove for a maid. Drew waited almost nervously for her approval.

"You've been busy," she finally said with a sigh, turning to face him. Her features looked drawn with worry and maybe weariness. "I thank you for your consideration, but it really is unnecessary. Unless she has changed greatly in the last years, my mother cannot tolerate company for long. That inclination has only worsened with her illness. Mr. Lithgow is looking for a place in the country for her. I will hope that at best, she'll only be here a night or two."

The name Lithgow rang bells, but Drew was more focused on the woman before him. "The earl left her no dower house, no place to call her own? That is beyond callous."

She shrugged. "She has the cottage in France. We had a flat here, but she preferred the cottage. If, as your cousin says, my uncle has no more than a watchtower, it would never have suited." Her gaze roamed the stout walls, carpets, and drapery of his home. "This is far less drafty than our old home, but. . ."

"It's not hers, understood. And if she cannot bear to live with her sisters either. . . I'll ask about, see what is available." And given the state of the lady's clothing, Drew assumed it would have to be inexpensive, not an easy task.

"I cannot expect you to deal with my problems," she protested. "She will travel slowly, so our solicitor has time to look around. I will feel. . ." She gestured at the enormous suite. "I am out of place in this luxury. I am only a governess."

"You are the daughter of an earl. Your aunts made that quite clear. I am humbled that they have allowed you to live here to deal with Simon's children, and I do not wish you to leave. I'll have Hugh add to the contract that you will receive an additional allowance for refurbishing your rooms as needed." He hoped she might spend it on herself, but he suspected she wouldn't. He didn't know any polite way of overhauling her wardrobe. He didn't understand why her aunts hadn't done so.

She rolled her eyes heavenward, then stalked through the suite in his direction, making his pulse race with anticipation as she approached.

"You are being ridiculous. There is nothing holy about being the offspring of a man with wanderlust who managed to get himself killed before he could provide for his wife and daughter. And my mother. . ." She boldly laid her palm over Drew's vest. "My mother may look like a dainty fairy, but she's *dangerous*. If you fear my aunts, you really do not want to meet the countess. Let us do something more productive and determine how we can persuade Drumsmoore to tell us about the Association."

~

PHOEBE DROPPED, EXHAUSTED, INTO HER NEW BED THAT NIGHT. SHE KNEW, IF she must share this suite with her mother, that the countess would claim this front room with the wide bay window. Her mother did not like enclosed spaces.

But for the nonce, the room was hers, and Phoebe tried to enjoy it. The featherbed was exquisitely new and soft, the sheets were like silk, and she had more space than an entire cottage could possibly hold. If only she could bring her books and. . .

No. She could not become too comfortable here. Simply going upstairs to the children invited trouble. She was on the same floor as her employer now, further from her rooftop retreat. She must learn to sit in the window and absorb the stars and listen for the night creatures from behind locked doors.

So maybe there was a little of her mother in her. She liked her freedom.

The mice noted a stranger in the alley. Wolf was alert to the stranger's scent. She showed him an image of waking Henry. Did she tell the men? She was in her nightclothes.

She listened to the low murmur of their voices as they climbed the stairs. As a lone unmarried woman, she hadn't been able to join them over dinner and drinks. She resented that they could discuss her ideas without her. The earl was *her* uncle, after all. Of course, the men apparently knew him better than she did.

She'd offered to speak with Drumsmoore but been refused. She'd offered to write a letter, and that had been rejected as well. She'd suggested they dictate the letter and have her aunts sign it. She was fairly certain Simon would prefer to take his dirk to the earl's throat before he'd let her aunts speak for him. The last she'd heard, Andrew was to ride out there and make inquiries about Mr. Glengarry, as if he were considering running for office.

She should simply go to sleep and not worry about any of it, but she was unaccustomed to letting down her guard. She felt *useless* in this pampered environment.

That was ridiculous. She'd spent the better part of her life running about, helping others, holding the tattered edges of her life together, free to come and go as she pleased. And now she had a grand home and people who looked after her—and she didn't know what to do with herself!

And she'd told Andrew *he* needed to expect more from his life. It appeared that making the leap from just surviving to pursuing a dream was harder than she'd realized.

She should apologize.

By all that was holy, she should not go near the man again.

He wanted to *court* her.

She could not begin to imagine any world in which she might fit as wife—and mother.

She sank down into her pillow and pulled the covers over her head to block out the memory of heated kisses and strong arms and an honest man trying his best to do what was right.

But it would be so lovely to have someone she could talk to when she didn't know how to go on—someone who didn't think her peculiar.

And there it was, in all its shining glory—she had never wanted marriage because she couldn't conceive of any man who might accept her as she was. She was a clatty coward.

And coward that she was, she let Wolf scare off the stranger rather than face Mr. Blair in her nightclothes.

～

"What do you mean there's a bloody great lien on the property?" Drew roared at his assistant the next morning. "Isn't that something we should have known *before* we signed the agreement?"

He'd postponed all his meetings for the day and was prepared to ride out to Drumsmoore. He didn't need any more disasters heaped upon his head.

Hugh looked even more upset than Drew felt. "Bennet didn't tell us of a lien, even though he had to have known about it because the lien holder threatened to sue. I would have checked the deed before I spent money, but the solicitor's warning sent me looking sooner. The previous owner has a *life lease* on the property. It's built right into the contract and deed."

"Then find the value of the lease and take it out of the funds of whoever was responsible for not checking before we made the agreement." Drew slammed his hat on his head and marched for the door.

"It's not that easy," Hugh called after him. "Negotiating the value could take months, while the place crumbles into a liability."

And his bank account emptied in the process. Seeing all his years of work turn to dust did not improve his mood. "One week," he shouted back. "You have one week to settle the matter or I'm out of the consortium."

Drew practically fled out the back door. He'd been driven out of his own home by a pair of tattered shoes and a tempting bosom he didn't seem able to resist. Even as he left, he could hear the governess's clear contralto teaching the children a song they enthusiastically, if less musically, belted out. Little by little, she was dragging the bairns from their gloom back into the happiness of childhood.

His horse was already saddled and waiting. So was Simon and his mount. Drew glared at his cousin. "You're supposed to stay here, guarding the children."

"No one will scale the walls of your fancy townhouse. And even if they tried, there's a wolf and a fairy to teach them better, and I've bribed the constable to keep an eye out. I want to look Drumsmoore in the eyes when he denies knowing of the Association."

"Lady Phoebe is not a fairy," Drew said in disgust, trotting his horse down the mews. "No more than that mutt is a wolf. And looking Drumsmoore in the eyes will not do more than rile your temper."

"Then I'll at least feel alive for a wee bit. I'm tired of feeling like the walking dead. Knowing what we know now, I want to look in the eyes of a bastard who would deny shelter to a grieving widow and her child." Simon's face set in solid stone.

"You've met the child and been warned of the widow," Drew reminded him, picking up the pace. He, too, wanted to meet the earl on more social terms than he had before. Phoebe's classification of her titled father as a man with wanderlust had made him seem more human and less the all-powerful lord wielding his will over others. Maybe the current earl had his own flaws. *Aristocracy* was no longer a remote concept to be feared but an obstacle to overcome. "The man might have good reason to keep the women out."

"Cowardice," Simon said in disgust. "Bigotry and cowardice. In which case, we can play to his weaknesses."

"A man so weak that he fears strong women isn't dealing in logic. Perhaps we should use superstition against him," Drew suggested, toying with an idea he'd had last night—when he'd been sleepless for thinking of the lady lying in a bed down the hall from him.

"Aye, right," Simon replied with a snort. "And we should warn him of dragons down the mine and witches in his fields?"

"It's an hour's ride out there. We have time to work up a fairy tale or two." Drew almost wished he had Phoebe here to help them. He'd wager she could add a realistically creative spin or two.

They had a suitable story worked out by the time they rode up the pitted lane to the medieval stone watchtower that gave Drumsmoore Hall the look of a castle. The long low building attached to it had originally been little more than a byre, but windows and a second floor had been added.

An ancient butler answered their knock. With misgiving, the servant took their cards and left them standing in the drafty foyer. Drew gazed up at the cobwebs on the ancient candle-lit iron chandelier overhead. "Housemaids are apparently not one of the earl's expenses," he whispered.

"Another good reason to keep out women," Simon said with a chortle. "They'd insist on a bevy of maids."

Drew would do well to remember that himself, if he chose to surrender his bachelor state—which he couldn't honorably do if his investment in the consortium fell apart. That left him balanced on a thin edge of frustration.

The butler led them back to a dismal office with a peat fire, a worn carpet over a stone floor, and a dark oil painting of a stag being murdered over the mantel. Behind a battered desk sat the earl, a man in his fifties with thinning, faded blond hair and the stooped shoulders of someone who spent his days at a desk.

"To what do I owe this dubious honor?" Drumsmoore asked, not inviting them to take a seat.

Not inclined to be treated as one of the servants, Drew dragged up an ancient carved armchair and sat. Simon did the same.

"As you're aware, my cousin here owns a large mining operation to the west and is planning on opening a manufactory that can burn coal more efficiently and profitably than shipping it elsewhere. I am planning on running for council office with the goal of expanding his business into Edinburgh." Drew crossed his tailored trousers and propped his silk hat on his lap. The earl couldn't miss the wealth his attire represented.

Simon leaned forward, with a straight face. "I, on the other hand, am trying to convince Andrew that the portents are against him unless he marries. He has the opportunity to court a woman of the same exceptional talent as my late wife, may she rest in peace."

"What the devil has this to do with me?" the earl asked irritably.

Drew didn't see a flinch of guilt, but he continued to study the man as he spoke. "The lady is your niece. If there are any unfavorable portents to fear, it would be in not asking your permission to court her first."

Instead of astonishment or anger, the earl's eyes burned with greed. "You're looking far above yourself, lad. If you want my agreement, we'll need to talk settlements. The daughter of an earl is a precious commodity worth a goodly sum."

Drew had to fight the urge to lean over the desk and throttle the oblivious old geezer, but he admirably restrained himself. "Lady Phoebe is, indeed, special. I'll have my solicitor speak with yours. I feared now that the countess is returning home, she might work a hex on you if you did not grant your permission."

He wouldn't have a ha' penny for settlements if the consortium crashed. So he'd best stay far away from the lady until matters were clear. But his true objective here was information, and his ploy appeared to work.

The earl looked alarmed enough to be fearing the countess might really bewitch him.

Humor restored, Drew sat back and crossed his boot over his knee. "That leads to the next question. I've been informed that Gareth Glengarry is the kind of man who can help me round up the votes I need. Do you know the gentleman?"

The earl's eyes narrowed. "He's a man of the land. He'd not support a vulgar upstart like yourself."

"Well, that's the matter at hand," Simon said smoothly. "Are you aware of the Association?"

The earl narrowed his eyes. "Maybe. Why?"

"I'm willing to give up the notion of a manufactory, if we can obtain the support of the Association. Andrew here is willing to buy an estate if that's what it takes. We need men like us in positions to keep a lid on rising labor costs or the profits from our mines will continue to decline. It's in our best interests to work together."

Drew watched the old skinflint's eyes gleam and understood at once why petitioning Phoebe's uncle to provide support for the countess would never bear fruit. Greed had dried the earl's soul into a lifeless husk.

"Marrying the witch won't help you," the old man snarled. "But if you can keep the countess off my doorstep, I can help."

EIGHTEEN

With the men scattered for the day, Phoebe decided to use the entire house as a testing ground for the children. Henry had said last night's stranger had run away before he could have a good look at him. Running away sounded ominous.

She didn't wish to risk anyone's safety by taking the children outside. But they could come to no harm in the attic or kitchen. They needed to be comfortable everywhere.

On the roof, Phoebe introduced them to Raven and the pigeons. Enoch experimented in helping the old bird lift a heavy stick to the nest he was building. Clare explored but said nothing, as usual. Leaning over the parapet, Cat, surprisingly, declared she saw a rainbow around a lady approaching and a black shadow around a gentleman sitting on a bench.

Not wanting to get too excited since Cat had quite an imagination, Phoebe studied the street below. "I believe the lady is Miss Higginbotham from next door. It's a cloudy day, and I don't see shadows. Can you describe what you see?"

"His light is *black*," Cat said defiantly. "Like yours is pretty red."

Oh dear, Cat saw auras. And that man down there had a black one? Phoebe tried to study the bowler-hatted gentleman but he had turned his face away. "I don't know the gentleman, do you?"

Clare crept up and clung to Phoebe's skirt before she'd lean over to look. "He's one of the bad men," she said matter-of-factly.

"Did your mama tell you that?" Phoebe asked, wary of the boogeyman theory.

Clare nodded.

"So your mama hasn't gone away?"

"She came back with daddy."

Phoebe didn't know if that was good or bad or even real. She studied the street along with the twins. The man on the bench did not look up.

It appeared Miss Higginbotham, though, was approaching Mr. Blair's door and not her aunt's. Phoebe was torn between wanting to greet her friend and finding out more about bad men.

Clare retreated to the chimney. Cat spoke for her. "Mama said people with black shadows are bad and to stay away."

Phoebe wished she could speak with the ghost, but she resisted teaching the twins to be mediums at this tender age. With a frisson of fear, she signaled the children that it was time to go downstairs. "We'll explore the attic after I see what Miss Higginbotham wants. Can you sit quietly in the nursery and finish your work until I return? Maybe we can ask for milk and biscuits to be sent up."

The children cheered and raced down the stairs. In the attic, Cat slowed down and grasped Phoebe's hand, letting her siblings run ahead. "Cousin Drew is a pretty red too," she whispered, before taking off down the stairs to the nursery.

More information she needed to retrieve from the librarian—aura colors. Perhaps she ought to make a trip to the castle library since she had yet to hear a reply to any of her other queries.

Resisting the urge to barrel outside and question a stranger, Phoebe proceeded to the parlor.

Miss Higginbotham—Dahlia—waited, practically glowing with joy. She rose to take Phoebe's hands. "It's my half day off, and I had to come to say how very happy I am and to thank you for giving me courage."

"Nonsense. It took a great deal of courage just to admit what you wanted. Do you have time for tea? I'd love to hear how you're faring."

Dahlia smiled in relief. "Could we? I don't think I've ever had a friend who understands me so well."

"And I've never had a friend so talented. Sit, and I'll let Abby know." Phoebe rang for the little maid. In a whisper, she asked Abby to send Mr. Morgan out to investigate the stranger, then sent her off to the kitchen.

Over tea, they chatted about Dahlia's lovely new chambers, her friendship with the other clerks, and her blooming success as a milliner, if not a sales person. And then her expression darkened, and she reached over to squeeze Phoebe's hand. "I don't want to say this," she murmured.

"Courage," Phoebe returned. "Life is not all roses, as I am well aware."

Dahlia nodded, and the flowers in her hat bobbed. "It is my uncle. He is quite convinced you are at fault for driving me away. He thinks you have set your cap for Mr. Blair and are jealous of me. He is. . . having you investigated."

Phoebe grinned. "If that is all, please do not worry yourself. I am exactly who I say I am, and Mr. Blair is free to court whomever he wishes. I know the situation is unlikely, but the children's father is here now, and my aunts have visited, and my mother will arrive soon. There is utterly nothing untoward in my teaching Mr. Blair's wards. They are very clever children, and I am enjoying myself immensely."

Dahlia looked partially relieved. "Then it is just my uncle being mean, I suppose. He says the children aren't normal and neither are you or your family and that you've put a hex on Mr. Blair. I've never heard him utter such rubbish, but he is meeting with men who are guiding him. . . Oh, I'm not supposed to talk about that. I've been listening where I shouldn't again, so this is all hearsay. My aunt isn't speaking to me yet."

Phoebe felt a flutter of fear. "You *are* speaking with your uncle, though? That is a good sign that he's coming around."

"No, he still thinks I should marry Mr. Blair. He does not understand at all. But he has been using my room above the shop to meet with his friends and had to explain why. I do not like that he's keeping his affairs from my aunt. I'm not sure what I should do."

Phoebe leaned over and patted her hand. "There is nothing you can or should do except keep the doors open for your family and hope they will eventually accept that you're happy. I do worry about your uncle's new friends though. If you should learn more of them, would you give me their names? People who believe the children aren't normal are a danger to them."

"Oh, I hadn't thought of that! If they really think it's necessary that I should marry Mr. Blair to advance my uncle's cause. . ."

"They might say or do anything," Phoebe finished for her. "The children have already lost their mother to a tragic accident that might not have been accidental. We must be vigilant."

Dahlia's eyes widened in shock. "Surely not! No one would harm little children, would they?"

"Some people think of children as little more than dogs or cats to be tossed aside if they're in the way. Mr. Blair is a very wealthy man. If people believe the children block their access to Mr. Blair. . ." Phoebe let her voice trail off as she considered this new aspect she'd just invented.

People could very well be trying to get at Andrew and his money and. . . his inventions?

"I will listen to my uncle and his friends and warn you if I hear anything," Dahlia said bravely, rising from her chair. "And I think I will also try to see my aunt. I know she cannot possibly be involved in anything remotely illegal."

Which might mean Dahlia knew her uncle wasn't quite so honorable, Phoebe reflected as she walked her guest to the door.

"The old clutchfist!" Simon swore as he and Drew rode down the mews later that afternoon. "He'd sell his soul for a few coins."

"Drumsmoore is not selling anything if I offer him money for nothing," Drew reminded his cousin dourly. "He doesn't own Lady Phoebe. He simply hopes I'll keep her and her mother and their *hexes* away from him. Offering a plump settlement simply dangled too much temptation for him to care what we'll do with the information he provided. He gave us names."

Glengarry had been one of them. And John Wilkes from his consortium—people whose favors Dalrymple was courting. Unease crept up Drew's spine.

"The earl is *afraid* of the women he should be protecting!" Simon said, still indignant. "I think it was your promise to keep them away from the estate that made more impression than your coins."

"Well, we did tell a few faradiddles about what they can do," Drew said. "After you mentioned war hawks and military mice, he'd have believed flying pigs."

As they rode down the mews toward the stable, a rubber ball flew past their noses, bouncing under the hooves of their horses, causing them to shy and prance. The toy bounced suspiciously high several more times.

Drew glanced up to the roof of his house—just in time to see the cascade of water. "Duck!" he shouted, yanking the reins of his mount so it stepped backward.

Simon didn't move fast enough. The waterfall hit his top hat, knocking it sideways, and drenching his hair and coat. He shouted and shook his fist, but the culprits weren't visible.

"I'm not thinking highly of your damned governess," Simon shouted, leaping down and leaving the reins to Henry, who'd run out of the stable at the excitement.

"She's unorthodox, but that was no normal water toss." Drew dismounted and handed over his reins, catching the garden gate his cousin had just shoved past.

Following in Simon's damp footsteps, Drew counted off the distance to the back door. He calculated how hard that water had to be flung to pass over the garden and reach the mews. Enoch's talents were broadening. If they could harness his levitation, that amount of pressure would create far more efficient fire hoses.

Inside, the children laughed and shrieked and ran down the stairs to greet their father, not caring that he was soaked through and hopping mad. They flung themselves into Simon's arms, all talking at once. No decent man could help but crouch down and gather them up in a hug.

Drew's gaze lifted to the woman drifting down after them. A smile teased at the corner of her lips as she observed the scene. She was wearing her split skirt, which he feared was a warning of sorts, but then, so had the water been. It was a bit daunting realizing he had come to understand Lady Phoebe. He sidled past Simon and his offspring and up the stairs. She halted and waited for him.

"What's wrong?" he demanded in a low voice.

Her skin looked dewy and fresh, and her eyes sparkled—but that could be anything from tears to fury. He waited.

"Dahlia reports that her father is warning her against me and the children, saying we're not normal. I have just learned that Cat reads auras. The twins believe that a black aura indicates a bad man. So they are not necessarily recognizing the men, just reacting to their colors. One has been spying on the house all day." She reported this crisply, as if conveying information of value but doubting he'd believe it. "Hugh was unavailable to question the bad man."

Drew had doubts about the twins' ability, certainly, but after Letitia, he would never ignore a warning. "The bucket of water?"

"I wanted to encourage Enoch to guard his sisters in unanticipated ways. He's too young to physically attack anyone, but he's clever. He thought of the water himself." Laughter lit her features now. "I didn't wish to discourage him."

Drew wanted to kiss her while she was laughing and looking merry. He needed to hold her and proclaim her as his very own enchantress. And if he were in the least superstitious, he'd believed she really had put a spell on him. But lust was a spell all men fell under, sooner or later. Except maybe dried-up husks like Drumsmoore.

Which brought him back to the task at hand. He didn't mention that her uncle was willing to sell her for coins and an exchange of information. Instead, he grew serious and contemplated the family tableau below. "We have names. The Association has apparently been revived and is intent on preventing parvenus like myself and Simon from obtaining a handhold on the reins of power. I haven't been a particular concern to them since they perceive me as little more than a mechanic. Simon is the one encroaching on their territory by buying lands and mines and expanding into industry while talking unionist notions."

"And he crossed swords with one of them?" she asked, following the direction of his thoughts. "Your cousin has a temper. Did he anger someone enough that he'd actually want to *kill* him?"

Drew nodded curtly. "Several people, including a local baron and a lord in Parliament. We have no proof. All your uncle did was provide us with names of people belonging to the Association, but Simon recognized some of his neighbors immediately. Wilkes and his cronies wanted to buy him out. Their wives visited Letitia occasionally to enlist her aid."

"She laughed at them," Phoebe said without hesitation, recognizing the tactic from the journal. At his glance, she shrugged. "We are not a family who cares about gossips and social standing, if you have not surmised. Malcolm women are raised to support our families and worthy causes and offer our aid to those in need. I believe it is ingrained into our souls from birth. Selfish old biddies clucking do not warrant recognition. It is no doubt a family failing and the reason we are often called witches. Centuries of defiance haven't changed us."

Drew fought back a broad grin. "You're teachers and librarians and you educate others in your defiance, which is damned dangerous in many eyes, including Dalrymple's, which is why my neighbor may fear you. I wager half your family has been burned at the stake, literally and figuratively."

She wrinkled her nose. "It is not a laughing matter. I don't think any of us have been brought down by a mob in centuries, but it has happened. As a consequence, my family has learned the safety of being social and powerful. In the old days, for protection, we married the most influential men available. These days, we are related to half the aristocratic families in the kingdom."

"Supportive family is important," he said. Which was why he didn't wish to be reduced to penury. Too many people—like Simon and the bairns currently, as well as his mother and a few other cousins—counted on his money. A lot of people had helped him over the years.

She nodded. "My family has been given talents we can use, if necessary. I could have applied my gift in any number of ways to earn coins, but I preferred to use it to help others. Perhaps that was foolish of me."

"That's a philosophical discussion we need to have some other time. Right now, we need to plot how to stop Simon's enemies. Has Hugh returned?"

"Not yet, hence our preparations to guard ourselves," she said. "Although I am not convinced anyone would invade in daylight."

Drew stood aside so Simon could pass by, carrying the twins under his arms, with Enoch on his heels, pelting him with questions.

It did his soul good to see his cousin returning to life after this last bleak year. And some part of that recovery had to do with this fascinating woman. Drew offered his arm. "We need to develop a battle plan."

The spark of relief and approval in her expression was ambrosia to his battered soul.

NINETEEN

PHOEBE WATCHED FROM HER BAY WINDOW AS MR. SIMON SAT DOWN ON THE bench and began sharpening his dirk next to the man with the black aura. The man took one look and scurried off. She tried to smile, but she remained uneasy.

Mr. Morgan had finally returned, and the men had had their heads together all afternoon. She didn't know the results of the discussion. She wasn't too concerned that Mr. Blair hadn't told her what had happened with her uncle. She'd accepted at an early age that the earl would never be part of her life. She'd never needed him to be.

But for the sake of the children, she hoped the discussion had led to some decision about catching the maggots who had killed their mother. She couldn't be comfortable while constantly searching shadows for danger.

The men rode in and out on various errands for the rest of the evening. As usual, she ate her dinner alone, then went upstairs to read a book to the children before turning out the lights. She kissed their cheeks, left them in Daisy's care, then retreated to her room. She was glad she'd brought a few of her own books with her because she'd not found anything except technical manuals.

She wrote notes in her journal summarizing the things the children had learned to do with their talents and adding a few notes of her own. The Malcolm librarian had finally sent a reply earlier in the day. The response hadn't been wholly satisfactory—she'd said there were too many passages in ancient journals about ghosts, auras, and levitation, and too few of value to bother copying at length. The Librarian had simply sent summaries. But she'd reminded Phoebe that she must turn in her own journals, that her notes might help to find the necessary volumes.

Occasionally monitoring the animals, Phoebe was reassured that no large creatures were stirring. She knew the men had talked to the police about patrolling outside. The rats didn't bother scurrying from the constable's familiar footsteps. They had talked about hiring a guard for the alley but hadn't found anyone suitable. At least one of the men was supposed to be here at all times during the night hours. She didn't know what was delaying their return.

She relaxed a moment, thinking she heard one of them returning through the back door. She sought Wolf for reassurance, but he was asleep. No pail crashed against a wall, so it had to be someone who knew about the latch. She ought to feel at ease. She didn't. Had the men locked up before leaving? They still didn't all have keys and had a bad habit of believing the latch was all that was necessary.

She got up from the table and held back a bit of drapery to look down at the street. She saw no furtive figures lurking in the shadows outside the gaslight, but she sent out mental feelers.

The rats under the street were in a panic, rushing in the direction of the park.

Alarmed, she sought the mice in the kitchen walls. They were scampering away from. . . a smell? Since when did mice flee smells?

And that's when she noted the smallest flicker of red and orange licking out from the coal cellar under the street—at the bottom of the kitchen stairs. *Fire?*

Sending out mental shouts to her pets, Phoebe grabbed Letitia's journal, stuffing it in her robe pocket as she raced upstairs to wake the children and Daisy. She couldn't know for certain that what she'd seen was fire, but it was enough to know the rodents were fleeing it.

"Put on your shoes and coats," she ordered. "Run down to the back door, but do not go out until I know if someone is out there. Hide as I taught you if you see anyone you don't know."

Wolf wasn't responding to her mental pleas. The horses were all gone, out with the men. She wished she could wake Henry.

The children bravely reached for shoes, not weeping but uncertain if this was another of her tests.

"Daisy, go below to wake the staff," she whispered as the older woman clucked and tugged on small coats. "I fear there is a fire in the coal cellar."

The older woman reacted with shock and concern and hustled out. The house was separated from the cellar by a stone landing, and coal burned slowly, but smoke was a danger.

And a diversion, Phoebe knew. Her fear escalated as she herded the children down the stairs. She could be driving them straight into the hands of kidnappers, but she couldn't leave them upstairs if there was any chance of a fire spreading.

"Daddy's sword," Enoch whispered as they reached the bedroom landing. He darted off down the hall.

While she waited, holding the twins' hands, Phoebe sought Piney and Kitty. The martin was sniffing suspiciously at a human presence in Andrew's office. Kitty was hiding under a sofa, wary of the scampering mice.

Someone was downstairs, and it wasn't anyone the animals knew.

Enoch ran out with no mere dirk but his father's *claymore*. He shouldn't even be able to lift the weapon. Phoebe released Cat's hand to grasp the ornate hilt. Changing her mind about taking them downstairs, she gestured back to the bedrooms. "Hide until I tell you it's clear."

The children started to look a little more worried, but Phoebe gave them a big smile of confidence. "You know what to do. You've practiced. You just need to learn new territory."

Given permission to invade the bedrooms of their elders, they raced into action.

Phoebe prayed she wasn't making a mistake. They were only one floor from exits to the outside, but she didn't know what was out there. Or downstairs.

She sought the creatures in the park and street to find out what was happening at the front, but they were in a panic and fleeing. She disturbed Raven, who swooped down to show her an image of Abby, Daisy, and Cook in their nightclothes, forming a bucket brigade and flinging pails of water on the coals. She and Raven woke the pigeons perched on the roofs so they squawked and raised a racket that ought to bring people into the street to help.

It was the stranger—or strangers—in the house, who concerned her now. In a stroke of brilliance, she sent a rat to bite Wolf's tail. The dog woke with a howl that made her smile. That should wake Henry.

She couldn't see the rear door from her position on the landing. The downstairs hall was dimly lit by a single gas light so people could find their way without bumping into walls. The office door was as far as she could see. It was directly across from the lamp and slightly ajar.

As she hesitated, a tall, hulking figure stepped out of the office, shoving papers into his coat pocket. Piney was right. Big and Burly wasn't anyone familiar to them. Phoebe shrank back into the shadows, holding the heavy sword blade over her shoulder.

Apparently confident that he was in charge—which worried Phoebe endlessly—the burly stranger waved at someone she couldn't see and headed for the stairs.

Mentally shrieking for her pets, she looked for the best grip on the heavy claymore. She didn't think she had the strength to stab anyone. The blade was far more likely to be swiped from her hands.

She decided to stand sideways so she could swing it like a stick. With luck, she might catch him by surprise and possibly knock him off balance and down the stairs.

Phoebe waited in the shadow of the landing, shivering, and trying to summon an alternative plan. She had to let the intruder come close and risk being seen. Surprise was her only hope, so her timing had to be perfect. Heart pounding so loudly she could hear nothing else, she waited until the prowler was two steps away—before shrieking at the top of her lungs and swinging as hard as she could.

Since she stood above him, the flat of the blade merely connected with his chest. Still, he staggered backward, shouting curses.

Appearing from the back hall, another man ran toward them. *Oh sugar and shame!* Outnumbered, Phoebe chose Plan B. She fled upstairs to the nursery, knowing the children were safely ensconced in the lower bedrooms. If nothing else, she could lead the cads astray long enough for the children to flee.

Wolf howled and battered the back door. The distraction didn't prevent Burly from catching up with her. He grabbed her by the arm and reached for her sword. Outraged at being manhandled so rudely, Phoebe screamed at the top of her lungs and switched the hilt to her other hand. She swung anywhere she could reach until he howled as loudly as Wolf. He tried to reach the hilt with his free hand, but she beat the heavy blade wildly over her head, risking both their necks.

When she connected with the side of his head, he cursed, hauled her off her feet, and flung her over his shoulder. Rough male hands held her backside as he lumbered up the stairs. Furious more than humiliated, Phoebe struck viciously at the back of his legs with the weapon until the second man snatched it away and flung it over the banister.

"Get the brats. I'll bet this one knows where to find the book," the man holding her ordered.

The book? The one in her pocket? Praying it stayed in place, Phoebe kicked and screamed, doing her best to unman the brute before they realized the children weren't to be found.

Lifted by an unseen hand, the brass lamp on the landing flew from its stand. It didn't rise high enough to reach Burly's head, but it had enough impact to make him go *oomph* when it smashed into his shoulder.

Enoch. Enoch was nearby.

The crass varlet didn't lose his grip but shook his head as if to wipe out the image of a flying lamp. Then he continued hauling her past the landing, toward the nursery floor. Phoebe bit back her shrieks and tried to be as calm as she'd taught the children to be. Enoch could do little while the *bad man* used her as a shield. It was up to her to escape this position.

Biting her lip to keep quiet as she bounced uncomfortably over the scoundrel's nasty shoulder, she sought Piney and Kitty. They were already sniffing the strangers' trail and in defensive mode. She needed to give them time to catch up.

Silently, Phoebe wriggled and kicked at the cad's knees while beating ineffectively at his back. She slowed him down while he tried to prevent her feet from unmanning him. The other stranger had pushed past and was in the nursery. She could hear his loud curses at finding empty beds. She hoped he'd head for the attic next. She could arrange that.

She sent her army of mice scampering up the stairs, under her attacker's feet and up his trouser leg. Big and Burly squealed like a little girl.

Piney chose that moment to scamper up the woodwork and fall on her captor's head, wrapping his tiny paws around his ears and biting at the villain's nose. With that distraction to aid her, Phoebe finally got in an effective kick, tumbling Burly to his knees in howls of anguish.

Upstairs, the other man's footsteps halted.

Wolf's howls reached ear-shattering levels.

As Burly tried to cover his privates while fighting the weasel clinging to his nose, Phoebe tore loose from his grip, tumbling to one side and scrambling away. Now that the intruder was down, Kitty leapt on the thug's back and clawed his neck. The brute tumbled over trying to fight cat and weasel and the mouse up his trousers, leaving Phoebe free to run.

She simply didn't know what to do next. How safely were the children hidden?

Before she could decide, both back and front doors crashed open and furious male voices echoed through the house. She nearly wilted in relief, before she straightened her backbone and raced down to the bedrooms where the children lurked. "Stay hidden," she called to the closed doors, praying they'd hear her. She didn't want them to watch whatever happened next.

Returning to the landing, she called, "One on the stairs and another in the nursery."

The children's father was up the stairs first, even though he must have stopped long enough to grab his claymore off the floor because he brandished it like a berserker Highland warrior prepared to lop heads.

Andrew was next, a pistol in one hand, a sgian dubh in the other. Mr. Morgan was close behind, holding a fireplace poker. Henry guarded the bottom of the stairs, hanging on to Wolf's collar. Phoebe felt her knees go weak, but she refused to crumple. Andrew halted next to her, letting Mr. Morgan run up with Mr. Simon.

"The children?" He nodded at the hall she guarded.

"Hiding in the bedrooms. I hope none of you have anything naughty in there," she whispered back.

When he slid his dagger into his boot, clasped her waist, and hauled her against him, she melted into his greater strength, clinging to his coat until her knees stopped shaking.

"If you're making jokes, then they're safe. How many scoundrels are there?"

"Only two. Is the fire out?" she asked anxiously.

"The kitchen is half flooded, and the servants from the entire neighborhood are having a fine old chat. I didn't linger. I damned near died a thousand deaths these last minutes." He held her closer, resting his chin on top of her head.

Safe against his broad chest, Phoebe closed her eyes, blocking out the horror of being hauled like garbage, trying to let this much better moment wipe away her fears.

Male laughter roared from above. "The one with the kitten on his neck has dirtied his breeches," Mr. Simon howled. "Good work, milady." His booted feet pounded overhead as he sought a better target.

"Bring me some rope," Mr. Morgan called down in disgust. "Make it one the mice won't eat."

Setting her back, Andrew quirked a questioning eyebrow. Phoebe shrugged and continued snuggling under his arm. She did, however, tell Kitty and Piney to chase the mice back to the kitchen.

Below, the stableboy dodged scampering creatures and waited uncertainly.

"Bring up the rope, please, Henry, and tell Cook to set milk and cakes on the kitchen floor," she called down to the boy. "Even rodent warriors should be rewarded."

A battle cry rang out on the floor overhead. Thuds followed, but not for long. Phoebe glanced worriedly to Andrew. "Should you see that your cousin is all right?"

Andrew snorted. "I should probably make certain he doesn't behead the fellow. It's damned difficult to get bloodstains out of carpet."

She giggled. It was probably hysteria, but she giggled. She was safe. The children were safe. The bad men would no longer bother them. She didn't care who they were or what they thought they'd accomplish. It was over, surely.

She very much wanted to ignore a ghost's request and hand the book to Andrew, but she'd yet to find any secrets in it..

As Henry ran up with ropes, Phoebe beckoned Wolf and sent him to find the children. She waited to be chastised for letting the animal run loose in the house, but Andrew only hugged her tighter. She buried her face in his shoulder so she didn't have to watch as Mr. Morgan and Mr. Simon dragged the intruders down the stairs rather than carry them. She supposed she should object to such mistreatment, but after all the terror the dastards had caused, she wasn't feeling particularly sympathetic.

"How did you all arrive at once?" she asked, to distract from the curses and groans.

"We were all patrolling the area. We were distracted by a carriage accident or we would have been here sooner. Your shrieking Raven brought us running," Andrew admitted. "You want to guess how many lives I lost after we saw the smoke and heard Wolf howling?"

"Not as many as I did," she said tartly. "I'm just glad you arrived when you did. I feared Enoch would try to throw beds at them next and hurt himself."

She pulled away from her safe haven as the children's father hauled his victim down the rest of the stairs by the feet. "Mr. Simon, you need to go in and reassure the children. They were utterly brilliant and did exactly as told. Enoch was an enormous help."

"I'll send someone to fetch the police," Andrew assured his still furious cousin. "You'd best not batter the *limmers* too badly. We need them to talk."

Mr. Simon glowered at the bound man at his feet. "Let's see if the girls can identify him. I know who he is, but I won't beat him into pulp until I know for sure." He stalked down the hall to seek his offspring.

Phoebe glanced back to see the children hesitantly peering into the hall from their respective rooms, while taking turns petting Wolf. At sight of their father, the girls scampered into his arms.

Enoch emerged with an oil lamp. At Phoebe's reassuring nod, he straightened and boldly marched out to the landing to shine a light on the two bound and trussed intruders. With Mr. Simon holding the twins,

Mr. Morgan took possession of his claymore, swinging it lightly as he hovered over their captives. Mr. Morgan's size alone would intimidate even Big and Bulky.

"The big one was in the office. I think he stole some papers and put them in his pocket," Phoebe warned. "He was confident you wouldn't be here. It's possible they arranged that accident."

Refusing to release her, Andrew nodded at his partner, who rummaged in coat pockets until he found the papers. In the light of Enoch's lamp, Hugh scanned them.

"Little bit of theft on the side," he said. "Bank letters, ways of conning funds using your correspondence, the contents of your cash box from the looks of it. You don't leave much valuable in your desk."

Mr. Simon kissed the twins' tawny heads. "What say you, my little cuckoos? Do we roll these two villains down the stairs?"

"Black colors," Cat said decisively. "They are very bad men."

Clare scrunched up her nose and clung to her father's jacket so he had to adjust her to a sitting position on his arm. The quiet twin buried her face in his lapel and whispered something only Mr. Simon could hear.

In the light of the one lamp, his expression darkened. He gently handed Clare to Phoebe and Cat to Andrew. "Cover their eyes."

Enoch and Cat, being of the bloodthirsty sort, refused to look away. Clare buried her face in Phoebe's shoulder and wept.

Their father took the claymore from Mr. Morgan, then using his boot heel, shoved both bound men tumbling down the last set of stairs to the hall below. Phoebe winced as their heads collided with treads and railing and their howls abruptly broke off at the bottom.

"If they haven't broken their necks, I'll call the watch," Simon said grimly. "Otherwise, I'll bury them in the park, then go after the shining examples of humankind who hired them. They're foremen of neighboring mines. Clare claims Letitia recognizes them, and that they were talking to the stableboy who fled, and that's good enough evidence for me."

Since she had found no such claim in the journal, Phoebe pondered why the men wanted the book. Had someone told them Letitia had evidence just to send them in here?

"They broke into my home, set fire to my kitchen, and terrorized women and children," Andrew said grimly. "Do as you will with them, but take the law with you when you go after their employers."

Mr. Simon saluted with the blade and signaled Mr. Morgan to follow.

Only after they hauled the intruders out of sight did Phoebe realize that she was standing in her employer's embrace and no one had commented.

And they'd left her alone with Andrew. Again.

TWENTY

Drew sat at the top of the stairs, guarding the nursery floor against any new intruders. Behind him, Phoebe gathered up her charges, distributed hugs, ordered warm milk and rolls, and let them chatter about their fears and excitement.

His gut churned in fury, but his blood raced for other, less rational, reasons.

He wished he could be as innocent as the children again. He'd like to forget the world with a few biscuits and nursery rhymes—and Lady Phoebe's caresses. Aye right, so he didn't wish to be as young as the children.

He settled for a shot of strong whisky from his flask and a rough slurp from a wolfhound. He didn't feel inclined to return to his work. He didn't belong in the nursery. He wasn't about to go to sleep while his fury brewed with a desire to commit murder.

The cowardly bastards had dared to lay hands on a *woman*. And not just any woman, but a good one, a lady who was kind to all.

He'd seen how the usually unflappable governess had looked when he'd reached her. She'd seemed horrendously young and frightened, with her hair tangled around her face and down her back. The gentle lady who sang lullabies to children had had murder and fear in her eyes and blood on her hands. Her already threadbare robe had nearly lost a sleeve, and there was a large rent at the hem.

If he didn't kill someone soon, he'd choke on his rage.

The quiet twin tip-toed down the hall and planted a sloppy kiss on his bristled cheek. He nearly wept at the gesture. She giggled and ran away before he could reach for her.

Wolf groaned in contentment as Drew scratched behind his ear. "Machines are easier," he told the dog.

The hound slurped at his hand.

Dog slurps weren't the same as a child's kiss. And definitely not the same as a woman's caress. He hadn't realized how much he'd come to enjoy their company until he was threatened with their loss.

But he damned well knew how good Phoebe felt in his arms. Holding her, guarding the children, had aroused more visceral urges than running trains and inventing typewriters ever had. Drew was pretty certain that machines were more important than playing warrior, but right now, he couldn't shake the primeval impulses racing through his blood.

So when Phoebe sat down beside him on the stair, only one reaction seemed reasonable, logical, and exactly what he needed. Drew pulled her close again, because she felt like the missing half of him. And he leaned down to kiss her.

Gratifyingly, she wrapped her slender arms around his neck. Her breasts pushed into his vest, and when he devoured her mouth, she responded with the same hunger.

All his primitive urges found a focus. Drew dragged his hands through her hair, scattering any remaining pins and luxuriating in the rich lengths of her soft, sweet-smelling mane. He deepened his kiss, and she moaned in response, arching into him, encouraging him to do all those things he'd dreamed of these past nights.

All the artificial divisions of class and temperament dissipated when he slid his hand over her breast and found her jutting nipple through the thin cloth. He didn't notice when Wolf trotted off. He was only aware of the lady's hand creeping over his vest, unfastening buttons to seek his chest.

He deepened his kiss, and her tongue against his blurred his mind.

He'd have to unfasten his trouser placket before he broke himself. As if sensing his need, the lady ran her long fingers down his shirt to his waistband.

Drew hastily removed his weapons and let her explore while he worked on her bodice. *Just one touch,* the imp controlling his primitive brain begged. Just one touch of bare flesh. . .

But when he held her breast in his hand and caressed the nipple, she whimpered and shivered and pressed into him in such a way that his brain snapped and his lower one took command. Without a thought to what he did, Drew swept her into his arms and carried her down to the suite he'd provided for her.

He lay her down on the bed in front of the bay window, recognizing the rightness of this placement. She belonged here, and he belonged with her. He bent and suckled at her breast, and she writhed in animal abandonment, pressing her hips upward as naturally as if they did this every day.

He pushed her nightgown upward so he could caress her bare thigh. He smothered her cries with his kisses and offered her the caresses her rocking hips demanded.

She grew silent as his fingers invaded her, and Drew froze. Was she a virgin? Was that possible for this reckless female who had no heed of propriety?

Fearing he'd gone too far, he reluctantly pulled back—until she moaned again and lifted her hips to rub against him. With relief, he found the wet nub that needed only the slightest flick. She bit the fabric over his shoulder, clung to his arms, and surrendered sumptuously to the primitive urges possessing them.

He released his prick, letting it free to brush against her wet lower lips while his mouth aroused hers, and his fingers plied her nipples into sharp points again. She writhed and pushed into him, eager for more.

Sliding into tight bliss, he hit an obstacle. In the back of his brain, warnings flashed, but the imp had full possession. Nights of ecstasy beckoned, and he suckled hungrily on a soft breast, lavishing her with appreciation before he plunged deeper into heaven.

Mindless from the most exquisite pleasure she'd ever experienced, craving the strength of this man who seemed to know exactly what she needed, Phoebe tore at Andrew's shirt until she could touch warm male flesh. Oh lordy, he was hard all over, with thick muscles that rippled when she caressed them and male nipples that responded when she tweaked them as he did hers.

His kisses were so hungry that she responded with eagerness, needing to offer him the same comfort as he'd given her. The urge to please fed her desire to feel useful. Fear had never been part of her constitution. Curiosity was. And denying herself basic human needs did not even come into consideration. She longed, she yearned, she craved to be filled in ways she could not comprehend but was willing to learn.

Until a thick hard part of him pushed between her legs and it all became momentously clear. But he distracted her from his invasion with kisses, caressed her breasts, and the longing ache in her lower body became part of the pain and she pushed upward, needing. . .

She muffled her scream in his shoulder as he ripped her asunder. The male animal above her halted his depredations to kiss her temple and her cheek, until she lifted her head, and her lips tentatively sought his for solace.

"Mo leannan," he whispered reassuringly, brushing the tears from her cheek.

Then he caressed her tenderly between her legs, as he had earlier, and the need built, and this time. . . she wasn't empty. She wasn't alone. He was part of her as their bodies bucked and fought and he finally filled her so completely that she thought they were done. Then he moved again, raising her to a new frenzy ending in a physical explosion that consumed her thoroughly, leaving her in a state of pure bliss.

After the exertions of the day, she simply fell asleep in his muscled arms, feeling safe and shielded from the rest of the world for just this one moment in time, for perhaps the only moment in her life.

A dog slurping his hand woke Drew from his slumbers.

An unhappy feminine hum from beside him jarred him half out of the bed.

"Guard, Wolf," the governess murmured beneath his arm, wriggling a little to free herself from his weight.

Drew didn't want to move. He knew if he moved, his brain would return, and everything that had seemed so right a mere few hours ago would be all wrong. But the dog trotted away, and he had to roll to one side to release her.

"We have company," she muttered, not sounding pleased. "I warned you, my mother is dangerous."

That got him moving better than a splash of cold water. Drew rolled from the bed and looked down at his disheveled clothing in dismay. Then he watched the goddess rising from the sheets, her hair tumbled, her nightgown around her waist, and he simply could not regret what he'd done. He kneeled on the mattress and kissed her, stealing a feel of her bare breast to give him courage. She fit his hand so perfectly that his confidence rose still another notch.

She caressed his bristled jaw, reminding him that he wasn't as civilized as he pretended, forcing him to back off.

"We're betrothed," he informed her. She'd been a virgin. There was no other honorable choice. "We simply anticipated the wedding night. It happens all the time. Bathe. Take your time. Let me be your fortress against the world for now." He kissed her hair and stepped away to straighten himself.

She lifted her heavy hair, giving him a tempting glimpse of alabaster breasts that would suit a goddess, before she raked the mass down over her shoulder and pulled up a sheet against the room's chill.

Drew hurriedly fastened his buttons, aware that sapphire eyes studied him as he did her. The situation was too fraught to care if she found him lacking in any way. They'd sealed their fates. It was all over but the shouting.

She remained so silent that he thought she might be communicating with her animals.

"I don't think your cousin and your partner came home last night. Wolf is disappointed. I've sent him upstairs to the children. I suspect

Abby is a little frantic, not knowing where to find you and afraid to go near Wolf."

"He's been guarding the door?" Drew considered a dog in the house more favorably if so.

"I believe so. You might save yourself if you can somehow pretend that you're just arriving home after a night of carousing, but chances are good that my mother knows better." She didn't appear worried, just attuned to the creatures in her head as he fastened his buttons and tugged his jacket into place.

"You'll never fool anyone looking like that," she said with a hint of amusement. "There is not a place on you that isn't wrinkled, and you're looking a little too. . . smug and irritated at the same time. Perhaps you should change and go pound on a machine a bit, let me greet my mother."

"How the devil do you know she's down there?" he asked—definitely irritated but acknowledging satisfaction. Last night had rubbed off edges he hadn't known he had. And the possibility that there might be more nights like it diluted the irritation considerably.

He was ready to put up a damned good fight for what he wanted.

"The creatures tell me there is a woman in the parlor, and the sun is barely up. Who else would it be? The question becomes, how did she arrive here so soon? My mother is a mystery." Pulling up her chemise and bodice to cover her bare shoulders, Phoebe slid her legs off the side of the bed.

Drew wanted to stay and see all of her. But he couldn't promise he'd stop at just watching, so he headed for the door. He cast a look over his shoulder and was rewarded with a glimpse of long, narrow feet. "Don't leave," he told her, not knowing where that thought had come from.

She glanced up in surprise. "I'll go nowhere without discussing it with you. I'm still your employee, and as far as I'm aware, the children still need me."

He wanted to shout and fling things, but he didn't have the leisure. "You are my wife in all ways but one, and I'll rectify that one as quickly as possible. Don't make me chase you to the ends of the earth."

He walked out without seeing how she took that. He'd meant it in the best possible manner, but he didn't have a way with words. He thought he might have sounded a little—intimidating. Which was fitting. He was feeling pretty damned dangerous.

He grabbed his weapons off the stairs where he'd abandoned them last night in his fit of depravity.

Then Drew washed, donned his newest suit and stiffest collar, found a polished pair of shoes, and stalked down the stairs to confront a countess. The nobility had to pull on stockings one leg at a time just the same as everyone else, he reminded himself. He was a powerful, wealthy man and her equal.

Mostly, he had to remember she was a furious mother. That was enough to cause trepidation and a desire to disappear into his workshop.

Entering the parlor, he recalled Phoebe's apt description of her mother as a dainty fairy. The countess had to rest her feet on a stool to prevent them dangling from his overlarge sofa. He'd bought the furniture to suit his own frame, perhaps a mistake, he supposed, but he didn't often have female guests.

The countess didn't sport wings, but her gauzy shawls had a similar effect. Pointed chin, wide eyes, and skin so translucent that it would put pearls to shame added to the impression. Her hair could have been spun gold for all he knew.

He bowed when she glanced up from her teacup. "Lady Persephone, I presume?" He'd looked up the proper address some time ago and recalled Phoebe using the honorific instead of the late earl's title. He didn't want to start out on the wrong foot.

The countess graciously nodded in a way that reminded him of Phoebe. "*Mister* Blair, I assume?" she returned in the same tone.

"Have you had a chance to breakfast? Cook serves promptly at eight " In an obnoxious gesture he'd learned from the stiff-rumped businessmen he dealt with on a daily basis, Drew removed his expensive pocket watch with its gold fobs and checked the time. "We're only a few minutes early."

"If that was disapproval at the hour of my arrival, please know your approval means nothing to me. Will my daughter dine with us?" She rose regally, without his aid.

Blood and thunder, Phoebe had never eaten with them. They'd barely cleaned the boxes from the table just the other day and had yet to sit down at it. Meals tended to be eaten wherever they carried their plates.

"She prefers to dine with the children, as is proper given our unusual household. I'll send the maid up to fetch her, unless you wish to go up and meet my wards," he added with only a hint of maliciousness.

"Send the maid," she commanded dourly.

The countess's hand was frail on his arm, and he remembered she'd been ill. "Have you traveled all night? Where are your trunks?" He wanted to ask if she needed to rest, but he'd left Phoebe looking tousled in an unmade bed. He couldn't produce a fresh room like magic.

He'd almost believe the woman was a witch to arrive at so inconvenient a time.

"My trunks are with my servants, awaiting a coach." She accepted his arm and did not enlighten him further.

Perhaps she'd flown from the port on fairy wings. Or a witch's broom.

He checked the dining room with a degree of trepidation as they entered. No books or machine parts littered the carpet. A stack of china he didn't know he possessed waited on the buffet, along with the usual hearty fare Cook prepared and left to congeal until he looked for it. He was on time for a change. The sausage smelled hot and tempting, and he had worked up a considerable appetite.

"We had a small fire in the coal cellar last night," he said apologetically. "We may not be up to our usual standards this morning," he added, lying through his teeth. He hadn't an inkling of how the table should be prepared.

"I am not helpless," the countess said stiffly. "I am capable of serving myself."

Which told him that a servant should have been hovering to fill her plate.

After she chose a piece of toast and a spoon of marmalade, she took a seat. "You will tell me now what happened last night. I will know if you lie."

Drew considering strangling himself with his cravat.

TWENTY-ONE

EVEN THOUGH SHE HADN'T SEEN HER IN YEARS, PHOEBE KNEW HER MOTHER well. So she didn't linger over her ablutions, much as she would have liked to do so. She was sore in places she'd never hurt before, even after a day on her bicycle. She longed for the luxury of sitting in a bath, reliving what had happened last night, exploring the implications of Andrew's rash declaration, but time wasn't on her side.

Throwing her ruined clothes in a rag bag and opening the window to freshen the air, she called Abby up to set the suite to rights. She sent Daisy to fetch breakfast for the nursery. Then taking a deep breath, she set out to rescue. . . *Andrew*. He was no longer simply her employer, but she could not quite call him her lover either. She hadn't been raised that way.

She had been raised to believe what they'd done happened on a wedding night. She wasn't at all certain that she wanted marriage, however.

Entering the dining room just as her mother played her family's favorite "I know it all" card, Phoebe shook out the folds of her best wool skirt and swished her one good petticoat as she leaned over to kiss her mother's cheek.

"Mr. Blair is a man of science, Mother. He won't believe you *know* everything. That is an old Gypsy ploy and used by too many silly mediums to work anymore. It's good to see you looking well."

She curtsied at Andrew, who looked so strikingly handsome in his double-breasted suit and immaculate collar that she wished she dared kiss him too. Or wipe the tiny bit of soap lingering near his ear after his hasty shave. "Good morning, sir. Abby is otherwise engaged. Shall I pour your tea?"

She didn't wait for a reply but set out cups and poured tea all around. It kept her hands steady and her mother occupied.

Filling up her plate, Phoebe took the seat on Andrew's right, across from her mother. "If you know all, then you know you have nowhere else to stay except with my aunts until Mr. Lithgow finds a place." She willed her mother not to mention the shame of her homelessness.

"My sisters are idiots. I cannot believe they let you throw yourself away on this—" The countess gestured abruptly, belatedly realizing her host sat right next to her.

"Children were at risk, Mother." Phoebe turned to Andrew, who seemed somewhat bemused, if not enthralled, by the conversation. Or the situation. A man who could withstand the tide of her strong-willed family was a rare gem. "Abby is preparing the suite. If you are sure you do not mind, we accept your kind offer of a bed for my mother until we find a new residence. I don't suppose you have heard from Mr. Simon yet?"

He looked relieved to be given an easy question. "Hugh will have steered Simon from pursuing and beating up the men who hired our intruders. It will be difficult to convict wealthy men on the basis of what a couple of scoundrels tell the police. We'll concoct a plan once my cousin's temper has calmed." He turned to her mother. "More toast, my lady?"

"More information, sir," she said tartly. "Is my daughter in danger?"

"Does it look as if I am?" Phoebe asked in exasperation. They'd lived in a neighborhood of scoundrels and rogues for years, but she didn't disturb Andrew with that knowledge. "Mr. Blair has provided luxurious accommodations. It is his cousin who has stirred trouble. You may rest easy."

As long as no more varlets broke in the back door. She shuddered imagining her mother arriving in the midst of last night's chaos.

"I welcome your presence, my lady," Andrew said smoothly. "It will be good for Lady Phoebe to have someone here besides the servants."

"Do not dissemble with me, sir," the countess said frostily. "I *felt* the forces disturbed last night. I have arrived too late. I accept my failure to protect my daughter from you and from my sisters' idiocy. I will not have Phoebe throwing her life away on a man. Life is too short, as I have learned. She will have her education now that I am well again."

Phoebe opened her mouth to protest, but Andrew was better prepared and spoke first.

"I have already spoken with Drumsmoore. Lady Phoebe has won her way into my heart and home. We are to be wed as soon as the arrangements can be made."

Heart and home, indeed. Bed was what he meant. Phoebe kicked him under the table. He merely removed his leg from her reach.

"I will not allow it." The countess threw down her linen and rose. "Show me to my room, Phoebe. We'll visit Mr. Lithgow after I've had a rest."

That her mother allowed herself to be housed by the gentleman she'd just dismissed spoke of immense weariness or duplicity. Or both.

Maybe she could run away to France, Phoebe thought as she led the way upstairs. Or disguise herself as a man under a new name and become a student at the university where no one would ever find her.

"This is all my fault," the countess muttered as they climbed the stairs. "I should never have left you alone."

"I am fine, Mama. I know how to take care of myself. And I *will* marry—or not—as I choose. You and no one else can decide for me."

"The choice will be made for you if a child is involved," the countess said gloomily, surveying the newly freshened suite.

A child. She hadn't had time to consider what would happen if a child came from what they'd so rashly done.

DREW DEBATED SHEDDING HIS SUIT AND POUNDING ON PHOEBE'S BICYCLE FOR a while, but he had a meeting soon. He hoped he wouldn't have to bail out Simon and Hugh.

They staggered in not much later—before Cook removed the breakfast plates. Snorting at their haggard appearance, Drew ordered Abby to bring up a pot of coffee, sat back, and waited.

"The bastards claimed they were just looking for blunt," Hugh said in disgust.

Drew knew his assistant well enough to know Hugh hadn't consumed an entire bottle of whisky last night, but pretending to keep up with Simon had taken its toll.

"I told the police they were stealing my children and molesting a lady, but they wish to come here to verify it. They wouldn't take my word." Simon slapped the table, then winced at the noise and reached for the coffee.

"I would demand the same," Drew said. "They don't know you. I don't like it, but I'm a householder. They'll have to believe me, especially if Lady Phoebe is willing to give witness. The real problem is how to stop the men who employed the villains." Drew chewed a cold piece of bacon and considered how that might be done.

"I think Dalrymple may have been involved," Hugh added grimly. "They knew how to unlatch the door to enter without disturbing the alarm—something Henry told his aunt who may have told her employer. The scoundrels are not from around here but knew where to find our coal cellar. Someone gave them information about this household. Unless one of the servants is involved, I have to suspect the neighbor seeking approval from the Association."

Drew grimaced. "Lady Phoebe said something of the sort. Apparently Dalrymple thinks she and the children are all that stand in the way of my fortune. Perhaps I should tell him my coffers are running on empty."

"I've not had time to renegotiate the deed terms, so they're not empty yet," Hugh said. "If you don't need me to maul killers today, I'll do that this morning."

"I'll take my leave of the weans and leave them in your fine care," Simon said sarcastically, holding his head up with one hand while holding his cup in the other. "I'll handle the bastards on me own."

"I'll gag and bind you first," Drew said, respecting his cousin's pain by not raising his voice. "We're in this together. Dalrymple is a weak link. We'll start there. I don't expect trouble immediately, but I've hired a constable to patrol and Wolf is guarding the halls. Sleep it off while I go about my business. And watch yourselves. The countess arrived an hour ago. She's upstairs now. I daresay she'd pierce an intruder to the quick with one look."

Both Simon and Hugh stared in shock. Hugh made a cutting gesture across his throat. Drew shrugged. The aunts might not mind if Phoebe lived with a bachelor. A mother would. He'd meant to marry anyway.

Lady Phoebe simply wasn't the kind of woman he'd ever imagined spending his life with. His nights—yes. His days—would never be the same. Maybe he could draw boundaries. Buy a bigger house. Start a business in the Shetlands.

He pushed away from the table. "No warfare until we have a battle plan, gentlemen."

That might be a good admonition for the matter of marriage as well.

AFTER LEAVING HER MOTHER IN THE SUITE, PHOEBE TUCKED THE JOURNAL into a satchel with the remnants of last night's nightclothes, then ran up to the nursery to assure the children that their world was still as it should be.

She'd heard the men arrive. Mr. Simon might be taking the children home soon. She couldn't stay here after they were gone, not and remain a free woman.

She needed time to *think*. She had never planned on meeting a man who made her heart race and her mind go blank. She'd never expected to even meet one who accepted that she talked to mice and birds.

She didn't care if Drew was a shipbuilder's son. What concerned her most was that he needed a civilized woman who stayed at home, tending the household, entertaining his guests, being his extra appendage.

She was not and never wished to be that woman.

To prove it, she called Abby up after she was done waiting on the breakfast table to find out what the men had discussed. Repeating every-thing she'd heard, Abby frowned in concern, but Phoebe just nodded reassuringly. "Don't worry. I know a few policemen. They're very nice people, for the most part, but I'd rather they didn't disturb my mother and the children. I'll take care of it."

With a plan in mind, she gave the children assignments Daisy could easily monitor. Then she slipped out the back door carrying the satchel.

She wished for her penny farthing, but she was wearing proper skirts and petticoat and couldn't ride it, even if had been repaired. She didn't own a crinoline—another of those reasons she'd never suit a respectable household. Walking around inside a cage just to prove she was idle—was the most ridiculous folly anyone had ever invented.

Carrying her satchel, she hurried down the street to the police watch-box. The helmeted constable, unaccustomed to being accosted by ladies, blinked at her in surprise.

"I've been told I need to testify against the intruders at Mr. Blair's house last night. I don't wish to disturb my ill mother and the children. Would it be possible to go to the station?"

She knew the police station in Canongate. She'd rescued a few neigh-bors upon occasion. She feared this more formal, respectable side of the city might not approve of her visit.

The policeman frowned, confirming her fears, but she meant to prove to herself and everyone else that she was her own woman. "I know the captain at Canongate. I will go to him, if necessary."

The man's eyes widened. Canongate was notorious, for good reason. Abject poverty did not bring out the best in people.

He escorted her the few blocks to an official-looking building, where he talked to a clerk. Then he waited nervously with her until another man in uniform led her into an office.

All the stiffly formal officers and clerks terrified her more than the raging drunks up the hill. She was out of her element among civil soci-ety, evidently, which was simply foolish. Perhaps she failed at obeying society's dictates, but she knew how to be a lady.

Phoebe straightened her spine in the chair she'd been offered and smiled at the officious gentleman who entered. "I have been told I must give testimony against the two scoundrels who broke into Mr. Blair's home last evening," she said in her best rounded tones, learned at her mother's knee. Sliding the journal into her pocket, she removed the rag bag and set it on the desk. "This is what they did when they attacked and mauled me as I attempted to protect Mr. Blair's wards."

She pulled out what had once been fine, if threadbare, nightclothes and showed the rips. "The scoundrels terrified the children into nightmares as well. I cannot have the little ones interrogated and frightened more. I hope this is evidence enough."

The officer took her name and her account of the intrusion. When he finished his report, he studied her with curiosity. "The villains looked as if they'd been run through a mill when they were brought in. They raved of rats and monsters and swords. We had to bring in a physician to bandage them. They're big brutes. Your account does not explain the damage done."

Phoebe offered her best complacent smile—this was not the first time she'd had to explain the inexplicable. "I am a woman, sir. That does not mean I am helpless. They are ashamed to admit that a woman and a dirk could hold them at bay until help arrived. They may have fallen down a few stairs in the process. Should I send the servants to give witness of their terror when they were smoked out of their rooms by the fire the scoundrels set? Mr. Blair will be fortunate if they do not all give notice. I am here to speak for them, if I may."

He rubbed his eyebrow and studied what he'd written. "Thank you. . . Lady Phoebe. I used to work up the hill. I've heard of you. I just never believed. . ."

"Believe, please." Phoebe rose. "Frightened men create boogeymen to explain their fears. I assure you, no monsters other than a dog and cat occupy our home. Those wicked men are the only beasts here."

She checked the pin in her pretty indigo hat and sailed out, only to almost bump into Mr. Dalrymple coming up the stairs of the police station. He started to step aside until he recognized her. Then he blocked her path.

"We are aware of your wicked ways," he said with a scowl. "You will not trick us or Mr. Blair much longer. Your time is coming, harlot."

"And a pleasant good day to you too, sir." Disturbed by his obvious agitation, Phoebe stepped to one side so she might squeeze past him.

"We could have all burned in our beds!" he cried. "The rats could have eaten us alive! Nothing of this sort has ever happened until you and those damned children came along."

She raised her eyebrows in disapproval. "Really, sir, your language is rude. Give my regards to your lovely wife and niece, please." She kicked at his ankle, forcing him off balance so she could push past and down to the street.

Shaken, she considered her next goal. She had meant to prove that she was still her old self, but Dalrymple reminded her that her independence came with risks. She must make the prize worth the risk.

Her mother was correct that she should not abandon her hopes of an education. Now that the countess was well, and they might have the upkeep of only one home, perhaps she could again entertain the idea of the university. It was in the old town, near her aunts, where she needed to go next anyway. The journal had become too dangerous to leave with the children.

She started up the hill, away from the vet school. Dick's would not have changed its mind already about women. She had little desire to masquerade as a man to attend if cattle disease and husbandry were all they offered. No school would tell her how to mend a pigeon wing. She would like to know more about diseases of dogs and cats. Would the university allow her to take biology classes?

Feeling more like herself, Phoebe aimed for the university. She was not just a governess—and she would *not* be just a wife, even if there were certain aspects of marriage she was inclined to enjoy.

While she was in the old town, she should check to see how her former neighbors were faring.

TWENTY-TWO

Drew returned from the meeting with the development consortium with the hope of working on his pterotype—and speaking with Phoebe. He couldn't think of her as *Lady* Phoebe after last night. She was *Phoebe*, goddess of the night, in his mind. Maybe mythology said goddess of the moon, but he was hoping she might be a little more constant than a silvery orb that disappeared regularly.

A note from Hugh awaited, asking him to meet at the Margaret's Wynd properties. Being part of rebuilding an historically important part of the city had its fascination, but he had new priorities.

He glanced longingly up the stairs where he could hear the faint laughter of children. Simon was here to guard them. He could pray the countess still slept. He probably shouldn't disturb Phoebe while she was with her students. If he wanted her to respect his work, he had to respect hers.

With a resigned sigh, he scratched Wolf behind his ears, clapped his hat back on his head, told Abby where he was going, and set out to the stable for his horse. He nodded at the constable patrolling past. He hoped the need for extra eyes was over, but they were taking no chances.

Dalrymple's carriage stopped in the mews. "A word with you, Blair, if I might."

Not if his neighbor had anything at all to do with last night, Drew vowed. He ostentatiously drew out his house keys and locked the back door. "I'm in a hurry, sir. Perhaps later."

And he crossed the garden and mews without a friendly handshake. He disliked turning his back on a man he'd considered his friend, but if Dalrymple had insulted his future wife, the man was no longer even a sensible acquaintance.

The ride across town gave Drew time to indulge in fantasies of Phoebe gracing his bed, presiding over his dinner table, perhaps even forcing Cook to prepare meals when he was ready to eat them. He needed to provide her with a more suitable wardrobe. . . and a wedding ring. He should talk to the local minister. Or was Phoebe Anglican?

He had to admit he knew little or nothing about Phoebe's background, just the information Hugh had dug out about her family and origins, and what little he'd learned in their encounters. He had to adjust his thinking from a meek, obedient wife keeping his house and children to a fearless one who defied convention, but after last night. . . Fearlessness had some redeeming qualities.

After crossing the bridge, he steered his horse down the busy Royal Mile in the direction of the narrow lane leading back to Margaret's Wynd. Once he turned off the wider street, towering tenements and clothes hung overhead, blocking what little sun the day provided. The cobbled alley didn't normally teem with people, but it seemed unusually busy for this time of day. Drew edged his nervous horse through the rushing throng until he feared trampling the children racing down the lane. What the devil?

Dismounting, he wondered how he was supposed to find Hugh in this mob. Was it a street fair? A carnival? He couldn't think of any holiday to be celebrated, and this didn't exactly seem to be a joyous lot.

He led his horse down the street in the direction the crowd seemed to be heading, forcing a path with his mount's hooves and his greater size. He frowned at people leaning against windows in the towering old stone buildings that formed this man-made canyon. He had visions of that badly-fitted old glass caving under the pressure of everyone pushing to see out. The boys on the roofs eight stories over his head shouted and waved their hats, and Drew had to look at his feet not to feel dizzy just imagining standing at that height.

He frowned when he realized the worst crush formed in front of the consortium's properties. What now? Had another front collapsed?

He picked out Hugh's familiar bellows near the partially collapsed building. Men shoving in that direction didn't want to give way, but Drew squeezed through using his elbows and his prancing, nervous horse. He wished himself elsewhere as he followed gazes upward, and the source of the disturbance became apparent. His gut churned from more than vertigo.

A child and her mother perched on the disintegrating edge of a floor six or more stories over his head. How the devil had they got up there? The structure was in such bad shape that Drew couldn't actually count the layers of floor and debris to be certain of the height. On the street, Hugh was attempting to build a platform of stones from the wall's remains. Men beside him held a ladder that was far too short to reach without a raised area to set it on, and even then, it would take a far stretch just to grab the woman's ankles. Precarious, at best.

"Jump, jump!" a few ghouls shouted. The inhuman cry had him gritting his teeth to prevent throwing punches.

The other half of the mob wept or avidly watched as if this were a circus.

Something had to be done. "Back stairs?" Drew demanded as he reached Hugh.

"Tried that. The whole floor tilts. We'd endanger our lives, and she'd jump before we reached her," Hugh replied curtly. "We need taller ladders so we can go up and talk her down."

Hugh could read contracts and calculate numbers, but he was no engineer. Drew studied the situation and shook his head. "Ladders are likely to disturb the timber too. We need a net to catch her." They had about as much likelihood of finding a net as a ladder.

Would the woman really kill her child too?

Fighting off his fear by applying his brain to the problem, Drew searched the upper stories, looking for anything likely—feather mattresses? Mounds of pillows? But from what little he could see, it appeared as if the flats had been stripped. He grounded his gaze on the lower levels again. Maybe there was. . .

A heavy mound of burgundy velvet plunged from above, landing on the men helping Hugh. The crowd gasped and heads swiveled upward. Shouts and finger pointing ensued. Despising his weakness, Drew forced himself to look up again—and wished he hadn't.

A woman who looked far too much like Phoebe in her bright blue gown stood in the shadows of the third story, using some sort of stick to push at. . . Drew leaned against his horse to study what in hell she was doing.

Another mound of burgundy parted from one of the ancient timbers that had once held a wall or window in place. Staying far back from the edge, she whacked and poked at the heavy cloth with her stick until gravity gradually drew the weight over the edge, tumbling it to join the other.

Even while he froze in utter horror imagining every conceivable tragedy that could come of this reckless endeavor, Drew's inventive mind grasped what she was doing.

"A net!" he cried. "Pick up the edges, spread it out between you. You, grab that corner." He handed his reins to a stout, bearded fellow in a faded top hat and pushed to the front to show Hugh's helpers what needed to be done.

The velvet drapery had once been thick and sturdy but was worn in places now. As another layer tumbled on their heads, Drew had the men crisscross the fabric to strengthen it.

The child wailing above provided all the incentive anyone needed to rush the task. More hands joined them, strengthening and tightening the unconventional net. He could wish for sturdy canvas, but the shore and any sailing boats were too far away. The crowd alternately cheered and jeered their efforts.

Swallowing hard, Drew dared another glance upward. The woman in blue had vanished. He had a horrible feeling he knew why.

It couldn't be Phoebe, he told himself. Even if the ridiculous bit of fluff on her head and the bright blue skirt looked familiar, his governess was safely ensconced in the nursery with his laughing wards. Yes, her aunts lived several blocks away, near the university, but Lady Phoebe. . .

Had probably been the charity worker he'd seen last time he was here. *Damnation.*

What were *velvet* draperies doing here? He might not know much about fabric, but he was pretty certain that velvet of this quality cost a king's ransom in some prior century. It did not normally hang on the windows of the poor. His own family adorned their few small windows with tattered remnants of lace woven by some distant ancestor.

The childish wail grew more frightened. The murmur of the crowd took on a more frantic note. Even the apes shouting *jump* ceased their cries and more men rushed to hold up the edges of the makeshift net. Hugh muttered imprecations under his breath as he directed the placement of hands and material.

Holding his hat on, Drew forced his head back.

The child was attempting to squirm out of her mother's hold. The woman on the edge continued to blankly stare down at the street. Thin to the point of emaciation, with lank blond hair hanging about her dirt-smudged face, the mother did not appear well. The round-faced little girl, on the other hand, appeared clean and well-cared-for, from what little he could see.

But it was the figure emerging from the shadows behind the pair that held the enrapt attention of the crowd.

And that's when Drew finally translated the heavily accented rumbles of the mostly uneducated mob. . . . *The lady will save them. The witch can fly. She's come back for us, you'll see. Don't be a tumphy, it's the ghost of the old lady. They're all witches. . . .Fly, lady, fly!*

And deep down in his heart, Drew knew there could only be one woman who would climb six stories in a collapsing building to save a crying child, one woman people would call witch because she bloody well had haggis for brains.

"Where are the stairs?" Drew demanded, looking for someone to hold his corner of the impromptu net.

"No time," Hugh said, interpreting the demand. "The front stairs are destroyed. The rubble can't be climbed without risking life and limb. You'd have to go down the alley and around to the courtyard. There's an outside tower. That had to be how they got up there."

Before Drew could debate how quickly he could scramble over the first-floor debris, the crowd roared, and a weight hit the velvet, sending up clouds of dust. His heart nearly stopped.

He didn't breathe again until a feminine voice cried from above, "I have Evie. She's fine. See to Mrs. Tarkington."

Drew's pulse didn't return to normal until he scanned the floor above and saw the woman had vanished. So had the little girl. How the devil. . . ?

He returned his attention to lowering—Mrs. Tarkington?—from the draperies so women in rags and tatters could reach the would-be suicide. They helped her to her feet, clucking and chattering, ignoring the men who had saved her.

Actually, one turned and spat at his once-shiny boots.

In shock, Drew simply controlled his breathing and waited for the woman in blue to return with the child.

"She'll have to come around the alley there." Hugh nodded down the street. "You might take the horse down."

After that amazing performance, he'd stupidly been expecting her to fly, he supposed. Drew recalled his brains, took the reins back from the portly fellow, and made his way out of the crowd. No one followed. Maybe like him, they were all expecting the lady to magically materialize —or fly in on a broomstick—carrying a child.

The woman he wanted for wife had made a spectacle of herself. No wonder the damned women were called witches. No normal female. . . No lady. . . No governess. . . would risk life and limb and. . .

He tried to calm his fury and shock but that was an impossibility. *She could have been killed. . .*

He'd kill her himself. He'd tie her in knots and lock her in an attic.

He didn't even know it was Phoebe. *Yes, he did.* He knew it with a deep-down certainty that had no explanation or rationale. Unless she had a doppelganger, that was his thrice-damned governess and future wife endangering life and limb and entertaining a mob. . .

He was definitely going to murder her with his own hands.

But his rage took a back seat when he saw her bedraggled figure striding down the filthy dark alley bearing the burden of a child who didn't seem so small anymore. The woman who had removed the draperies from a crumbling wall had appeared as an omnipotent goddess earlier, but Drew knew her as a tender female who broke as easily as any other.

Leaving the horse at the entrance, he jumped over fallen stones and trash of the alley until he was close enough to haul the heavy, weeping child over one shoulder, then encompassed Phoebe's fragile waist with his other arm. She leaned into him, crying inconsolably.

All he could do was hold her as she shook with sobs.

He had no experience with weeping women and suicides and children who mumbled incomprehensibly into his neck. He knew machines. Machines could crush, but he'd never endured anything to the immensity of the discomfort he suffered now. Helplessness was not a state he could tolerate for long.

He had only instinct to guide him as he led her toward the horse. He lifted Phoebe into the saddle, and amazingly, she swiped at her eyes and quit weeping to hold out her hands for the child. Drew handed over the golden-haired, nattering baggage, saw them settled, then thanked the heavens for his well-trained horse since he had to back it out of the rubble-filled alley before he could turn it around.

"Where to?" he asked.

"My aunts. They'll know what to do. Mrs. Tarkington is too ill to look after Evie. That's the reason she was up there. She knows she's dying, and she had nowhere to go and no one to leave Evie with." She sounded as if her strength were returning.

Drew had ten thousand questions, but they could wait. He understood desperation.

He'd strangle Phoebe *after* they delivered the child.

"SHE MAY BE SIMPLE, BUT SHE'S THE HAPPIEST, MOST HELPFUL CHILD YOU'LL ever know," Phoebe told her aunts, rocking Evie in her lap. "She's old enough to learn to help in the kitchen. She's too pretty to stay with a mother who can no longer protect her."

Phoebe knew she didn't have to explain what she meant. The only occupation for single women in these streets was prostitution. And the kind of men who sought out an ill woman for their perversions wouldn't hesitate to use a child instead, even one who was obviously simple.

She felt Andrew stiffen with shock, but it was far too late to worry about what he thought. Had she wanted to be the pleasant little wife he needed, she'd have stayed home today. She was perfectly aware of the tragedies on every corner in this part of town. She could have gone straight home after she left the journal with her aunts earlier, or after she left the university, but no, she'd had to check on her neighbors.

The question became. . . what was *he* doing here?

Evie gabbled happily, crumbled the cake she'd been given, and licked it off her fingers, the past hour of terror forgotten. Phoebe wished she could forget so easily.

Cousin Olivia had been in the parlor when they'd arrived. She leaned over now to take Evie into her lap. "I'll take her if no one else will. I. . . knew a child with odd features like Evie's. Looks are deceptive. He was slow, but he learned to talk and eat properly, and he was the most loving child you'll ever know. I'll put a trundle bed in my room."

Olivia marched out, letting Evie rub her sticky fingers in her hair.

Phoebe didn't know Olivia's story—they were distant cousins and didn't know each other well. But it was apparent her aunts understood. They looked sad but didn't go after her. Her family was known for meddling, but on the whole, they did not tell tales.

Relieved that she'd found Evie a home, Phoebe breathed easier. She was still shaken by her brush with death, and the thundercloud looming over her rattled her more than she liked. She wanted Andrew to *understand*. She feared he didn't and never would.

"Well, that's settled then," Aunt Gertrude said. "Now, have you told your mother that she no longer has a home? Should we prepare a room for her?"

Phoebe hastily stood up and shook out her filthy skirt. She didn't want to have this conversation in front of Andrew. Besides, he had some explaining to do.

"Never doubt that my mother knows everything," Phoebe replied. "She's fine with us for the moment. Mr. Lithgow will show her about. I really need to go back and change. I fear I've breathed enough pigeon droppings to give me lung fever. I don't need to be carrying it around on me."

Her aunts protested. Andrew didn't. Still scowling, he offered his arm and escorted her to the street.

"Why were you here today?" she asked before she lost the courage.

"I ask myself that often." Without her permission, he threw her into the saddle, where she had to cling to the horse's mane and pray she wouldn't slide straight off again. She'd been too numb while holding Evie to remember how she'd stayed in the saddle earlier.

The horse's mind was pleasantly blank, at least.

"Which means what exactly?" she demanded, uncertain why it mattered.

"I have an idea for a machine that will aid in carrying loads to high places."

She couldn't find a way to argue around that if he meant to put his machine to good use. Rebuilding those houses had to happen.

As they traveled back to the main road, the professor lifted his hat to them. She'd sought him out at the university earlier. He hadn't discouraged her aspirations. Now that her mother was well, she might dip into their funds. She could move back here somehow, become a student. . .

On the corner where Mrs. Mac sold pencils she didn't know how to use, the old lady lifted her clouded eyes and gray curls to wave as they passed. The morning's excitement well over, everyone had found their way back to their usual humdrum lives.

Only Phoebe still vibrated with agitation. And Andrew—Mr. Blair, she probably should call him. He had to understand now why what he wanted was impossible. She couldn't not be who she was. And people would never forget.

"You've been living with your aunts since your mother left, haven't you?" he asked, innocuously enough.

Except she knew the question was loaded with explosives. She could lie, but she wouldn't. "I've been living in the family flat," she said—flatly. "Our family has owned it for centuries. I had an ancestor who was once lady-in-waiting for Queen Mary."

He digested that as if she'd offered him frog's legs—edible but foreign to his taste. She pointed out a few buildings from that long ago time—once proud mansions that had deteriorated as old Scotland lost its independence and the palace and fort fell into disrepair.

"You knew how to unhook those draperies," he said, almost accusingly, as they reached the bridge.

"I used to watch the maids remove them to beat out the dust," she countered. "And I had to climb up them occasionally to rescue my kittens."

"*That* dump was your mother's home?" he asked, barely able to contain his horror.

She almost felt sorry for him. She felt sorrier for herself. She might never find another man who almost accepted most of her idiosyncrasies —because he foolishly wanted to believe she was a sheltered, aristocratic lady.

"It's my home," she declared boldly, casting aside any hope of happiness. "We owned the entire flat. It was quite grand, actually, until the walls fell. Evie and her mother lived in a room several floors above. Everyone else rented."

"You lived in a tenement that housed the destitute," he said as if the words were mud in his mouth. "One that was so derelict that the whole damned wall fell off!"

"Fortunately for you, yes," she said pertly. "Otherwise, I'd never have met the children and agreed to live in your place."

"You're daughter of an earl!" he roared, causing staid passersby to stop and stare. "You could have died in there! The whole clatty building could have fallen on your reckless head!"

"Well, it didn't," was all she could say to that, because of course, he was perfectly correct—as always when one points out the obvious.

In defiance, she offered her heart on a dish. "Would it make you any happier if I move back in with my aunts and remove my spectacle-creating self from your presence, or would you prefer that I change my name and pretend I'm not daughter and granddaughter of nobility so you can excuse my behavior?"

TWENTY-THREE

Spectacle-creating self? She thought he wanted to *change* her? Of course he wanted to change her—bashing his head against walls was a favorite sport. He should stop and pound his skull against that iron lamppost just to warm up.

Drew didn't know how to contain his rage and confusion. The last harrowing hour had imperiled every notion he'd ever conceived of delicate females, the nobility, and propriety.

He'd spent these last years learning how to behave in polite society so he might get ahead in the world and provide for his family.

And Lady Damned Phoebe was throwing all his notions of respectable behavior arse over ears. He'd be reduced to sputtering in Gaelic shortly.

He needed to put his world back to rights, return order out of chaos, or his brain would implode.

As they crossed the bridge from the old town to the new one, Drew studied a prim young lady strolling by, gleaming curls adorned by a piece of fluff like Phoebe's. Except this elegant creature wore skirts that billowed and swung in the breeze above neat ankles encased in lacy pantalets above her shiny shoes. She wore neat kid gloves and a frilled shawl and cast him a sideways glance that once would have caused him to tip his hat. *That* was how a lady should look and behave.

Interested only in comparing the stranger to the woman he was determined to marry, Drew grunted in dismissal of the flirtation. Lady Phoebe was freezing him out, not responding further, rightfully so, he supposed. He might explode if she made one word of excuse for nearly killing herself.

He led his horse past the fashionable establishments on Prince's Street, with Lady Phoebe's tattered, filthy skirt blowing in his face.

She'd ruined more of her wardrobe. No wonder the damned fool woman always went about in tatters. "How filthy were those stairs you climbed?"

"As filthy as you expect, I wager," she said, still sounding like an irritated princess, but apparently unsurprised by the direction of his thoughts. "They've been well used this week. It appears everything that could be cut up and hauled down has been. The neighbors will have expensive firewood this winter. Most of our furniture was cherry and mahogany."

He could swear he almost heard the sorrow behind her brittle words. He'd never had fine furniture or been attached to material things, but he had an old pocketknife his father had given him that he'd hate to lose. Magnify that by a few thousand. . .

"Or maybe Mr. Bennett sold access to the stairs. He should have locked them." There was the bitterness he'd expected.

He could have ordered the stairs locked and the building protected, had it occurred to him that anyone cared one iota about the stinking, crumbling pile of rocks. It hadn't. *He* was responsible for leaving that rat trap open for a woman to throw herself off.

And Lady Phoebe owned a flat in that building—one she didn't know he owned. *That* was a conundrum he'd ponder when his head wasn't on fire.

He reined in his horse outside a shop he'd passed a thousand times on his walks to meetings. Tying the reins to a hitching post, he lifted Lady Phoebe from the saddle.

Taken aback, she didn't protest, just grabbed his shoulders to steady herself. Drew enjoyed that gesture a little too much.

By all rights he should be hauling her home and yelling sense into her. Except he'd seen her weep and shake even as she was accomplishing the most impossible, illogical feats. He was still furious, but he'd found a more practical outlet for his temper. He shoved open the dressmaker's door. A little bell tinkled over his head. Phoebe tried to yank from his grasp and retreat, but he wasn't having any of it.

Holding the lady's arm firmly, Drew glared at the women behind the counter. "Do you have anything made up the lady can wear today? She's had a bit of an accident."

"I cannot go shopping like this," Phoebe practically hissed, trying to swing back to the door.

He refused to release her. "Something simple, like she's wearing, so she can hide in plain sight and fly off roofs without showing her underpinnings."

Phoebe smacked him, but Drew had suffered worse spider bites. He glared down at her. "Unless you say what you want, I'll choose your clothes myself."

"The gray, in the window," Phoebe said in irritation, unable to cope with one more shock on top of another. "Now, may we go?"

She was not only heartbroken and shaken to the core, but she was filthy and felt like one of the beggars Andrew so obviously despised. Her hair was all about her shoulders. Her shoes were worn thin and so was her underwear. These clerks were accustomed to dealing with wealthy women garbed in fine silks and jewels who probably bathed in milk and perfume before arriving here. She had never been so humiliated in all her life.

"Not the gray," Mr. Blasted Arrogant commanded. "Bright blue, like she has on, or a nice green. Better yet, yellow."

"Yellow is impossible," she cried, knowing the ridiculousness of this argument but unable to help herself. "I'd have it filthy before noon. I do not intend to sit in a parlor with my feet on a cushion all day!"

One of the younger clerks timidly stepped out from behind the counter to the shelf of fabrics. "We have a lovely brown and gold merino that would hide dust. You could have a yellow bodice and cover it with a brown jacket if the need arises. It's all the fashion to dress a gown up or down and use two colors."

She pulled out a bolt of striped material of sumptuous merino that all but glittered in the sunlight through the window. Phoebe longed to stroke the fabric to see if it was as soft as it looked.

"She'll take that. What do you have ready in blue?" Bloody Arrogant demanded.

"Perhaps milady would be more comfortable if she freshened herself in our wash room?" the young clerk said with just a hint of defiance.

Phoebe started to like the girl. Glaring over her shoulder at her tormentor, she punched his arm until he gave in and released her. Head high, she followed the girl back to a private room with a wash basin where she could at least rub the grime off and restore some of her hair to pins.

While she was at it, she took off her filthy shoes and stockings and threw them in the trash. She was fairly certain people had been using the tenement's outside tower as a privy. Lord Knows-it-all would have a real paroxysm if he knew that.

Outside the washroom, a bevy of young girls awaited her with pins and fabric and stacks of ready-made garments. They'd included chemises and pantalets and all those things she did not normally concern herself over because no one else ever saw them.

What she needed was *shoes*. Striding barefoot back to the front room, Phoebe pointed at her feet. "If you truly wish to be useful, my boots need replacing. Do you have a magic shoemaker in mind?"

Unfazed by her request, Andrew spoke to an older lady wearing a permanent frown of disapproval. "She needs sturdy brown walking boots. Send one of your girls to fetch a shoemaker."

Phoebe almost giggled as the old crone gaped at his audacious command. Let someone else suffer his male arrogance.

Another eager young clerk curtsied. "I'll bring Mr. Ledbetter, sir. Might I suggest a pretty pair of kid slippers for around the house as well?"

"Excellent. Tell Mr. Ledbetter to bring samples." He glanced down at Phoebe's bare feet as if deciding what else he could demand.

She pulled up her skirt and daringly pointed her toe at him, almost laughing at the sudden blank expression of lust softening the furious tension in his jaw muscles. She wasn't averse to vicarious thrills, and that look went a long way toward preventing her from killing him. "Stockings. While you're behaving like Napoleon conquering Austria, order stockings, sturdy ones."

"Silk ones," he countered, not tearing his gaze from her toes.

The hatchet-faced older woman finally stepped in. "A trousseau?" she suggested in disdainful tones.

Phoebe supposed it was the disapproving hauteur of women like this that had kept her out of fancy shops. She disliked being judged for the clothes she chose. Used clothing could be purchased without snotty clerks and tossed aside without a qualm once damaged. And generally plain gowns didn't require hampering corsets and crinolines.

But she loved pretty fabrics as much as anyone. And really, the old woman was no more than a shopkeeper. Did it really matter if a clerk was accustomed to wealthy clients and disapproved of impoverished nobility? *Filthy* impoverished nobility. It stung to be humiliated, so possibly it mattered a little, but now that she was here, she'd make the best of it.

"A trousseau, yes," Andrew said with such satisfaction that he begged to have a bolt of wool flung at his head. "Silks and lace."

"No," Phoebe corrected. "I want two pair of plain, sturdy stockings, a new chemise in good calico, flannel knickerbockers and matching petticoat for the winter, to go under the striped gown." She dropped her skirt to hide her feet and headed back to the dressing area and the waiting seamstresses.

"A complete trousseau in silk and laces and frilly nightwear," Andrew countermanded. "And a blue gown immediately, with whatever frippery it requires."

Phoebe swung and glared. "No crinolines or gowns requiring them, *ever*. And if you demand anything else, I shall order a new split skirt and *wool* stockings. I can buy my own clothing, thank you, so you need to toddle on to your *meetings*."

"It's not what you *can* do that concerns me," he replied with equal emphasis. "It's what you *won't* do. So I'm not going anywhere until I see boxes of fripperies sitting on that counter." He crossed his arms, leaned against the wall, and crossed one booted foot over the other as if he meant to become part of the furniture.

Phoebe lifted a hand mirror to fling at him, but the young clerk hurriedly presented a stack of chemises and distracted her. "If you'll step behind the curtain, we can take your measurement, and you can try these on while we pin up the blue gown."

Torn between wanting to beat the obstinate man about his thick head, and the allure of pretty fabrics and new attire, Phoebe thought she might rip right down the middle. Instead of following the clerk, she studied the ridiculous stack of delicate underthings with longing and demanded, "Why are you doing this to me? Is this some perverted revenge?"

"Aye right," the annoying man agreed dryly. "The woman takes years off my life and dumps her biddy of a mother on my doorstep, and it's revenge I need. Torture her, ladies. Cover her up from head to foot in frills and furbelows so she remembers she's female. And then figure out how to make that split contraption so she isn't showing her knickers to all the kingdom while flitting around on that dratted penny farthing."

A reply to that just wasn't possible. Phoebe allowed the clerks to push her back into the dressing room while her frazzled nerves and muddled mind tried to make sense of this day.

She had savings. She could certainly buy her own clothing. She just didn't, because there were better ways of spending her limited funds. Besides, she only destroyed anything she wore.

But her feminine soul cried out for a bit of pretty ribbon or lace every so often. She loved her silly new hat. New boots would be practical, she told herself. They'd last for years. It was just. . . She studied the fancy underpinnings she'd never worn and simply couldn't see the point.

She reached for the blue flannel on the bottom of the stacks the clerks were piling around her. At this concession, a young seamstress shook out a frilly confection and held it up to Phoebe's front while others divested her of her best gown. She'd worn her newest gown this morning to impress her mother and Andrew, and because she was to see their solicitor this afternoon, and. . . after rescuing Evie, it looked like every other rag in her wardrobe, only worse.

And she was just a little bit tired of doing everything herself. She'd almost cried in relief when Andrew had materialized out of the crowd and started ordering men to hold up the draperies she'd flung down. The men might never have worked out what she'd intended if he hadn't been there to organize them. He'd saved Mrs. Tarkington's life and probably Evie's. And she'd been grateful to have his broad shoulder to cry on when the horror had caught up with her.

Against his will and in a state of fury, the man still offered the aid she'd never known.

Which made this wardrobe feel like charity. Or payment for what she'd given freely, which terrified her. He couldn't still mean to marry her, not after today.

That fear took a little of the pleasure out of the pretty clothes the seamstresses kept producing from the depths of their storeroom. She let them take her measurements and tighten seams and hem a gown to wear now. She agreed to the brown striped merino because she simply couldn't resist. It seemed horribly wasteful, but she agreed to a pair each of calico and flannel undergarments. She refused a new corset, even though the design looked to be marvelously more comfortable than her own and had adorable embroidery. Determinedly, she donned the sturdy new stockings with the new blue wool gown and insisted that the bill be sent to Mr. Lithgow.

She'd forgotten the shoes until it was time for her to leave, and she realized she had nothing to protect her new stockings.

"The shoemaker is waiting, my lady," a young clerk said. "Your gentleman is right. The blue looks beautiful with your eyes. Not many dark-haired ladies have such light eyes. It's quite striking."

Malcolm blue eyes, Phoebe knew, inherited like the other odd traits her family often passed on. Her looks had never meant anything to her—until the moment she stepped out of the dressing room, into the shop, and Andrew's eyes lit as if she'd just invented a flying machine.

She suddenly felt shy. Her stylish new dress emphasized curves she'd never displayed in her ill-fitting second-hand gowns. She was much too aware of the way her bosom pushed against the ruffles of her bodice and her nipples brushed the soft cotton of her new chemise. She'd never paid much attention to her clothes before. They were merely there for decency and warmth.

Andrew's hungry gaze made her feel as if the garments were intended to be stripped off and cast aside. Which was when she began to understand his perverse commands for lingerie she'd never wear.

The shoemaker distracted her by offering a pair of butter-soft tan boots with good sturdy heels and soles. A lad waited patiently by the door with a box of different sizes and shapes. The tan ones fitted perfectly, and Phoebe refused to take them off to try any others on.

"Send the bill to Mr. Lithgow," she said crisply, walking back and forth on the carpet, enjoying the way the leather cradled her foot—and the soles that didn't flap.

"Send the rest around to the address I gave you, and she can try them on at leisure," Andrew ordered. "Come along, my lady, before your mother sends out search parties."

He could tempt her all he liked, but she didn't have to buy anything more. In all likelihood, she'd be moving in with her mother to a new residence soon. She reached for her gloves, realized they were in her old gown, and didn't have time to call for them before Andrew handed her a lovely pair to match her new blue dress.

He handed out gold coins as if they were water. The staff bobbed and curtsied, and Phoebe had to bite her tongue, knowing how much those rare coins meant to ill-paid clerks.

Plastering on a smile, she thanked everyone, made certain they had her solicitor's address, and with one last glance in a mirror to see how Dahlia's hat complimented the new dress, she stalked out.

"You may go on about your business, sir," she informed Andrew once outside. "It's only a short distance to the house from here. I can walk it."

"The horse must go back in its stable. If you won't ride, I'll walk with you. The clerk is correct. That dress sets off your beautiful blue eyes. What is the chance we can talk privately without your mother breathing fire down our backs?" He unfastened the reins of his horse from the post.

His flattery shouldn't go to her head, but unaccustomed to anyone noticing her eyes, it did. Phoebe was intensely aware of his broad form even as he stayed to the street with his horse. He'd managed to keep his silk hat through all the morning's travails, and his elegantly tailored suit scarcely looked rumpled. She didn't know how he did it, which made her grumpier.

"Almost none," she replied curtly, although the steam had finally seeped from her temper. Consequences had a way of doing that. "Mr. Lithgow is probably with her now. You are far better off finding a meeting to attend than accompanying me back to the house."

"If you'll take the front stairs when we arrive, I'll take the horse back to the stable, and we'll at least avoid the questions about where we've been. But we *will* talk," he said firmly, pointing her toward the pretty walkway by the park.

"That's *all* we'll do," she reminded him, marching away before she could give in to weakness and ask if they could just run away to the Americas.

TWENTY-FOUR

Hugh, unsurprisingly, had reached the house first. He had papers in hand before Drew even took off his hat. Simon paced the hall and practically dragged Drew into the workshop before he'd divested himself of his coat. Apparently his cousin had recovered from his drunken stupor and was in full battle mode.

Drew was more interested in listening for feminine voices in the front room, but Hugh waved the documents in his face, as always, to command his attention.

"The consortium wants *us* to negotiate with the lienholders. That's why I called you out there before all the rumpus began. Then I come back here and the lawyer we're supposed to consult on the negotiations is sitting *right there in the front room!*"

"Talking to a countess," Simon said in disgust, before heaving his battleax into the fray. "I'll be taking the children and finding a safer place for them. Just because we caught the culprits doesn't mean the ones who give orders won't try again."

Having spent a day fighting fear, himself, and Phoebe, Drew grabbed the metal rim of Phoebe's bicycle in his bare hands. He twisted spokes sufficiently to settle his frustration without beating his cousin over the head. "You'll not be going anywhere without a governess to mind the weans."

And he damned well wasn't sending Phoebe away unless he went with her.

He swung on Hugh, avoiding the stack of papers. "The lawyer is out there because he is solicitor for Lady Phoebe and the countess, who just happen to be the *lienholders* with whom we must negotiate."

His brain might be a muddle, but he'd finally assembled that nugget of certainty. She'd *owned* a flat in that wreck of a building. He let the news smack his partner in the face.

Hugh gaped, then slumped into a chair, digesting the magnitude of the problem with his usual mathematical precision. "We can't cover the cost of a lien."

"And we can't ask Phoebe and her mother to take less than the flat is worth. They need the funds to find another place to live," Drew said, whacking a spoke back into place.

His governess, an earl's daughter, was *homeless*.

"Which means paying more than we have," Hugh said miserably. "Or taking in another investor."

Simon threw up his hands. "Don't look at me! I've sunk everything into that mine they're trying to shut down. I have more than I can manage already."

"How the devil did we end up in this witch's brew?" Hugh asked, crumpling his papers in disgust.

Simon laughed without humor. "You called on Letitia's family, remember? The School of Malcolms? They should have called it the School of Magic."

Magic or not, Phoebe's aunts probably knew about the sale of any property relating to their family and had deliberately stirred the cauldron. He could almost respect their perspicacity. Drew whacked another spoke into place as Abby timidly knocked on the door frame.

"Cook asks if you be wanting a luncheon sent up," she said into the frustrated silence following Simon's remark.

They stared at the maid in astonishment.

Cook *never* asked. It was well past the hour when she sent up the meats and breads that went stale and attracted mice before they got around to looking for food. Drew's stomach was eating him from the inside out, but he'd expected to forage.

This change in routine had to be the work of the magic women in the parlor—ones accustomed to ordering servants about and expecting to be obeyed.

Drew flung down his hammer. "Serve it in my office, if you would, please."

Knowing Cook's predilections better than Simon, Hugh raised his eyebrows in query.

"*Phoebe.*" Drew stalked for his office, trying not to appear too desperate. "I'll have to marry her just to get fed."

Following him, Simon laughed hollowly. "Better you than me. Once the bairns start coming, she'll forget you exist, just wait and see."

That was bloody rubbish. Letitia had doted on him. But if it made Simon feel better. . .

But the notion of children spun Drew's head around, and he didn't try to answer.

"If you marry Phoebe, you could make her partner. . ." Hugh hurried after him, plotting.

"If I marry, I'll have to throw the lot of you out on your maggoty heads," Drew countered, unable to focus without a hammer in his hand. "I'll have to find a real workshop and an office, and I won't have funds for investing in foolishness. So let's plan with what we have and not wish upon stars."

Simon hooted in derision. "You'll not have a life to call your own. Give it up, man, and go beg the girl for her hand and her flat, and I'll handle the Association on me own."

"It's all over but the shouting," Hugh said gloomily, helping himself to a sandwich before Abby could set her tray on the desk. "I'll go live in the slum and supervise the project."

"Where's the whisky? We need to mourn the man's bachelor state and congratulate him on his upcoming nuptials." Simon rummaged among the bookshelves, hunting for Drew's hidden liquor cache.

Recalling Phoebe's joyous acceptance of his lovemaking, her trembling body as she cried into his shoulder, her naked toes defying his notion of propriety, Drew savagely devoured his sandwich and blocked out the mockery.

He'd built his wealth on sheer stubbornness and a refusal to stay knocked down. He simply had to decide on a goal and go after it. He'd like more time for that decision.

He didn't have time. Hugh had worked hard on obtaining those properties. He needed an answer now. Simon was in danger of losing himself inside a bottle if he couldn't see his children safe and his wife avenged *now*.

And Phoebe. . . Phoebe could be carrying his child. She might take wing and fly at any moment, before he'd had time to work through all the ramifications of marrying well beyond his station or his imagination.

Marriage and children should prevent her from attempting any more reckless stunts like today, right?

"I'll make the women see reason," he decided, saying it aloud so he would believe it.

His friends' hoots as he set down his sandwich and headed out the door warned he was only fooling himself, that his cock was doing the thinking for him.

PHOEBE ALMOST CHOKED ON HER WATERCRESS SANDWICH WHEN ANDREW stalked through the parlor doorway, looking like a condemned man.

He'd shed his tailored coat and was in shirtsleeves, his form-fitting waistcoat and trousers indecently exhibiting his broad shoulders, muscled chest, and narrow hips. She gaped, unable to disguise a surge of lust and the need to examine the placket. . . Swallowing, she focused on his cravat, rumpled from the morning's adventures. But then her gaze followed the strong column of his throat to the square jut of his jaw and his grim expression. . .

She was sitting here in all her new finery, looking like a proper lady for a change, and he appeared to have done a morning's work in a stable. She sipped tea to stop gaping.

"Mr. Blair," Lady Persephone said sharply. "Your coat, please?"

Ignoring the countess, he turned to Mr. Lithgow. "Sir, I believe we have a lien to discuss. Once that is resolved, the ladies can make their decisions."

Phoebe's stomach dropped to her feet, and she set her teacup aside. Why would he know about the lien?

The friendly solicitor stood to shake his host's hand. "I represent the ladies, you understand, sir. You'll need your own man to handle this properly."

Phoebe narrowed her eyes. "Mr. Lithgow, you have told Mr. Blair about our private conversations?"

The solicitor beamed, his eyes bright behind his wire-rimmed spectacles. "Of course not, my dear lady, of course not. I have done my very best to keep your current situation and your business completely separate. I have not revealed your names. Apparently Mr. Blair has learned it from another source."

How could he possibly know. . ."Tell me again why were you in Margaret's Wynd today?" she demanded, her gut knotting before he gave his answer.

"Because Hugh and I *own* those buildings." His expression was stern and unapologetic. "If you'll excuse us, ladies, I will attempt to rectify the situation. The children are being unusually quiet, are they not? Should I send Simon to check on them?"

He was the one throwing people from their homes? Not the landlord?

Only because he'd asked about the children and offered to send Mr. Simon instead of her kept Phoebe from killing him. "They are coloring with the new paints I ordered. By all means, send your cousin to admire their handiwork. But Mr. Lithgow remains *our* solicitor, and we will hear any discussion of the lien we have placed on the property *you* wish to destroy."

Her mother simply sipped her tea with a frown of disapproval. Or maybe she plotted. It was hard to say. Phoebe had been much younger and more naïve when she'd last seen her mother.

"It is not diplomatic to discuss settlements in front of ladies," Andrew insisted. "You have appointed Mr. Lithgow to discuss your interests. Let him discuss them."

"Settlements?" Lady Persephone said in a dangerous tone. "We merely wish to be paid what we're owed so we may seek another residence."

Once her mother became involved— Phoebe thought it might be safer to go play with the children and wait to see who was left standing. She'd almost rather be back on the sixth floor, clinging to a pillar, and reaching for Evie than waiting for her mother and Andrew to rip each other up. *Settlements.* She was fairly certain Andrew meant marriage settlements—involving her home, apparently. Or lack of one.

Which meant she had to stay and join the fray. Really, it was more than enough for one day.

"Lady Persephone, I am willing to provide you with a residence, within reason," Andrew said, confirming part of Phoebe's suspicion about settlements. He shoved his hands into his pockets and leaned forward in emphasis. "But this also involves my contract with my investors, my partnership with Mr. Morgan, and my offer for Lady Phoebe, none of which concerns you, countess, until the discussion is done."

"Provide *us* with a residence?" Phoebe corrected warily.

"If I know the type of residence your mother requires, I will be better able to calculate whether we can continue with our plans to rebuild. If we cannot come to terms, then we'll have to let the property go, and you may negotiate with someone else."

He sounded cold and unflinching, and Phoebe didn't know whether to flee or fight. How had she not known who owned the building?

And what could she have done differently if she had known?

Not gone to bed with the man to start with.

"*You* let that building fall apart?" she asked in incredulity. "*You* are putting hundreds of people out of their homes?"

Before he could respond, her mother stood. "My daughter wishes to attend the university. *We* will prefer a similar flat in that location. I daresay the choices are limited, but they should be sufficient parameters for negotiation. Come along, Phoebe, let us leave the gentlemen to their talk of money."

"No, I don't think so," Phoebe said, surprising even herself. "I don't wish to be tied to another empty flat when you return to France. I loved our home because it was a home. But that's gone now, and I don't want another. And I certainly don't want one from *him*."

"I won't be returning to France," the countess said stiffly. "I have sold the cottage to my nurse and her new husband. She wished to remain there. That sale will give us funds for new furnishings. Come along, leave the men to their boring talk."

READING PHOEBE'S FURIOUS LOOK, DREW REFUSED TO CRINGE, DESPITE THE quagmire of guilt he wallowed in. He changed the subject before anyone could come to blows. "Lady Phoebe, we have a more crucial problem that you and your mother might be able to assist with."

When Phoebe glared but didn't rise, the countess disapprovingly returned to her seat.

"For safety's sake, we must remove the children from this house until we have the real villains behind bars." Speaking of Simon's problems in front of the countess and her solicitor seemed worth the risk. Drew preferred enlisting their aid than having them oppose him.

Phoebe looked as if she'd take off his head, but they'd not had that talk he wanted. She'd simply have to work things out for herself. He was pretty certain she would. He hadn't been alone in that bed, after all.

"I thought the children were safe now that the criminals are caught," she said cautiously, not looking at her mother.

Drew shook his head. "We only caught the hired help. The real criminals are still at large. It will take them time to regroup, but last night made it apparent that they are seeking a book they think the children possess."

"That's simply ridiculous," Phoebe protested. "They are four years old and talking of ghosts, for pity's sake! No court of law will listen."

"The court of public opinion might do otherwise," he said. "Letitia was liked and respected and her abilities were well known. The mine owners in the Association are universally despised. Simon's neighbors will *want* to believe the children. The miners are ready to walk out anyway. It only takes a small match to start a large fire. If Simon had a mind to do it, he could stir entire villages to riot and march against his enemies. There is a reason someone tried to kill him, and it had nothing to do with the children."

"What on earth is this about?" the countess asked querulously. "Who is Letitia? What do small children have to do with miners? *And what have you dragged my daughter into?*"

Even the merry solicitor was starting to frown behind his spectacles.

Drew had never meant to be a politician, but he practiced his best diplomacy now. "I will let Lady Phoebe explain later, my lady. Right now, my concern is that the children be removed from this house. I am hoping Lady Phoebe will go with them. They need her."

"Where?" Phoebe demanded. "Where will you take them that is safe? Because I am assuming you do not intend to go with them. They need people who will guard them as well as you and their father do."

"Guard them from *whom*?" the fairy countess demanded in a voice that thundered more than should be possible.

"The Association, my lady," Drew replied, choosing his words carefully. "I do not expect you to be familiar with an organization once thought defunct, but they are wealthy and powerful. My cousin and I can halt their depredations if we are not spending our time attempting to safeguard the children."

The countess's fine eyebrows lifted. The muscles under her soft cheeks firmed, and her lips formed a thin line. "The Association should be *dead*. The abomination should never be raised again."

Before Drew could react to the stunning news that a countess knew about the dirty dealings of her peers, she turned to Mr. Lithgow. "Is the duke at home these days or in London?"

"I believe he resides in Sommersville currently, my lady. As always, Castle Yates is the residence of various relations. That's a most excellent notion. Shall I telegraph your arrival?"

Drew felt as if he were in a runaway carriage and someone else had taken the reins. "Duke?" he asked warily.

Phoebe looked surprised but not quite as shocked. "A distant cousin," she explained. "We are related to all manner of people. I don't believe I have visited Yorkshire though."

The countess waved a frail hand. "You did, but you were very young. Previous dukes helped build one of the first railroads through that part of Yorkshire. It would be a simple task to take the train and stay at the castle. Even the Association would not dare anger a duke."

Drew was fairly certain his head was coming unscrewed. "The Association was once comprised of nobility," he argued.

Both the countess and Phoebe gave him scornful looks. Drew comprehended immediately and waved a hand in surrender. "Of course. The duke is one of *your* family and would not approve of profit above people." A duke with the weird abilities of the women? His world became a little stranger. "I take it he would also understand the children's abilities?"

Wearing her new gown with the frilly lace and looking like the lady he had expected her to be, Phoebe nodded curtly, still not happy with him. Had Drew not spent the morning dying a thousand deaths watching the fool woman flit about a condemned building, he'd have groveled at her feet for daring to enter her noble presence. He was the one with haggis for brains.

The woman he wanted to marry had a *duke* in her family, one who believed in witches and superstition and women who made magic happen. Phoebe inhabited a rarified world he'd never meant to enter. And she was rightfully furious with him.

When she stood, he feared she'd tell him he'd never see her again, and he almost agreed she was right to do so. The pain that caused almost erased what she was saying.

"I will go up and talk to the children. They will be excited to visit a castle where they might ride ponies. Castle Yates also has a dovecote for messenger pigeons. It's quite fabled among the family. The children will be much assured by sending and receiving private messages from their father. You should have said something sooner."

When? his scrambled brain demanded. Before or after she'd entered crumbling buildings and shaken his world to the core?

"I will not, however, be going with them." She was gone on her errand of duty before he could find his tongue and roar.

TWENTY-FIVE

"You will explain to me how Mr. Blair is involved with the Association," the countess commanded, pointing out items to her maid that she wanted in her trunk.

"I know little. Apparently someone has revived an old name for a new purpose." Phoebe finished off a quick missive to her aunts and entrusted it to Abby to send off with a messenger. "I believe Lady Gertrude still occasionally corresponds by pigeon with Castle Yates. Anything too private for telegraph can travel that way."

Her mother waved a dismissive hand. "I refuse to act as nanny for small children all the way to Yorkshire."

"Your sisters have an entire household of teachers who will happily join you. I'm sure they'll choose someone far better than I am at managing children. Do you think you will know any of the family at the castle?"

"I will know all of them," her mother responded peevishly. "That is not to the point. Where will *you* be?"

"Do you really think I would leave the men to fight bullies on their own? Mr. Blair and his friends are honest businessmen. They don't hire criminals to do their dirty work. They don't think like we do. They will want direct confrontation, and that can only be messy." Phoebe tried to speak calmly as she jotted more frantic instructions to go with the children.

She didn't know what she was doing. She simply knew—no matter how furious she was with him—that she couldn't leave Drew to fight this battle alone. Fighting a common enemy was far preferable to fighting each other, which was next on her agenda, if he thought he could direct where she lived. And once she fought that battle, the one over the tenement still loomed.

"The men seem perfectly competent to lop heads," the countess replied in scorn. "It's time you met more of your family. I was seriously remiss in keeping you to myself for so long."

"We didn't have money for travel," Phoebe countered, rejecting her mother's self-criticism. "Mr. Blair is wealthy enough to send everyone without thinking twice about it."

"I could have asked—"

Phoebe folded the instructions. "I loved our home. I had you and my aunts and the professor and countless others to teach me what I wanted to know. I was given a freedom I never would have experienced if cooped up in a castle with prim governesses and dancing instructors and other such foolishness. Do you really believe I would have been happy making a come-out and going to balls and simpering like a schoolgirl?"

"Not any more than I would have," the countess confessed with a sigh. "But I'm still not convinced that wasn't a mistake. I loved your father, but had I met a wealthier man—"

"You might not have been as happy. And I would not exist. The world is changing. Women have a right to make their own choices. Mr. Blair is building a machine right now that will allow women to work at home, printing up documents for offices. Can you imagine? And the university is allowing us to take classes and study medicine. No, I am exactly where I want to be." It sounded like a battle cry in her head, but when she said it, it was with satisfaction.

Andrew might not realize the full extent of who she was and what she could do, but so far, he'd only quailed at her lack of proper attire and carelessness. He seemed self-assured and intelligent enough to overcome his disbelief and see her point of view. She hoped. At least he wasn't thundering and storming and hauling her to the train station—yet.

And surely what they'd shared in bed meant more than a moment's pleasure. That night had held such promise. . . And reminded her that the world was beautiful.

She ran upstairs to calm the children, who were bouncing with excitement at the idea of ponies and castles, just as she'd predicted. Even silent Clare announced their mother was happy and hoped she could ride the train too.

Phoebe wished she had the power to speak with ghosts, but she had to make do with curtsying in the direction Clare indicated and assuring the phantom that the children would be receiving the best possible care with family who understood them. She hoped the breath of air lifting the curls at her nape meant approval, but it sent a chill down her spine.

She settled the children in their chairs to eat their dinner. It was too late in the day for travel. Even with the extra patrols outside, the entire household would have to be on guard for another night. Surely the Association hadn't had time to regroup yet.

After reading them stories, she left Daisy to bathe the children and tuck them into bed. The nursemaid was pragmatic about the journey— she'd arrived on a train, after all. But the thought of a castle had her flustered. Phoebe promised everyone was very nice, and Daisy would make new friends, and she'd be back home in no time. She prayed she wasn't lying.

By the time Phoebe returned to the suite she shared with her mother, the dressmaker had sent over the first of her boxes. They spilled over with practical flannels and ridiculous silks. The brown gown wasn't ready yet, but they'd sent a blue silk she'd rejected as too costly. Beautiful, but she was not accepting any more gifts from the damned man. Phoebe packed it back into its box, but her mother caught her in the act.

"I'm so glad you're being sensible, dear! That gown is very attractive. Wear it to dinner tonight, and the men will do anything you ask." The countess shook out the silk and examined it with a critical eye. "It's far behind the fashion, but I doubt men will care."

Trapped. Phoebe couldn't tell her mother that their host had paid for the blasted silk.

Grumpily, she opened the message that arrived from her aunts. It improved her humor. "Perfect," she said, scanning Aunt Gertrude's scrawling penmanship. "Olivia has agreed to accompany you and look after the children. She is much more experienced than I am. Correct me if I am wrong, but I believe she sees auras like Cat."

"That's what I recall," the countess said, poking through the rest of the boxes. "These are lovely kid shoes. They should go well with the gown. Hurry. I told Cook to serve promptly at seven and to inform the men to be ready."

The image of dining with her mother and three barely civilized men entertained Phoebe enough to try on the shoes she hadn't ordered. They were completely impractical and wouldn't last six months under her use, but they were soft and the lightest things she'd ever worn. She'd have to repay Andrew when she declared her independence—after the battle was won.

"I don't think they're accustomed to dressing for dinner," she warned her mother. "They are not accustomed to sitting at a table at all. Cook despairs of improving them."

"Compromise. With a little warning, they should learn to disengage from their activities to join us. I'll not expect more than that. One can't leave men to themselves for too long or they return to caves and gnawing on bones." The countess rummaged in her jewelry box. "Here, wear this. It is time you wore jewelry, and this will look better on you than me."

With the lure of possibly preventing open hostilities, Phoebe managed the lace fripperies. She winced at the notion of adding her battered corset—until her mother's maid produced the pretty embroidered one from the stacks of boxes. With a sigh, she allowed herself to be tugged into it. She was too skinny in all the wrong places to ever have an hour-glass figure, but the corset mimicked feminine curves better than the old one.

Which was a good thing, she realized, when the blue silk was pulled over her head. The bodice was the most immodest piece of work she'd ever worn. She stared at her cleavage in dismay.

"You chose your seamstress well," the countess cooed, admiring the lace spilling from the silk neckline. "That's the perfect chemise for that gown. I don't know why you insist on going about as a flower seller when you could accomplish so much more as a lady. When you present

Mr. Lithgow's list of available properties, your Mr. Blair won't be able to take his eyes off you to read it."

Phoebe had no intention of using her non-existent feminine wiles to persuade anyone to anything. And she'd already made her position clear about living with her mother. So she remained silent and allowed the maid to fasten the sapphire necklace around her throat. The stones were small and threaded on a thin gold chain, the sort of thing a debutante might wear. She calculated how much rent it might buy and concluded it wasn't enough.

But she hoped the gown would make her look mature enough to make her own decisions.

Drew tugged the tight cravat, glanced worriedly in his shaving mirror, and gave up. The countess had seen him without a coat. Phoebe had seen him in less. He didn't need to dress up for the battle at hand.

Simon came in tugging at his tie and Drew straightened it. "Do you good to practice refinement for a change. Do *not* hit the whisky."

Simon grimaced. "I'd rather be taking my sgian dubh to a few throats than choking to death to suit the ladies."

"You will not be taking knives to anyone's throats, and the ladies are taking care of your children for you, so behave. They have connections to a *duke*. We don't have to fight the Association with tooth and nail if we can threaten with money and power. We just need time to formulate a plan."

Hugh arrived with a page full of numbers and names. "Your best choice would simply be to buy the mines the Association owns. I've written up an estimate of costs and potential investors."

"I like that plan, as long as it doesn't require *my* dwindling funds. It's almost seven. Let us proceed, gentlemen. We can practice our manners before pursuing investors." Drew shoved his cousin and his assistant toward the door.

He didn't give a damn about numbers and names. He wanted to see Phoebe and hear her reaction to the boxes he knew had been delivered. He hoped the seamstress had managed to prepare at least one evening gown. Maybe the gift would make her more amenable to his plan.

So, he was deranged. A man was entitled to go off his head at least once in a lifetime.

He could hear the low murmur of feminine voices as he descended the stairs. It was a very genteel sound in his crude bachelor household. He'd chosen a respectable neighborhood and a staid residence in order to establish himself as a gentleman, but he'd never really lived as one.

The workshop in the withdrawing room was proof of that. The ladies had nowhere to repair before or after dinner except the formal visiting parlor.

He found them in the parlor. He barely managed a bow without strangling while trying not to stare too openly at the lady he'd so stupidly thought to call governess.

Lady Phoebe in an evening gown. . . Drew wildly imagined the heavens opening, the sun beaming down, birds singing. . .

He was barely coherent as she directed him to take her *mother's* arm, while she took Simon's. Hugh trailed behind as they paraded into the dining room to the law of some etiquette of which he was hardly aware.

Cook had found linen to cover the table. China and crystal that he vaguely recognized glittered in the candlelight. Candles! He glanced up at the gaslit chandelier. It was still there but hadn't been turned on. First salvo to the lady. He was speechless.

"So, this is what civilization looks like," Simon said heartily, pulling out a chair for Phoebe on Drew's right, then taking the one on her other side. "Ladies, you look charming this evening, more beautiful than the stars in the sky."

"Which you can't see through the fog," Phoebe replied. "And this isn't precisely civilization. We are wearing poor Abby to the bone. I asked Cook to hire some help for the evening. I hope that was not too brazen of me, but I feared you might not be aware of the difficulty of preparing a proper table."

Since Drew intended for her to preside over this table for the rest of his life, he had no objection. His turn to fire the next shot. "Feel free to hire whatever help is required, but we'll not need much over the next days while you and the countess are in York."

Lady Phoebe smiled and changed the subject to the children. It gave him an opportunity to adjust to seeing Phoebe in this new-found aspect of proper lady. The shiny bauble around her throat drew attention to firm high curves he'd held in his bare hands. *That* thought caused trouser constriction. He sought less volatile distraction.

While Simon and Phoebe discussed ghosts—blessedly keeping his cousin from drowning in fine wine—Drew watched the new. . . footman? She had hired a footman to serve the table? Or was he a butler? The lad looked too young and brawny to be a staid butler. Did butlers serve soup?

The countess slid a folded piece of paper over to him. Was trading notes instead of conversation a habit of the nobility?

He waited for Lady Persephone to speak.

"Suitable residences," she said curtly, without further explanation.

Ah, the price for his stupidity. Or his lust. "I'll have Hugh assess them," Drew replied without opening the note. If that was her contribution to the battle, it failed. His turn.

He engineered his way into the conversation during a lull. "We wish to smuggle the children out unseen in the morning. To that end, Lady Persephone, we'd like to appropriate your trunks."

"I am to wear only my travel clothes while staying at the duke's home?" the countess asked acerbically.

"No, of course not. We have crates that can be carried to the station separately in a wagon. You may pack as much as you wish into them. But it seemed better to have the children traveling in the carriage with you and Lady Phoebe, even if they are hidden."

"That will not work," Phoebe announced without hesitation. "If you fear we are being watched, I'll need to be seen standing on the front step, waving my mother off."

Hugh frowned and nodded agreement. "I'll have another crate delivered. You can ride in that. Once you are on the train, it will be simple enough—"

"No," she said firmly. "I have already explained to the children that I must stay here, and that my cousin will go with them to teach them to ride ponies. I do not ride."

Protests erupted. Drew sat silent, prepared for that declaration of war.

If that was the way she wanted it. . . He clinked his wine glass against his china until everyone shut up.

"If Lady Phoebe is to stay here without chaperonage of mother or children, then I'll purchase a license and we will marry immediately. We'll have the celebration after the children are safe and your mother returns." Gauntlet thrown, he met Phoebe's startled gaze with equanimity.

TWENTY-SIX

Phoebe's fine and fancy dinner disintegrated into argument after that. In denial, her mother tried to draw attention to her list of properties, but no one had any interest in discussing real estate with a juicier bone like marriage to chew on.

Simon wanted to toast the impending nuptials. Andrew ordered the new footman to remove the wine decanter. Hugh wanted to leave the table to look up laws regarding marriage and joint investments. Andrew ordered him to sit down and shut up, although it sounded more like *Haud yer wheesht*.

Phoebe strained to maintain mature, ladylike decorum, but she may as well have been sitting with the children and telling them not to scrape their chairs.

When all else failed, the countess insisted that she wouldn't allow Phoebe to ruin herself, and she'd send her back to stay with her aunts until sensible heads prevailed. "Ruin" in her mother's mind meant "marriage," but the comment confused everyone else.

When all her attempts at polite conversation failed, Phoebe chose to believe it wasn't *her* failure. She had done her part. She wasn't meant to be a leader of men. She could live with that. Her alternative was to send mice running up their trouser legs. She would resist—for now.

Finishing the delicate sole and Brussels sprouts Cook had prepared, Phoebe drained her wine and stood. "I will check on the children and help mother's maid with the packing. Good evening."

The men scrambled to reach their feet, but she was out the door before they'd moved their chairs back.

She climbed straight to the nursery, where order might prevail. To her satisfaction, she found Enoch and Cat sound asleep, as they should be. Quiet Clare, however, was curled on a pillow on the floor, wrapped in blankets and cuddling the kitten.

"Can we take Kitty?" she whispered as Phoebe lifted her from the floor and settled her on her lap in the rocking chair.

Perhaps she could not control a dinner conversation because her mind worked on childish levels. Needing kitty comfort was serious business that she could handle.

"If you think Kitty wouldn't mind the train." She rocked child and cat, soothing herself as well as them. "He doesn't know what a train is, so I can't ask him. Why aren't you sleeping? Morning isn't far away."

"Mama worries about Daddy. She's afraid of the train." Clare burrowed into Phoebe's arms. It was difficult to know how much of this might be ghost or Clare's own fears.

"Will you talk to your mama for me?" At Clare's nod, Phoebe gathered her thoughts. "Tell her that you will be safe and happy. I am sending someone older, stronger, and wiser than me to go with you. Can she hear all that?"

Clare nodded. "She hears you. She asks if you'll help daddy."

"That is exactly what I hope to do. If your mother stays here, can she help me in your place?" Phoebe wasn't certain what she asked. But she'd heard her cousins talk and thought some spirits could make themselves known.

After a moment or two of silence, Clare giggled. "Mama says to send the villains to the roof, and she'll take care of them."

Villain definitely sounded like a more adult word than little Clare would use.

Letitia would have a lot of incentive to shove her killers from the highest precipice. Phoebe just didn't think it was likely.

"I'll do my best," she told both child and ghost. "Now, will you sleep? If Kitty is to go with you, he needs his nap."

"I like your pretty dress," Clare murmured sleepily as Phoebe tucked her in.

"Thank you. Some day, you may have one like it." She kissed the child and slipped from the nursery, ruefully regarding the now-wrinkled silk. She simply wasn't made for fashionable gowns.

She didn't even have a pocket to carry treats in for Piney and Raven. Or time to visit with them much anymore. Her nights were full now instead of lonely. She wasn't certain how she felt about that yet. She knew what she had done with Drew was wrong. She knew he meant to right it. She didn't know how she felt about that either.

Not wanting to harm Drew's lovely gift of evening clothes and shoes, she couldn't even retreat to the roof to think. She was being pushed into propriety, whether she liked it or not.

In that melancholy mood, she drifted back to the suite she shared with her mother to help repack clothes from trunk to crates.

"I cannot leave you here with him," the countess protested. "He will turn you into a meek housewife."

Put that way—Phoebe laughed. "There is little likelihood of that. I know I should be worried about what other people think, but it takes up all my time worrying about those I love." She hugged her mother's frail shoulders.

The countess sighed in exasperation. "You are so like your father that I cannot say no to you any more than I could to him. Be careful you do not go the same way I did."

Phoebe considered that. "I wore this gown for Mr. Blair because it was important to him but not to me. But I will not be sent away because he thinks propriety is necessary, while I believe people matter more. He knows as well as I do that he needs me."

"You don't have to *marry* him to prove that." Her mother snapped a case closed in disapproval.

"That's between Mr. Blair and me and is not up for discussion until matters are settled. I do like him a lot, Mama," Phoebe admitted.

The countess engulfed her in a perfumed embrace. "I know, darling, and that worries me. You may be more like your father than me after all."

"Is that why you came home? Because I worry about you living in this cold damp climate."

"Once this little contretemps is straightened out, we shall have a good talk. Now remove your rodent from my nightdresses so we may finish packing."

DREW CLIMBED ALL THE WAY TO THE ROOF EXPECTING PHOEBE TO TRY FLYING off. Only the raven greeted him. He fed the creature a piece of Cook's fish in the interest of solidarity. If he wanted Phoebe, he had to accept her pets.

He wanted Phoebe, no question about that. It was the marriage part that daunted him. He'd be finding mice in his machines and birds in his attic and eventually, children underfoot. And Phoebe wasn't exactly the sort to stay home and keep order.

But she would see that everyone was fed properly, order the servants, and grace his bed with enthusiasm. That last part covered a multitude of sins—if he could only persuade her to the same.

He traipsed downstairs and halted near the door of her suite. He heard women talking. There would be no having Phoebe to himself this evening.

Drew sought Simon and Hugh, finding them in the workshop, playing with his newly re-arranged pterotype. "I just read an article saying an American has solved the key problem and sold the patent. I'll make no fortune off that after all my work."

"But think of what a machine like this can do!" Hugh pounded out letters with two fingers. "If you received a printed document, wouldn't you believe it was official?"

Drew shrugged and sat down with the bicycle wheel. "Anyone can have a document printed. How is this different?"

"Because we can do it right now and with no one to observe. Look, see what you think." He yanked the paper out of the carriage and handed it over.

Simon peered over Drew's shoulder. "I think you need more ink and lines that run parallel instead of slipping about like drunken sailors."

"I was learning how it works," Hugh said defensively. "The carriage slips and needs tightening."

Instead of criticizing the poor quality of the print, Drew read what Hugh had written. "This is genius. And probably criminal."

"Not that I can see. It's not really official. We can't help it if they believe it is. We'll send it to Wilkes. He's supposedly an Association member. As one of the more powerful mine owners, he has the most to lose from Simon's newfangled ideas. If this doesn't draw out the cads, we'll try a different tactic with another suspect." Hugh rolled another piece of paper into the machine.

"Let me fix that carriage first." Drew handed the paper to Simon.

Simon read it properly this time and whistled. "Can we hire an army? You really want to send this to Wilkes? The baron has had his way in the district since I was in short pants."

"I really want to put Phoebe in a crate and send her to Yorkshire," Drew growled from his machine. "But where would we be without her mice?"

"This time, we'll be here and prepared," Hugh added. "And after receiving this, the real scoundrels are likely to walk through the front door."

Drew pointed his screwdriver at his cousin. "And you are not allowed to lop off their heads. We will have witnesses on hand who will testify to anything they admit."

"They won't admit to killing Letitia," Simon said, slumping in the chair.

"Once they see a transcript and believe their hired hands are telling all, we'll be lucky they don't turn tail and run. We'll let you decide whether you want them locked up or forced to sell their mines." Drew tightened the carriage and gestured for Hugh to try again.

"I want them hanged," Simon growled.

"Not bluidy likely," Hugh said, sliding paper into the typewriter carriage. "The Association has too much money and too much power. Just convincing a policeman to arrest one of them would require blood dripping from their hands. It's how the Association gets away with what it does."

"One step at a time, gentlemen," Drew insisted. "We bring the varlets to our doorstep and proceed from there. May I suggest another document verifying that Wilkes' mine is encroaching on Simon's mines? We'll put a fancy inspection seal on it and hand it to whoever arrives, just to see the fireworks."

His cousin began to smile for the first time in months and reached for the stack of paper. "I like it. I'll scribble the wording I've seen used and Hugh can type it up too. It will look as if it came from a government printer."

Drew thought scribbling lies might be safer than Simon sharpening his dirk. "And after that, someone needs to check those properties for Lady Persephone. Can we do that while waiting for the Association to arrive?"

"Don't send the letter yet," Hugh suggested. "Give them a day or two to stew first. Make certain the children are safely settled in York."

"You'll be as dangerous as they are one of these days," Drew complained, watching the keys as Hugh typed. "Remind me never to cross you."

Stewing villains meant hostile warfare in the near future, and he returned to pounding another dent from the bicycle rim.

Although warfare might be easier than finding a home suitable for an interfering mother-in-law.

TWENTY-SEVEN

Rubbing at the tears streaking her cheeks and half-wishing she were traveling with her mother and the child-bearing trunks, Phoebe stood on the steps and waved at the departing carriage.

"We cannot sit about waiting for villains to appear. Should we take a tour of your mother's property list?" Andrew asked as the carriage vanished around a corner.

Without the children, her only purpose now was to find the men who endangered them. She had hoped her aunts would let her know if they found anything of interest in Letitia's journal, but they hadn't. "Do you not fear the house will be attacked at any moment?"

"They may have scalawags lurking in the shrubbery, watching for the children, but they'll see nothing." Andrew gestured down the street.

Phoebe tried to unobtrusively scan the park, but the shadows were long at this early hour. The rats saw nothing unusual.

He took her arm and steered her inside. "Hired thugs are of no matter. We want the big guns, but it will take time to draw them out. Meanwhile, I've set all my business on hold. First, we must decide if we wish to marry by registrar or church. Once we've signed the papers, I thought we could look at properties to honor that lien."

"I have not even signed my employment contract," she argued. "I don't see the point in a lifetime commitment over a night spent together, especially to a man who flings his tenants into the streets."

"The building fell down—the tenants have to move! I am working on relocating them. I am only one very small part of the consortium that owns those buildings." He dragged her inside, presumably so they weren't arguing in the street.

She had no reason not to believe him, but she was terrified of a step she'd never prepared to take. "I shall see about that. Since I am apparently not needed here, I shall slip away and stay with my aunts. Then you will not feel obligated to marry me. We've known each other much too short a time and should not act hastily." She shook off his hand and aimed for the stairs.

Andrew grabbed her by the waist and yanked her down the hall into his stuffy, dark office, slamming the door behind them. "Thunderation, woman! What do you mean you're *not needed*? Do I need to go down on my knees and beg?"

Phoebe stared at him in astonishment. The wealthy, handsome Mr. Blair stood there in his tailored suit and immaculate linen, looking the very personification of proper gentry—and a fierce Highland warrior at the same time. How did he do that? Overlong dark curls falling on his forehead perhaps. No fancy whiskers concealing his blunt square jaw and cheekbones. And a gaze that pierced her soul and weakened all her defenses.

"You are being ridiculous," she said, not as firmly as she would have liked. "We do not even know each other."

"We have lived together for almost a fortnight. We have gone to *bed* together. That is far more than most couples know. How much more is there?"

She'd spent the better part of the night creating rational arguments against last night's declaration—not proposal—of marriage. But all logic fled in the face of Andrew's earnestness. She *wanted* to share his bed again. She rather enjoyed living here and having a warm room and servants. But she should not be seduced from her purpose by creature comforts.

"I have a gift," she announced with more fortitude than a moment ago. "I have to believe I was given that gift for a reason. I know it does

not mean much to you that I can understand the minds of mute creatures. But think how you'd feel if you knew a child suffered and you
could do nothing? I have been bumbling along, learning the hard way
how to find nests, protect eggs, fix wings or bandage paws. I have
reached the limits of what I can do on my own. I need the benefit of
learning from others."

He listened. She could see he tried to understand. She waited, hoping
he'd find a solution so she could have it all.

He scowled and shoved his hands into his pockets. "We both need
time to adjust our thinking. You have never considered marriage. I have
never considered a wife who spends her time with books and classes
and. . . animals. I'm sure we're both smart enough to work it out."

"You mean you think you can seduce me into your way of thinking,"
Phoebe replied pragmatically. "I'm not a romantic. I do not expect
promises of love and undying devotion." Although she supposed they
might be pleasant to hear, but she'd never *expected* them. She was odd,
after all. She was still amazed that this perfectly normal, respectable man
considered her at all. Obviously, he was as seduced by lust as she was. "I
do expect a man who keeps his word."

"I am working on your tenants, I promise." Like a prized thoroughbred, all muscles and grace, he paced his study, coat pulled back, hands
in pockets. "I will be faithful," he added. "I will shower you with everything your heart desires."

She almost smiled at his earnestness. "I might believe you mean the
first two, but not the last. You'll forget I exist while you're working on a
project. I *am* being practical. I do not want to tie us together for a lifetime
if we cannot tolerate each other's habits."

There, that sounded very logical and well-reasoned, when all she
really wanted to do was fling her arms around him and ask if they could
go to bed now. And even she knew that impulse was a very bad idea.

Grimacing, he studied her words and bent his head in acknowledgment, if not acceptance. "I need you here. I *want* you here. I will be very
unhappy if you return to your aunts. So let us spend this day together
and work at compromise."

Phoebe laughed. "Ever the businessman, ready to negotiate. *Life* isn't
negotiable. Life just happens. But if we're not to expect any visitors yet,

by all means, let us visit my old neighbors, then find a place to store my mother."

Before she left the house, she warned the creatures to watch for strangers. She could not hear them if she traveled too far, but Raven flew long distances. And Wolf was awake and eager.

A pity the university could not teach her how to help the animals communicate with each other—but even people had difficulty with that.

DISCOURAGED BY THE SLOW PROGRESS OF MOVING OUT THE CONSORTIUM'S tenants, dejected at the lack of decent property anywhere in the old town, Drew examined the next unprepossessing building on their list. He'd hoped to woo the lady with his engineering expertise, but they'd not seen a single building worth repairing, including this one. At least he'd been able to ascertain that no scalawags followed them.

Unlike him, Phoebe had been encouraged that some of her old neighbors had found new homes. And she seemed excited by this abandoned dump situated on a leafy lane near Georges Square, not far from the university. Georges Square had been developed about the same time as the neighborhood where he lived. But this ugly barn wasn't one of the elegantly terraced mansions a few streets over.

"At least it's not medieval," he said, not hiding his doubt.

"It has a roof," Phoebe added with laughter.

The last property had pigeons roosting in the attic.

Phoebe wore one of her old, colorful gowns today, with her new boots and new hat. Drew found the effect both rakish and charming, and he was having difficulty concentrating on matters at hand. "Your solicitor must think I am some sort of miracle worker if he thinks I can restore any of these properties to habitable."

"My mother and I have lived our lives in a medieval tenement with no latrines or running water or gas lighting. We can manage. I simply do not believe she should live like that again. Do we go in?" She examined the multitude of dirty mullioned windows. "It will take an army just to clean the glass."

Drew juggled through the keys he had been given. "At least the door on this one seems solid. I could have kicked in the others." He set the key in the lock and felt the strong tumbler action. Someone knew how to make locks.

He opened the door and allowed Phoebe in first. She laughed again as she entered the front room. "This is perfect for you."

"Me?" That didn't sound promising. He entered, letting his eyes adjust to the gray light. Once cleaned, the windows would illuminate this front room nicely—if one could call it a room.

"What the devil did they do here?" He examined the thick plaster walls adorned with hooks, the solid timber workbenches, and the enormous stone fireplace.

"It may have been a kitchen for one of the grand houses." Phoebe crossed the filthy stone floor to peer through a doorway. "This seems to be a pantry. Lots of lovely shelves and drawers."

Drew followed her, scowling at the lack of lighting. Phoebe moved through the next doorway and twirled around in the rear room, scanning the high ceiling and windows.

"I suppose the cook and her family could have lived back here. These old houses are not always cut up the way the new ones are. Look, there's a sink. There must be plumbing. Did you see any in the front room? Kitchens require water."

"Probably a pump system, maybe a cistern." Drew studied the seemingly sturdy stairs to the next level. Unable to resist curiosity, he climbed up.

"Divided up here," he shouted down. "Most likely servants quarters. That back room you're in may have been for horse tack or other equipment storage."

"Stable in back," she called up to him. "A good lane for deliveries or leading to the main house, which is apparently no longer there. That appears to be an official building down the lane now, brick and new."

Drew poked around this second floor, noticing the fine construction someone had put into the place. Ideas stirred. "The windows are deep enough that glazed glass could be fitted to the interior. If the flue works, braziers could be added for better heating."

Phoebe climbed up to join him, poking dismissively through the maze of small rooms. "They're no bigger than wardrobes."

Drew studied the walls and the ceiling, then hunted until he found stairs to the attic. "Walls can be removed to make four good solid bedrooms. Or suites with maid rooms in between. Or offices."

"You sound interested," she said in incredulity, following him upward.

"Georgian construction is far superior to that medieval abomination you lived in." Entering the attic, he examined the timbered gables and stomped his boots on the thick plank floor. "Gas pipes can be run through here and down to the rooms."

At her silence, Drew glanced up and found Phoebe testing a ladder. "Not until I try it first," he warned. "The roof tiles could be rotted."

"The treads are very sturdy." She stepped away from them anyway, allowing him to go first.

He hated heights, but if he didn't look down, he shouldn't get as dizzy. Drew climbed up, testing the ladder treads. He crowed at the first thing he saw on the roof, a dovecote. "I don't suppose one of your family might have lived here?" He stepped out to test the roof, which had a walkway and parapet wider than his own. He stayed to the middle so he could look out but not down.

Phoebe's head peered around the door. "Oh, my. Oh, yes, it's very possible. Look at that! Isn't it cunning?"

She emerged to crouch in front of the ornamental stack of boxes currently inhabited by pigeons and probably mice. Or rats. And squirrels. Drew watched one scamper toward a ragged pine shading the side.

"Your rodent might like that tree," he said tentatively, still working ideas through his mind.

Phoebe stood up, her willowy figure firm against the wind. Her skirts blew around her. Her hair tumbled in artless curls. But she remained steadfast against the elements, admiring the view. Drew's heart nearly exploded at the sight. He didn't know how to make it work, but he knew this was where she belonged.

Her generous lips spread in a smile as she studied the pine. "Piney would love it! And maybe someday I could find him a mate." Then the smile dissipated. "But my mother would hate it here. She likes formal parlors and dining rooms and elegant furnishings. And she really shouldn't be living in the north at all."

Drew didn't want the house for her mother. But they had other matters to settle first. He drew her into his arms and kissed her. "We're all alone. There is no one to watch. And I am having difficulty keeping my hands off you."

He kissed her throat, and she moaned and wrapped her arms around him.

Not all of his ideas were about construction.

TWENTY-EIGHT

FEELING WILD AND FREE ON THIS MAGICAL ROOF, PHOEBE SANK INTO Andrew's kisses as easily as she accepted the wind and sun. When his big hand covered her breast through her bodice, her nipples ached for more. Evoking the forbidden delights he'd taught her, her hips pressed into his, seeking satisfaction.

The children were safe. The villains hadn't returned. There was no one but the two of them. . .

Still, she tried to protest when Andrew half-carried her back to the attic. He kissed away her fears. A man of many talents, he kept kissing her as he stripped off his coat and flung it to the floor. Her head spun so senselessly, that she was barely aware of being lowered to the fine satin lining. The luxury of hot, hard man leaning over her made the world and all their differences go away. She grabbed the back of his head and tugged him down until he kissed her breasts through the thin fabric, tantalizing her with memories of nakedness.

She ran her fingers beneath his linen. He unfastened her bodice and untied the ribbons of her chemise. With sensitive flesh finally touching flesh, she arched into his invading hand. He caressed the ache of her nipples, sending liquid rivers of desire shivering to the place between her legs.

Understanding better what they did, Phoebe tried to be sensible when he tugged at her skirt. But he suckled at her breast, and she wept with desire.

"We can't make babies," she feebly protested as he unfastened his trousers. She avidly watched him release himself from layers of clothing. The attic light was dim, but she could see enough to almost be frightened.

"I want to," he growled in her ear. "I want to see you swelling with my pups. But I can wait."

His visceral growl trembled her womb, and she insanely wanted babies too.

He rummaged in his pocket for a square of linen he unfolded. Phoebe watched with interest as he rolled a thin membrane over his male member. In curiosity, she reached out to stroke him, and he groaned and pushed against her hand. Enjoying the power to do to him what he did to her, she helped him with the sheath, then explored more. He grew even larger.

"How is this even possible?" she whispered.

He slid his fingers between her legs until the river became a flood. "Like this." Apparently having studied feminine engineering as thoroughly as mechanical, he pushed more fingers inside and kissed her breast at the same time.

Phoebe cried out as every nerve ending came undone. Lost in the bliss, she eagerly accepted the push of his male organ. The tension built again, but she knew what to do now. She rocked her hips, dug her fingers into his back, and demanded all he had to give.

She felt him so far inside her that she feared he'd cleave her in two, and then her world shattered with his, and she really understood what it meant to be as one with a man, why women through the ages had lost their heads and virginity and themselves for the satisfaction of a man's bed.

She'd been thoroughly seduced.

DREW WASN'T PARTICULARLY PROUD OF HIMSELF AS HE LED PHOEBE BACK TO his waiting carriage. No gentle lady should be ravished in a dirty attic. But this lady seemed serenely unperturbed by their lovemaking, to the extent that he wanted to make love to her again in the carriage—except he was driving.

Amazingly, this confusing woman possessed the healthy nature of his peasant ancestors *and* the civilized veneer—when she wished to apply it —of the genteel society he now cultivated. His need to be proper didn't have to war with his upbringing when he was with her. He wasn't about to let this prize go.

"Registrar's office," he said grimly, taking up the reins.

"We really can *not* make babies immediately?" she asked, sounding a little less certain than she looked.

"We can *try* not to make babies. Nothing is ever a hundred percent certain. Your family can probably teach you more ways than I can." Relieved that she hadn't raised instant objection, Drew directed the horse back to the Royal Mile. "Do you wish to visit with your aunts now?"

Visiting her aunts was the last thing he wanted to do. But marriage wasn't all about what *he* wanted, he recognized.

She was silent for so long that Drew wondered if he should stop the carriage, go down on one knee, and grovel. But he'd like to have a ring in his hand when he did so.

She studied her hands, avoiding his eyes. "The twins had a book, one of Letitia's journals."

That was not the rejection he'd expected. Drew tried not to levitate like one of Enoch's victims. "And you didn't tell me, *why*?"

"Because Letitia didn't wish it," she whispered. "Malcolm journals are very private. Had I found anything applicable in it, I would have told you, I promise."

He clutched the reins, not knowing what to expect from this woman who held his future in her hands. Letitia—a *ghost* didn't wish it? "And why are you telling me now?"

"Because I gave it to my aunts for safety. And I know they are going through it far better than I had time to do. And I suspect their Latin is better."

"Latin? The journal is in Latin?" Without thinking, he shook the reins and set the carriage in the direction of her aunts.

"In incredibly tiny writing. I only read the pages at the end, where I thought she might have entered dangerous information, but there were only the bits about neighbors telling her she needed to persuade Mr. Simon to sell. I found nothing incriminating. I thought. . . before we go home. . . we should see what progress my aunts have made."

He relaxed his shoulders a little. "You thought I'd take the book and not believe about Letitia's ghost?"

She nodded. "It does not sound sane to most people. And you did not really seem to believe in her. But if. . . if we're to learn each other, you need to believe what I believe."

"That works both ways, you know," he said, thinking this through. "If I believe you're in danger, you need to listen."

She wrinkled her nose, unhappy with the concept. "I will *listen*. But I will keep my own counsel," she decided.

And he'd have to accept that from a woman who had survived these filthy streets and who had taken down two sturdy thugs without his aid. "And I thought I wanted a sweet woman who stayed home and let me take care of her," Drew said with a sigh.

She flashed him a cautious smile, and he felt better. They were both uncertain about this relationship, but they were *learning*. He was an excellent student.

The aunts welcomed them in the front parlor, with the journal prominently displayed on a table as if they had been expecting them.

"We had our Latin teacher translate," Lady Agnes said.

"And your journalist writes in *code*," Lady Gertrude added. "One needs to understand the proper declensions and when she strays from them. A very extraordinary lady. I wish we'd known her."

"Then there is the matter of the initials. We had to send for information on the neighbors."

Drew feared his head would spin off his neck if he tried to follow this conversation. Phoebe seemed resigned, so perhaps he wasn't the only one.

"But we think she's discovered a conspiracy involving the baron, John Wilkes, a Mr. Glengarry, and a Lord John? We're told they all live in Mr. Blair's area and have mining interests?"

"Is there anything that might be considered proof?" Drew asked skeptically.

Lady Gertrude handed him a sheaf of papers. "This is the translation with the private parts deleted, the ones that would only cause her husband greater grief. She is protecting him, even in death."

Drew looked at Phoebe. She squeezed his hand and nodded. So she knew what Leticia concealed—it must be a woman's thing. And now that he had a woman of his own that he wanted very much to shelter, he had a flash of understanding. *Letitia may have been with child when she died.* That's the only thing that would drive Simon even madder with grief.

In shared sorrow, he squeezed Phoebe's hand back. Papers in hand, they departed soon after.

"Thank you for understanding," she whispered, holding his arm. She checked the sky and added, "Raven is circling."

He glanced up but couldn't tell one bird from another. Still, Drew helped her into the carriage, climbed in, and urged the horses into a trot. "He's not close enough?"

"Not yet. I'm sorry. It could be nothing. And if there is no one home, then it may not matter at all. I never said that my gift is useful to others." She crossed her hands in her lap.

Drew covered them with his and squeezed. "Since I'd rather not have anyone burning down my house, we'll head there instead of the registrar's."

She squeezed his hand, then sank into silence, presumably communing with her creatures.

With any other woman, he would have laughed at the conceit of believing she connected with animal minds. With Phoebe. . . anything seemed possible. A woman with an open mind, who enjoyed a good round of bedding, was worth any number of women who could sit demurely through a social occasion. He felt as if a heavy weight had been removed from his shoulders, and he was free at last.

"Wolf isn't happy with some strangers in the mews. Raven is seeing. . . men in suits on your doorstep. Were you expecting company?"

"No. We were waiting until we heard that the children and your mother are safely in Yorkshire before inviting trouble. It's broad daylight.

Perhaps they're neighbors." Although his closest neighbor had some questionable companions these days.

He steered the carriage into the mews but didn't see any strangers. Henry ran out as usual to take the reins, Wolf trotting at his side. Did that mean Phoebe *wasn't* reading the dog's mind? Drew shoved aside niggling doubt, climbed down and held his hand up to assist her. The dog came over for a head rub, then turned in the direction of the far end of the mews and growled.

"Whoever was here left when we drove up," Phoebe whispered, pulling nervously at the gloves she'd donned once they'd crossed the bridge into this part of town.

She'd asked him to believe her. He wished he could read minds so he'd know from what direction to expect trouble. "And the men in suits?" Drew took her arm, wondering if he ought to send her elsewhere.

"The mice show they're inside with Mr. Simon. Kitty left with the children, and Piney is asleep. I have no other useful spies."

Drew thought this might be one of the more nonsensical conversations he'd ever indulged in, but he opened the back door with caution and attempted to keep Phoebe behind him. "The mice?"

"Are hiding mostly." Amusement tinged her voice. "Perhaps we should acquire a parrot."

That *we* gave him hope. "Would you care to go upstairs and primp while I see who is waiting?" He exchanged his coat for one hanging beside the door. The attic floor had not been clean.

Phoebe hesitated, glancing down at her old gown. He'd wrinkled it in his enthusiasm, and spiderwebs clung to the wool. And he'd stupidly thought once that he wanted a lady who wore crushable silks and untouchable underpinnings!

"I doubt the new dress has arrived. Just give me a moment to tuck my hair up." She removed her hat and swiftly pulled at pins and tresses, putting them back together again using the aid of a mirror in the dark hallway.

Drew admired the skill of this swift rearrangement, but he preferred her tumbled curls. He brushed off the back of her skirt, removing dust as best as he could. Once Phoebe stepped away from the mirror, he used the glass to straighten his cravat but the linen was hopelessly wrinkled. His attire would start matching Phoebe's at this rate. Remarkably, he didn't care, even if the Queen herself waited for them. He buttoned his coat, then offered his arm. "Shall we meet our visitors?"

"*Our*," she whispered, shaking her head. "Yours, more likely."

"Any visitor of mine is also yours. Remember, we are married in all but one way." He could be stubborn when needed.

She glared at him but wrapped her fingers around his arm. So, she wasn't on the same page as he was yet, but he'd bring her there. Confidently, he led her down the hall.

Male voices emerged from the front parlor. Drew recognized Dalrymple's, and his gut clenched. But Simon spoke next, and he didn't seem agitated.

"Last chance for you to escape," Drew warned as they reached the stairs that divided the house.

"No, I am curious. And I definitely think we need a parrot." Her gloved hand clasped around his arm, Phoebe strode into the parlor at his side—as if they were truly a couple in the eyes of the world.

Drew nodded at Dalrymple as they entered. The older man glared in disapproval, probably of Phoebe and Drew's dishevelment. Responsible businessmen did not look as if they'd been rolling in the gutter. Dismissing his neighbor, Drew studied the other two well-dressed businessmen. Simon offered a frozen smile of welcome. Drew's gut did not unclench. He recognized their guests.

Simon performed perfunctory introductions. "Lady Phoebe, this is Lord John, Sir Charles, and Mr. Wilson. I believe everyone knows my cousin, Andrew Blair."

Phoebe offered her hand. Standing, the strangers bowed politely over it.

Dalrymple scowled. "If you'll excuse us, my lady, we need to borrow Blair for this discussion."

She began removing her gloves, one finger at a time in a tantalizing strip tease that had Drew salivating. "I shall order tea, gentlemen. We are expecting my uncle, the Earl of Drumsmoore, momentarily, so I'll have them send up the crumpets as well."

Even if Drew hadn't known her uncle's reclusiveness, he'd know Phoebe was lying by her prim hauteur— the disguise with which she met his world. In rags and dust but bearing the air of a countess, she tugged the cord to call Abby, then settled into a wing chair as if she owned the place.

Drew didn't know whether to hug her or strangle her.

PHOEBE WASN'T ENTIRELY CERTAIN WHY SHE WAS BEING DELIBERATELY provocative. Drew had business callers. Her place was to order refreshment and retire out of sight. Well, factually speaking, her place was in the nursery. But even if she really were Andrew's wife, she'd have to leave the men to business.

But *Lord John* matched one of the names in Letitia's journal.

The men sat down after she did, although Andrew lingered behind her chair, assessing the situation. Abby entered with the tea tray. Even the servants were better behaved than Phoebe.

"Sir Charles is offering to purchase my mine," Simon offered as Phoebe poured tea. "Wilson is the banker I use at home. He verifies Sir Charles has the funds."

"Very convenient," Andrew said smoothly, taking the cup she handed him. "The earl warned us about selling to the Association." He squeezed her shoulder in warning.

"The Association is a myth," Dalrymple said with a derisive gesture. "Drumsmoore is feeding you nonsense if that's what he told you."

"My uncle is not inclined to telling tall tales," Phoebe said, smiling over her cup and recalling Dahlia's warnings of her uncle's secret meetings. Another person from Letitia's code fell in place. "And where is Mr. Glengarry today? Did he not introduce you to these fine gentlemen?"

Andrew squeezed her shoulder again, but provocation came so easily. . .

Two of the new gentlemen shifted uneasily. They seemed like nice men. Sir Charles was portly, his stomach straining at his respectable gray vest. Mr. Wilson, the banker, was younger and ungainly tall, with spectacles, and seemed very earnest.

Lord John appeared to be a wealthy man in his forties, with a weathered, healthy look that spoke of time outdoors.

"We are here at the behest of Glengarry, yes," Sir Charles admitted. "He is acting for a few other businessmen who prefer not to be known. They have all assured me that the mine is active, and that Mr. Blair is no longer interested in exploiting his assets."

Phoebe sipped her tea, leaving that topic for the men. Her attention was diverted to the mews, where Wolf was growling at the returning strangers.

Drew excused himself to fetch some papers in his office. She took that opportunity to follow him out.

"They may have thugs in the mews," she whispered. "Where is Hugh?"

"He may have left to find a constable when this crew showed up. We have. . . constructed. . . documents showing the two mine owners Simon suspects—not the gentlemen in the parlor—have been illegally digging into the mines of others." He waved a sheaf of papers. "We were hoping to draw them out, but not until we had authorities on hand."

He glanced worriedly at the locked and latched back door. "Go upstairs and find Simon's claymore. Leave it in the umbrella stand by the back door, if you will, please. Is your new footman still about?"

"In the kitchen. I hired a lad from my old neighborhood. He's a little too good with his fists and needed to be away from the streets. I hate to send him into the fray here." She frowned, not wanting to attack strangers before they knew if they were dangerous.

"Just have him up here so he can fetch help if needed. I need to return to the parlor. We can hope Hugh will be back soon." He kissed her cheek. "Sit on the roof where they won't find you," he suggested.

Phoebe smiled at the suggestion and senselessly thrilled at the proprietary kiss. "Most excellent idea, sir." She kissed him back, then darted for the stairs before he could reach for her.

Like a general who observes from the best vantage point, she would use the roof to direct her troops. She hoped Drew had understood that when he sent her up there.

Phoebe found the claymore, left it in the stand by the back door as promised, and ran down to the kitchens to warn the servants that danger might be imminent. She stationed Dougie, their new footman, in Andrew's workshop where he could hear and not be seen. She picked up a few tools to use as weapons for herself, then climbed up to the roof.

She really should have set up a signal with Henry in the stable, using Wolf as her communication channel. She made her way over to the rear of the roof and gazed over the edge. Henry held a growling Wolf by the collar with one hand and a pitchfork in the other. Good boy, she thought to herself, meaning both boy and dog. Wolf tossed his head in acknowledgement of her approval. Henry glanced up, and Phoebe waved her hammer at him. She couldn't tell from this distance if she'd reassured him, but he held his post.

She couldn't see the strangers from this vantage point. Wolf's sense of smell indicated they weren't close. Cautiously, she worked her way around the roof's edge, debating whether she could leap from the parapet here to the one on Mr. Dalrymple's house. It would be awkward in skirts, but doable if necessary, she concluded. The front of the house revealed a pair of horses tied to the post but no sign of Hugh or policemen.

She mentally reached out to the pigeons on the chimney and the ones on the front fence.

Alarmingly, the ones on the chimney were following human movement on Dalrymple's roof.

TWENTY-NINE

DREW ONLY HALF-LISTENED TO THE INTENSE ARGUMENT BETWEEN HIS COUSIN and Simon's Association neighbors. He had the nagging feeling that the meeting was contrived for a purpose he couldn't discern. If the villains still thought the children were in the nursery—

Wolf howled in a spine-tingling, eerie pitch that had Drew out of his chair before he gave it any thought. Oblivious to the dog's warning, Simon scowled when Drew headed for the door. His cousin continued his war of words, waving the typewritten papers they'd drawn up the previous evening.

Drew noticed nothing unusual in the corridor. Phoebe should be standing guard on the roof. Perhaps she'd seen something and had the dog howl the warning. The weasel scampered down the stairs and toward the back door, confirming his fear.

He was actually treating her weird ability as if it were a normal, scientific reality!

Grateful he didn't have to worry about Phoebe running about, trying to hide the weans, he pulled out his sgian dubh and eased open the back door. Had they left it unlatched earlier? Possibly, since he'd assumed the enemy was inside.

The stableboy practically fell into him. Henry gestured frantically at the roof, keeping his hold on Wolf, who was struggling to be free. The weasel scampered up the vines on the back of the house.

Drew gazed upward and nearly expired of fright.

Hanging backward, half off the parapet, Phoebe struggled with a well-dressed gentleman who held a cane to her neck. Her raven flew overhead, shrieking and attacking the man's top hat. Phoebe seemed to be beating her assailant about the shoulders with a. . . hammer? But she was so slender and the brute was so large. . .

Strangling on a furious, unvoiced, battle cry, Drew thought quickly. Their enemies wanted the journal and the children. Phoebe had said there were *two* strangers. One of them could already be inside, ready to take over if Simon didn't give in. Returning inside might be a trap. They wouldn't be expecting attack from the outside. . . or below.

Which meant. . . he watched the weasel scampering up the vines. Drew almost lost his nerve and returned inside to fight an army rather than do what needed to be done. But that was Phoebe up there. He needed to reach her *now*, without risking being outnumbered.

He quietly commanded his one soldier, a stableboy. "If you can, have the new footman send Simon up through the attic. You go with them. All hands on the roof, understood?"

Henry nodded, his eyes wide with terror, and ran into the house with Wolf at his side. Drew hoped he didn't send the lad into danger.

He needed the element of surprise.

He needed to fly.

His mind frantically tossed up suggestions of how the hell he would accomplish flying—but the weasel has already showed him the way.

While mentally creating one increasingly inventive flying machine after another, Drew instinctively sought purchase in vines and trellis and downspout as if they were the rigging on the ship he never wanted to sail again.

He'd half scaled the wall when the voice in the back of his head sang *Don't look down.*

He swallowed hard and started up the second story. The vines at this level weren't as thick as the ropy trunks on the ground. He hauled himself higher. *Don't look down.*

At the attic level, the vines ripped off the wall under his grip, nearly flinging him backward. Extreme vertigo struck. The weasel chittered scolding, from the parapet, urging him on. Desperately fighting dizziness, Drew dug his fingers into a brick, propped a boot on a narrow windowsill, and sought other purchases.

A few yards and a universe out of reach, Phoebe choked on screams, driving him to foaming insanity. He didn't dare glance in her direction. Her life depended on him concentrating on the next toehold for his boot, the next grip for his hand. He prayed she couldn't see him, because that meant he still had the element of surprise.

Don't look down. . .

Drew sent up prayers to a god he'd long abandoned. He made promises to the heavens. He wept and cursed and clung on for dear life —*because Phoebe was his life*. That bastard held his entire world in his hands. If Drew couldn't save Phoebe, he had no reason for existence.

He had a glimpse into the bloody black void of Simon's soul after the devastating loss of his beloved wife. At least Simon had had a few good years. . .

The vines were no more than loose tendrils by the time Drew reached the attic story. His head spun. He couldn't find a grip at the top of the wall to pull over the parapet. If he'd had a damned normal roof—Phoebe wouldn't be out here. He had to look down, find a better foothold. . . The alley below whirled. His sweaty hands slipped and all it would take was one loose brick. . .

A slender vine blew past his nose, of no use as support. He needed a hand hold, anything. Despair filled him.

The tendril blew harder, smacking his cheek. Annoyed, he brushed it aside, and discovered a hole in the mortar just large enough for his fingers. Without the vine, he had no other support, but if he could hold on long enough. . .

He gripped the brick, found a foothold, and put all his strength into surging upward to grab the parapet's edge. A loose stone crumbled beneath his feet.

Phoebe screamed louder, as much furious as terrified. Her attacker roared a curse.

Drew threw his leg over the edge and prayed the decorative wall held his weight. As he tumbled over and onto the slates, he could swear he felt a tug on his coat yanking him to safety, but he was on his feet before he could consider invisible hands. The weasel chittered approval and scampered off.

He finally dared look past the chimney, to where a top-coated gentleman strained to push his struggling victim over the edge. The weasel ran up his trouser, but the madman didn't notice.

Kicking and screaming, Phoebe had apparently lost her hammer. Instead, she gripped her attacker's coat sleeves, seemingly attempting to pull the scoundrel over the edge with her. Righting himself, Drew stifled his cry of horror at the scene.

The weasel bit at the scoundrel's cravat. Phoebe's new boots connected with a shin. The bastard released one end of the cane, making a fist to hit her.

On his feet now, Drew lunged. Using his body as a bludgeon, he bashed Phoebe's assailant aside, yanking her back to the roof in the same motion. His goddess slid safely to the slates. With both hands free and red rage filling his head, Drew swung at the fiend stumbling to catch his balance. Instead of putting up his fists, or even his cane, the dastard ran for the attic door.

And tripped over the rodent. Sideways, *as if pushed*.

Standing protectively over Phoebe, Drew watched in shock and disbelief as the man he recognized as Wilkes, one of his investment partners and Simon's mine-owning neighbor, slipped impossibly toward the parapet.

"Go, Letitia," he could swear he heard Phoebe whisper.

Before Drew could react in any sensible way, the would-be killer fell against the low parapet. Wilkes was taller than Phoebe, and the wall hit him at thigh height. He grabbed for the parapet but apparently off-kilter, he fell backward—and over the edge.

The baron's screams echoed through the mews—just as a contingent of rescuers surged through the attic doorway, Simon leading the charge, waving his claymore.

Drew knelt to take Phoebe in his arms, willing his heart to quit ripping its way out of his chest and to settle down where it belonged.

"Letitia is here," he thought she whispered in his ear, before passing out.

Had the baron succeeded in throttling her?

Panicking, Drew ripped the aging fabric of her bodice to reach her corset. With his pocketknife, he sliced the ties so she could breathe more freely. While Simon's adolescent array of servants raced about, hunting the enemy, Drew covered Phoebe's mouth with his to breathe air into her. Her lungs heaved. He could feel her heart pounding as hard as his. "Talk to me," he whispered, praying.

"What the hell is going on?" Simon shouted at the skies. "The wolf has a blackguard cornered in the nursery, and you're up here having your way with the governess?"

Phoebe stirred in his arms. She lived!

In relief, Drew replied, "*Your wife* just pushed John Wilkes over the parapet." Now that he could breathe again, he enjoyed shaking up his cousin as badly as he had been. Even better, he relished Simon's shock at his insane declaration.

Letting his aching legs collapse under him, Drew pulled Phoebe into his lap and cuddled her against him.

He thought she giggled in understanding. The weasel scampered up his arm and settled on his shoulder. Overhead, the screaming raven settled on a chimney and shut up.

"My. . . ?" Simon peered over the edge, which was more than Drew could make himself do. "Why is Dalrymple down there? I thought we left him in the parlor. And what's he. . ." He grew silent, then abruptly ushered his small troop back toward the attic.

Trying to peer over the edge, Henry and Dougie lingered. Simon gestured at them with his sword, forcing them ahead of him.

"Is he dead?" Phoebe asked uncertainly.

"If he's the bastard who had Letitia murdered, then I sincerely hope so, but do you really want me to look down there to see?" Drew thought he might just sit here for the rest of his life. Let Simon handle his adversaries. Let Hugh swing papers in faces. He was good here, with Phoebe in his arms.

And a raven watching from the chimney, a weasel curling around his neck, and pigeons circling.

"The baron was crossing the roof when I came up. I think he and his friend planned on entering the nursery and taking the children out this way.

Or pushing them off." She shuddered and wrapped her arms around his waist, burrowing her nose in his shoulder. "He sincerely believed Letitia and the children were witches who read his guilty mind and wrote it all down."

Drew held her tight, trying not to think how close he'd come to losing her. "I am never letting you out of my sight again."

"That could be awkward." She chuckled and kissed his jaw, bravely pretending she wasn't shaking from head to toe, although he could feel her shivers. "How on earth did you climb that wall? I thought I'd lost my mind when I saw your head appear. I thought he'd blocked my breath, and I was seeing apparitions."

"Vines are no worse than ship rigging. And maybe Letitia's ghost helped me a little the last step of the way. I don't want to talk about it. I just want to sit here and slowly freeze to death as night arrives and never have to think again." He hugged her as close as he could.

"I don't believe freezing would be pleasant, and you have ruined a second coat this morning. I may be a bad influence." She fingered a rent in his sleeve and a smear of filth.

"We will hire a seamstress and tailor and install them in that building by the university," he vowed. "Along with a nursery for your pets and a workshop for me so mine isn't cluttering the drawing room."

"And install my mother upstairs?" she asked with a laugh. "Living over a barn couldn't be worse than living with some of the animals who slept around us before. One tenant used to keep goats in the cellar."

"I can't believe you're laughing." Reluctantly, Drew stood, refusing to release his hold on her.

"Give me a minute, and I'll have hysterics, I promise," she said, clutching her gown closed. "But I've never fainted before, so I'm trying to catch my breath and not think about anything. I suppose we must go down to see if any part of the house is left. I fear your cousin was looking for battle."

"Oh, most assuredly, which is why I'd rather not take you down just yet. Simon may be beheading whoever your dog has trapped in the nursery. Will you promise to stay in your rooms until I tell you it's safe?" He kissed the top of her head, valiantly trying to resist temptation.

"I cannot go anywhere until I have changed into probably my last gown. So you have a little time to mop up the blood." She limped along beside him, still clinging to his waist.

"Are you all right? Do I need to call a physician?" he asked worriedly.

"I am fine. I twisted myself into a puzzle attempting to hammer the madman's head, gouge his eyes, step on his toes, knee his nether parts, and kick his shin while dodging raven wings. Ravens are not very effective weapons," she said mournfully.

Drew had to stop, close his eyes, and hug her harder to be sure she was solid and breathing. "You learned to fight in the streets?"

"Of course." She started for the door again. "I can't use a knife, I fear. It makes me squeamish. But I had good neighbors who taught me how to look after myself. I never expected to be attacked on the roof by a *baron*, in a nice neighborhood like this."

"People are people no matter where they live or how they dress or what they call themselves." Drew thought about that. "Titles and tailoring may conceal a criminal better, but that doesn't make him any less evil than ragged thieves in the street."

"Clothes do not make the gentleman, *or* lady," she agreed. "But generally, I'd think a gentleman would find better means of stealing than throwing women off the roof," she said tartly. "I am glad Letitia shoved him."

Drew threw a last glance back to the place where the baron had gone over. A trick of light played a shadow on the wall where there should be none. "So am I," he said in heartfelt relief.

PHOEBE COMFORTED A DISTRAUGHT DAHLIA AS POLICEMEN LED MR. Dalrymple away with his companions. "He's only a witness, you'll see," she said, hugging the girl, hoping she wasn't lying.

She feared the gentlemen who had accompanied Mr. Dalrymple were a great deal more than witnesses, but they had not stopped Simon from running to her rescue. Without evidence, they'd never be convicted for soliciting murder or attempted kidnapping. For all she knew, the baron had simply known of the meeting and taken advantage of the distraction.

"But my uncle admitted he *knew* that awful man who tried to kill you," Dahlia said through sobs. "All those men! He met with them in secret in my room. That can't be good."

"They were part of Andrew's consortium, so that means nothing. Your uncle is innocent until proven guilty. Maybe only the baron and his mine manager planned to harm the children. We don't know. You should try to see your aunt. She must be terrified. Tell her my mother, the Countess of Drumsmoore, will be returning from Castle Yates shortly, and I'd love to introduce her."

Dahlia wiped her eyes with a handkerchief and offered a half laugh. "Phrasing it like that might actually help. Do you think your mother would be interested in charity work?"

"I do not, but don't tell your aunt that. Now, go, before she has time to work herself into a state. Mr. Blair will tell her what he hears as soon as he has word." Phoebe ushered the girl out the front door since the back lane was still full of officials and gawkers. She hoped someone had washed up the blood, and she shuddered anew. She'd have nightmares for years.

Abby brought up a fresh tea tray and a thimble-sized brandy. "Cook says she'll hold dinner until Mr. Blair is ready. Should we wait for the other Mr. Blair and Mr. Morgan too?"

"Keep a cold collation ready for them," Phoebe suggested. "I have no idea how long they will be at the police station."

Abby didn't depart immediately but crossed her hands in her apron. "May I speak, my lady?"

Phoebe poured the brandy into her tea and raised her eyebrows. "Of course. I fear I do not stand on propriety. Nearly flying off a roof has that effect."

The maid stifled a smile and bobbed a curtsy. "We. . . all of us. . . want to thank you for thinking of us when all was topsy-turvy. The gentlemen are very brave, but they do not always remember us belowstairs. With your warning, we had time to sharpen our knives and bring out heavy skillets in case we were invaded."

Phoebe tried not to muse too hard over Cook, who could barely manage the stairs, arming herself with kitchen hatchet and skillet to thwart a killer. "I am very sorry you had to be put to the trouble. I shall ask Mr. Blair if he can't add a little to your wages as recompense for the fright his cousin's enemies have given you."

Abby beamed and curtsied again. "I do hope you will stay, my lady." She scurried away.

Phoebe sipped her doctored tea and considered that plea.

Andrew had climbed three stories—on *nothing*—to rescue her. She saw little difference in that insanity and her escapade with Evie. Perhaps he disguised his madness a little better, worked a little harder to fit in, but underneath the proper suit and cravat was a strong man capable of impossible feats for those he. . . loved? Would he have climbed those vines for Dahlia? She didn't think so. No more than she would consider bedding any man but him.

They were dreadful influences on each other.

She glanced down at the new gown she'd changed into. Perhaps not completely dreadful. Clean clothes and pretty underwear weren't quite as confining as she had feared. And she'd discovered that failure was how she learned and wasn't all bad, as long as it didn't involve lives anyway. With the support of a good person like Andrew, she could pick herself up over and over again until she accomplished what needed to be done.

Her hero entered the parlor looking unshaven, frazzled, and still filthy, but his eyes lit with what appeared to be genuine delight upon finding her waiting. "I feared you would flee to your aunts before I could shake off queries from half Edinburgh."

"I should have," Phoebe admitted. "I simply didn't think of it. I needed to be certain everyone was all right and to bail you out if the police decided you must have flung that awful man over the wall." And because she belonged here with him, she realized. She might occasionally even be of use to him.

"For some reason, the officer in charge believed your testimony," Andrew replied, pouring himself tea. "Thank you for not mentioning a ghost. The bruise on your neck spoke loudly enough."

She touched the scarf she'd donned to conceal the purple marks. "Perhaps we should not call my mother back until the bruise is gone.

Now that she's well again, she wants to treat me as the child I was when she left. She will fear you did this or that I must leave the city to be safe or any number of preposterous things."

He set his teacup aside and unexpectedly dropped to a crouch by her chair. Taking her hand, he bowed his head against her knee. "Don't leave, Phoebe. I know you have no reason to believe I can keep you comfortably, or even pay you the attention you deserve, but you are my heart. I will be an empty shell if you leave me."

Before she could recover from shock and find words, he dug in his coat pocket and produced. . . a bent nail holding a tie clasp?

He slid the iron ring over her finger so the diamond clasp sparkled like a real ring. "I didn't have time to run to the jeweler, and I'd rather have you with me when I go. But I needed proof that you will be mine, however difficult you might find me. Please, Phoebe, will you do me the great honor of marrying me?"

Seeing this gallant man kneeling at her feet nearly crushed her. She probably wasn't in her right mind or in any condition to make life-long promises, but finding freedom in accepting what her heart told her, she slid off her chair to kneel with him. "I am not a comfortable sort of person, sir. I don't expect you to change me. But if you can love and respect me as I am, then I am not so foolish as to turn away the most perfect man for me in existence, and I shall return your love and respect with all my heart and soul."

"Thank you, *mo chridhe*, my heart, I love you as you are and will always do. And after today, I don't think I'll ever let you out of my sight again." He crushed her in his embrace.

Relaxing for the first time in hours, Phoebe rubbed her cheek against his coat. "Did you just speak Gaelic to me? Will you teach me? I know French and Latin but no one—"

He laughed and shut her up with kisses.

THIRTY

"PLEASE HURRY, THE TRAIN WILL BE HERE ANY MINUTE," PHOEBE—LADY Phoebe *Blair*—pleaded.

The love of his life had actually signed the registrar's papers and said her vows before a minister. Drew was so proud, he could burst, but he still couldn't gallop a carriage down crowded Prince's Street.

The odd wedding ceremony she'd insisted on had been puzzling, but she'd claimed it was old family tradition to vow to love, honor, and *take thee in equality*. He had no argument with that since she'd vowed the same.

"You do realize the children will not be with her?" he said, admiring the pert gold confection perched on his wife's thick hair. The hat matched the gold-and-brown stripes of her new gown, which had lasted all of the morning without ruination.

"I know, and I'm so glad they're enjoying Olivia and the ponies. And I hope your cousin untangles all the scandals and the labor problems and whatever else troubles him, but it's my *mother* we need today. I have to tell her that none of the properties Mr. Lithgow suggested are suitable and persuade her to look in a warmer climate. I love my mother, but I do not really wish her to live with us."

"Are you planning on putting her on the next train south?" he asked in amusement.

She pulled off her glove to admire the new ring he'd bought for her— and probably to wave it like a red flag at her mother. He was learning his beloved's foibles.

"No, of course not. But now that she doesn't need to worry about a home for me, she may be more reasonable about the lien, and then you can build new buildings and people can have homes again."

The ring she helped him choose looked nothing like the fancy diamonds other ladies wore. She'd fallen in love with one with chips of different-colored stones set into a gold band to form a discreet infinity symbol. And then she'd insisted that he have a tie pin just like it—so everyone knew they were a couple.

Drew was fairly certain all of Edinburgh knew it by now. If the ravens, mice, and pigeons hadn't carried the word, her aunts had. They'd had half society calling ever since the news leaked out. He didn't need to worry about losing investors any time soon, even if gossip said he'd pushed one off his roof. Marrying into aristocratic circles apparently excused eccentricity.

"We are relocating the tenants as quickly as we can," he assured her. "There just aren't a lot of empty rooms to be had for the rent they can afford. I've found employment for a few of the men, but the women. . ."

"I know. I understand. It is a lot of people, and some of them are so incapacitated that they really belong in the hospital. But everyone should have a home. It is breaking my heart that I am so happy, while they're so lost! The world isn't fair." She checked the pins in her hat as the carriage drew up near the station.

"I've addressed the council about the situation. We'll have to take each family one by one and see what can be done. We may be living on short rations for a while, but I won't tear the buildings down until everyone has a place," he promised.

She kissed his jaw as he flung the reins to a boy to hold.

"And so I must do my part and persuade my mother not to ask too much for our lien. It would be even better if she would decide to live at Castle Yates, although Yorkshire is too cold for her, I fear," she said as Drew climbed from the carriage. She took his hand and leaped down after him, showing the pointed toe of her half-boot and a glimpse of lacy petticoat.

She still refused to wear crinolines, but for him, she'd gone out of her way to look the part of lady when necessary. In return, Drew had hopes of pleasing her as well, but his plans relied on Lady Persephone.

"Who is that with her?" Phoebe asked as her mother climbed off the train in a billow of petticoats.

Drew studied the older gentleman in graying side-whiskers and excellent tailoring. The man was slender and not much taller than Phoebe, an almost perfect match for the petite countess. "I haven't the slightest. Considering the gold fobs and diamond pins and monocle, I'd say royalty."

Phoebe laughed under her breath and rushed to greet her mother.

Drew steeled himself for the confrontation to come. Phoebe was his. No one could part them. But her mother could make his life damned uncomfortable if she chose.

"MY DAUGHTER, LADY PHOEBE," THE COUNTESS SAID TO HER ELEGANT companion, accepting Phoebe's enthusiastic hug. "Phoebe, may I introduce Lord Percival, a friend of mine I met in France. My, you're looking lovely today!" She stepped back to admire Phoebe's new attire.

Phoebe bobbed a wary curtsy at the stranger and gestured for Andrew to join them. "Lord Percival, this is my husband, Andrew Blair."

She'd written her mother of the marriage and her wish not to waste funds on a fancy gathering. Her aunts were waiting to throw a small reception now that her mother had returned. That was more than enough for Phoebe.

She waved her hand under her mother's nose so she could admire her wedding ring while the men shook hands.

"It is lovely, dear, and if you're happy, I'm happy." The countess smiled up at Lord Percival, who had a proprietary arm around her waist. "And before we are swarmed by my sisters and all their relentless infants, let me say that Percy and I have announced our engagement."

Phoebe stood stunned while Andrew slapped the stranger on his back and congratulated him. Lord Percival continued to smile through the beating.

"I. . . I wish you happy, of course," Phoebe stuttered. "It's just so. . ."

Her mother patted her arm. "Sudden, but it's not really, dear. Percy has spent these past years in France recovering from a near-fatal illness, and we came to know each other well. He is a good man. We thought we'd take you with us when we move into his estate in Sussex, but I see you have found your home here."

"Sussex? Will that be warm and dry enough for you?" Phoebe asked anxiously.

Andrew ushered them toward the waiting carriage. He kissed Phoebe's cheek. "Sussex is said to be lovely. Perhaps we could visit when the snow becomes tiresome here."

Travel. . . Phoebe had given it little thought. She shook her head so the ribbons on her new hat swung. "Now that the university has agreed to let me take classes, I do not mean to miss any. I have a *schedule* to keep! I feel very grown-up."

"Well, I'm sure we can work out something, dear." With the help of her fiancé, the countess climbed into the carriage. "Now may we wash off the dust before we descend on my sisters?"

"You'll be staying with us, of course," Andrew said, snapping the reins and setting the carriage in motion. "I've arranged to have your trunks delivered. With the children still in Yorkshire, you'll find we're a quiet household these days."

"I was rather hoping to meet the ghost," the countess said dryly.

Phoebe bounced in her seat and turned around to speak. "Even Andrew believes he felt her, but I think she went home with Mr. Simon. It's rather romantic, don't you think? His wife lingers to watch after him and her children?"

"I think I wouldn't want to be his second wife." Lady Persephone grimaced.

Phoebe returned to sitting properly to study on how a ghost might affect a relationship. But she could only think of the children and hope they'd be happy having an invisible mother.

Once they reached the house, she wriggled with impatience, but she'd promised to let Andrew handle all mention of finances. And now that her mother had a fiancé who might concern himself in her affairs. . . Phoebe tried not to bite her fingernails.

Her new parrot squawked a greeting as soon as they set foot through the front door. Phoebe ran to his perch, mentally saying *hello*, until he repeated it with a flourish of feathers. She fed him a bit of dried apple from her pocket and beamed proudly.

Hello, hello, the bird continued squawking, looking for more treats.

Oddly, her mother and Lord Percival declined her offer of tea, asking to go directly upstairs and rest.

Andrew kissed away her disappointment. "Not everyone appreciates watch birds," he reminded her.

"But I taught Macaw more tricks," she protested.

"Maybe they'll appreciate Wolf better. We'll introduce them later," he promised.

So she showed her mother to the suite they'd once shared, while Andrew showed Lord Percival to the chamber upstairs near the nursery where Simon had slept. Phoebe preferred not to think of her mother welcoming a stranger into her bed, but Lord Percival was a very elegant stranger, to be sure. She prayed he made her mother happy.

While their guests rested after their journey, Andrew drew her back into their private suite. She didn't have any instincts for nesting, so she hadn't changed his very masculine décor except to add her wardrobe and vanity items. She leaned appreciatively against his strength.

"Do we have Lord Percival investigated?" she whispered.

"I'm sure Mr. Lithgow will be happy to do so. He treats your funds as his own, so he'll not let a gambler empty your account. And your mother seems a very sensible sort. I think she'd know by now if he was after her rather limited funds. Do you need to dress for the evening's affair? Can I help you?"

The look in his eye was very wicked. The thrill had not grown old. Phoebe turned her back to him so he could work the fastenings of her gown.

Her husband had very skillful fingers and grasped the construction of her garments with a mechanic's ease.

Later, lying languidly amid the tousled sheets, Phoebe ran a finger-nail down Andrew's broad bare chest, admiring the scattering of masculine hairs adorning sculpted muscles. No statue in any museum could compare with his chiseled musculature. She kissed his nipple, then dodged out of his reach.

"If you want me to look like a lady tonight, I need to bathe and start dressing." She was making him teach her all the words for what they did in bed. She felt jolly well rogered at the moment and feared her aunts would know it the moment they saw her.

Andrew climbed from the sheets, and she admired his physique a little more, until he noticed and headed for her. Phoebe squealed and ran for the washroom.

"Do I have to call you Lady Phoebe all evening?" he asked, reaching around her for a washcloth.

"When I am dressed like a lady, of course," she said primly. "And I shall call you Mr. Blair. And we will giggle over the punch."

He pinched her backside and kissed her ear. "Then we'll end up shocking that house full of children and teachers. Let us pour your mother full of champagne and present her with our ideas and hope she approves."

"Or Lord Percival approves," she said anxiously as he left her to her ablutions.

"If he can hold his own in that house full of women, he's smart enough to understand. We will hope he's not counting on riches."

Phoebe loved sharing a home with Andrew. He *understood* so well.

At her aunts' house, all the teachers and distant cousins were waiting in the front parlor to greet them. They'd transformed the School of Malcolms into a bridal boudoir of white lace, netting, flowers, and potted trees. If she'd been Cousin Max in this sea of femininity, she'd have run away too. His prolonged absence was the only sorrow hovering over the celebrations.

Phoebe admired the traditional Malcolm addition of forestry and hugged both of her aunts.

"We are so happy for you, dear," Lady Agnes cried. Her gray curls were caught up in a white feathered confection, and her sparkling earrings suited a ballroom. "We knew you were never meant to be a teacher. You and your pets would absolutely ruin our lessons. I'm so glad Mr. Blair worked as well as we hoped."

"Do not try this marriage ploy on Olivia," Phoebe warned with a laugh. "She has enough on her hands with Evie. Andrew's cousin still has a wife haunting him. Leave Olivia with his children in York, please."

"We shall see." Agatha patted Phoebe's shoulder and turned toward her sister. "Now that Persephone is finally seeing sense, perhaps she'll let go of that medieval dungeon she buried herself in. I shall speak with her."

Phoebe blinked as her usually rattle-pated aunt swept off to greet the countess.

Andrew circled her waist and watched as her aunts cornered her mother and her new fiancé. "I like your family, but I think I'll stay well away from them when I can."

"It's difficult to know if they're meddling like normal people or using whatever psychic gifts they possess."

"Psychic?" he asked.

"I read the word in an article about mediums. The author coined it from the Greek *psykhikos*, meaning *of the soul, spirit, or mind*, I believe. It seems very suited to who we are. I'm not sure if my aunts and my mother are mind readers or simply understand the human soul, but they are quite frightening in what they know sometimes."

Lord Percival joined them, looking puzzled. "The ladies are having an argument about a dungeon. I think there are a few things I have not learned about my intended."

Andrew laughed. "Just accept that every day is a mystery, and you'll do fine."

Phoebe pinched his arm through his coat sleeve, knowing he didn't feel it. "Every day should contain a little surprise. Has my mother spoken to you about the lien she has on the building Mr. Blair is purchasing? I've tried to persuade her that we don't need to buy a flat, and the consortium could pay the lien on the tenement in monthly installments, if she'd like."

"That is the dungeon of which they speak?" he asked, lifting a graying eyebrow. "Your aunts seem to think it should be given to you as a wedding gift. I don't think a dungeon is very appropriate."

Laughing, Phoebe leaned over and kissed his cheek. "It is a perfect gift! Please persuade her to do so."

She turned and flung herself into her husband's arms. "Can we truly buy the workshop then? And once it's fixed up, Hugh can have his own office near the construction. And I can have a place close to the university for studying. And if you're there working. . ."

Andrew swung her off her feet in front of all her family and company. "I shall ask rent for your studio and your pets and demand payment in lewd ways." He nibbled her ear until she shrieked, laughed, and escaped —nearly running into her mother.

The countess frowned at them in disapproval. "You wish to exchange our family home for a *barn*?"

"Mr. Lithgow said he'd obtain a mortgage so we can make payments on the property. The alternative is to make payments directly to you to repay the lien, but it's not possible to obtain a mortgage on a lien," Andrew explained.

Aunt Gertrude sailed up, her overly-black tresses stacked precariously beneath a white fascinator. "It is not a *barn*, Persephone," she scolded her younger sister. "It was built by our great-grandfather for his wife. Her baking was often called sorcery, but she produced enough bread to feed the hungry during years of deprivation. And he used the other half to train students of animal husbandry. The students lived upstairs. It is a Malcolm property and should be preserved as such."

"I have an ancestor who taught animal husbandry?" Phoebe asked in disbelief. "Why has no one ever told me of this?"

Lady Persephone opened her mouth to object, but her older sister spoke right over her. "Because he was a Jacobite, of course. He would have been arrested had anyone known who he was. They lived quietly in the shadow of the palace, helping where they could. It's silly to hide that fact after all these years."

"I want to teach animal husbandry to women! I shall follow in the shoes of my ancestor and start my own rebellion," Phoebe crowed. "I'll be on my home ground again!"

Andrew hugged her. Her mother rolled her eyes and glared at her sister. "*This* is why we did not tell her. Whatever happens is on your head, Gertrude." She turned back to Andrew. "And yours, sir. I will gift my share of the lien to the two of you as a wedding present, but you will set aside Phoebe's half for your children. I will have our solicitor draw up the agreement."

Phoebe broke away from her husband to swallow up her mother in an embrace. "Thank you, thank you, and you will not regret this. We can have an entire chain of Schools for Malcolms."

Her husband lifted her away and whispered in her ear, "Your first students will be our children, *mo chridhe*. Now come away and have some punch before you shock the other teachers anymore."

Smiling so hard she thought surely she'd shatter, Phoebe covered his face in kisses, then turned to the other startled young women who formed her aunts' school. "We will educate the world, ladies, see if we don't!"

One of the younger ones cheered. Before long, the others joined in, and the champagne flowed.

Once the party was in full swing, Phoebe took her husband by the hand and led him out into the chilly evening, where she covered his square jaw in kisses. "I love it when you speak Gaelic to me. And I love that you like to touch me. And can we *not* wear fancy clothes when we're in our barn?"

He chuckled and ran his hand over her breast and waist. "You have to ask? Let's take you home and out of all these ridiculous fripperies so I know there's a real woman under them."

"And you can learn how I work and together we'll improve each other like your pterotype," she said in satisfaction, dragging him toward the carriage.

He laughed, and the pigeons flew up from their roosts with her joy.

LESSONS IN ENCHANTMENT
CHARACTERS

Andrew Blair: Inventor and engineer
Lady Phoebe Malcolm Duncan: daughter of late earl of Drumsmoore
Lady Persephone, Countess of Drumsmoore: Phoebe's widowed
mother; younger sister of Agnes and Gertrude
Hugh Morgan: Andrew's partner; accountant
Simon Blair: Andrew's cousin; mine owner, industrialist
Letitia Blair: Simon's deceased wife, mother of his children
Enoch Blair: six-year-old son of Simon Blair
Catherine and Clare Blair: four-year-old twin daughters of Simon Blair
Lady Agnes: Phoebe's aunt; part owner of School of Malcolms
Lady Gertrude: Phoebe's oldest aunt; part owner of School of Malcolms
Earl of Drumsmoore: Phoebe's Uncle Albert
Mrs. Dalrymple: Drew's neighbor
Miss Dahlia Higginbotham: niece of Mrs. Dalrymple
Thomas Lithgow, Esquire: Phoebe's family solicitor
Merry: one of Phoebe's many younger cousins
Olivia: another of Phoebe's distant cousins, widow
Rose: Drew's ex fiancée
Bennett: Phoebe's landlord
Abby: Drew's maid

Henry: Drew's new stableboy
Dougie: Drew's new footman, young lad good with fists
Gareth Glengarry—Dalrymple's political aide
John Wilkes, Baron: Simon's mine owning neighbor
Lord Percival: Lady Persephone's suitor
Cousin Max: Lady Agnes's son who disappeared in Africa

ABOUT THE AUTHOR

With several million books in print and *New York Times* and *USA Today's* bestseller lists under her belt, former CPA Patricia Rice is one of romance's hottest authors. Her emotionally-charged contemporary and historical romances have won numerous awards, including the *RT Book Reviews* Reviewers Choice and Career Achievement Awards. Her books have been honored as Romance Writers of America RITA® finalists in the historical, regency and contemporary categories.

A firm believer in happily-ever-after, Patricia Rice is married to her high school sweetheart and has two children. A native of Kentucky and New York, a past resident of North Carolina and Missouri, she currently resides in Southern California, and now does accounting only for herself.

ALSO BY PATRICIA RICE

The World of Magic:

The Unexpected Magic Series

MAGIC IN THE STARS

WHISPER OF MAGIC

THEORY OF MAGIC

AURA OF MAGIC

CHEMISTRY OF MAGIC

NO PERFECT MAGIC

The Magical Malcolms Series

MERELY MAGIC

MUST BE MAGIC

THE TROUBLE WITH MAGIC

THIS MAGIC MOMENT

MUCH ADO ABOUT MAGIC

MAGIC MAN

The California Malcolms Series

THE LURE OF SONG AND MAGIC

TROUBLE WITH AIR AND MAGIC

THE RISK OF LOVE AND MAGIC

Crystal Magic

SAPPHIRE NIGHTS

TOPAZ DREAMS

CRYSTAL VISION

WEDDING GEMS

AZURE SECRETS

AMBER AFFAIRS

MOONSTONE SHADOWS

THE WEDDING GIFT

THE WEDDING QUESTION

THE WEDDING SURPRISE

Historical Romance:

American Dream Series

MOON DREAMS

REBEL DREAMS

The Rebellious Sons

WICKED WYCKERLY

DEVILISH MONTAGUE

NOTORIOUS ATHERTON

FORMIDABLE LORD QUENTIN

The Regency Nobles Series

THE GENUINE ARTICLE

THE MARQUESS

ENGLISH HEIRESS

IRISH DUCHESS

Regency Love and Laughter Series

CROSSED IN LOVE

MAD MARIA'S DAUGHTER

ARTFUL DECEPTIONS

ALL A WOMAN WANTS

Rogues & Desperadoes Series

LORD ROGUE

MOONLIGHT AND MEMORIES

SHELTER FROM THE STORM

WAYWARD ANGEL

DENIM AND LACE

CHEYENNES LADY

ABOUT BOOK VIEW CAFÉ

Book View Café Publishing Cooperative (BVC) is an author-owned cooperative of over fifty professional writers, publishing in a variety of genres including fantasy, romance, mystery, and science fiction. Since its debut in 2008, BVC has gained a reputation for producing high-quality ebooks. BVC's ebooks are DRM-free and are distributed around the world. The cooperative is now bringing that same quality to its print editions.

BVC authors include New York Times and USA Today bestsellers as well as winners and nominees of many prestigious awards, including:

Agatha Award
Campbell Award
Hugo Award
Lambda Award
Locus Award
Nebula Award
Nicholl Fellowship
PEN/Malamud Award
Philip K. Dick Award
RITA Award

World Fantasy Award
Writers of the Future Award